THE HISTORY OF
VICTOR CLÉMENT

A novel by Edd King

Copyright © Edd King 2018

For

Katie, Andrew & Timothy. 2018

Other books by Edd King:

Nelson's Law

Set Up!
[A sequel Nelson' Law]

1

CHAPTER 1

THE PATIENT'S MEDICAL RECORD, held on a clipboard by the bed, identified the man as Ted Willis. Date of birth December 1945. Age 73. Next of kin: Unknown. Case: Victim of robbery and knife attack.

The nurse looked up as the doctor entered the ward and approached the bed.

"He's gone, Steve."

"What?"

"He's gone. He's dead. The monitors are all blank."

"Oh shit!" The doctor moved to the patient's bedside and felt for a pulse. "No, he isn't dead. Someone turned the monitors off. Probably some bloody cleaner using the mains sockets, and not plugging everything in again. Wouldn't surprise me. They shouldn't be allowed in here, anyway. Let me deal with it. And would you please stop any bugger just coming in here and interfering. He's my bloody patient, okay? Now go and get some lunch."

"Okay, doctor. It's only a matter of time, anyway, isn't it?"

"Time for what?"

"Until he dies."

"Probably."

As the ICU nurse left the ward side-room, Doctor Steve Grant looked down at his patient. He needed this guy alive. He fished out his mobile 'phone and made a call.

"Hi, is Andy there? … Oh, right. Steve, here. Steve Grant. Royal Derks. Regarding our earlier discussions and meeting, I think I've got something for Andy, so if he can make the necessary arrangements then let me know. Has he got the other side of things lined up yet? … Okay. When he can. The sooner the better. It's your end that's going to have to move fast, so let's get this one set up and all prepared. I can fix things here in no time, but it can't wait forever. I'll call again later." Grant picked up the patient's notes. He'd read them a few times now and could recall the facts.

Male. Born 1945. No known relatives. Unconscious when brought in. Occupation unknown. Victim of a stabbing in Reading. Fought off a couple of muggers. Apparently, one of them had his arm broken and a smashed knee but his mate had a nine-inch kitchen knife and had stabbed the victim multiple times. Injured attacker apprehended; other one got away. Address ... some place in Marlow, the notes said, 'Oaklands' or something like it and a post code. He'd had no visitors since being admitted two weeks ago. Grant knew there was nobody to ask whether they could switch off his life-support. The doctor threw the notes onto the bed. Then out loud in the otherwise empty ward, "Fuck it. We'll give it a go." He left the room to go to the canteen, just as the nurse appeared with a sandwich and a coffee.

"How is he, Doc? ... I brought this for you."

"Thanks Rosie. No change. He's my patient, so please, as I've already said, make sure nobody else takes over. He's mine, okay?" The very last thing Grant wanted was to get back to the ward to find someone had arbitrarily decided to switch off his patient's life-support. Grant desperately needed to keep this one alive.

"Of course." Doctor Grant took the food and the drink over to the nurses' station and sat at the desk to make some notes while he ate his sandwich. He noted in capital letters, that only he and nurse Pollard were to deal with the patient. He then underlined that note, signed off duty and made his way home. His flat was virtually across the road from the hospital. Once there he shrugged off his clothes while making another call to Andy.

"It's me. I called earlier. Is Andy there? ... I want to refer this patient to Professor Vennuchi and if he wants to go ahead with it, we'll need a private medivac to Milan, okay? Also need an ambulance transfer to Heathrow or maybe Wycombe ... no, it's my decision. The guy I have in mind was ... is ... obviously well-heeled, and I've done a little background on him. The med notes are crap. The guy's fuckin' ideal. I've been to his house as well and I've got his passport. Nobody mentioned as a person to contact. From what I found out, he's a professional guy, so there's no doubt he's a bright old bastard, so we really need to give him and us a chance. Let me know soonest, and I'll do things here, as I said. I'll give you a full background as soon as I can get back to his house again and do a bit more poking about. Can we talk money later? Cheers." Grant had a shower and dressed. In the evening, he would check out the Marlow address for the second time. He had to be sure he was going to do this one properly.

The doctor drove over the Marlow bridge, past the Compleat Angler and into the high street. Left at the 'T' junction, past Waitrose then the little garage on the corner, and then into Spinfield Lane and up the hill, with his satnav taking him through the gates into the property. There was a small, white van parked in front of the double garage, and a man walking across the front lawn, which was bordered with neat, colourful flower beds and the acre or so comprising the front garden was interspersed with mature oak trees. He stopped the car as the man approached him.

"Can I help you sir?"

"Oh, yes. Probably. I'm Grant, Doctor Grant ..."

"Oh, yes. You were here before, weren't you? I recognise the car. You looking after my Mr Willis, then?" Without waiting for an answer, the man continued. "I hope he's gonna be okay! Dreadful business isn't it!" He then stuck his hand through the window. "I'm Alf, Alf Gardner. That's what I am, see, the gardener!" Grant took his hand.

"Nice to meet you. Yes, I am his doctor. I've just come along in the hope of finding whether he had any family we could get in touch with, really. And of course ..."

"Don't the Social people do that?"

"Well, yes and no. There's a degree of urgency about it and it takes a lot of time to get them moving ... thing is, we need to know for various reasons ..."

"Yeah, my wife knows all about them social buggers ... he had nobody. He had a brother many years ago, but he died overseas somewhere. He had loads of friends. No kids. His wife's also dead. Died a good few years ago now. Got keys, have you?"

4

"Yes."

"Never been any family. Ever. He was a real gent. Always asking after my lot. My family, like. Generous at Christmas. It's a bad business. Anyways, better let you get on, I suppose. I'll just shut the garage and be on my way. Nice to have met you, Doctor!"

"Yes. And you." Grant drove round the central fountain in the circular drive, then parked his car and walked to the house. He felt now that his look round the property was unnecessary. As far as he was concerned, if Willis were moved to Italy, there would be nobody particularly keen to trace his whereabouts. Ideal. In the lounge, he again took down the photo albums he had seen on his first visit. This time, he was looking for family. He picked up a few of them, the latest he could find, and sat down to leaf through the A4 sized pages. There were pictures of Willis in the uniform of a naval commander, with, he thought, pilot's wings, and next to that a caption *'Me in Germany open-day visit to 3 Sqn Harriers with wife Deborah [died 2009]'*. There were certificates showing he was enrolled as a solicitor in 1982 and various press-cuttings about his involvement in a number of Courts Martial cases. He pulled a few more albums down, then found a marriage appointment card for the reading and Wokingham Register Office, at Yeomanry House. His wife's maiden name was Soul, Elaine, widow. He made a note of the name. There were some pictures of the couple. She was a very attractive girl. There were no pictures or references to any children or other family members. It was all good enough for Grant. It seemed that after his wife's death, Willis hadn't kept up with his family history. In fact, with no family, what was the point? As far Doctor Grant was concerned, Willis would be going to Milan.

Back at his flat, Grant spent an hour doing searches on various Willis hits, but there was nothing on his patient. He was the ideal candidate. He then searched under Soul. He found that she had first married into a family who built up a chemicals and drugs business, and her husband had been killed in a road accident, which also killed their two children. On his death, the business was sold to a well-established, Chinese company for an estimated twenty million pounds. Grant noted the irony of that, after his set-to with the business in Manchester which currently motivated him to deal with Willis. So, no wife, no children, no known living relatives. No problem. He sent a text to Andy. *'All clear my end. I hope this one it is the same deal as the victims in 'Moving Target' without the nigger in the woodpile. No-one to take any interest in the guy. As far as I can see, it's now up to you to deal with things at your end. I expect that we can have Willis with you within seven days. Give me a day and I'll book through Medical Air Services and sign off as fit to travel. You arrange payment please. Regards SG.'*

Within twenty-four hours, Grant had the date for the move. 17th May. He signed on for duty and visited his patient. Rosie was at Willis's bedside.

"Hi, Rosie. How's our patient?"

"He's okay. What's happening now? We can't just leave him forever, can we?"

"We're not. He's going to Milan in two days' time. Ospidale San Raffaele. I think their guys want to take a look at him. He's being taken to the airport then onto the medivac Lear Jet. It's only a two-hour flight."

"Who's footing the bill for that?"

"Some well-wishers ..."

"Isn't that a bit odd? Wouldn't it be better to let him ... die in peace?"

"Depends on your point of view. Anyway, it's not up to us, is it! Just make sure that he's all ready to leave on Thursday, pick-up at about midday. I'll have all the paperwork ready, okay?"

"Yes, Doctor ... but I ..."

"Just do it ... please." Rosie turned away and left the room. She couldn't understand why the doctor was suddenly become so ... what was he? Not his usual self? She just decided to shut up but at the same time do all she had to do for the guy. But she couldn't but feel a little uneasy about the whole business.

By midday on the Thursday, Rosie and her assistants had their patient on a trolley ready to go. The nurse looked down at him and stroked his face. He was not a bad looking guy for his age, and he had obviously taken good care of himself, not an ounce over-weight and with a firm, muscular body. She put her lips close to his ear and whispered to him. She saw his eyes flicker again. He had beautiful blue eyes.

"Bye bye, darling, I hope somebody can bring you back here to see me, your Rosie Pollard at the Royal Berks." She took his hand and kissed it, and, walking slowly backwards let his fingers slip out of her hand.

The private ambulance drove away from the hospital yard to Heathrow airport. Grant accompanied his patient and would do so until he was safely handed over to Professor Vennuchi.

Three hours after G-ABMM took off from London Heathrow, Willis was wheeled into the Milan hospital. Andy Vennuchi was there to receive them and after he and Grant checked-over the patient, Grant signed away his charge to the Professor.

"Looks okay to me, Steve. Got his passport there? ...Thanks. I'll get the death certificate signed and you can take it back with you just to close the case, alright? Organ failure and dementia do?"

"No problem with that, Andy. If your staff can register the death with the Consul, it'll be a great help."

"That's no problem."

Okay, then I'll get my arse back to London. Just let me know how things, go please, and don't forget, we're a team so don't forget my little part in it, will you?"

"Of course not. In fact, you look a bit like Leonard Nemoy ..."

"Who the fuck's he when he's at home?"

"He played the part of David Kibner, the doctor in Invasion of the Body Snatchers, the 1978 film ... I thought you were the movie buff?"

"What makes you think that?"

"Didn't you mention the film *'Moving Target'*? Hopefully this patient here'll be no bugger in the woodpile, as you said!"

"Yeah, so I did. Anyway, if you get me a taxi I'll get back to my hospital. Just keep me in the picture, and we'll discuss money at some more convenient time." Grant took the death certificate and his patient's passport, then made it back to the airport.

The next morning, Grant was back at work. His ICU nurse was sitting at the nurses' station, writing up her records. He stopped with his hands on the counter top, and saw Rosie look up at him.

"How's Mr Willis, Doc?" Grant just handed her the death certificate. It was written in Italian, but she knew that whatever language it was, her patient was now dead.

"Organ failure. Brought on by trauma. I suggest you tell the cops. The little shits who attacked him are now murderers." Grant collected his duty sheet to see what he was doing for the rest of the day. He didn't see Rosie again until Monday morning. To him, everything was back to normal. But not for Rosie. She felt uneasy about the whole Willis business, but was desperately trying to put it down to her being unable to ever detach herself from all her patients' suffering. But she tried to forget.

A few days after Rosie Pollard informed the police of the death of Ted Willis, the Reading Chronicle ran a short article about the death. There was a picture of him, looking a lot younger, saying he had been in the Royal Navy, that he had no family his wife having died some years previously. A Mr Alf Gardner who worked for the deceased, said he was a 'lovely man'. The nurse now assumed that the usual authorities would go through his house to deal with his possessions, find his heirs if any, and then clear everything up and move on to the next one. She tore the article out of the paper and put it into her office drawer in the little house she shared with Sean, her partner. She had no doubt that everybody else who read the article, would just turn the page and forget it.

Back at work, Rosie had a message to contact Steve Grant. She found him in reception just packing off a patient.

"Ah, Rosie. Had the Registrar's office on the 'phone wanting to know if we have anybody asking after your friend Willis. They want to put his affairs to bed or something and need someone to do the usual. Want to give them a call? I don't think he ever had any visitors, and anyway, they wouldn't be allowed into the unit unless they were family, bearing in mind the circumstances. It's a Mrs Blake. There's a note of the number somewhere at the nurses' station, where I left it. Are you ..."

"Yeah, I'll give her a call. Seems so bloody sad, doesn't it?"

"It's called, life, Rosie. Get used to it."

"Thanks ... I'll go and make a call." Rosie got through immediately.

"Mrs Blake? Rosie Pollard here. I'm returning the call you made to the hospital regarding Ted Willis ... yes that's right, I was looking after him with Doctor Grant ... before they took him to see Professor Vannuchi. How can I help?"

"Mrs Pollard, Rosie, we need to deal with his estate. Social services will have to get into the property to try and find details of any relative or somebody who can help them on that score. Can I give your name to the right department? They will need to access his house. Were there any keys or anything else left by the deceased at the hospital?"

"Er ... I don't know about that. I will check in his property bag, but I think everything he had went with him to Italy ... Doctor Grant went with him, so I can ask if everything was handed back to him when he died. You see, he died when the doctor was actually with him. So, there is just a chance ..."

"Thank you. We'll have to hand it all over to the death admin team ... they are busy people you know, it's not uncommon for men living alone to die with no relatives or anything." Rosie wondered what 'or anything' meant exactly ... "so whatever you can do to help would be appreciated. Thank you. If I leave it for a while before I call in the team it'll give you a chance to do what you can ..." Mrs Blake rang off. Rosie went to find doctor Grant.

"Steve, I've spoken to the Registrar's office. They want to know if we have any of Willis's stuff. I assume you brought it all back with you after the Italy trip?"

"I didn't take anything except his passport, and I brought that back. I put it away in the main office as usual. If you get it, everything should be there."

"House keys?"

"Yes. I dropped in a couple of times to try and find any traces of a relative or somebody, in view of the plan to move him. I suppose I was really trying to find out if there was anybody who might have the authority to make life-changing decisions ..."

"Like a person with a power of attorney for ... health and welfare? Is that it?"

"Something like that." Grant was beginning to feel uncomfortable with his senior ICU nurse's enquiries. He decided to shut up before he let anything slip and she became a real nuisance.

"Thanks, Doc, I'll get the stuff and hand it over to the people the Registrar mentioned. I'll let you know if anything crops up, okay?"

"Thanks, Rosie." As she turned away, she heard the doctor add under his breath, "I hope the fuck nothing does turn up." Nurse Rosie Pollard assumed it was not intended for her to hear.

Rosie was more disturbed. It was not that she had become attached to her patient over the nearly two weeks he was in her care, but the actions of Steve Grant seemed somehow odd. Why did he have to go to Ted Willis's house twice? Why didn't he get the police to do it? What was all this about the Italian doctor or whatever he was, getting involved when they had in England the best surgeons and A&E doctors in the world probably? Why was the move so sudden, especially where there was no deterioration or improvement in the patient's condition? Why was organ failure and dementia listed on the death certificate when the patient had been stable for two weeks, and how could dementia be included when there had been no indications and no history on his medical records? She wanted it all to make sense. She wanted to forget it and move on. But she couldn't. Was it just Steve Grant? He was sometimes a bit abrupt and he hadn't been at the RB for very long, but he certainly knew his job.

With a serious need to deal with a failing economy, the Beijing government stepped up its investment in transplant surgery. There were two reasons for this. Firstly, it was a very lucrative branch of medicine and secondly, China had an almost unlimited supply of organ donors. The order handed down to the Beijing surgeons was simple; we want to sell our expertise to the world. It started with getting up to speed on basic transplant operations. Anything would do; whole arms, legs, eyes … then head transplants … then brain transplants. Not known for it's adherence to accepted medical ethics or appreciation of human rights, many political prisoners or members of persecuted minorities were dragged out of their camps to finish up on the operating tables of the various medical facilities and universities throughout China just so the surgeons could carry out their gruesome experiments. Very few of the wretched souls ever opened their eyes again once the scalpels and bone-saws got to work on them. The failures were just incinerated, as were the few successful transplants, as, once carefully monitored, they too were given lethal injections or just shot. It will never be known just how many thousands of these poor souls were used. The marked lack of success was frustrating. Maybe, some medics thought, we should be using Europeans … better fed and stronger, so better able to withstand the highly invasive surgery, so they might have more success and so open a massively lucrative market in Europe and the Unites States.

So they set up a top secret, state-sponsored people trafficking business to abduct healthy Europeans to be sent to China.

That was how Ted Willis and a young French foundling, now twelve years old, finished up on operating tables nest to each other … and the result for the survivor, became his ultimate identity crisis. How would he react?
If Willis, a widower with no children and no will, how would he

11

recover his estate? Or would it be taken by the UK government as bona vacantia? If Victor, would he ever learn who his parents were? And would his appointed mentor, Angelica, the Italian psychiatrist, help him to find his old life or try to detain him in the Milan hospital where he was being looked after?

Synopsis ?

Why here ?

CHAPTER 2

Nobody at the SOS Children's Village at Plaisir, near Paris can recall when or how Victor Clément came to be in their care. He was dumped as a child, then aged no more than three months, in a Paris *Zone Urbaines Sensibles* and his name and date of birth 1st December 2007 was written on a piece of paper left in the pocket of his little blue dungarees. It is believed he must have been born somewhere near Montée de là Cure St. Marcel Bel Accueil, where he was found, but nobody had the inclination or resources to pursue it. The authorities found it convenient to believe he was abandoned because he had never cried. He was dumb. He grew to be a beautiful little boy, with thick blonde hair and lovely blue eyes. Over the years, he displayed two main characteristics. One was a hatred of school work and the other was a keen interest, a real passion, for gymnastics which he had once seen on television and thereafter it was all that interested him. Every waking hour he devoted to either watching or doing gymnastics. It was his sole method of expression. At school, his teachers had no time for his sullen attitude and disdain for anything academic. When he was told to sit and learn maths or to learn to write, and as he could not, or would not, talk, and as they assumed, he was also, or appeared to be, deaf, they just packed him off to the gymnasium where his gym teacher, Jacques Grévstoch realised he had a phenomenal potential as a gymnast and which Jacques encouraged. By the time the young lad attained the age of eleven years, he had the strength and ability sufficient for him to travel with the French national junior team to championships all over Europe. Although too young to compete, his potential was such that he was regarded by the French national coaches as a mascot. And then as a possible Olympic Champion.

Then the gym teacher was summoned to see his boss, André Marais.
"Yes, you wanted to see me".

"Jacques."

"Yes André"

"The boy, Victor ... I think you should take the sullen little bastard to China when you go. It will be good for him to see real competition, live."

"I agree. But the sports council won't pay for it, so who will?"

"Already organised. Put him on the list. I'll organise the passport. Unless he learns to listen and to speak, he's no damn good to anybody, right"

"Alright. At least he'll get to see and experience the robust methods the Chinese apply to their own sports teams, especially the gymnasts. Might do him some good!"

Everybody loved Victor. The Chinese saw his potential. He had a superb body for his age, strong with muscle in the right places. Even standing still, with his looks, his shape and his infectious smile, everybody, even the hosts, knew he was a star. To the China team coaches, he was also a threat. After his arrival at the sports venue, the Chinese doctor insisted that Victor be allocated a room of his own. He said it was because he was technically 'disabled'. The French team manager could not argue.

At approximately two the next morning, the lad woke to find two men standing over him. He could not shout out. One of the men grabbed his left arm, holding it flat on the bed, while the other plunged a syringe into his upper arm. Victor managed to twist in his bed, and he plunged a finger into the eye of the man leaning over him, his finger nail cutting deep into the aqueous humor and severing the upper zonule fibres. The boy then grabbed a handful of the attacker's long, black hair which he pulled out of the attacker's scalp. The man let out a shout, followed by a stream of abuse. The other assailant tried to silence him, but to no avail. The entire contents of the syringe was emptied into Victor's body. Then the two men left hurriedly. One of them was now permanently blind in one eye. The little French boy fell asleep.

14

Early the next morning all efforts to wake Victor failed. The team coach was called by the boys who had tried to wake their friend. The first thing the team coach noticed was a plastic needle-cover on the floor of the bedroom, and some tufts of long, black hair in the boy's right-hand. So as not to alarm the other boys, the coach removed the tufts with his handkerchief and shoved them and the syringe-top into his track-suit top pocket and zipped it shut. After establishing that the boy was alive, and failing to wake him, he called for the team medic, but he feared the worst. The medic could do nothing and confirmed the coach's worst fears. The tournament doctor was called, and he arranged for Victor to be transferred to their hospital A&E unit. It took about an hour for the A&E surgeon to arrive at the hospital, but he knew before he arrived that this was the boy he was told to expect, knowing full-well the circumstances of his young patient, injected with some unidentified fluid. He professed to be unable to treat the boy and insisted on his removal to the Harbin Medical University. This was a job, he told the team coach and medic, for their esteemed surgeon, Xia Renchuan. The surgeon had been expecting the call. He didn't say it, but he also knew it was extremely likely that, and within possibly hours, the lad would be brain-dead. The French team manager told the surgeon at the hospital that the lad was an orphan, and that if he died, there were no funds to fly the body back to France, so the hospital was to dispose of the corpse in any way they thought fit. Victor was taken to Harbin. Xia knew what he had to do. He had to ask no-one; in the university and in the medical department, he was king. He informed the French team members that Victor would be confined for at least two weeks, that he was going to get the best treatment, and if they just brought all the lad's possessions to the facility, there would be no need for any of their team to remain in China. He would take personal responsibility for their boy and would keep them informed. The French contingent could do no more. A brief physical examination told Xia that the boy was in superb physical condition, better that he could have possibly hoped. So far, things were running to plan. To the Chinese plan, that is.

15

Xia retired to his office in the university and dialled the number for the Ospidale San Raffaele. He asked for Professor Vennuchi. He was put through. The 'phone rang for a long time. Xia looked at his watch. In Milan, the time was 0524 am. Bloody hell, Andy wouldn't be pleased

"Yes!"

"Andy. Xia ..."

"Do you know what the fuckin' time is? ... Sorry, did you say Xia?"

"Yes. We need you here like now to look at a case. So, don't fuck about. Bring everything you've got. This is a no-duff message, so get your arse out here pronto. I'll email the patient's condition. There will be a few issues which might ... just wait to see my diagnosis. We'll get an Air China jet into Milan within an hour or so. I'll send you the flight number as soon as I know it. But you can get moving like now. You'll fly into Taaikpaania International Airport ..."

"Into where?"

"You'll know it as Taiping. It's only about forty kilometres from the university."

"Got it. Let's not screw this one up, eh? We've done a lot to make this possible. It's a one-shot job."

"We bloody won't fail. Can't afford to. If we do, then kiss goodbye to all the funding. I've got to go now. Cheers Andy." The Italian surgeon leapt out of bed.

"Fuck fuck fuck!" Short-notice jobs tended to disorientate him. He was actually quite excited. If he pulled this one off with Xia, if between them they managed to bring this one back from virtual death, the team would be all over the medical publications world-wide. There would be no stopping them. He showered and by the time he had dressed and had breakfast, he was ready to go. He had the flight number texted to him. The message was that CA847 was a training flight specially diverted to Milan for the job. There would only be a spare crew on board, and all necessary facilities for the team could be accommodated. The estimated take-off Milan time was 1330. By six the next morning he would be at the university. He called his team together and told them to get their arses into gear.

Transport had been laid on at the airport. Xia was there to meet Andy Vennuchi and brief him. Beijing had been informed of the consequences of a successful operation. If it failed, nobody would be any the wiser. The two top surgeons had *carte-blanch* to do whatever they felt was necessary, but the pressure was on them to succeed. The visitors were to rest for the remainder of the day, and the operation would commence by 0700 hours the next day, to give the teams time to prepare everything. The estimated time for the procedure was put at eighteen hours.

By 0745 hours both teams were ready. The lead surgeon was Xia. As was his habit, he talked out loud about what he was doing, and this operation was no different. He looked up at all six of the cameras positioned round the theatre. He then approached his patient's now unconscious form. The lad's head had been shaved clean of all hair.

"My patient. Eleven-year old male. General physical condition is excellent. Total paralysis brought on as far as I can establish by a cerebral seizure induced by drugs. We do not know how the drug was administered." He lied. It was for the benefit of the cameras, and for his guests from Italy. "In time the brain will die. I intend to remove this organ". He looked at the second team. "Ready, Andy?"

"Ready."

"Good ... follow me through. I am going to open the skull by cutting through the coronal sagittal and lateral sutures, separate the left and right parietal bones. I may not need to remove the occipital bone. Once done, I will remove the parietal then the meninges layers. Clear?" The surgeon held out his hands for the theatre nurse to give him the medical saw. Cutting through the bone was a noisy business. After some three hours, the bones were removed, and the brain exposed. "Done? Excellent. Now, we have to remove the brain, and to do this the spinal cord must be severed." He nodded to Professor Vennuchi. "The brain must be frozen of course. This will serve two purposes." The teams knew the procedures, but he was speaking now for the benefit of the recordings, which would be an integral part of the presentation to the world, about how advanced were the transplant technicians of China. The best in the world. "Without freezing, it will otherwise die, firstly, and secondly we can only attach the electrical female connectors when the brain is frozen. The male connectors will be connected to a living body and this is the tricky bit. It will take hours. We have perfected this technique probably after hundreds of attempts. This will be the first live operation." He again lied. He knew there had been hundreds of failed attempts on individuals from China's prisons, and, when preparing for the world-exclusive exposure about their break-through in performing what was hitherto thought to be impossible, on European guinea-pigs. The failures had been quietly incinerated; the recordings destroyed. Xia continued. "This is the job of my assistant surgeons here. This is their specialisation." He indicated the team of four men standing to one site of the tables. We can relax while this operation is performed. We will do the body first so leaving time for the brain to freeze."

"Now Andy ..." The Italian professor stepped forward to give his brief presentation.

"Now we administer some methylprednisolone to preserve some motor and sensory function. If all the white matter in the same cord segment were destroyed, there could be an interruption in signal transmission, especially if the connectors were not functioning properly. This could cause paralysis in the hands and lower limbs and loss of control over urination and defecation. This is a second level of damage, progressive enlarging of any lesions and thus exacerbating functional impairment. This can encompass several spinal segments around any original wound."

"Excellent. Any damaged axons become useless, disconnected stumps and their severed terminals disintegrate. Or could remain intact but are useless due to loss of myelin. And the glial cells proliferate causing glial scars. These could form a barrier to any

18

cut axons that might somehow try to regrow and connect to cells they once energised. Some may remain whole, myelinated and able to carry signals, but their numbers are usually too small to convey useful directives to the brain or muscles." Professor Xia broke off to peer at the operations of his four-man team. "So, tell us what that would mean, Andy."

"It means gentlemen, that the small operation you see before you is undoubtedly the most important and innovative operation in any brain-surgery, and if we can carry out this correctly the patient will have full, normal functions. If botched, or if our scientific theories are incorrect, we have been wasting our time and a great deal of money. If we get it right, then you gentlemen, are on the brink of a breakthrough which the rest of the world will queue up to learn. It will represent a great deal to the economies of the participating nations, Italy and China, and of which you should all be justifiably proud."

"Thank you, Andy. I couldn't have put it better myself." Professor Vennuchi looked up to the Chinese surgeon and smiled. If the Italian had known how the two patients had come to be where they were now, or just how many bodies had lain where those two did now, it is extremely unlikely that the Milan doctor would have done more than walk out of the operating theatre.

Thirteen hours after the first incision, the skull rebuilt, and resealing operations commenced. Professors Renchuan and Vennuchi's tasks were complete. They could do no more. Xia then addressed the teams again.

"Right, finish up, clean up and get everything over to the ICU. Twenty-four-hour bedside observations please and I want to see a complete record of readings when I get back. Thank you all." They left the theatre and took some refreshment. They then had to review the video recordings and do any voice-overs the editors deemed necessary. And Beijing wanted to see the result, but only if the surgeons could prove beyond doubt that their work had been successful. Otherwise as far as Beijing was concerned, and true to form, it never happened.

CHAPTER 3

Willis had the feeling that he was rising to the surface of a swimming pool. The feeling was one he had experienced only once before, when a dentist had given him an anaesthetic and it was actually quite an agreeable sensation. His first two thoughts were that he was alive. The second was 'where is my car'? He'd left it in the car park opposite the old Ramada hotel, and it was probably the car which attracted the muggers to him in the first place. Any bright yellow muscle-car would do the same, but his was the first such car he had bought since he flogged his old Dodge Charger. Now it was a new Mustang. He had the 5.3 litre because he liked the exhaust noise, a very stupid reason to pay an extra five grand on a bloody car. He remembered flooring the first mugger who came at him in the car-park, but he had not seen the second one coming up from behind. But he would not forget this face. He was a short-arse, with short hair, and a scar running across his face from his left ear to the corner of his mouth. Ugly, chubby bastard, probably about thirteen stone with a small pot-belly. He would have to get hold of an artist to draw him. But he would like the chance to dish out his own punishment before the police picked him up.

The next thoughts Willis had were that his eyes were covered, and he was unable to move his arms or his head. Maybe he was dead after all. But then he heard some people talking. He could not understand what they were saying. That's okay then. He was obviously in an NHS hospital. Then he felt someone touch him. He also noted that the language he was hearing was Chinese. He couldn't open his mouth, so he just let out a few loud 'Hmms!' to attract attention. The result was instantaneous. A sudden gaggle of raised voices, as though some startling emergency had taken place, then he felt someone touch his face through his bandages. He carried out another appraisal. No, he was not dead. Nor did he think he was in China. Everything went quiet for a while then he felt hand gently removing the bandages from his face. His eyes fluttered open, and he blinked in the brightness of the room. He licked his lips. He could not move his head to either the left or the right, but he detected a movement above him and off to his right. Then a smiling face appeared above him and looked directly into his eyes.

"Zao!"

"What? I do not speak Chinese. Do you speak English or German?"

"Bù. Bùshi German. Děng yîxià." The face disappeared. After a short interval, another face appeared.

"Hello. How are you?"

"As well as can be expected. Who are you and can you tell me what the fuck's going on?" Willis's voice sounded alien to him. He put it down to not having spoken for a while, and he had no idea exactly how long that had been.

"Of course. I am Professor Xia Renchuan and you have been in a nasty accident. We hope to get you home soon ..."

"You'll have to untie me first. Why am I secured like this...?"

"All in good time. We have to ..."

"Thank you. The sooner the better I have a great deal to do. What's the date?"

"Oh, yes. Today is the 31st of May ... but we must get you back to your own hospital. They will deal with all the other medical issues. The surgeon turned to the doctors and nurses who had flooded into the room behind him. He spoke in Chinese. "Make sure you get this recorded, and as soon as it's obvious that this is our patient, we can get him taken back to Professor Vennuchi to deal with. We don't want any embarrassing scenes, got it?"

"Hǎo!" They all bowed and nodded. Willis thought. The end of May? When was it he drove into Reading? Weeks ago! At least he was alive. Possibly. His situation seemed to him unreal to say the least.

Back in his office, Xia called Andy telling him that the patient was conscious, and now all they wanted to do was get him back to the Milan hospital. He made it clear that the patient was now under the care of Ospidale San Raffaele, not Harbin. He was also to write up the operation and monitor the patient and as soon as they had all they wanted, and whatever happened to him thereafter was Milan's concern. He continued. "Once the guy appears in all respects to be normal, he's your problem. We've done our bit and we'll arrange transport. I'll send on the details as soon as I can. We can move on to the next operation."

"Of course, Xia. That was just as agreed. And thanks". Xia went back to see the patient to tell him he would be going to an ICU under the care of his surgeon, Professor Vennuchi. Willis thanked him. He also wondered what was going on as this was clearly not an NHS deal.

"Will I be able to move around? Or get up and dressed?"

"No. You've had quite a serious operation, and you will have to be restrained for a while. Once your physician gets you back under his care, you might well be able to do all that. In the meantime, we'll get all your clothes and personal belongings together ready for your move." Without waiting for any response from his patient, Xia turned on his heels, and was gone. Outside the door of the ICU room, he instructed his staff to not converse with the patient. "He must not learn of what has happened to him. Let the other team deal with all that. It is no longer our business. Our bit is complete, and we have all necessary information to send to Beijing to secure our future funding."

Shortly after Xia had left, a nurse buzzed around for a while, and Willis remembered nothing until he woke up as he was being carried off a plane. He recognised the smell, the goings on, and the sound of engines starting up or shutting down or 'planes taking off. He still appeared to be bound as he was unable even to move his fingers. He was carried to an ambulance, and then the smell of a hospital filled his nostrils. Then he fell asleep again. He woke up sometime later. It may have been just hours, or it could have been days. Somebody was taking the bandages off his head, and this time he could turn his head left and right. To the right he saw the stiff, white uniform of the nurse who was attending to him. She said something to him in Italian, but the only word he could make out was 'Vennuchi'. He had heard the name before.

"You speak English or German?" The voice came from his left, so he tuned that way and saw a slim, dark man who reminded him of Heinrich Himmler.

"I prefer English. My German is a bit rusty and certainly lacks any medical terms."

"Ah. As I thought. I am Professor Vennuchi. Andy. I expect you have a few questions to ask?"

"Just a few. Like where am I for one and ..."

"You are in Italy, Milan. You were brought here from England because your condition was regarded as untreatable there, so your doctor had you airlifted here."

"So, what the fuck was I doing in China? Hoping to harvest my bloody organs, were they?"

"Oh dear no. It was just that there they were able to ... to deal with your problem ..."

"Which was?"

"I'm afraid I couldn't go into that, but your condition was quite severe ..."

"So, when am I going to be able to go home? And when will I be able to get up?"

"Subject to a few checks, pretty soon. You might have a few problems with your memory, such as identity and so on, and for a while be somewhat delusional, but that should soon pass. It's only natural, and we have psychiatrists on hand to assist you." Willis's eyes narrowed. The bloke was talking tosh.

"All I want to do is go home."

"Of course." Vennuchi looked at his watch. "I'm sorry, I have to go now." Within a second or two, the surgeon was gone. Willis was in serious need of a piss, and assuming the hospital staff had thought of that little problem as well, he just let it out. He thought it felt pretty good.

Andy Vennuchi picked up his mobile and sent a text to Steve

Grant. *'Call me when you can. Andy'.* Grant heard the 'ping' indicating an incoming message, but he was too busy to see who had sent it, but he picked up the message about two hours later when he finished his morning rounds. He had left his 'phone at the nurses' station, and Rosie, who had accompanied Steve Grant on his rounds, saw the message on the screen before the doctor returned from the canteen. She knew it was Andy Vennuchi, so she decided to stick around just in case Grant called the guy somewhere where she could listen into the call, so she moved into the little office next to the station and busied herself. She heard the doctor return. With his back to the ICU nurse, she saw him pick up his mobile, and look at the screen while he called up, she assumed, the Italian surgeon.

"Hi, Andy, Steve … Oh, yes, Willis … Hey, that's great news … look, can't talk now. I'll call you again later." The doctor disappeared down the corridor. He had not seen Rosie. She wondered what *'the great news'* could be … about a dead man. She went into Property and claimed Ted Willis's belongings, explaining to the department head why she was asking for the bag. She had promised to have them ready to deliver to whomsoever Mrs Blake's Register office decided should have them, the police or the death admin team. Having recovered the property, she called Mrs Blake again.

"Rosie Pollard, Royal Berks … yes, that's right, Mr Willis … I have his property. There's not much, two sets of keys, one for a car, and house keys. A mobile 'phone and some cash. Hankies, no rings or jewellery and a note which I think is a book title …"

"Any missed calls on the 'phone, Rosie?"

"The battery's flat so I …"

"Could you do me a favour? Can you hold onto the 'phone and recharge it and let us know if anybody has rung or does ring? I know it's a bit unusual to ask you, but we are really busy, and as you know about his circumstances, we do need to find someone who can help …"

"Of course. I'll tell Property that I'm doing this. I'll be happy to do anything to help. I'll also call the police regarding the car. I imagine it's been towed away by now, if he had parked it in the town centre ..."

"Thank, Rosie, that's very helpful." Rosie called the police HQ and explained the reason for her call.

"We have picked up a car registered to a Mr Willis. A nice Ford Mustang, new it is. We've got it in our compound ... I think under the circumstances, we ought to return it to his house. The address we have is ... 'Oaklands', at Marlow, would that be right?"

"Correct. I suppose you'll need the keys?"

"It would be helpful, yes. Do you know who's dealing with Mr Willis's estate?"

"Yes. At the moment it will be the death admin team until we find a relative ..."

"Okay. Let me take your details again, and if anything else crops up we'll call you. We can send a traffic officer to collect the car keys ..."

"That's fine, as long as he gives me a receipt for Property." Looking across the car park, Rosie saw Doctor Grant, mobile clamped to his ear, his right-hand gesticulating wildly, as he walked up and down. The nurse reckoned he would be talking to Professor Vennuchi. She was right.

"Okay, Andy, how's things with Willis?"

"He has no idea yet what's happened. Sooner or later we've got to let the bugger up and as soon as we release him from the restraints, he's gonna get one hell of a shock. I'm planning to play it so our psychos can deal with him and get him sectioned, 'cos otherwise, imagine the consequences if he gets out? I don't think anybody would believe anything he says, but ..."

"I think that's your little problem, Andy. How's the China side?"

"They're over the moon. They are getting all the stuff sorted so they can do a press-release. No bugger'll believe them, of course, so it'll put us back to the Doctors Head and Wu, Sarah Wu, and their patient Jose Ivanovich O'Malley, the 2008 April Fool's joke!"

"Well, it's no joke now. So, we just untie the bloke and see what happens?"

"That's the only option ..." Andy Vennuchi decided that tomorrow would be the day. He would give the patient a full medical, then release him. His muscles would not have been too adversely affected by what was a fairly limited time strapped up, so the guy should be able to walk and move normally after a few hours. The surgeon was both excited by the idea, but he did not underestimate the problems.

CHAPTER 4

On Wednesday, 6th June, Professor Andy Vennuchi called his team together and briefed them.

"Right. I want a full health check. If everything looks OK remove all support and monitoring services. Then I want the patient to be allowed to get out of the bed, and on his feet and into a surgical gown. By this time, he will be fully aware of his ... er ... his situation. I want him in my surgery where we will show him the result of our work. I want two psychologists, one female the other male, to attend as well. We can't delay this any longer. Any questions?"

"Yes. What do we call him?"

"Willis. Mr Willis. Okay, let's get on with it."

Willis lay naked on the bed. His only covering was a bandage over his eyes. The nurse cranked up the head-end of the bed, so Willis was sitting up. There were about ten medical staff standing round the bed.

"Mr Willis, please try standing up." Willis lifted his knees and twisted his body to his right. He ran his right hand over his face and then his head. Clearly somebody had been shaving him. And his hair was very short. And that was not all. He felt different somehow, but he could not figure out what it was. Maybe he had lost a bit of weight. He swung his legs over the side of the bed, assisted my many unseen hands and onto his bare feet. He felt what he supposed was a hospital gown being placed over his naked body, then he was gently propelled forward so he had to walk a few paces. All OK so far. He was then helped into a wheelchair and felt himself being pushed across the floor. He reached up to uncover his eyes, but hands prevented him from removing the bandages. The movement stopped. He heard a door close behind him, but he felt the presence of people in what he judged was a fairly small room. He placed his forearms on each of the armrests of his wheelchair and waited.

"Mr Willis. Do you know what you've been through over the past few weeks?"

"Yes. Some bastards attacked me and knifed me in the back and chest. Then I went to hospital ..." He could hear some whispered conversations in the background. It occurred to Willis that whatever was going on, it might be wise of him to hold back. It was never smart, he had learned over his long career, to let anybody see all your cards, so he added, "or I assume I did. I suppose you are now going to tell me otherwise?"

"How old are you, Mr Willis?"

"Er ... I think ..." Careful, Willis.

"What do know about yourself?" Watch it!

"I'm a bloke."

"Where are you now?"

"In a hospital?" The surgeon produced a card from his desk drawer and beckoned to the nurse to remove his patient's eye coverings. Willis blinked. Vennuchi passed the card to the nurse.

"Mr Willis, can you read what's on that card please?" Willis took the card. He immediately noted that his arms were totally hairless and did not look like he remembered them. His personal observation was *'fuck me, I've lost some weight'*

"No, I can't."

"Vennuchi looked up at the other people present in the room.

"Why not?"

"It's gobbledegook, that's why not." He dropped the card onto the floor, and the nurse picked it up and handed it back to the surgeon who looked at it. It was written in Italian.

"Oh, I gave you the wrong card. Try this one." He handed over another card. Willis took it from the nurse's hand.

"Yes, I can read it."

"I wanted you to read it to me."

"You should have asked me to then. Shall I read it to you now?"

"Yes."

"Say please."

"Please."

"The first part of the process is to demonstrate that you have a

29

deep level of understanding of your ... have I read enough?"
"Yes, thank you."
"Mr Willis. When you came to this hospital, some time ago ..."
Willis knew exactly when it was; 17th May but he knew that to say
so, and that he also knew the call-sign of the air ambulance which
brought him to Milan from Heathrow was G-ABMM, which he heard
the flight crew use on their radio calls. He also knew that Professor
Vennuchi was the bloke who had signed his death certificate and
had told Doctor Steve Grant that cause of death was organ failure
and dementia, and Grant's reply *'No problem with that, Andy ...
now I'll get my arse back to London. Just let me know how things,
go please, and don't forget, we're a team so don't forget my little
part in it, will you.'* Willis knew that to say anything which showed
he had a firm grasp of his situation, would not be to his advantage.
He knew, too, that to be shown to be something other than an idiot,
in the old sense of the word, might be suicide. It was easy to kill
someone in a hospital, especially where nobody would, or could,
question the circumstances of a properly-certified death, then a
cremation. Vannuchi was droning on "... you were a hopeless
case, so we took the only course open to us." He gestured to the
nurses to bring Willis to his feet, which they did. Andy stood up and
moved over to his patient, and gently removed the theatre gown,
leaving Willis standing naked. Willis looked down. At first, he
thought he was looking at the body of a young girl, but in a nanosecond realised it was a male child, a very muscular male body.
He saw a mirror on the wall to his left and pushed the two nurses
out of the way to look at his reflection. The first thing he noticed
was the force with which he moved the two men, and secondly that
the reflection showed him to be a nice-looking kid, with a head of
blonde hair, albeit it very short. He ran his right hand over his
scalp, feeling the slightly raised lines where, he assumed, the left
and right parietal bones had been reattached at the sutures. He
had had a brain transplant. The enormity of what had happened
suddenly became apparent to him. Then he cried. He turned away
from the mirror, and a nurse gently replaced his gown, then he sat
in the wheelchair again.

"I'd like to get dressed please."

"Of course. Take Mr Willis back to his bed. I think all his clothes are in a bag in his locker."

"And then I'd like to go outside and get some fresh air."

"Sir," one of the staff addressed the Professor, "I'd like to chaperone your patient if I may. I'm happy to look after him until … until he … er … until you've decided what to do with him."

"Of course, Angelica. As a psychiatrist, and as you speak English it's a good idea. But I want you to keep a full record of what he does and take some pictures, for the record, but of course, his face cannot be shown in any pictures which are released to the public. Anyway, that's not a problem for you to deal with. I appoint you immediately to look after him."

"Thank you, sir. I'll take him back to his room and find his clothes." Willis was stunned. He may well be safe in his current situation, and it was only some innate sense of unease which convinced him that he wasn't. He would review his situation daily and look for a chance of escape. He determined to apply his mind to his flight and to take every opportunity to effect it.

"Here we are, Mr Willis ..."

"Please call me Ted. Can I call you Angelica?"

"Okay. You are Ted and I will be Angie." Willis supposed Angie to be about late twenties, and not actually a bad looker. "Now, your clothes." The girl rummaged around in the locker beside the bed and pulled out a large green bag. She peered inside and handed the bag to Willis. He looked inside.

"They whiff a bit." He pulled out the clothes which all appeared to be sports clothing. There was a pair of new-looking white trainers, a tracksuit emblazoned with the French colours, a few sets of underwear and a baseball cap, again in French colours. Then he saw at the bottom of the bag a French passport. "Angie, if you wash it all, I'll wear it, and maybe tomorrow we can go and buy some proper clothes?"

"I'm okay with that."

"Let me see what's here first. I want a proper look at them! If you get another bag, I can keep my shoes in this one." Willis noticed

31

that the bag was liberally marked with Chinese characters, and it could be of value when he wanted to get to the bottom of his very recent history. Angie disappeared, and while she was gone, he put the trainers into the bag, where he left the passport, rolled it up and slipped it back into the locker, leaving the clothes on the floor. Angie came back. "I see there are no socks, Angie. Maybe we can get some as well tomorrow?"

"Of course. I'll wash all this stuff now, and it'll all be dry by tomorrow. Then we go to town."

The couple did not walk into town. Angie was convinced Ted needed more time on his feet after being in bed for perhaps two weeks. Ted however, felt fine.

"I have no idea what size I am. I suppose we could look at the clothes I have on to see the sizes."

"Don't worry. We'll deal with that."

"And I hope you aren't having to pay for all the stuff we buy ..."

"I'm not. I have been given the department charge card. I'm actually on duty looking after my toy-boy!"

The little town they drove to was, Willis reflected, about the size of Marlow, his home town, and virtually everything they needed was available. They entered a shop which looked like an Italian Primark, but the stock looked pretty good quality. They had some fun choosing what they wanted.

"You'll need something for casual wear, not too tight, and something to put on in colder weather."

"I agree." What Willis wanted was something he could wear when he made his escape. Some of the stuff was very bright and conspicuous which he could maybe dump once free of the hospital and change his appearance to avoid any CCTV trails. He didn't want any police who might be called to find him, looking for a bright red and yellow hoodie. So, he needed some stuff which would blend in after he had dropped the bright gear. Obviously, he wanted some head-wear and a pair of sunglasses. In fact, between the various shops, they bought quite a lot of stuff. When it came to pay, Willis insisted on using the card which Angie pulled out.

"What's that?" Willis feigned ignorance. Can I do it please?"

"You'll need the *numero di codice segreto.*"

"The what?"

"The PIN number." Willis's finger was poised above the keypad. "Seven – eight – four – seven."

"Et voilà!"

"That's French!"

"It is. I know some more as well. Try *'Je voudrais un café'*"

"You should learn it in Italian."

"No, Angie." He was serious now, "I first have to learn to be a little boy again." Angie put her arm around his shoulders.

"I like you as you are. A little boy with a brain full of … full of life. You are one in a million. Probably a billion." She was closer than she thought, was Willis's reaction to that comment.

They found a small café and sat down. Angie ordered.

"Tell me, Angie, what are they going to do with me?"

"I have no idea."

"Look me in the eye and say that."

"I can't, Ted, because I don't know."

"Then I suppose I'll have to take things into my own hands, won't I?" The two sat and had two coffees and a Pizza. It was an age since Ted had had a pizza. He got the impression that Angie was a sensitive girl, and in the time that had together he grew fond of her.

"Why don't we take all this stuff back to the car, then wander around town and you can hold my hand and pretend that I'm your little boy!" Angie laughed.

"What a super idea! Let's go and do it now!" It was Willis's intention to get hold of Angie's card and see how much he could steal from a cash machine.

"Okay. I'll go and pay for the coffees." Angie handed over the card again.

When Willis returned from paying, he collected the shopping bags while Angie popped into the toilets. When she returned, he was standing with both hands full. They made the car-park and dumped their purchases. She didn't ask for the card. If she had, he would have said that he left it in the car. Willis needed about ten minutes alone with the card and a cash machine. He soon got his chance. He saw a bookshop, and asked Angie if he could pop in to have a browse. He wanted to see if they had any books in English, subject, Russia.

"Anything in particular?"

"No, Russia would do as I have this sudden urge to read about the place". He also thought it would be an interesting comment when she wrote her report about how the patient behaved when away from the hospital.

"We've just passed a book shop. You go in there and I'll go and do a little shopping. Whatever you do, stay in the shop until I collect you." Willis turned around and made for the shop. He had seen it as well, and across the road from it was a cash machine. He entered the shop. On the way in, he removed his baseball cap and his dark-blue track-suit top so he was left in his white 'T' shirt, then he crossed the road to the ATM device. The 'show balance' facility showed there was over 6,000 Euros in the account; he asked for another service and dialled up 700. The cash came out. He recrossed the road and entered the book-shop again and replaced his cap and track-suit top. He felt perfectly justified in doing what he had done. The legs on his track-suit pants were tight elastic, and he dropped the cash half into each trouser leg. Then he went to the 'foreign language' department and waited tor Angie to collect him. She was away for about half an hour, and she found him with a copy of Luke Harding's *'Mafia State'*. He looked up as she approached.

"Did you know that Putin is a fuckin' crook?" He wanted to see how she would react. It says here in chapter nine ..."

"Hold it, Ted. Firstly, *'fuck'* is not a good word for nobody ... sorry, anybody ... to use. Secondly, you read very fast, and finally that book is not normally what an eleven-year old ..."

"An eleven-year old? How do you know that? And a fully-grown male brain would very probably not fit into the skull of a an eleven-year old. A skull does not reach full size until about sixteen years ..."

"Not true. It can be pretty much full size at that age, with normal development ..."

"You know more about this bloody business than you let on, don't you? Maybe you should come clean with me!"

"Maybe. Maybe not. Either way, I'm not going to discuss it in a 'fuckin', as you say, bookshop. Now let's go home ... back to the hospital."

"I'd rather go home with you. Despite your disgusting language, I rather fancy you, Angie!" The woman looked straight into Willis's eyes for an almost embarrassing fifteen seconds, a long time he thought, before she burst out laughing.

"Okay, then, let's go home!"

Willis sat staring through the windscreen of Angie's little Fiat Panda as she drove to her house. He again addressed his situation. To him the most important issue he had to deal with, and any decisions he took would mean, probably, on how long he lived. He didn't really know how to play his hand. His concerns were simple. If he appeared fully conscious of what had happened to him over the previous weeks, then he could be a threat to not only the Italian connection, but also to the China set-up. The latter, he knew for certain, would be very happy to disappear him. What would the Vennuchi crowd do? Probably hand him back to the China team on some pretext. He had no doubt, none, that firstly he was an experiment and secondly, if successful, somewhere along the line, a lot of money was to be made. What he struggled with was why China had him returned to Milan ....

"You are deep in thought, Ted." Angie was pulling into what seemed to be an underground car park.

"Yes, just knackered."

"Knackered?"

"Tired."

"Okay. That's understandable. Let's unload the car and get up to my flat. The lift is over in the corner."

Angie's flat was on the first floor of a large block, two bedrooms, a large kitchen-diner and a substantial veranda accessed by two sliding doors.

"This is nice. Do you share it with anybody? Like a boyfriend or husband?"

"No thanks. I am too fussy to have anybody live with me. For the moment it's just you, my new boyfriend."

"I would have thought that a girl like you ... with everything going for her, couldn't avoid marriage ..."

"Don't go there. Let's just talk about you."

"Yes." Willis had to be careful. He knew that Angie was on the side of the hospital, and she must also know that what had been done him was very probably unofficial and he could, if he were judged able, cause the whole business some serious embarrassment. "Talk about me. Tell me in simple terms, what the fuck's been going on!"

"You sound angry."

"I am angry at knowing nothing about me ... either of me!"

"I understand ..."

"But you are assessing me? What happens if you tell your bosses that I'm just a stupid kid. Will your experiment have failed? Or is that what you want me to have no idea about me from the day I arrived at your hospital?"

"I don't know really ..."

"It is important to me. I feel my history is all tied up in a language I do not understand, like searching for a word which I might know well, but I just cannot annunciate. It bugs me like hell. Where did I live, apart from the fact that it was somewhere in England? I have no idea. Similarly, what did or do for a living ..."

"Ted ..." Angie moved up to where Willis was sitting and put her arm round his shoulders ... "Look. You are alive. You are a good-looking guy, and you have a superb body. Everybody's going to love you ... you've got everything going for you. You have to make a new life for yourself. I am sure you can do things which no other person of ... of your age can do ..."

"No, Angie, you're wrong. I am a nobody. I'm made up of spare parts ... I'm neither one thing nor the other. Where do I live? In an orphanage? Who is my body? Who is my brain? I do not have the wherewithal to find out the answer to either of those questions ... if you as a psychiatrist think this is anywhere near a satisfactory situation, then you ought to try it! Do you love me?" Willis thought he would be bold. "If you and I had sex would it be with me? ... Or me?"

"Ted! Don't be unfair! ... You know I can't answer that question! You're putting me on the spot, aren't you!"

"Yes, I fuckin' well am, Angie, and I am because I am going to have to live with the question for a good few years yet!" Angie stood up.

"Let's get back to the hospital ..."

"No. I want to stay here for the night. And if you say I can't, I'll throw a tantrum!"

That night, Angie had sex with an eleven-year old boy. Whether it was in her mind only or not, was, to her, neither here nor there, as she put it. Oddly, the same thought was running through Willis's mind.

Doctor Angelica Scrito's report to her superiors stated simply that the patient had little or no clear memory beyond when he was delivered to their hospital, but he had an overall basic appreciation of his environment, social niceties and inter-personal skills. Her conclusion to the six-page report, was that Ted Willis could be rehabilitated and have sufficient grasp of the Italian language to enable him to live independently after a period of no more than six months, and that she, Dr Scrito, was happy to do whatever she could to facilitate that transition and he, Willis, regarded the hospital's interest in him as normal procedure after his recent trauma, especially in view of the extreme invasive interventions he had undergone and he was grateful to the hospital staff for giving him a new lease of life.

The Vennuchi team bought it hook, line and sinker. They in turn concluded that once everything had been documented and otherwise recorded, their patient represented '*... no threat to the innovative nature of the transplant, and which, in view of the fact it was carried out in China, it was not, under the laws of Italy, a breach of the patient's human rights, of any medical ethics or such thereof as applied in that country, nor was there any evidence that the approximately thirteen million Euros [equivalent] expenditure in developing the technique applied in research inter alia was not in any way financed by this hospital.*' The administration chose not to touch on the fact that many hundreds of unwilling participants had been sacrificed and had undergone some most unethical, as judged by any decent society, cross-transplants which although had no hope of survival, had provided the various teams with valuable experience and data. Willis, had, it seemed to Doctor Scrito, been extremely fortunate. Her private thoughts were that SS-Hauptsturmführer Dr. Josef Mengele would have been proud of them. She was also aware that had the operation gone badly, the Harbin Medical University hospital would have incinerated two bodies, not just one. And, as with all the others, nobody would be any the wiser.

"Angie, is there any chance that I could move out of the hospital?" Willis waved his hand at the pile of clothes on his bed. "I don't think living like this is conducive to rehabilitation, do you?"

"No, I don't. Provided you have no ulterior motive, then I'll see what I can do."

"Where did you learn your English?"

"I went to university there."

"Which university?"

"Portsmouth. Do you know it?"

"Er …" Willis caught himself just in time. "No. Not really. You speak it well. Why don't you go and live there? In England, I mean."

"Because your NHS is shit." Eager to keep up his pretence of ignorance, Willis responded.

"What's NHS stand for?"

"National Health Service … It's where everybody in the whole world goes to for free medical treatment."

"Oh, I see!" Willis didn't take the bait. He was more keen on furthering his plans to escape. Getting out of the hospital, away from prying eyes, was a first priority. He had clothes, cash and a passport. He would need a rucksack, a mobile phone and the location of the nearest railway station which was, he guessed Milno Porta Garibaldi but clearly, he couldn't just ask anybody how to get there, nor would a taxi would be the solution. He had some homework to do. He chose an arbitrary escape date of 27th June, a Wednesday. He had two weeks. He decided on a 'phone first.

The station was not a problem. According to a map in hospital reception, the main station was in an approximately south-west bearing from the hospital, and there were so many train-lines running from the station that it would be hard to miss. His route would be via Brussels, then onto the fast train to London St. Pancras, which was roughly a 75-minute journey. The trip to Brussels would be about ten hours with, he imagined, at least one change. He budgeted about two hundred Euros for the fares. He planned to travel first class.

"Ted!" It was Angie. "We want to move you to the nurses' lodgings block. It's close to the hospital. I can check up on you and you can call me if you need me …"

"How will I do that? Is there a 'phone in the room?"

"No, silly. Use a mobile 'phone … Oh I don't suppose you have a mobile 'phone?"

"No. Shall we go and buy one?"

"No need to. I have a spare."

"Show me how to use it. Will I need your number?"

"Don't worry. I'll show you everything. Let's get you moving, shall we?"

The accommodation was on the ground floor. Much easier than being in the hospital's neurological department, sector 'C' on third floor. Things seemed to be falling into place. Once settled in, he checked he still had his passport and cash. He needed a safe place to hide it. There was a dirty-linen basket in the room, with a heavy plastic rubble-bag lining it. He lifted out the bag and placed the cash and the passport in the bottom of the basket, then replaced the bag. He then used some suture thread he found in the small first-aid box fixed to the wall of the bathroom, to fix the bag at various points inside the basket so to all intents and purposes, the bag was a permanent fixture. Willis was satisfied that is was a more than adequate hiding place, especially when he had chucked into the basket a few bits of dirty washing. Going back to the first-aid cabinet, he sorted out anything he might want on his journey and stacked what little he thought he would need onto a separate shelf. Now he wanted that 'phone Angie had promised, and a backpack.

CHAPTER 5

Willis stripped off and dumped his dirty clothes into the linen basket; the fuller it was, the safer his money and passport. He looked at himself in the full-length mirror. His hair was growing well, and he could see no sign of the suture repairs showing through, though he could just feel them. The lad had a fine, muscular body which Willis thought was indicative of a life of hard labour or a deliberate work-out programme, the latter he considered unlikely. He wondered about the lad's family, his academic progress, his ambitions, his loves. There was no doubt he was attractive and must have been an awful loss to his parents and siblings. He determined to trace the family as soon as he had sorted out his life back in the UK. And that would not be a five-minute job, either. He showered and pulled on clean socks and pants when he heard a rap at the door.

"Come in!" It was Angie. Willis stood up to pull on his new jeans.

"Hi, Ted. Wow, that's some body you've got!" She moved in to stroke his stomach and feel his biceps. Willis continued dressing.

"Just what I was thinking ... the lad must have been really hard worked. What nationality was he, any idea?" Willis thought it was odd, discussing that point. It was more like asking about a car or the origins of a cheese.

"No idea, and I don't think it's too healthy for you to dwell on that, either. Now, I've come to take you out to dinner. You need a balanced diet, one that gives your body the nutrients it needs to function correctly. Like fresh fruit and vegetables, whole grain, legumes, nuts and proteins. According to the USDA ..."

"What?"

"The United States Department of Agriculture ... guidelines, a person of your age needs 1600 to 2000 calories a day."

"What about a real Italian dish? Like the stuff we were eating the other day?"

"No. We'll have some real Italian spaghetti Bolognese. And, unless you want a two-hour lecture on diet, the subject of my master's from Portsmouth, you won't argue about it. And I'll show you how to use my mobile 'phone!" As Angie poked about in the room, Willis finished dressing. Diet? It was all tosh. For years he had survived on one tin of soup at lunchtime, and a whole tin of beans on toast for dinner. With plenty of cups of decaff coffee in between. But he couldn't tell Angie that, could he?

Willis had always been a fan of POW escape stories and knew enough to know that thorough planning was the key to success, as indeed it was to everything. The advantages he had were that nobody was going to shoot him if he got caught and nobody would be surprised at his lack of French or Italian, and the use of his mother-tongue would arouse no suspicions. The one problem he might have, would be with the passport at possibly Brussels and London, but as far as he knew, the hospital staff were not aware that he actually had a passport. But it was always possible that, once Willis had gone missing, and perhaps concerned about his safety or more likely that he might somehow alert certain authorities as to what had been done to him, so effectively screwing up their plans, they instruct the police, either the *Carabinieri*, the military police, or the civilian *Polizia di Stato* in which case a photograph of him would be all they needed.

Willis remembered some time ago reading an amusing, but he believed true, account *'Ridiculous Italy'* by one who identified himself, possibly, Willis thought, to avoid being assassinated, as Marcus Tullius Cicero. After some research Marcus had concluded that *'... the Italian police organization is so arcane, that it does not operate properly. Not even by accident and as Italy has a weak parliamentary system, one does not need to be brilliant to conclude that coordination among the Italian police forces is remarkably complex, maybe impossible ...'* However, notwithstanding, and as they were all bigger than he was, he decided that he would avoid getting involved with them. He would have to lay a false trail. He would suggest to Angie that he wanted to see the *'the famous tower in Rome'*, which he hoped would give her a continuing impression of his lack of basic knowledge as far as towns ... and towers … were concerned.

Now he wanted a rucksack, aka a bookbag, kitbag, knapsack, rucksack, pack, sackpack backsack. He was beginning to think that life as a real eleven-year old was a lot simpler. He had noticed a store-cupboard of sorts in the hallway just down from his room, so he had a good rummage around. He found two 'sacks. One was nearly new and the other smaller and a bit tatty, but it suited his purposes. He took it to his room and gave it a good washing in the shower and hung it up to dry. Unless Angie wanted to shower, she wouldn't know he had it. His excuse would, anyway, be that he wanted to go to see 'the tower' and hopefully it would, or might, help perpetuate his apparent helplessness and lack of grasp of his situation. Further, everything he did from now on must be justified by some simple explanation. Next, he deliberately flattened the mobile 'phone battery by leaving the torch facility at the 'on' position, because he wanted Angie to give him a charger. His plan worked.

"I'll give you one of mine. Ted, you must be careful. What would you have done if you needed to call me? Make sure that if the phone tells you the battery is low, you must immediately charge it up!" Willis didn't pursue the issue with some inane remark to further his desire to appear somewhat dim. He thought Angie was already convinced.

"Anyway, you didn't just pop in to ask about my 'phone. What are you going to do today?"

"You are having full medical check-up today. They will be looking at everything. A full service. Then you will be in the clear for about another two months if you pass. What do you want to do?"

"I would like to do some exercise. Running, or maybe go to a gym and pump iron? I just feel I ought to be doing more than eating pasta. I need a work-out!"

"Great idea. I can take you to the physio department, they've got a small gym there and you can be looked after by our trainers. It'd be nice to see how you get on." All Willis wanted to do was make sure he could manage the walk to the station in a week or so's time. If he managed some training every day, he should be pretty fit. Or fit enough.

For Willis, the fitness assessment was easy. He was amazed at his lung and muscle capacity, and the trainer, Marcel, a Frenchman, was impressed. Willis was invited to turn up every day for an hour's workout. After the training, Willis went back to shower and change. It was very hot, so he donned a T shirt, shorts and trainers. He met up with Angie again for an evening meal. It was a Bolognese again. Willis was happy with that.

"So, what happens to me now, Angie? I can't stay here forever, and nor can you pretend you're my mother. And I suppose that, sooner or later, I should go to school? At my age?"

"School's out of the question. Until we're totally happy with your condition. Regarding our relationship, I'm kind of your doctor. Then if all's well, you can be integrated into society here, not too far from the hospital in case ... in case there any complications."

"Like what?"

"I don't really know ..."

"Like legal issues? my identity?" Judging by Angie's reaction, he had hit the nail ... or one of them ... on the head.

"I don't think that's an issue, Ted, but ..."

"Maybe you don't!" Willis raised his voice putting the accent on 'you'. "And what if I don't want to live here in the shadow of the hospital? What if I wanted to ... live in Rome for example?" He could see Angie was getting upset. But he ruthlessly drove his points home. Other people in the restaurant were looking over to their table. All the better, thought Willis. "Do you think I give a fuck about the hospital? Or my doctors? Or you? What about the patient? Should he spend the rest of his life as a convenient little experiment to be written up in your surgical journals? Wouldn't you rather have me stuffed into some fuckin' jar on the lab shelf, so you could just pull it down when it suits you? Or chuck it into the fuckin' furnace when you've all finished with me? Is me, being a sentient, living entity, going to be too fuckin' inconvenient for you and all your fuckin' messing about with me? Well?" She looked really pissed off now and was also welling up. He really had hit home. She stood up abruptly and disappeared towards the back of the restaurant. Willis got up and went outside into the street. He would damn well walk back to his room. He was entirely happy with what he had just done, and now he wanted to see how the 'team' would react when Angie reported back to them.

He stood on the kerb, waiting for a gap in the traffic so he could cross the road. Then he heard "*Ehi, piccolo screanzatto!*" and a firm hand grab his shoulder. He knew within a nanosecond that it was not Angie. Instinct took over. All the years of his karate training. He didn't have to even think about it. He whirled round to his right both of his arms bent at the elbow, forearms vertical, about a foot from his head. He saw the guy who had grabbed him, and the force of Willis's spin and strike, made the attacker bend forward and to his left. Willis followed-up with a double strike to the man's ribcage. The attacker sank to his knees, and before he finished the job with a Maegeri kick to the man's neck, which might well have killed him, he heard Angie shout out.

"Ted! No!" The kick did not make contact. Instead, Willis stood over the man who seemed to be in pain, both of his arms hugging his rib-cage, head hanging down. What a target! "What are you doing!"

"This guy assaulted me ..." Angie spoke to the man.

"He said he was going to rebuke you for shouting at your mother!"

"Tell him to fuck off!" She gabbled away in Italian as the man got slowly to his feet, still in pain, probably with a good few broken ribs. He inched towards Willis, extending his hand.

"Angie, tell him that if he touches me again, I'll finish the job and really hurt him!" She spoke again.

"*Ha detto che gli dispiace.*" A small crown had gathered. The big man spoke up.

45

"*È inglese? Anzi, per me è pazzo!*"

"What did he say?"

"He said sorry, Ted. Let's go please!" She took Willis's hand and crossed the road to walk back to the hospital. They both walked in silence until they were almost back at the hospital, then Angie turned to him.

"Ted, what the fuck do you think you're doing? You could have killed the guy if that kick had landed! And if ..." Willis had to lie again.

"I've no idea what came over me, Angie. I was angry. And you really piss me off. I meant every word I said to you in the restaurant."

"We'll have to discuss it."

"No, we won't '*have to discuss it*'. He mimicked her voice. "What you will do is find some answers. There will be no discussion, okay?"

"You're upsetting me, Ted ..."

"Well, that's tough. Don't you think I'm just a teeny-weeny bit upset? I don't think your fuckin' team did a very good job. I think they left a few wires loose ..."

"That's impossible! We're here now. Go and get some sleep." Willis was determined to keep up the pretence of anger.

"Yes. Now you leave me alone. I don't want to see you again until you've got some answers." He walked into the accommodation block leaving Angie standing alone outside.

What Angie did not know, was that Willis thought he had behaved very badly, and was equally upset. His justification was simple; he had to get some answers, firstly, and secondly, when he did disappear, he didn't want it to come as a surprise for Angie or anybody else. He also thought his karate instructor would have been proud of him. He was glad, now, that he didn't land that kick because if the pigs got involved, it might well have gone rather badly. For everybody.

Willis didn't see Angie for nearly a week, but she had obviously asked some of the nurses to look after him, because he was invited to eat with them in their little communal kitchen. He also attended the physio department, where Marcel gave him a good workout. He was pleased that every morning after a session in the small gym, his thigh and arm muscles hurt. The Frenchman didn't speak much, but he would sometimes give Willis a few odd looks. Then he started asking questions.

"Teddy, you live Paris, no?"

"Non, Marcel. I live in London."

"I sure I see you before. In Paris. Yes?"

"Never been to Paris." Had Willis been truthful and said he was there about forty years ago, he doubted the Frenchman would have believed him.

"Do you know Jacques? Jacques Grévstoch?"

"Non. Never heard of him." However, Marcel's questions alerted him to raise the point with Angie.

The other nurses in his block were all very nice, and very tactile. They would put their arms round him and cuddle up to him when they sat in the adjacent TV room to eat their fast-food takeaways, or more often, the pasta supper they had prepared for him. Willis enjoyed the attention. While he could. He was now due to make his escape in only four days. He knew how to leave the accommodation block without alerting anybody. He planned to leave at about four in the morning. It would be light, and he would just take the next Brussels train out of the station. He hoped that any searches would concentrate to the south of Milan. He racked his brains for anything he had forgotten. He could think of nothing.

Then Angie turned up. He stood up to greet her as she entered his room, and she embraced and clung to him.

"Ted, please don't do that to me again. I've been worried about you. I know we've taken advantage of you terribly, but you must understand I want what is best for you, darling Ted."

"It's okay, Angie. It's not your fault ..."

"I've been pestering the team for ages now, and they're going to make a decision soon. If you can just wait a little longer, then it should all be sorted out ..."

"I have no option, do I really. And by the way, Marcel seems to think he knows me. From somewhere in or near Paris? Perhaps when ..." He was about to say 'when I've gone' but just in time he stopped himself ... "when I know what you've got in store for me, you could ask him how he thinks he might know me? He asked if I knew a **Jacques Grévstoch**."

"I will take that up with him, of course. Now I have to rescue you from those nurses. They all fancy you like mad and I don't trust any of them not to try and drag you into bed ..."

"Really? You should have told me that before! I think it will ... or should I say ... would have ... been an interesting experience for ... for them!"

CHAPTER 6

Just after lunch on the 26th June, Willis did a final check on his 'escape kit'. He laid everything out on his bed. From the linen basket he recovered the passport and the money which he planned to secure in small amounts in different trouser pockets and in his rucksack. He had two full sets of spare clothes apart from the set he planned to wear during the early stages of his flight from Italy, and as the weather was hot, he had no concern about taking any heavy warm or waterproof items. He packed the sports clothing and the bag from the Harbin Medical University. Mobile 'phone, fully charged, and the charger, all carefully tucked away. He must remember to switch the 'phone off until he was at least in London. He had no food, but he planned to remedy that problem by raiding the nurses' fridge in the kitchenette, but he would leave some money on the work-top to pay for it. As far as he was concerned, he was ready. By the time Angie called on him to take him out for his evening meal, the kit was stashed away under his bed. He was not going to leave her any notes when he went, as he would call her once he made it to the UK. It was to put her mind at rest, because he had grown rather fond of her ... and he would miss her.

During the meal Angie had some news on Marcel. He had been involved with the French national Gymnastics team, but there had been some hoo-ha about the use of drugs, and he had contacted the authorities as a whistle-blower and as a result, he was sacked, so he moved to Italy with his Italian wife to take up the hospital job.

"That's all very interesting. Can you look into that for me? It would be an amazing coincidence if in fact he had seen me before. It is an avenue to pursue ..."

"Do you really want to go there, Ted? It might open up a huge can of worms ..."

"Angie, how the fuck can you say that? Isn't the biggest can of worms, by any chance, what has been done to me and to the poor lad? Was he knocked off just to facilitate the god-damn awful Frankenstein experiment?"

"Ted!"

"Which you and your co-conspirators got involved in ...?" And for good measure he added for the benefit of the now distressed-looking doctor, "Isn't it just bloody fortunate that I have no recollection of just how the hell I finished up in your bloody hospital? What would you do about it all if it turned out to be a massive, totally illegal deal done for the benefit of a few surgeons who will doubtless cash-in hugely on their success and which, if it had failed, or will ultimately fail, they would just bury me or cremate me and destroy all the paperwork?"

"Ted ... I am a small cog in all this. I really don't ..."

"Angie that's bollocks! You are part of it. You are just as guilty if you know what's going on and keep your mouth shut. What about the Hippocratic Oath? *'I will use treatment to help the sick according to my ability and judgement, but never with a view to injury and wrong-doing ...'*. Don't you think, like Marcel did, that you have a duty to contact your regulators and ..."

"Stop it! We're going nowhere on this. What do you think would happen to me if I did that? Where's the evidence!" Willis looked up sharply. For a long time neither Angie nor he said anything. He reached across the table and took her hand in his. She looked straight into his eyes. Then very quietly, Willis broke the silence.

"What do you think you're looking at, Angie? I'm the evidence. I'm too young, now, to drink, to drive a car, to fly an aeroplane, to have sex with you, to get married, to inherit money from somebody's estate, to go to university, to have a bank account ... I can't even fly as a passenger in a bloody 'plane without being accompanied by an adult! So, when the shit hits the fan, what will they do? To me, I mean?"

"I understand Ted. But let me tell you something. I will look after you. Somehow, I will look after you. Let me tell you something else. Looking at you and hearing an apparently young man talking like a fuckin' lawyer. I find it incredibly sexy. I really do hope that I can get you into a school because I think all the teachers ... will learn a hell of a lot ... from you." He saw the tears well up again in her lovely blue eyes. For a fleeting moment, Willis was thinking twice about leaving her.

"Come on, love, let's go home. Back to the hospital."

"Ted ... don't ..."

"Don't what?"

"Nothing."

Willis's alarm went off at 0345 the next morning. He rose from the bed and dressed. All he had to do now was nip into the kitchen and lift some food. He found two small bottles of energy drinks, half a cooked pizza, some cooked ham slices and three chocolate bars. He left a ten-Euro note inside the fridge on the now empty pizza dish. Returning to his room, he stuffed his booty into his backpack. He opened his bedroom window, dropped the pack onto the ground below, then jumped down, pulling the window shut behind him, and set off out of the hospital grounds. He had a good idea of distance and direction, as he and Angie has passed the station a few times on their various trips out.

As he approached the station, he stopped at a bench, and took off his jacket and turned it inside-out, now the bright red which probably showed on the hospital security cameras was gone. He pulled up his hood and put on his sunglasses. The sun well up, rising fast, and the air was warming up. There was not a breath of wind. He took off the black trainers, and pulled on his new, white slip-on shoes and also put a small pebble in his right shoe, so he had to walk with a pronounced limp. Another ruse to avoid being traced. He limped into the station concourse shortly after five. The arrivals and departures board told him that the next train to Brussels left at 0600 hours, probably long before anybody at the hospital realised he had gone. At the booking office, speaking very bad French, which he was sure clerk could barely understand, but knew only that it was French, Willis paid 90 Euros for his single, first-class ticket to Brussels. Arrival time was 1547; there was just one change. It was all printed out on the ticket. He found a shop in the station, from which he bought a newspaper, one with the biggest headlines if French, so that any perusal of surveillance cameras would clearly show the lad reading it, but the hospital staff would also know that he didn't speak French. Another move to put them off the scent.

At 0545 and after sitting on a bench and spending most of the time with his paper held high in front of his face, he moved onto the designated platform, and boarded the train's first-class carriages. Most seats were reserved, but he found a window-seat. Ideal, as he could turn to face the window and pretend to sleep, thereby not permitting fellow-travellers to provide any identity information if asked, which he thought was a bit unlikely anyway. But everything big is made up of little parts. His clean escape was something big. He removed the pebble from his shoe, put his pack onto the floor, with one leg through the straps. He didn't want to get it stolen. His passport and most of his money was on him. It was safer that way. Soon, most of the reserved seats were occupied. According to the station clocks, the train left on time. There was an English couple in the compartment, and from what they were saying, they, too, were going to London via Brussels. There was about a two-hour wait for the London connection, departure 1656 hours, arrival plus about two hours, he heard them say, so he knew that was also his train. He would keep them in sight. Willis turned to the window. Then he went to sleep.

He woke with a start. The English couple had left the compartment, but their luggage was still on the rack above their seats. The only other occupant was a chap who had stretched out on the seats opposite Willis and he was fast asleep. Willis had been dreaming that he was fighting with a roomful of teachers.

Perhaps it was because he had on his mind the inevitability of him having to go to school, and that conjured up in his mind the almost inevitable battles he would have with not only the teachers, but also the other pupils. He mused that nobody with even half a brain could get to my age and not have strong opinions about every damn thing, likes and dislikes. He ran through a few of his own *bête noires*. There were many. Facial hair, tattoos, smoking, drunkenness, gold medallions and neck-chains. The compartment door opened, and the English couple came in and sat down. The lady smiled at him. She wasn't a bad looker. He supposed that he should now shout at her, something like *'Fuckin' paedo!'* which is what he used to get when he told kids, of both sexes, some also of indeterminate gender to not chuck their cans into the river at Marlow, or when any adult had to approach anybody under the age of twenty years for any valid and wholesome reason. It seemed to him to be the *de rigueur* response to any admonishment served up to youngsters of a certain age and minimal intellect.

Willis decided to follow the Brits across the platform at their stop to pick up the onward connection to Brussels. No sweat. Willis had wanted to know the time, but he was not going to turn his 'phone on as he knew it could be tracked. Instead, he would wait until he could see the station clock. The train pulled into the Brussels Midi station, and he glanced at the station clock. He wouldn't use the 'phone until he was well past Dover on the way to London. He planned initially to send some text-messages. He reckoned a few people would get one hell of a surprise. Somewhat perversely, he was looking forward to surprising quite a few people. Even more perversely, he was getting a faint notion that he might get to enjoy being eleven … again. He followed the English couple, and the signs, to the platform for the Eurostar service. He bought his ticket, showing his passport to confirm his age. The cost was a whisker under 50 Euros. As Willis predicted, the train to London left on time. He had bought a copy of the Times at the station and settled down to read it on the journey. He shared a compartment with the

English couple again and noticed them looking at him.

"Excuse me, young man ... are you English?"

"No. French. Can I help you with something?"

"Er ... no. But you're reading the Times!"

"Yes. I have been for a few years now, actually"

"Wow! How old are you?" Willis decided that, had he said 73, it would probably be more of a shock that his saying eleven. He chose the lower age.

"Eleven."

"Very impressive! So you speak good English?"

"Yes. And I hope that from my accent you would not be able to tell I am French, would you?"

"No. Very unusual for a Frenchman not to give away his origins ... the accent is usually very strong. And they usually do not pronounce their aitches, either"

"What you say is so true, madam. And, like the Germans, rarely pronouncing their double-u's" Willis returned to the paper. He appeared, however, to still be an object of curiosity to his fellow travellers. He just hoped that when they got to London, the station would not be plastered with pictures of him above a notice asking *'Have you seen this boy? If so, please contact Interpol'* If there were any posters, he hoped that they might have had the decency to add *'Do not approach him; he is highly dangerous!'* He also resolved not to show off again, as it could lead to all sorts of cross-examinations with possibly disadvantageous consequences. Willis finished as much of the newspaper as interested him. He decided not to attempt the Times crossword puzzle, as he didn't want to further alert the Brit's interest in him.

The Eurostar train started reducing speed to pull into London St Pancras station. Willis made his way through the barrier. He needed a hotel and a *Bureau de Change*. No problem. He had something approaching 500 Euros on him and he needed English pounds. He also wanted to book into an hotel, as he was a bit knackered. He sat on a station bench and turned on his mobile.

The History of Victor Clément

There was an ICE Bureau at St Pancras; the hotel was a Premier Inn at 88 Euston Road. He changed 300 Euros into pounds sterling, then walked to the hotel and booked himself in. A standard room came in at £89.00. He approached reception. There was a woman fussing around at the back of the reception area, and a young man seated behind the counter. He looked up at Willis in a way which made him think, *'Oh, fuck, now what?'.* Then it started.

"Yes, sonny?" Here we go. Willis knew he needed volume. He leaned as far towards the employee as the counter would allow.

"I'd be very much obliged if you would not call me 'sonny'. My name is Victor Clément ..." Willis made it sound as French as he could, and he thought, too, that the volume was perhaps a bit over the top ... "I would like to book a single room for the night." The youth looked a bit startled, and the woman had turned round to see what was going on.

"Sorry, mate I didn't know your name ..."

"I am not your mate. Is it not good form for a man in your position to address your guests as sir?" The woman had had enough. She wrenched the youth from his chair.

"Mike! Into the office!" Then she turned to Willis.

"I'm sorry, sir. He is just a trainee. He'll learn. A single room, was it? Of course. How do you wish to pay? Cash? Thank you. Just complete the visitor's card. I'll get your change." Willis signed. She handed him his change.

"You've given me too much change."

"No, that's right, sir. I've given you a discount ..."

"There really is no need ..."

"I insist. Thank you. Here's your room card. The charge included breakfast. Anything else you want, just give them your room number. There's a selection of drinks in the mini-fridge in your room."

"Thank you." He smiled at her. She beamed back. Willis thought, *'Shit; once all my blonde hair grows to any decent length, I'll be fighting off the birds!'* He went up to his room showered, changed then went down to the restaurant.

Willis ordered boned lamb medallions, in red wine sauce with shallots, garlic, rosemary, spinach and baby new potatoes. To drink he ordered an Erdinger alcohol-free wheat beer. Having placed his order, he switched on his mobile 'phone. There were six messages from Angie, all of them asking him to contact her, each message seemingly more desperate than the other. He sent one reply. *'Call me in one hour when I've finished my dinner. Ted XX'*. He then sent another text to his own mobile number 07532 066440 which he had had for years. *'Sir, Madam; if you are dealing in any way with the affairs of the late Mr Ted Willis, would you please contact me on this number any time day or night. Urgent. Thank you'*. He knew it was a long shot. He knew, too, that if it didn't work, the next thing to do was to pitch up at the royal Berks and confront their Steve Grant and nurse Rosie Pollard.

The meal was excellent. Willis ordered another Erdinger and looked at his mobile. The hour was nearly up, and he knew that Angie would call him very soon. He was right. He saw the screen light up showing *'Angelica S'*. He let the ring-tone twitter away for a good few seconds, then pressed the green 'answer ' button.

"Hello!"

"Ted? Where are you? What are you doing for God's sake! I've been worried sick …!" Willis let her rant on.

"Sorry, who is this?" He thought he would let her wind herself up even more.

"It's me, Angie! Where are you? What's going on?"

"Oh, Angie! Some of your nurses kidnapped me and they are holding me as a sex-slave in the London Hilton ..." He talked a bit quieter, as several guests at nearby tables turned to look at him.

"Ted! I'm serious! Where ..."

"I'm in London. I've just had an excellent dinner and a couple of whiskeys and ..."

"You are too young to drink ..."

"Yes, thanks to you and your bloody hospital! There are some things I've got to do here. One is to get my life back together … before …"

"I knew you were up to something. Did you nick a load of money from the charge account? I had to ..."

"The official answer is no. The truth is yes. Probably ..."

"Well, I told the office that I gave the card to you and you lost it. So, you owe me one. What are you going to do now?"

"I'll tell you. You can tell your Professor Vennuchi, Andy, that I'm going to drop in on the arsehole who dropped me into your bloody hospital. After that, I don't know what I'm going to do."

"Ted, be careful. Really careful. Please liaise with me before you do anything, please! Don't forget the Chinese are involved as well ..."

"I think you have a better grasp of what's been going on than you let on, haven't you?"

"Ted, I can't understand why you are behaving like this ..."

"I'll fuckin' well tell you why! ... Whatever the outcome was ..." Willis had raised his voice again, and he knew people were listening in, but he was beyond caring. "... you can't hurt someone, for example, then expect to not be called to account for it just because the victim might have enjoyed it or some of it. And it's for the probably hundreds of poor souls who finished up on some filthy operating table somewhere in China just to further their vile experiments which you know full well could not be done in any other country in the world, not North Korea 'cos they don't do anything civilised medical wise, not Russia 'cos all the rich guys there fuck off to the UK or America for their operations ...!"

"Ted! Stop! I know you're right! I'm on your side ..."

"Alright. Just do me a favour. Don't warn anybody here, or in Milan or in China about what I am doing, or where I am. Let me deal with it here. And just to put your mind at rest, I do not have any problems about looking after myself." Then as an after-thought, "I love you, Angie."

"Just take care, Ted. You're a great kid!"

"That just about sums it up ...a great kid... Bye, Angie." Willis cut the connection. Then he went to bed. Tomorrow he would be on the train to Reading, departing Paddington at 10.27. arriving Reading 11.22. First class fare £22.45. If he hadn't received a reply to the text he sent to his mown 'phone, he would take a taxi to his house and ask Alf to let him in.

CHAPTER 7

Willis was up early, the sun streaming into his bedroom window. He showered, put on clean clothes. Then went for breakfast. All he wanted was croissants and some decent coffee. He returned to his room, cleaned his teeth, packed and returned to reception to settle his account. Mike was again working reception.

"Morning, sir. Can I help?"

"Morning, Mike. I'd like to settle up please …dinner and a few beers last night." Mike poked about on his computer screen.

"Thank you, sir. No charge. It's all been taken care of. Courtesy of the management."

"Well that's very kind of you, Mike. I must say the food was excellent, and the rooms clean and fresh." Willis pulled a £20 note from his pocket. "Here. Please add it to the gratuities pot." Mike stood up.

"Thank you, sir, very much. I'll pass your comments onto the manageress." Willis felt good. Starting the day on a high was usually indicative of having a good day. He followed the signs to the underground. A few stops on the East London Line would soon have him at Paddington. He bought first-class ticket and a copy of the Times, passed through the barrier to his platform, and sat on a bench until his train pulled in. At 10.05 his 'phone pinged. It was a text from his own mobile. It read *'I am Rosie from the Royal Berks hospital ICU dept reading Mr Willis was my patient I have his belongings prior to handing them over can I help'*. Willis responded immediately. *'I would like to talk to you. Face to face. I assure you it is very important. Please keep this to yourself. I am perfectly happy to meet you at work; this is work-related. I shall be in Reading at about half-eleven if that is convenient for you. Thank you'*. He nearly signed off *Ted Willis* which would almost certainly have caused a few problems, not least of which would be Rosie cancelling the meeting and probably calling the police, so instead he left the message as it was. Rosie's response was a brief. *'OK'*. Willis's train pulled up to the platform. He climbed aboard, sat down. Again, his rucksack was on the floor, one of his legs through the straps. He opened his paper and began to read.

Rosie Pollard was shaking. She could not concentrate. She called Mrs Blake's office, and explained what had happened.

"All you can do, Rosie, is meet the person. Make sure that you meet in a place where there are other people around you. Then let us know if anything positive comes of it, alright? Thanks for letting us know." The nurse was wondering if she should call Steve Grant, and maybe meet this man or woman with the doctor present. She decided not to. She would meet the person in hospital reception, and if necessary, then move to a private consulting room. She found a small note pad and slipped it into her pocket. She also pocketed a personal alarm device.

The train's late arrival was no surprise. Neither the French nor the Italians were up to much on most things, but they managed to run their trains and buses to their timetables. So, rather than walk to the hospital, Willis got a taxi. The weather was warm, so the taxi was a good idea on two counts. He opened the door of the first cab in the rank. It stank of cigarettes, so he just closed the door again and moved up to the second car. The driver shouted at him.

"Wassermatter, mate?"

"Your car stinks. I don't want to use it!"

"Fuck off then." The second driver was only too happy to take him.

"Sorry about that, we keep telling him. The bloke's a pig. Where to?"

"Royal Berks please." The journey took only five or so minutes. He paid off the cab-driver and entered the hospital. He got out his 'phone and sent a text. 'I'm in reception. Newspaper in one hand, knapsack in the other. Willis sat down and waited.

He saw a nurse enter the reception area and gaze around. He caught her eye and stood up.

"Rosie?" The nurse looked at him and extended her hand.

"Yes. Are you the guy who texted me?"

"Yes."

"What can I do for you? You said this was about Mr Willis?"

"I did."

"And you are ...?" For a moment, perhaps for too long, he didn't reply.

"Er ... Victor Clément."

"Is that a French name?"

"It is." Rosie thought that, for a mere kid, the guy was very self-assured, very positive beyond his years. She felt no concerns about being with him.

"Rosie ... if I may call you Rosie, could we go somewhere private?"

"Of course. I'll just check in with reception first. Rosie walked to the desk and had a brief word with the receptionist, then she returned to Willis. "This way please. We can use this room." The consulting-room wall facing reception was mostly glass, so the staff working on that floor could see right into the room. "Please, do sit down." Willis sat. He placed his rucksack and paper onto the table. "Well? How can I help?"

"Rosie, I called you ... because I remember what you said to me before I left this hospital, and now ... I want to take you up on that invitation ..."

"I'm sorry, Victor, I don't recall ever meeting you before, let alone inviting you anywhere ..."

"Rosie you are wrong, but I cannot blame you for saying that. What I am about to tell you will come as a bit of a shock ..." The nurse looked to her right, through the glass wall facing the reception desk, as if looking for help.

"I can't blame you for feeling nervous about the way this little chat is going. Please listen. This is what you said to me." Rosie sat stock-still, looking straight into Willis's eyes. You said, and this is word for word, *'Bye bye, darling, I hope somebody can bring you back here to see me, your Rosie Pollard at the Royal Berks'...*"

"When did I ... when did I say that?" Rosie was beginning to look uncomfortable now. Willis extended his hand and placed it on top of hers. She didn't draw back.

"You said it ... and this may come as a shock to you ... you said it to me before Doctor Grant bundled me into an ambulance ... and had me flown to see Professor Vennuchi, in Milan." His words hit the nurse like a slap in the face. The nurse slumped forwards and she would have slid to the floor, had not Willis caught her. He held her and knocked hard on the glass and beckoned for somebody to help. Two figures ran into the room, a male and a female nurse.

"Rosie. It's Sandra? What's happened ... Sandra held her friend. Rosie started to stir, then attempted to sit up in her chair. "Has this lad hurt you? What..."

"Oh, God! No! No! Just please leave me with him. Leave us alone!" Rosie started to cry. She struggled to talk. With the other two still present, she managed to blurt out "I knew there was something going on. But I could never have believed it!" She gestured to her friends to leave the room. Rosie left the tears to run down her cheeks, then she moved to Willis's side of the table and pulled his head to her bosom. She ran her hands over his scalp. She had an immediate grasp of the situation. "Please God, don't blame me for all this ... how ... how do you remember everything?"

"Rosie, I remember ... I remember when you said to Doctor Grant, *'He's gone'* then Grant said *'What'* then you again, *He's gone. He's dead'* and Grant saying, *'Oh shit'*. Rosie, I remembered everything right up until I was wheeled into an operating theatre ... in China! Rosie, I am Ted Willis. I am in the body of an eleven-year old."

"I want to believe you. But I can't. Stay here just a moment." The ICU nurse left the room and had a quick word with the reception staff. She disappeared for a while, that came back with a small bag.

"I'm going to test what you say. I've signed off duty and I am going to drive you home. We'll soon see if all this is a try-on."

"I'll take any test. But please do keep this to yourself for the moment. I have a great deal to do."

"If you are operating some kind of fraud, you will pay the price." She looked through the glass, to see a man walking into the hospital. "Ah, here's my Sean. He's coming with us." The man came into the consulting room, and walked towards Willis, holding out his hand. Willis shook it. He turned to Rosie.

"You ready to go now?"

"Yes."

"Okay, let's hit the road. I have my car outside." Willis sat in the back with Rosie. The car was obviously a police car, unmarked. "We are taking you home. Rosie will ask you a few questions on the way." Sean stopped the car at the hospital exit.

"Right, which way?"

"Right. We should aim for Marlow." Rosie was fishing around in the bag.

"When were you born?"

"December 17th, 1945."

"Where?"

"In Ismailia, Egypt, but as my grandmother didn't want me to have an Arab birth certificate, she had my birth registered in Motherwell, Scotland."

"What car do you drive?"

"My lovely yellow, 5.3 litre Ford Mustang."

"How old is it?"

"Brand new.

The questioning continued. Then Willis called a halt. "Look I really must tell you. My situation could alarm a number of people, so I really do not want to introduce myself as Ted Willis, so I'll use Victor. And I have a good contact in the hospital in Milan who I think will confirm my story. She is a psychiatrist who, because she speaks good English, was looking after me. In fact, this is her 'phone. She lent it to me. But maybe we can deal with all that at some other time?" Sean spoke up.

"What's the postcode, Vic?"

"SL7 9EF'"

"Name of the house?"

"Oaklands. Look, Sean, please don't ask these questions. I suggest what you do is get to the place, open up then ask me to go and get something which you might think is in the place.

63

Otherwise, this examination-in-chief could go on forever."

"That seems reasonable to me, Sean" said Rosie. "Personally, I think he's genuine."

"Still, I'd be a lot happier if we can prove it to our satisfaction."

They crossed the Marlow Bridge where, not all that long ago, Doctor Grant had steered his car. Eventually, they pulled into the property. Willis saw his Gardner's white van.

"That's Alf. My gardener."

"What's his second name?"

"Gardner."

"What do you pay him?"

"Whatever he bills me. Depends on what he's bought, how long he works ... and do not tell him that Ted Willis is dead. I do not want anybody to know just yet." Alf left the wheelbarrow he was pushing and came over to the car.

"Can I help you?"

"Yes. Alf, isn't it? I'm a police officer ..." Sean pushed his warrant card out of the window. Alf took it and then handed it back.

"Doctors, then the police again ..."

"Again?"

"Yes. They returned Mr Willis's car. Been collecting parking fines for over a week, then they towed it away. Came back about a week ago, I think it was."

"Where is it now?"

"In the garage, over there ..." He pointed to a double garage, half hidden behind some trees. "They put it away. I didn't want to drive the beast. Huge bugger it is, new. American job."

"Thanks, Alf. If we can just pop into the house for a quick look round ..."

"Got keys, have you?"

"Yes thanks."

"Okay. I'll just carry on. If you want me again, I'll be somewhere round here."

Sean, Rosie and Willis entered through the front door.

"Right, go and get me … an encyclopaedia please, Vic!" Willis moved forward, then into a large triple-aspect room. In less than a minute, he returned with the book.

"Medicine cabinet."

"I have two. One in the downstairs loo by the front door, the other in the master-bed en-suite." They all went to look.

"Any money hidden in the house?"

"Yes. There's some in a small box under the dresser in the master bed, some in the kitchen behind all the cookery books, right-hand side of the shelf and another lot in the airing cupboard, upstairs."

"How much roughly?"

"Probably as much as three thousand pounds, but not less than two."

"Go and get it please." Willis did as he was asked. Rosie took the money to the large dining table and counted it.

"He's right. About £2,750."

"Where will I find empty plastic bags?"

"Cupboard under the stairs." They looked; Willis was right.

"Can you think of anything, Rosie?"

"Yes. The kitchen. Is the cooker gas or electric …?"

"Gas."

"What else is in the kitchen?"

"A microwave above the oven, a dishwasher, double sink, small table and four chairs, small TV, double-doored larder unit."

"No freezer?"

"No. That's just off the kitchen with the washing machine and a load of my small tools."

"Beyond the kitchen is my office …"

"Any computers in the office?"

"Yes."

"Come with me." They walked through the kitchen. There was a stack of mail on the kitchen table, he assumed put there by his cleaner, Connie.

"Right, Vic, turn the PC on and open your email account. I assume you know the passwords?"

"Just watch." Willis turned the computer on. To open the screen, he entered his password *'QueenBee747'* The screen opened. "Now my email account." Willis tapped *'Harrier365'*. The 'in box' looked pretty busy. "How's that, Sean?"

"Fine. What are all these books on the table there?"

"I'm doing a doctorate through Exeter University. The thesis is on money-laundering."

"Why Exeter?"

"So I go down there for lectures, then spend a few more days sailing at Salcombe. Stay at the Ferry Inn."

"Pass. Now, where are your children and when did your wife die?"

"No kids. Elaine died in 2009."

"Where did you marry her?"

"Registry office, Reading." Sean look at Willis, then to Rosie.

"I'm happy. But just one more thing. If I went to the boot of your car, what would I find?"

"Nothing ... But on the back seat, nearside, you would find a heavy-duty reflective jacket, some gloves, a hat and some wellies. In the centre console you'll find all my credit and debit cards."

"Okay, let's go and look." The policeman made to go outside.

"Er ... we can open the garage from here." Willis put his arm behind the coats hanging up in the front porch. The door started to roll up. Willis indicated a switch just inside the front door. It's here because from here, you can see the garage. There's another buzzer thing with the car keys."

"We can lock up the house now, because we can close the garage from outside. Let's go to the car, okay?" Alf was still pulling up weeds or something which pleased Willis, when Rosie pulled up sharply.

"Hold on, did Alf say that a doctor came here ... twice?"

"I think that was what he intimated, why?"

"Why did he come here at all? If he needed stuff on next of kin, he could have asked the police or any other agency to look into it. It's not his job, is it?"

"No, it's not" said Willis, "but perhaps I can tell you why. In fact, no perhaps about it." Willis stopped. Both Sean and Rosie looked at him expectantly.

"Well?"

"When I was taken to the hospital in Milan, their professor and Grant had a conversation that went something like this. The Professor. *'You look a bit like Leonard Nemoy'* Grant. *'Who's he when he's at home'.* The Professor again. *'He played the part of David Kibner, the doctor in Invasion of the Body Snatchers, the 1978 film … I thought you were the movie buff'.* Grant again. *'What makes you think that'* The Professor. *'Didn't you mention the film 'Moving Target'? Hopefully this patient here'll be no nigger in the woodpile'."*

"What was that moving target thing?"

"It was a piece of nonsense where, for half a million dollars, they … the business ... would arrange for a client to hunt down and shoot some poor sod who was offered a hundred thousand dollars if he could escape to a certain point, I think it was a river, but that's irrelevant. The point was that the person they chose, had to be a person who had no relatives, or anybody who would try to find out about the guy who gets killed." Willis looked at Rosie and her partner.

"Ah! So Grant wanted to check you out, is that it? Because he had some notion that you could be disappeared, and as you had nobody … you looked like an ideal candidate!"

"So then Steve … Doctor Grant … gets the death certificate, comes back to the hospital and dumps in on my desk. Case closed! So his visits were to make sure that there was nobody!" Sean lifted his right hand, index finger pointing at Willis.

"Vic, do you realise what you're saying?"

"Of course, he does, darling! And I knew something fishy was going on! I suppose Grant was paid for all this?" Willis answered that one.

"Yes, but before I mention that, Rosie, what did you do with the death certificate which Grant gave you?"

"Nothing. It's still with your medical records."

"Good. Please do not do anything with it, and if anybody gets a bit pushy about it, just stall them. Anyway, money. There was mention of money, just as Grant was about to go back to the airport. Thing is, anybody who can do successfully what the Milan and the China team have done, is set to make billions. After their successes, everything becomes possible." Just then, Willis's 'phone rang. He looked at the screen. It was Angie. Willis called out to Sean and Rosie.

"It's my psychiatrist from Milan!" Willis pressed the 'accept call' and the loudspeaker buttons. "Hi, Angie. Anything your end?"

"Yes. I interrogated Marcel. He knows that you ... Victor that is, was at the SOS Children's Village ..."

"Which is?"

"It's what you in the UK call an orphanage ... the children's village near Plaisir, not far from Paris. Thing is, nobody knows anything, but they think he was dumped as a baby in a Paris *Zone Urbaines Sensibles,* which before you ask, is like a slum. Anyway, he never spoke and hated school work but was a really good gymnast ..." Willis looked up to see if the others were getting the message. They both gave the thumbs-up.

"So, the poor sod was again, just used somehow. Any idea how he got to China?"

"No. Apparently all the kids at the home all had to give DNA samples, so they should still be on record somehow so if you need confirmation, you can just send a sample. But I don't think there are any issues on that front, because like you, he was a real darling little kid ..."

"We're putting two and two together, but are we not making six?"

"No, I don't think so. Just bear it all in mind. It might come in useful someday."

"How is the team taking my disappearance?"

"They are really pissed off. They wanted to put you under full surveillance in case of any ... complications. They were also supposed to send reports to Xia, the Chinese head of research. They'll just have to make them up, now. And another thing, if all this looks like getting out, there are some guys who stand to lose a great deal. So, for fuck's sake watch what you say and to whom, savvy?"

"Loud and clear. Maybe I'll have to do all my digging in secret?"

"You will. Must dash. Bye darling. Miss you!"

"Yeah, you too, love" Rosie spoke.

"Well, it all makes sense now. What do we do with Grant, Sean?"

"No idea. It's way above my head. Let me think about it ..."

"Yes, Sean but please think about it on your own. I have somehow got to get my old life together and convince HMRC that all this is my property. Before it all goes *bona vacantia*!"

"What?"

"The bloody government take it. No heirs, no will."

"That's not the only issue. Let's look in the car, then I suggest we get back to Reading." Just as Willis had said, everything was in the back of the Mustang.

"Let me get my cards. Do you think I could take it for a drive, Sean?"

"No, you bloody can't! ... but that's not the only problem you have. We can chat on the way back."

The little party drove back to the Royal Berks. On the way, Willis set out his problem.

"Officially, I'm an unaccompanied minor, with no family member or legal guardian who can take care of me. However, this designation refers explicitly to non-EU citizens, so precisely where I fit in is difficult to establish ..."

"So, what you need is ... hang on, if you were kept in an orphanage in France, and I assume nobody wanted to adopt you there because you never spoke, you were dumb, couldn't somebody here in the UK to apply to adopt you? ... Would that work, Sean?"

"I don't bloody know, Rosie, I'm a copper not a social worker!"

"Well, why don't we try it? I mean, with all the DNA stuff held by the people in France ..."

"Ah! But by now, I expect that the home will think I'm dead ..."

"They might well do, but if we produce DNA evidence to prove you aren't ..."

"It might come as a bit of a shock to them..."

"Why is that relevant, Vic? Clearly, they made a mistake. It might work, but who would want to adopt you?" Rosie broke in.

"We would of course Sean! ..."

"I don't think all that is my problem. The main problem is making sure that I inherit all my own property. After that, everything gets easy. So it might be easier if I got Angie to go to this home in France to collect all my records and stuff. In the meantime, I will find a way of ensuring I get my property back. I can't just pitch up once the estate has been advertised in the national press as seeking people who might be entitled to inherit and say 'Hello, I'm actually Ted Willis ...'"

"So how do you do all that?"

"I'm working on it now ..."

"So why can't you stay with us as a guest?"

"He'd have to go to school, Rosie ..." Willis took up that point.

"I probably would, but I think if what you suggested is possible, we should get that sorted out. Then I can deal with the estate issues, and once done, there is no reason why I can't go back to my house and live there. In fact, I see no legal reason why I can't live there now, but I obviously can't just pop into any old school and ask to be enrolled as a pupil, so regarding that, I might have to ask you to do that. Of course, ..."

"Why can't we do that, Sean?"

"I see no reason why not, but first of all, make sure you find out the procedure. I think Vic will actually enjoy going back to school ..."

"I'm sure I will! But perhaps we ought to first have a discussion re. the details, and the order of play. May I respectfully suggest that I deal with my property first. So I will want to go back and live at Oaklands while I sort that out."

"But how the hell will you sort that out, Vic?"

I'll tell you. But firstly, I am glad that you call me Vic, because to call me Ted when my passport has another name might just

70

complicate matters. Anyway, to answer your question. I have a very good relationship with my cleaner, more so than with Alf, my gardener ..." Willis was not going to be too candid about his relationship with Consuela, or Connie, as he called her, because she was not just his cleaner. She soon became aware that her employer after the death of his wife wanted a little more doing for him that looking after his house. She was not a bad looker, was an unmarried mum. As a result, he paid her substantially more than any other cleaner. He knew he could get her to look after him again ... "so I should be pretty comfortable there, and as there will be no other beneficiaries of my estate, nobody has the *locus standi* to make me leave the property ..."

"The what?"

"It means legal capacity to challenge a decision. *Somerset District Council, ex parte Garnett*, 1998 and *Pemberton and Southwark, 2000 ...*"

"Fuck me, Vic ..."

"Sean! You mustn't use that kind of language in front of Vic!"

"Sorry, Rosie, couldn't help it. I was gonna say that if he gets to school, and talks like that, he'll be taking all the bloody classes! Somebody is bound to get suspicious ..."

"Of what, for God's sake Sean? Suspicious of what?"

"I don't know, but I'll tell you something, love! I'd pay a million bucks to be in his class!"

"Right. Let me get the will thing sorted out. I'd prefer to do that at home. And in the meantime, as there are some good schools in the Marlow, perhaps you could get me enrolled in one of them?"

"What about fees ..."

"Don't worry about that. Because once I get my credit cards back from the car, I can just carry on using the accounts as, so far anyway, my death hasn't been reported, I can access them.

"Then what?"

"Then, and if necessary, we can get on with the adoption. Or guardianship. If we actually need to. I must have an adult ..."

"I understand. If we dropped you at home now, would you be alright?"

"Yes. I can talk to Alf and to Connie … they'll come round, and if there's any shit from anybody, I can refer them to you?"

"Of course, Vic. There you are Rosie; Vic's language is just as bad as mine!"

CHAPTER 8

"The schools' issue is urgent, Rosie, as they all break up in late July. There are a few good schools around Marlow we could apply for ..."

"Yes, Vic, but you will be going to a grammar or secondary school, as it was in my day. You're a big boy for your age. In fact, I imagine you'd pass for probably twelve or older?"

"Let's just try, shall we? Nothing to lose. Once I'm booked in, I can start work on the estate thing."

"Okay. I'll start making enquiries. Leave it with me for a while."

There were a few suitable schools in the area. One was fee-paying, the other a state school. Rosie made appointments to visit them both. She had explained to each that she was Willis's guardian, and was hoping to adopt him. The headmaster of the first school was Mr Reid. Rosie explained that Vic had had no formal schooling but was mostly self-taught.

"It's most unusual, Mrs Pollard. We have very high standards here. I doubt that this young man will manage to keep up. I mean, does he speak any foreign languages?" Mr Reid laughed. "What books have you read recently, Victor?... Sciences? Any idea about the theory of flight? ... Poetry ...?" He looked a bit smug. And held both hands out, wide, as though the boy was about to rush at him for a hug. "Well?" Willis looked at the headmaster.

"*Herr Page. Ich habe fast perfect Deutsch. Ich war auch fur ungefär zwei Monaten bei der Weltberümpta Red Baron Staffel und dabei habe ich eine kürtze historische Papier geschrieben und ...*" Mr Reid held up his hands.

"Enough, enough! Very good." Willis knew his German was not actually perfect, but what the hell.

"Books, sir? A few. First, '*The Battle of Trafalgar.* Then N. A. M. Rodgers, *The Command of the Ocean. A Naval History of Britain, 1649 to 1815'. 'Russia'*, by Robert Service. '*How the Red Army Triumphed'*, by Michael K Jones. Poetry, sir? *Shakespeare's histories and poems.* Pick one of them for me, sir?" Page was looking a little uncomfortable.

73

"Er ... shall we say ... King Henry?"

"Would that be King Henry the fourth, fifth or sixth, sir?"

"The fifth!" Without taking his eyes off the headmaster, Willis began his recitation.

"We few, we happy few, we band of brothers; for he today that sheds his blood with me shall be my brother; be he ne'er so vile, this day shall gentle his condition; and gentlemen in England now abed shall think themselves accursed ..." The headmaster held up his hand, but Willis ignored it ... *"... accursed they were not here and hold their manhoods cheap whiles any speaks ..."* Willis rose to his feet and raised his voice for the last few words ... *"... that fought with us upon Saint Crispin's day!"* Willis sat down. When he first heard that speech, in an old black and white film, with Laurence Olivier, he had gone home to learn it

"Well, upon my soul, young man! Er ... Act 1 scene ..."

"No, sir. Act four, scene three ..."

"Of course, of course! Excellent. Well I never! Do read your bible?"

"No, sir, but I thoroughly enjoyed reading that most excellent book by Richard Dawkins, *'The God Delusion'*!"

"Young man, you don't believe in God?"

"Sir it would hardly credit your position in this school if, just because I have read that book, as well as *'The Way of All Men'* that I am not a believer." Willis thought Mr Reid would choke. If he wasn't now, he would be in a few seconds. "But as it happens, I think all religion is pure, unadulterated tosh!"

"Well, you certainly know how to make friends, Vic! Anyway, I didn't like the bloke."

"Nor did I. But give him his due, if I had said that at my school in my day, I would have been flogged. Ditto, if I had not read history and poetry and had at least one language, I would still have been flogged. And frankly, the education was screwed up by your Tony bloody Blair!"

"Well, Vic, I expect at this rate they should just have made you headmaster! Now, the next school is fee-paying, and it's our only other option, so please, take it easy on the headmaster?" Willis laughed.

"Okay, I promise."

"Here, on the left. Turn in through the gates, right to the end then park."

"How do you know that?"

"Because I have walked past here thousands of times." Rosie pulled up, and the two visitors walked into school reception. The receptionist knew they were to see the headmaster, so she buzzed him to say that Mrs Pollard and Victor had arrived. They were taken to the head's office on the first floor.

"Do come in and sit down. Willis thought the head was scrutinising him a little too closely for his liking. He didn't sit, but moved behind his visitors, and placed a hand on Rosie's right shoulder, and his left hand on Willis's left shoulder, gently massaging it. Willis's first thought was that if he didn't stop it, he was going to rip his hand off. But he'd promised to go easy. This was his last chance. "Welcome to our College. I understand you are wanting to enrol … young Victor here for next term?" The head moved to his side of the desk, sat down and beamed at Victor. "Tell me about yourself young man? What are your interests?"

"Russian history, aeronautics and WW1. And I read a lot as well."

"Interesting. Are you good at maths?"

"Very good. And I am told my writing is very mature … for my age, sir."

"Do you know your nine-times table?"

"Yes."

"Sport?"

"I do a little self-defence. I'd like to do some martial arts, and I see that karate is on your curriculum?"

"It is. Can you run through your seven-times table for me? We are great believers in all out students knowing their tables."

"Seven, fourteen, twenty-one, twenty-eight, thirty-five, forty-two, forty-nine ..."

"Excellent. Now, Mrs Pollard, tell me your relationship with Victor here." Rosie explained.

"I'm sure I won't regret having a nice lad like Victor. Now, as you are aware, we do charge fees. For the first term, the fee is £2,500 ..."

"Mr Dyson, that's not a problem, and should you take the boy on, we will of course pay in advance." There was a bit of chit-chat, and Willis pretended to be bored by it and just gazed around the room. Eventually, both parties seemed satisfied.

"Would it be possible for Victor to attend the open-day coming up at the end of July?"

"Of course! I'll get my secretary to send some invitations. Just you and Victor?... and your husband?"

"Yes, that's three in all. I look forward to receiving the invitations in good time to add it to my diary."

They were soon back in the car.

"I think that guy's a bloody creep ..."

"In what way?"

"Like he can't wait to get his hands into my underpants. I don't think I'll be wearing short trousers with him around!"

"I'm sure you'll know how to handle him if he tries it on! Let's get back to Oaklands..."

"Good idea. I think Connie'll be there now, so we can explain our plan. I'm sure they'll go with it." Willis was damn sure they would. He would discuss things with them that only they and Willis knew, and it would either freak them out, so they would get the clear impression that there was some very intimate connection between their old Mr Ted Willis, and this new kid. He knew old Alf would be the hardest to convince, but by the time he had finished with them, there would be no doubt; they would be on-side, 100%. Willis needed to be in the house if he were to have access to all the documents he would need to prepare a will, leaving his entire estate to ... him.

At Oaklands, Rosie and Willis stepped out of the car. The van was there as usual, and so was Connie's little VW Golf. Willis could see the two in the kitchen, sitting at the table talking.

"I'll let you go and see them on your own, Vic. I don't want to be seen to be interfering in what is likely to be a pretty emotional scene."

"You're probably right. Pop up the garden and have a look around the veggie patch and in the greenhouses." Willis entered the house through the back door, which was between the kitchen and the office, opposite the door to the freezer and tool room. He turned into the kitchen. Connie looked up at him, and Alf introduced Willis to her.

"Ah Connie. This is young Vic. He's was here with the police a while ago, now he's back." Connie smiled.

"Hello, Vic. Are you anything to do with our Mr Willis?"

"Connie, I most certainly am. But I do not come here as a complete stranger. I have just a few days ago, come here from Italy, and before that I was in China, and before that in France, near Paris. I am eleven years old. Your twins Jade and Bella are now seven. Their birthdays were about a week ago, but I can only apologise that they didn't get their usual cards and little presents." Connie looked shocked.

"How did you learn about my children?"

"I've known all along. Mr Willis kept me up to date with all that stuff. And you, Alf? I hope Eunice has got over her sciatica by now, it can be pretty painful. And I hope you've been looking after the cats' graves, up there, by the greenhouse." Alf didn't look impressed.

"Is this some kind of trick, Victor? 'Cos if it is ..."

"Alf, Connie. You can ask me anything about Ted Willis's life. I know absolutely everything there is to know about him, his wife and ... about you ... ask me anything. Then I'll explain once I have convinced you that I am absolutely genuine."

"How much did Ted Willis pay me before he went and got stabbed?"

"I ... he gave you £120 in cash."

"When did he pay me, on what day of the week?"

"Usually Fridays, but sometimes a day early, or sometimes a day late." Connie piped up. Alf had fixed Willis with a stare. He looked more frightened that intrigued.

"Where did I get my car from?"

"Mr Willis bought it for you because your other one, a very old Volkswagen, failed its MOT. And it had a cracked windscreen. Connie, I know everything about you, about Mr Willis, about Alf, my neighbours, as though I were he. I am here ... because I am here to look after his affairs. In the meantime, nothing will change, provided you are willing to carry on as you are, you can stay here working as you have both done. You, Alf for over seven years, now, and you Connie for about three. And Connie, as I will need a little more looking after than Mr Willis did, I want you and your daughters to move in here. Free board and lodging, increased salary. You can take over the annexe. Treat it as yours, and you can give up the tenancy you have on the little terraced property at Marlow Bottom. Alf, I won't be able to help you in the gardens as ..." Willis very nearly said 'as I used to' but managed to blurt out ... "as I will have to go to school so I would like to engage you full-time, on a proper pay, but of course you can still do all the other jobs you currently do."

"...Thank you, but who's the lady? The one walking around the gardens now?"

"You've met her, Alf. She came here with the police officer. They might also be the trustees of Mr Willis's estate, as I am too young to take any absolute interest in it. Not until I'm eighteen."

"You talk like you're well over that already!"

"Thank you, Connie. Well, that's it. Those are the offers, and I will be moving in in a couple of days. And may I remind you. I am totally familiar with the work you both do, as though I were Mr Willis reincarnated. And you can ask me any questions, at any time, about anything, okay?" Both nodded assent. Willis moved into the garden and found Rosie in the greenhouse.

"Lovely garden, Vic ..."

"It is. Perhaps I should get Alf to make sure that all the produce he grows is kept for you and Sean, that is, the stuff we don't use here. Now, I need to pop into town to see the state of the bank accounts. As far as I know, nobody has any idea that Ted Willis is dead, so I'll continue to use the accounts and I'll draw some cash to pay Connie and Alf. As far as school fees are concerned, I can transfer as and when. Fortunately, when my wife died, we didn't need probate because everything we owned was held jointly, so we didn't even inform the land registry about her death. Or the banks. She and I still joint owners, and we shared joint bank accounts so even if they do hear of my death, her use of the accounts will continue. Frankly, Rosie, I just couldn't bring myself to deal with it all. If you leave me here, my kitbag's in the car, I'll stay at 'Oaklands' for now. Then I really must work on writing my will!"

"Okay, Ted. Just one thing. Sean and I are committed to helping you sort out this appalling business. Totally committed."

"Thanks, Rosie. I'm seriously thinking of getting Angie, from the hospital in Milan, you remember, getting her over here to help me with it all."

"It could be a good idea. Anyway, you have a lot to be getting on with, so I'll leave you."

"Just one thing. I want you and Sean to keep an account of your expenses. I don't want you to be out of pocket … I insist. It's not as though I'm gonna be on the bones of my arse, exactly, is it?"

"Er … alright. Let me deal with it. I'll see you later."

Willis was glad to be home. He was falling into his new role, and he had plenty to do. Connie was very helpful, and Alf helped her move her stuff into the Oaklands annexe. It seemed odd to Willis having the two little girls around, and in the hot weather, naked, totally unselfconsciously, running in and out of the water sprinkler. He wanted to join them, but firstly, he thought it would be inappropriate, and secondly, he had too much to do. The first few days were spent paying the bills, and from time to time he would wander down to the banks and draw cash, which he also did when

Connie took him to Waitrose shopping.

After a week of reorganising his new life, he started work on the will. He had drafted hundreds of them. His main concern was to find two witnesses, preferably dead, so there would be no bitching about due execution of the document. He went into the lounge and dug out the visitors' book. He wanted the document dated just before his wife died. He found two likely witnesses. Mr and Mrs Pete Coates had been his neighbours, and they had attended one of the many garden parties, usually held on the same day as the Queen's bash, and they were very well attended, and plenty of drinking. He found them in the book. Both were now deceased. As usual, Peter had been a little sloshed, as was his wife Daisy, and as usual, both had written scrawling messages. Peter had written his name, and Daisy had signed her full signature, little more than a scribbled 'X'. He would use them both. His draft was done on the basis that his wife was still alive. They were mirror wills. He left all to her, she left all to him. On the death of the survivor of them, the estate was to be held in trust for a child known as Victor Clément, at the date hereof and as far as was known residing at SOS Children's Village Plaisir, France. It continued ... '*but should the said child not survive the survivor of me and my wife or should he not attain the specified age of 18 [eighteen] years at which time the estate would vest in him absolutely, then the estate or such thereof as remains after any advancements to the said child prior to his attaining the specified age would go to the SOS Children's Villages International charity of Brigittenauer Lände 50-54 1200 Wien'.*

Willis also inserted a generous power for his trustees to benefit the child ...'*to any extent the Trustees shall consider reasonable for his education, maintenance or benefit generally as they in their absolute discretion decide and without limit'.* And the Trustee appointments were to be ...'*any blood parent should the same come forward by the 5th birthday of the child and is by DNA confirmed to be the parent of the said child or any parent by legal adoption or otherwise legally or by default appointed or in the absence thereof any person whether in the UK or in France and subject to satisfying all prudent checks takes on that role ...'* And so it went on. Willis was to hand-write some notes to his wife, which on the face of it, referred to her occasional visits to Plaisir, and other homes. Her interest in Victor ...*'arose out of her seeing Victor when he was at the home, his disability, yet keen interest in sports, and the free expression of affection he seemed to show for her'.*

The 'problem' of Willis's turning up in the UK was an easy one; he proposed to say that he was told by the Milan staff of a vague connection to the hospital in the UK, as confirmed by his medical notes, and he had made up his mind to abscond, and pitch up at that hospital. The name Rosie Pollard was also lifted from the same notes. He considered, that, as his DNA would prove who he was, there would be no arguments as to his identity. The only fly in the ointment would be if the French people tried explaining how he was now alive, when they had abandoned him in China. He needed to secure the DNA and any other records from the SOS home in Plaisir. He needed Angie. He called her.

"Angie? It's me, Ted." He explained the purpose of his call.

"Ted, I can't just drop into the home and pick them up, can I!"

"No, maybe not, but would Marcel do it? If they destroy all that stuff. I'm sunk. Ask if he has any friends who would lift it for him. He can explain that the option is starting an enquiry into why they just abandoned Victor in China, when in fact they had a responsibility to contact the French embassy and arrange for his body to be brought home."

"Maybe, but a PM would probably ... no probably about it ... be embarrassing for the home and everybody else involved, for one, and secondly, they don't have a body ... unless you went. They would recognise you. You wouldn't have to speak, and you could go with me and demand your records which you are entitled to do ..."

"Sounds good. You know, Angie, why don't you get out of Italy ... it's traditionally inflationary, fiscally its hopeless. The cops are idiots and you have no proper government. High unemployment

81

..."

"And it gets involved in dodgy medical practices as well, I suppose!"

"Yes, it does!"

"Well, I might just pop over for a holiday. But, Ted, you must come over here first. We can work out how to get all your documents. You and I can go with Marcel."

"Done. Just tell me when, okay? And maybe Marcel could come with you, so he can give me a fitness-programme, and set up a little training room in my house!"

Willis returned to the will. He typed in the names of his witnesses in the usual attestation block. He practised writing the names he needed. He knew that the plain, written name of Mr Coates was adequate for his purpose, as per the recent Court of Appeal case, *Payne and Another -v- Payne*. He printed off the draft document, read it several times, made corrections then closed it down. He was bound to find more errors when he read it again tomorrow. It was a good day's work. He sat in the lounge and turned on the TV. As a kid, he enjoyed the cartoons, Tom and Jerry, Road-Runner. These days, most TV was rubbish, Too many soaps, too many quizzes, too much bloody gardening and cookery, too much shit comedy. Bring back Bob Hope and the Two Ronnies. Documentaries, yes. Willis mused once again, as was common, that TV was having an adverse effect on the youth of today. Do away with 24-hour TV ... Oh what the hell, it'll never happen, so why did he get so wound-up about it? He really must behave like an eleven-year old. He went to the fridge and got out a couple of cans of Guinness.

The invitations for the school open-day arrived. Willis slipped into his little office and 'phoned Rosie. He had had a brainwave.

"Hi, Rosie. School open-day tickets are here. Now, why don't we put Sean on the insurance for the Mustang? I don't really want it

82

sitting in the garage rotting ..."

"Wow! He'd love that! And imagine us turning up to the school open-day in that! We would look really cool, and you'd be the envy of all the kids!"

"And probably all the parents as well! I'll take it that's a done deal then?" Willis had a few things to do. He would edit the draft will, go down to the town and draw out more cash, then list all the 'things to do' to further his theft of his own money. He now had about five thousand pounds in cash in the house. He looked up and saw Connie.

"Hi, Connie. What's the programme for today?"

"Firstly, you are too young to be drinking beer, and you left the cans in the lounge. Mr Willis wouldn't like it. Secondly, we have to buy you some decent food. You can't just live on pizzas and pies and beans ..." Willis stood up.

"You're right, Connie. Give me a hug!" She gave him a hug. Early in the day though it was, he had the urge to do with her what he had done as Ted Willis, but he knew it would be stupid to even try it. "Thank you, love." he felt her stiffen.

"Why did you call me 'love'!"

"Wasn't that what Mr Willis called you?"

"Yes, but how did you know?"

"As I said, everything he ... knows, I also know!" He just avoided saying 'knew'.

"It's kind of creepy ..." She gave a little laugh, then, he hoped, shrugged it off.

"Anyway, do whatever you need to do. And of course, you have to take care of Jade and Bella, so just carry on as though you were at home. I can be your third child."

Willis opened the draft will again. He had an addition to make to the trustees' clause, to the effect that ... *'there shall be no professional trustee or trustees appointed, but any person who shall act under the terms hereof shall be entitled to reasonable remuneration ...'*

And so it went on. He had no further issues with it, but still he didn't print it off as an engrossment. He'd have another look tomorrow. Knowing how any will could become contentious, he wanted to make sure that the Registrar at the probate registry found nothing wrong with it. There were, he reminded himself, no other valid claimants on his estate.

On the day of the school visit, Sean backed the Mustang out of the garage. The exhaust noise made the hairs on the back of Willis's neck stand up. He knew that buying the car was a ridiculous expense, utterly unjustified by any standards, but as he thought at the time 'What the fuck, why not?' It was a toss-up between that and learning to fly, then buying his own para-motor. He thought that now he'd buy the para-motor anyway. The only bitch he had with it was that the advertising spiel said it could on one tank of fuel on a para-motor *'cross the channel five times'*. He thought four times, or six times would be better, so there was no chance of getting stuck in France. Behind the wheel of the Mustang, Sean was grinning like a Cheshire cat.

"Wow, Vic. This is some motor!"

"Well, just don't write it off!"

"No chance! Let's get down to the school, shall we?" Rosie got into the front passenger seat, after Willis had strapped himself into the back. It wasn't ideal, as there was limited room at the back, which was something he hadn't needed to consider when he bought the car. Childish as it was, Willis felt pretty cool, rolling up the school drive in his beautiful, canary yellow Mustang. Yes, there were BMWs and even a Rolls Royce or two, one a brand-new Silver Spirit convertible, hood down, which Willis thought looked vulgar, and whoever owns it was in his opinion, a plonker. But it was the Mustang which got all the attention. Sean loved it too.

First on the menu was a brief history of the school. Boring. Willis wanted to know about sport, karate and any opportunities to go flying. He knew there was an arrangement with Wycombe Air park at Booker, where there were some interesting 'planes. He did not anticipate any problems with academic work, but he did anticipate serious problems with the teachers and with other pupils. But he could handle both. After a snack lunch, and a meander through various classrooms, Rosie informed Willis and Sean that she had booked a meeting with the school's resident chaplain

"Rosie, I bet you did that just to annoy me?"

"No, dear!" Rosie was more often calling him 'dear' just to, he supposed, play out the mother and guardian role. "He's a quite harmless old duffer." But Rosie was leading him on. Her first comment as they sat in front of the 'harmless old duffer' was inflammatory to Willis.

"It is so refreshing to know that the spiritual side of the pupils' welfare is such a feature of the syllabus, don't you think so dear?" She was addressing Sean. This was a conspiracy. Willis was however, not going to take the bait. "What do you think, Victor?"

"You know my feelings about religion. We should start as with everything else. Don't believe it until you see it, and if the particular faiths can convince me about why theirs is the best, or if Charles Darwin's 1859 scientific work '*On the Origin of Species by Means of Natural Selection, or the Preservation of Favoured Races in the Struggle for Life*' has a better argument, then I should be free to choose." The chaplain looked at him, open-mouthed.

"Er … Indeed … you have such a mature outlook for one so young, Victor!"

"I do, sir, like you just don't know!"

"That's enough! Victor. Excuse us, we must dash along to the sports hall. Come along, Victor!"

"What did I tell you, Victor? I wonder how many more members of staff you're going to thoroughly piss off, even before the open-day is over! And Sean … it's not funny! This is the last school-choice we have in Marlow!"

CHAPTER 9

The gymnasium was, actually, 'pretty cool' in kids'-speak. Willis approached the 'P.Ed' teacher, as it said on the label stuck to the front of his little desk just inside the door. He looked at the list of games available *'for pupils keen to improve their physique, develop inter-personal skills, strength of mind and respect for their instructors and teachers. A healthy body means a healthy mind'.* Apparently, a 'selected few' could obtain a grading in karate; even fewer could *'take to the air and fly a plane; a moment you will savour for the rest of your life'.* Willis noted the apostrophe was missing from the front of 'plane'. Maybe a healthy body did not, after all, lead to a better standard of written English. Willis thought he was turning into an eleven-year old grump.

"Rosie, I think I might like to come here ..."

"Yes, Victor, I have a gut feeling that you will, too ..."

"You will, mate" added Sean, "... go easy on the pupils. And on the teachers! Let's go back to see the headmaster, tell him we ... you ... are keen to join the school in September." Then to Rosie, "I don't think the poor old bugger knows what he'll be letting himself in for!"

"Vic, I'm going to ask Doctor Grant about your death certificate. I don't know whether we should report the death to the police just yet, do you?"

"This is a somewhat surreal conversation! ... I don't know what the protocol is on that kind of thing, but if you raise it with the hospital when you get back to work, I'll manage to sort out all the paperwork regarding his ... my ... estate. I tell you what might cause him a little problem. Ask him where the body is. And tell him that, as I believe to be the case, it should be returned to us ... you ... here?"

"Hey, you two, this could get very messy, you know that, don't you? And if the Milan people come up with some excuse as to why they can't produce it, or drop the problem into Grant's lap, there might be a few cracks opening up all along the line to China. We'll have to be really careful. Frankly, I wouldn't want to be in Grant's shoes!"

"I get that, Sean, so I really ought to get my Angie to sort out all my ... Vic's ... records and stuff before it becomes an issue. The China end won't give a damn, but France, Italy and probably the Royal Berks could become swept up in one hell of a scandal, which really is the last thing anybody wants. As far as you know, Vic, were any of the Milan crowd in China?"

"Yes, they were obviously. But if I can get Angie and Marcel ... he's the bloke who thinks he knew me from SOS ... to come onto our side, it'll make things a lot easier for all of us."

"Okay, Vic, let's work on that for a start. Here we are. I'll drop the car back into the garage. I think, Rosie, that the first thing is to mention it to Grant. If everything starts to unravel, when everybody starts ducking and weaving, I have no doubt that he will be one of the first to know."

"Could it get ... serious?"

"When piles of dosh are involved, yes, of course. Depending on the amounts and the people involved, depends on what they will do. Some blokes will kill for £500, so for a few billion ... get my point? Vic? Rosie?"

"Loud and clear! Right, I'll let you get away now, and thanks for today. And, for God's sake let me know what you get up to. I'll call Angie again and get things moving their end, okay?" Willis called the doctor again. After the usual pleasantries, he got straight to the point. "Angie. We have to get all the stuff on Victor ... I know it isn't going to be easy but imagine what's going to happen if your team there know I'm on the loose, and aware enough to blow the whole murky business wide open."

"So, what do we do?"

"You tell Andy, Professor Vennuchi who ran my end of the deal from San Raffaele, and who signed the ... my death certificate, that I stole your 'mobile and sent a text from London. Which I did. Also say that Marcel told you that there might be some records of mine still at the home near Paris. You and Marcel could collect them. You can show them a picture of me, which Andy will no doubt give you, and that you need all his records for the hospital in Milan. I am sure they will play ball. All they've done wrong was to abandon me in China, being told Vic was dead. Clearly, there were no charity funds to return Vic's body to France. Make sense so far?"

"Yes. But ... what will happen to the records when they get here? Do you think they'll hang onto them?"

"No, they will be destroyed. So he must not get them. You will have to bring them here with you. And Marcel."

"Why do you need the stuff?"

"Firstly, it belongs to me anyway, under the EU regulations, and secondly ... I have for various reasons, to prove that I am actually Victor Clément. I assure you, it is very serious. I promise I'll explain to you and Marcel if you do come over here, and I will of course pay all your expenses."

"No need for that, my love, but I promise to do what I can."

Willis had two jobs to do in town. He wanted a passport photograph, showing him holding up a copy of Le Figaro for date purposes. Then he needed to get his new 'old' will documents certified as true copies. He wrote the instructions long-hand, but didn't date it, then stuffed the original will and the written instructions plus a £50 note into an envelope. He knew that one of the solicitors' firms had a photocopier in reception, so he would know if the receptionist ran off copies for the firm to keep, as was sometimes their policy. He had dated the wills 2008, one year before his wife had died; he again checked the attestation. It all seemed okay. By lunchtime, he was back at Oaklands. He now had to call Rosie to see about getting a DNA sample.

The small package dropped onto the mat just inside the door to Doctor Angelica Scrito's flat. Alerted by the sound of the letter box snapping shut, Angie moved from her bedroom to the door and picked up the post. It was from the UK. She knew it was from Ted Willis, and that it contained evidence of Victor being alive, all the necessary information for her to persuade the SOS Children's Village to release the information they held on Victor Clément. The picture of 'Vic' was an original; a copy would have been easy to forge. She already had a letter from Professor Andy Vennuchi saying that the lad had been sent to them for treatment which the professor did not specify. As a result of the interest the Milan Team had in the boy, Angie and Marcel's travel and accommodation expenses to Plaisir were paid for by the hospital. In addition, the China team were chasing for updates on the progress of their patient, and for that they will, as they reminded the professor, need evidence that the subject was alive and well. A copy of 'Vic's' photograph was a good start. They had adequate records of the operation, now they wanted the results. The Milan team wanted their money. So did Doctor Steve Grant.

Angie called Willis.
"Hi. Package arrived, so we can start things moving. I'll copy everything of course, as I suspect the blokes here'll probably destroy all traces of you, or try to ..."
"Angie, do you actually know the full extent of what's been going on? I mean, really?"
"No, love. But I am getting the impression ... that it's something I maybe shouldn't get involved with. The China link frightens me because there is no authority in the world which can deal with them, whatever it is they get up to. But obviously, somewhere along the line, they needed ... shall we say, European material to give a great deal more credence to what they have been doing. For one thing, I need to know how it was that you, I mean, Victor, were picked out ... I have some ideas, but when I get to the UK, I intend that you have some blood tests ..."
"Why? Do you think that ..."
"That Vic was deliberately er ... sacrificed? Yes, I do!"
"Maybe I should have some tests done now?"

"Yes, if you can."

"Okay. I'll deal with it."

"I also want to know why you, at your age, were used and why a kid. I don't think someone was ... was ... I don't know ... why didn't they use people of the same age? I understand why it was male to male, that's obvious ..."

"Angie, don't agonise over that. I can tell you one thing, though love, I think I'm going to enjoy my next few years. I don't know if I now have a limited life-span ..."

"Don't even think about it ..."

"Well, I do, Angie. For one thing, I am into older women, yet maybe I should be going for girls of roughly my own age but somehow ..."

"Ted! That's not a problem ... I'm sure we can work something out!"

"I bloody hope so! Anyway, you've got stuff to do, so I'll organise a blood test."

"Bye, love." Angie rang off.

Willis sent a text to Rosie about organising a blood-test. About an hour later, Rosie called.

"Why do you think you need a blood-test, Vic?"

"Because it has been suggested that the lad might have been drugged to render him basically brain-dead. And it's also possible that he was taken to China just for that reason. Don't forget, he was also basically an orphan, so he, like me, was easy prey for these buggers who organised all this. Rosie, it could be a massive deal involving organ-harvesting, provision of bodies ... obviously, they couldn't just keep using local people, because sooner or later someone would catch on. But if you imported them, no problem!"

"I see what you're saying, Vic ...".

"Good. All we can do at the moment is to see what Angie digs out, from the SOS home, I mean. Then perhaps we could do a little digging around Milan, then your mate Grant ..."

"He ain't my mate, Vic, but I understand what you mean. Some

90

discreet enquiry into his background might be useful, but I can't access his records, no way!"

"I don't want you to, Rosie. In fact, I think you should be conspicuous by your lack of interest. Now, another matter. I think you could get the hospital to inform the authorities that old man Willis is dead. However, I don't think it would be a good idea to tell the local papers. If I can have a certified copy of my death certificate, I can start a kind of correspondence with the hospital, *et al*, about the facts behind his move to Milan. That ought to stir things up a little. Just keep your eyes open. But also speak to Sean about this, 'cos he might have a few ideas, okay?"

"Got it. I can take a blood sample maybe tomorrow, also for the DNA people, I'll get the results back within a week. But there's only a very remote chance of their being any drug traces in your blood after this long. Unless it was a sizeable dose, but that might have killed you. We can only try."

Within a few days, there were two pieces of good news. Firstly, the blood test results came through, delivered by Rosie, and while she was at Oaklands, Angie rang. She was excited. Willis put the 'phone on loudspeaker.

"Ted? Listen up. We got all your records from the home. The hospital, that's Andy and his team, has copies only, which I told him that was all that was available 'cos the originals were destroyed after being put onto a computer. I lied. I've got the originals. Also, I was speaking to Marcel on the way up to Paris, and guess what? I filled him in on exactly what's been going on, and he came up with something. They had a boss there, some bloke called André Marais who'd been mixed up in all sorts of strange goings-on, amongst other things letting some of the children get involved in pretty shady deals. Marcel didn't go into detail, but I think it involved iffy adoptions and probably a lot worse. He was the guy who sacked Marcel when he brought up the drug connection. Nobody liked him, but we think he was the one who was keen for Victor to go to China as he, Vic, was apparently a likely candidate for some sports team. His records show he couldn't talk, that he'd been dumped as a child. No parent traced, possibly because he was born to illegal immigrants, now no doubt back in the home country or working in the black economy somewhere in France. They think he, Marais, might have been contacted, and a deal arranged. It just stinks. The bloke has now been placed under police investigation and suspended from work. The lad died when in China ... or so they believed, after he was taken to Harbin, the university hospital where you were. The staff at the home were delighted that you ... Vic, that is, survived. It's possible that he'd been poisoned by someone when staying in China on this sports thing. Probably all pre-arranged, then shifted to Harbin on the orders of Xia, the surgeon. We need the blood test results, Ted. It's just possible ..."

"I've got them here, Angie. Also, my DNA ..."

"What do they show?"

"There were tiny traces of Zyprexa ..."

"Ha! ... A psychic drug! Seventeen out of twenty-three psychiatric poisons in the FDA adverse reaction section feature brain death. They could induce a coma by reducing blood-sugar levels, then brain-death, and even though there could be signs of life, the doctors often believe they are only primitive reflexes and didn't mean anything ... by which I mean the patient could be classified as brain-dead, but the patient can be more or less fully aware of what's going on. Xia only had to turn off the support systems as soon as he wanted ... wanted the ... your ... body!"

"Angie, I've got Rosie here. She'll know about that stuff, maybe talk to her?"

"Of course, Ted, but wait, there's more! When we were in Paris the gymnastics team coach was informed, and he when he knew why we were at the home, he came to see us, and you'll never believe this, but he gave us his sports top, a kind of tracksuit thing, and in his top pocket was a syringe cover and tuft of hair that he found in Vic's hand. He said that when he went into the boy's bedroom after being told his guys couldn't rouse Vic, he found the syringe-top on the floor, and with his hankie he wiped off the hair tufts from the boy's hand with his handkerchief. He didn't want to his upset his lads by screaming murder. He'd just forgotten about them, and he hadn't worn the top since."

"Wow! I suppose he's very happy that the boy is alive?"

"Yes, he is. And, he gave me the bits, so I can get the plastic cap sourced, hopefully, and the hair can be analysed again to find a DNA and also hopefully, a geographical fix ..."

"I bet a hundred quid it's all Chinese!"

"I wouldn't argue with that, but I get the feeling that Vennuchi's team are getting a bit jumpy. I think they want to wash their hands of the whole deal, basically because they've lost control of you! But they can't, in reality, because it'll mean that the blokes involved, from the arsehole at SOS right to, I imagine, that bloke from Rosie's hospital ..."

"Doctor Steve Grant."

"Yes, Grant, won't get paid and as soon as you mess with people's money, they get angry and start making waves ..." Rosie butted in.

"So, Angie, Rosie here ... does that mean that the China people won't cough up? Or that your guys have the money but want to keep it?"

"Don't know. But I intend to keep an eye on things."

"Just be careful, then ..."

"I will be. I've got Marcel on side now, so he'll look after me."

"Going back to the Zyprexa stuff, and organ harvesting. That's best when the body is still alive, even though it dies during the harvesting or the patient is finally allowed to stop breathing when they turn the machine off. There's no anaesthesia provided because the patient is supposedly unable to feel pain since their brain is, supposedly, dead, but according to the cases generally, the patient could feel pain, and hear what was going on. Very much like Ted here when he was with me in hospital, or Vic as we call him. We cannot but feel sorry about the cases who had their organs harvested, when they could hear what was going on ... so it's possible that poor old Vic knew exactly what was happening?"

"'Fraid so, Rosie ... Anyway, it seems we've done all we can at the moment. May I suggest that you look carefully at the history of your Steve Grant? He might have done this before!"

"Already in hand. And of course, we'll be discreet. Don't want him to do a runner!" The 'phone conversation ended.

"Well, Rosie ... where do we go from here?"

"I think it's time we got Sean and his guys seriously involved ... It's getting way too heavy for you and me to deal with and we can't just leave it!"

"Maybe we should brief him, then let him get on with it?"

"I agree ... now can we now let the authorities know about your death? I mean to let you wind-up your estate?"

"Yes. I've done all I can at my end. There'll be a load of inheritance tax to pay, but I had an insurance policy to sort that out. I'd better start writing letters ..."

"Yes. But be careful. I wouldn't deal with any enquiries on the 'phone. You might inadvertently give something away!"

"Okay. If you can get the original death certificate copied and one of your doctors ... try Grant ... to certify them as true copies, I'll take it from there. Also, Sean will be able to do a fingerprint check on him ..."

"Wow! you ain't thinking like an eleven-year-old, are you ... Vic!"

"No. But just imagine having the brain of an eleven-year-old in a seventy-year-old's body! Also, I know it's dodgy, but any chance of getting a look at his personal file? I frankly can't imagine that he hasn't done something like this before. Maybe he's in serious debt, or ... I dunno, maybe something else? And what about checking his bank accounts? The last thing we can do is access all that stuff without either him knowing or somebody tipping him off."

"As I said, Vic, this is way above our heads. I'll discuss it with Sean. If there is something, we can do to get into his history ..."

"Well, fingers crossed, if it's all going to unravel from the Milan end, everybody concerned ... that is the French end, Milan and, of course, Doctor Grant, are all gonna be jumped on at the same time. Can't do anything about the China crew ... they'll be untouchable!"

CHAPTER 10

André Marais pulled up in the car park of the Aushopping, Grand Plaisir. As he fished in his glove-compartment for his wallet, he heard a tap on his window. He wound it down.
"Oui? Est-ce que je peux vous aider?"
"André?"
"Oui, je suis lui!"
"Okay. I have a message for you, from Pierre. You have been to police HQ? About your business with Pierre? He says you keep your mouth shut. If anybody approaches him about your dealings ..." The messenger put two fingers to his head. "Bang! You're a dead man!"
"Tell Pierre to fuck off! And also tell him that *les flics'* interest in me is nothing to do with anybody else!"
"Okay. I'll tell him. But just remember. 'Bang'!" The man moved away from Andre's car, back to the big car which had pulled in behind him. After shopping, the man from SOS returned to his car. He was worried. He got out his mobile and dialled.
"Pierre? ... Who's this thug you sent to talk to me? If you think that I would do anything ..."
"André ... I have no idea what you're talking about. I don't employ thugs. Sorry. Goodbye." André sat in the car for a moment, staring at his 'phone. In his rear-view mirror he saw the messenger again. he opened his door.
"What now?"
"Pierre says don't be so bloody daft, mate. Don't you know the cops listen in to his fuckin' 'phone? He wants to meet with you. Here." The man passed a note to André. Usual place. Time as it says. Be there, okay?"
"Okay. Now you fuck off."

The 'usual place' since Pierre got jumpy with André was a bus ride. It was a bloody drag. Nevertheless, he made the meeting. Pierre got onto the circular town route bus a few stops before André was supposed to get on and climbed onto the top deck. He was with his minder. André joined him a few minutes later, four stops down the route.

"Okay, Pierre, what the fuck's going on?"

"Some bastard's poking about, mate, that's what. From now on, until further notice, we stop trading. The last job you did for Pierre has gone sour ..."

"That Victor job?"

"Exactly."

"Where did he finish up?"

"It was an Italian job."

"What, a bank robbery? How the hell does ..."

"No, you idiot, not The Italian fuckin' Job, the film ... I mean the destination. The destination was Italy."

"That's bollocks. I was asked ... told rather, to get him onto the sports trip to China. I had him taken to China, remember?"

"Course I remember. But by all accounts, whatever happened to him didn't happen. And some guys from some hospital in Milan had been poking about, but I suppose you knew that, didn't you?"

"Yeah. Well, no, not really, but I didn't connect Milan with China ... some doctor came here with Marcel asking about Vic. She, the doctor, works at the same place Marcel does now. The bloke I sacked."

"But he's back in France somewhere apparently."

"Who, Marcel or ..."

"No! The boy!"

"Maybe he is, but he can't talk. He's dumb."

"He doesn't have to talk ... look, I'm not going to bandy words with you, mate! Just clear your desk of all the shit. Don't call me. If I need you, I'll call you, alright?"

"Okay."

"Right, I'm getting off now ..." Pierre looked out of the rear window of the bus to check if his car was following. "Just remember what I said. If this gets out were both fucked. But I'll make sure you'll be more fucked than I will be, got it? Somehow, they've picked up on you. Not me. You." Pierre stabbed a finger in André's direction. "The only way they'll get onto my back, is through you, André. So I'll know. D'you know what that means?"

"Of course. You always explain things so clearly, Pierre, your one and only redeeming virtue."

"You're a facetious bastard, you are!" The big ugly bastard that Pierre was, got off the bus with his minder, who gave André the finger as he followed his boss into the street. André waited until the bus got to his original pick-up point on it's circular route, then he, too, got off. He had some serious thinking to do. He would call Marcel. He still had his mobile number in his contacts folder.

Marcel was not too pleased about the call.

"Yes André."

"Marcel we've gotta talk. I've had that Pierre onto me ..."

"You mean that fat greasy bastard who's always hanging around you? Why, is that my problem?"

"You were here last week or sometime asking about the lad Victor Clément? ... Pierre was the guy who had him shifted out to China ..."

"Yeah, so?"

"Well he's supposed to have gone to hospital in Italy after that, and as far as I know, it was all above board ..."

"All above board ... like all the other poor kids you had removed? Well the chickens have come home to roost now, haven't they André?"

"Marcel, I want to help. I have no idea what the hell's been going on, but I want to help ..."

"To save your own skin? Well, I suppose that greasy sod Pierre is worse than you."

"At least I am co-operating with the *le flics*. And he, Pierre, has warned me that if they get to him, I'm a dead man ..."

"Well, bearing in mind what they did to Victor, it would be a kind of poetic justice!"

"Fuck it, Marcel, I really want to help ..."

"I'll tell you what then, mate, talk to Angelica, the doctor who was with me up there. She'll tell you what's been going on. But first, I think you should write down everything about what you and Pierre have been up to. Then I'll let you talk to Angelica. Email the lot to me. If you mess me about, André, you're on your own. We need the full story, André, the full whack, no bits left out. And I also want you to say why you had me sacked, about the drug stuff, remember? Maybe you should have called a halt to your dirty business then. Now clear the line, I've got work to do and so have you, okay?"

"Okay, Marcel ... and thanks." Marcel called Doctor Angelica Scrito's number and relayed to her his conversation with André.

"Well done, Marcel. If we can get a complete picture from him, I'll then get to work on Andy. I don't think he had anything to do with Vic, because the lad didn't come anywhere near here until he flew in from China. But I know bloody well that he had a lot to do with Ted Willis! And I'd bet a pound to a penny that Andy and the guy from the UK hospital damn well knew each other, and set up an arrangement ... if I can see what conference and stuff they both attended, maybe we could make up the link?"

"Makes sense to me, let's go for it."

"And I also want to see who the lead surgeons are in normal transplant ops. I know there's been discussion of some pretty serious transplant experiments, but none of them that I know of were using live donor and recipient, but who knows what goes on in bloody China? I'll have a word with a few of Andy's team to see just what went on with Ted Willis ... one of them is bound to know about him if he started his journey from here."

Angie knew she had to work to a plan. Firstly, she went onto the Transplant Society website, which showed they were running about ten meetings per annum. There was the American Society of Transplant Surgeons, but on the Transplant Surgery Conference website, she found there had been a conference in Madrid and another in Berlin. She made a note of the dates. Next, she accessed Professor Vennuchi's diary entries; he had attended both, first in Milan in July then the conference in Germany in November. Both ran over four days. Now she had to find out whether the English doctor, Grant had also attended one or both of the same meetings. She knew it was a long shot, but she wanted to run it past Ted. She called him.

"Hi, Ted! ... yes, I'm fine. Right, Marcel is working on the France end of the deal. Apparently, the bloke who sacked Marcel ... yeah, André, is coming under a lot of pressure from the guy who had been involved with him in various ways with some of the kids from Vic's home ... and I think you can imagine what that means. This bloke, Pierre, is by all accounts a nasty piece of work threatening to kill our André if he leads the police to Pierre's door ... anyway, we've asked André to set out a full statement of exactly what's been going on and to co-operate with us ... reason being is that I have a notion a lot of pretty heavy stuff's been going on. But, the heaviest of the lot of course, involves you and young Vic. Now, can you ask Rosie ... I don't have her 'phone number ... if she can find out whether your Doctor Grant was attending any conferences? The first was in Milan over the dates 13th to 16th July last year, and the other was in Berlin, 7th to 10th November? We need to make a connection. Also, ask Rosie if Grant ever expressed any interest in transplant surgery?"

"Got that. let me give you Rosie's number ... but don't call her until I've checked with her first. Now, re China's involvement. That country is no miracle economy. They need foreign currency like, seriously, to deal with its massive debt problem so I'd like to bet that once all the ducks are lined up on this bloody business, they'll be exploiting it for all it's worth. And we are looking at billions! It might be wise to keep an eye on your Andy. Also, we'll keep an eye on Grant. Now, more news. We're gonna get organised on dealing with my estate. I'm getting Rosie and Sean to apply on my behalf ... I'll keep you informed!"

André had been busy. Within two days of his talk with Marcel, he had emailed a first draft of his report. It was a surprisingly well-written and detailed missive, and it shocked Marcel. He called André.

"So, to your knowledge, you have dealt with seventeen children? And you say, Pierre has been dealing also with other homes? Look at this, André ..."

"Marcel! ... I have been very open with you! Look at the actions. Recruitment, transport, transfer, lodging and receiving. Of all those stages, I was involved only in the first one. I always thought I was doing the best for the children. Then, when I found out about what Pierre was doing, I wanted to stop, but he threatened me. He told me some of the children were dead ...!"

"Yes, and look at what happens to them! Look what it says in your own report. Forced labour, begging, domestic servitude, slavery, sexual exploitation, incitement to commit crimes and ... look carefully at this, André ... organ removal and trafficking! Remember Vic? was he just going to be another failed experiment?"

"Marcel, please! Listen! ... all I knew about Vic was that he was going to China for this sports thing ..."

"What about the money, André? What did you make? What did Pierre make? If, as he once told you, he reckoned he made roughly twenty thousand Euros per child depending on age and sex what the fuck did you get?"

"About a thousand ... I had to do all the paperwork ...!"

"And this Pierre bloke, he made what? About 340k Euros from your home alone?"

"I reckon, yes. But child trafficking goes on all over the bloody world. Look at South Africa. There's some book due out shortly about key members of Botha's government picking up street kids to involve them in sex-rings, flying them to some remote island so people could sexually abuse them. God only knows what happened to them afterwards ... but what the hell do I do in my cases, Marcel? Help me!"

"I think you'll have to go to the police ... but I think it will have to be EuroPol ... because we've got the UK and Italy all mixed up in this ..."

"Let me think about it."

"Okay. But fill me in more about Pierre, so if he gets to you, we will at least know how to get him."

"Okay. I'll do that!" Marcel put his 'phone down. Then he looked up *'Invisibles. Child victims of trafficking in France'.* André had obviously been there before him. The content shocked him. He copied André's report to Angie, with a link to *'Invisibles'*. She copied it to Ted Willis.

"Rosie ..." Willis filled her in on Angie's call. "... so, we need to know if Doctor Grant attended those meetings as well and if he met up with the professor. And the next thing. looking at my estate. I want you to handle it all ..."

"Never done that, Vic. Have no idea what to do ..."

"Don't worry. All I need you to do is get a grant of representation, which solicitors can do for you, then you hand everything over to me to do. I doubt I'll be the first guy to do his own probate, but I bet I am the only genuine one. All the others were probably insurance frauds! I'll talk you through the process. I know a good lawyer in Reading. Ex-army guy. No worries on that front. Now, the next thing is, could we find enough on Grant to get the police involved?"

"Probably not ... but all I can think of as a possible route being his removal of you ... Ted Willis ... to Milan. Also, his death certificate might not be kosher ..."

"It's a long shot. Maybe I'll spend some time on the internet to see what I can dig out. What's Grant's full name, any idea?"

"Steven Edward Grant. He came here, I think, from Manchester."

"Okay, Rosie. Just a few more things. Can I give your number to Angie? It's mainly so you two can talk medical stuff, and if you can get the death certificate copies certified as true copies, it would be helpful, and keep a copy for Sean just in case he can find anything on the fingerprints. Then if you pop down here for the weekend, we can have a kind of 'where are we now' session, okay?"

"Yes, Vic. I'm okay with both of those. How's Connie and Alf these days?"

"Both fine. I just love having Connie's girls around the place, I really do. Just as well I'm into older women!"

"You just be careful, Vic ... that could get the older women into big trouble!"

Nurse Rosie Pollard went to patients' records and collected the *'Willis, deceased'*, file and extracted the *Registrazione Morte* which Doctor Grant had handed to her all those weeks ago. She ran off six copies on the admin office copier, then stamped each one with box 'Certified to be a true copy of the original seen by me' 'Signed' 'Date' 'Full name [print]' then 'Occupation' 'Address' and finally 'Telephone Number'. Rosie wrote in all the details of Doctor Grant. Then she went to find him.

"What's all this, Rosie?"

"We need it for various reasons, the usual. And of course, we have to get someone to deal with his estate, I suppose."

"He had no family, did he?"

"Er ... pass." Doctor Grant signed the copies.

"Here." he handed them back to the nurse. Don't forget to put one copy on the file, okay?"

"Of course." Grant watched Rosie as she left the rest-room. He had a sudden thought. Who would get Willis's estate? It would be interesting to keep tabs on that. He drained his coffee, then went back to work.

The following Saturday, Rosie and Sean dropped into Oaklands. They all sat down to a coffee, fussed over by Connie and her two girls. Alf had a basket of vegetables and a big bunch of flowers for Rosie.

"Right, Vic. I've got all the stuff certified. All my and Sean's details are there as well, just as you asked. So where do we go from here?"

"I'll send it all to my lawyer friend, and he'll get you two the authority you need to deal with Fred's estate. I'll actually do all the work. No sweat. Now, your friend Grant. Looking at the Companies House records, he appeared to have a business with a co-director, a woman. He removed himself as a director because there was an exposé into what they were doing ..."

"Don't tell me it was something to do with organ donation?"

"It was. Grant resigned immediately, because he stated that he didn't know what was going on. He thought it was just a registration facility, but it wasn't quite that!"

"The company was called SOXMIS which stood for Sperm & Organ Exchange Management and Information Services. In fact, in military terms, it stands for something else, but that's not relevant. Anyway, Grant dropped out saying he'd agreed to work for the company in good faith, but after the revelations, he repaid all his consultancy fees and resigned from the firm. He pleaded ignorance, saying he'd been duped."

"But that seemed a reasonable thing to do ..."

"It did. However, there are other issues. Firstly, did he actually cut off from the business? I put myself in his shoes. They were making oodles of cash ... in the UK, that is, and I think what happened was that Grant got together with Andy, the professor bloke, and set up something between them."

"In the UK again?"

"I don't know. But I think Italy."

"Why Italy?"

"It's only a hunch ... I mean, there's transplant stuff going on all over the world, but most civilised countries are really tied down by laws and regulations like you wouldn't believe ..."

"And some aren't?"

"Exactly. Like China. So the arseholes who control the money and the power in places like Burma and North Korea, where the medical services are such crap, and stuck in the middle-ages, all go there and send their families there for their transplant surgery ..."

"So ... no wonder they seem so keen to add the latest deals to their catalogue! And with Andy and his crew working closely with them, they'll also benefit!"

"Nails and heads come to mind, Sean! Now, in view of what happened to me, I reckon Grant is feeding what he can to the Italy guys. And another little medical fiddle. Referrals to care-homes can be very lucrative, and I wouldn't be at all surprised if he, *et al*, was also into that!"

"Right, Vic, if you're right, how do we prove it?"

"Good question, Rosie. We can't just confront him, obviously, but I would love to see his bank account to see if there are any credits from other sources. It'll be difficult to hide income into his, let's say, normal account, which could be bank to bank, or he could draw out cash then pay it in. If he gets careless then there might just be one or two receipts from another source ..."

"Or he might just use it for on-line banking to buy stuff, and not let it get anywhere near his real account."

"It's a tough one, Vic ... one possibility is to see what cards he has in his wallet ..."

"If he does carry it on him ... another option is to get into his flat and have a good rummage around ..."

"I think the first option is to see ... somehow ... what he has in his wallet ... and if that doesn't work, then ..."

"Arrange a break-in, Sean ..."

"Good heavens, that's illegal! But I have a few guys who owe me a favour!"

"Sean!"

"Yes Rosie?"

"You wouldn't do that ... would you?"

"Of course not, love. We don't do things like that."

HAPTER 11

André was worried. He would take Marcel's advice and come clean. He ran off a copy of his confession statement, and then drove to town, parked up, and walked into the police station. The desk clerk looked up.

"Yes?"

"Can I speak to Inspector Enzo Gabin, please." The clerk looked down at his desk.

"He's not in. You can talk to Adele Bonfasse ... what is it about?"

"I'll tell her."

"Okay ... wait a moment ..." The clerk picked up the 'phone.

"Adele, a Mr ..." He looked at the visitor.

"André. Mr André ... André ... okay." He looked up again at the visitor. "Through the door on the right, then second on the left." He nodded towards the door.

"Thank you." André found the door open. He knocked, just the same.

Despite France's generally lax ethical standards, as a member of the Council of Europe and the Group of States Against Corruption, the dishonesty levels in the police forces of France, except those in Marseilles, which, due principally to the high migrant numbers, is off the scale, are not much more corrupt than most of the other forces in Europe. However, it only takes one bad apple. Deputy Inspector Adele Bonfasse was one such. It is possible that her mother loved her once, probably, but nobody has since, and it was a fair bet that nobody would in the future. But Bonfasse had more than a few issues. She was seriously overweight, which she blamed on a genetic problem. She suffered with hyperhidrosis, so she smelled rather bad. In addition, she had an over-generous amount of facial hair. She also regarded herself as untouchable, and, if she were sacked, she would claim that whatever the reason the police gave, she would say that it was because she had a medical condition and sacking her was therefore unfair. In an entirely different sense, her co-workers also regarded her as untouchable. Unsurprisingly, nobody would share a car with her. Some police officers had threatened to shoot her if any of them were forced to pair-up with her for any duty, a threat taken so seriously, that the Chief of Police had been forced to isolate '*Madame Boudin*', as she was affectionately called, which isolation was effected by promoting her to deputy inspector so she could be confined to her own room. Further, the force generally considered her so singularly unattractive, that there can have been few men in the entire universe with such perverse sexual preferences that they would be naturally drawn to her.

As a result, the only sex she had apart from a suitably robust mechanical device, she had to buy or otherwise procure in exchange for information relating to the progress of certain police investigations. Many regarded that the favour had to be pretty substantial for them to agree to share a bed with her, made worse by her particularly distasteful, a fair description, sexual preferences. Her other problem was that she was overly fond of gratuitous flattery, which she received in copious amounts from some of the biggest crooks west of Paris. Officer Bonfasse was, then, a willing and rich source of information for the local 'Mr Bigs'. She was also kept up to date on some significant local crimes, especially where the perpetrators had trodden on the toes of the criminals further up the food chain. Hence, the police were reluctant to sack the woman as she was good for their 'clear-up' rates.

All in all, André didn't feel entirely happy talking to officer Bonfasse about anything, and certainly not about his business, so he just gave her the basics. And hurriedly.

"I have been dealing with Enzo. I have more information for him regarding ... er ... our business. Some bloke, Dauphin, Pierre Dauphin, is giving me a hard time, so I want to give Enzo, this note. Here ..." He passed a sealed envelope over the desk. Had André been more attentive to the facial expressions of Ms Adele, an omission for which he could hardly be blamed, he would have seen the name 'Pierre Dauphin' ignite a spark of interest in her eyes.

"Of course, Monsieur André. This is naturally a confidential matter? I will make sure that he gets it, certainly. He knows where to contact you?"

"Yes. It's all in there. Now, if you'll excuse me, I have another appointment. I am already late ..." He looked at his watch. It was seventeen minutes past one. Adele Bonfasse was getting used to interviews being terminated with that excuse. And anyway, she was hungry. On his way out of the station, André passed through reception, and the clerk booked him out at 1320 hours and noted too, that the visitor no longer had the buff envelope he had been carrying when he arrived. On the visitor's departure, '*Madame Boudin*' ripped open that envelope. She scanned the pages and it was immediately obvious to even her, that her 'mate' Dauphin could be up to his neck in shit, if, that is, Enzo got hold of that information. She fished out her mobile 'phone and with her fat but surprisingly dexterous fingers, sent a text.

André also used his 'phone. He called Marcel to tell him that, just as he had been advised by his former friend, he had gone back to the police. And that he had seen some fat, smelly policewoman and handed in a copy of the same statement he had sent to Marcel.

"Jesus, mate! Not her! I bloody hope you didn't tell her you'd sent me a copy! Those buggers *les flics* ... hey, hang on a minute, this line is shit ... call me on my land-line please." Marcel passed the land-line number to the caller. He had the wit to realise that this conversation ought to be taped. His land-line rang a minute or so later. Marcel picked up the receiver and pressed the 'record' button.

"That's better. Now what were you saying?" André repeated

what he had already said.

"You wanna be careful, mate. Old tubs is as bent as fuck! It'll be all over bloody France by now! For God's sake clear your PC stuff onto a stick, and bloody hide it. And all the 'phone texts you sent to me and to anybody else! Just hope that the fat tart doesn't pass it on to her bloody mates! Who were you dealing with before her? Who was the bloke who pulled you in initially?"

"Enzo ... shall I send the stick to you?" Marcel didn't want to nursemaid his old adversary, but he felt the guy was desperate. He really had no-one else, divorced and living in a crap bedsit.

"Enzo's a good guy ... yes, send the shit here. Do it today. But just watch your back, for God's sake, okay?"

"I will, thanks Marcel." When André rang off, the hospital personal trainer made some notes of the conversation. He was worried for his old enemy, in fact more than a bit sorry for him. He had good reason to be.

Not a great deal happens in Plaisir to interest the *Plaisirios*, but two weeks after André's visit to the police, the *Etang de Saint-Quentin,* a substantial body of water, by no means a pond but a lake, gave up a grisly secret. Somebody had launched a small rowing-boat into lake and had then dropped a concrete block through the bottom of the little craft, which sank taking with it the body of a man, later identified as André Marais. He had been tied across the seats, face up and flat out, and by all accounts, he was alive when the boat sank. He had therefore died by drowning. Even though having been underwater for the best part of twelve days, with his immersion having been unkind to his body, the *médecin légiste* established that prior to his death, he had been severely beaten.

Marcel learned of the death two days after the body was found. He concluded that the whole deal he, Angie and Fred Willis were engaged with, had moved up a notch or two. He thought it was time to get in touch with his friend Enzo, but first he wanted to run a few things past Angie. He called her.

"Angie, I think it's time to approach the professor's team. You remember the guy I spoke about, the one who effectively sacked me? André Marais? Well, he's been murdered, and I doubt that even *le flics* could get away with a suicide verdict. According to his statement, remember, the one he emailed to us? Well, the real villain of the piece is that bloke, Dauphin. But the main issue is, your Andy knows bloody well about Vic and Ted, and where they came from. Indeed, both of them I imagine!"

"Marcel, I doubt he will want to do anything until the Chinese guys have paid him ..."

"How much is he ... or the hospital due, any idea?"

"About two million Euros, Marcel, a lot of dosh but I think it will be to the research unit, or in other words, Andy and his crew. But he's got to get some tests done on Ted first ... And according to one of the team, the China guys have been agitating for that information for ages now ..."

"Okay. Let's say he gets all the stuff. Do you then think he'll shut the business down? ... do you think he ..."

"No. He won't. There's too much money to be made ... unless the authorities here, I mean in Italy, stepped in, and it won't be a case of money, it'll be him getting slung into jail ..."

"Okay. Why don't you find out exactly what it is the guys need, then maybe we could approach Ted and ask him for it? I know Ted will love to get involved ..."

"Possibly. But we have to be careful, because if Ted ... or if they think Ted will open his mouth ... then between them and your French police friend, that will open a massive can of worms ..."

"So, what exactly are you saying?"

"I'm saying, that once they've got what they want, Ted, certainly, could become expendable."

"True. We'll have to be bloody careful. But I doubt Dauphin will go so far as to knock off Enzo ... that matter has already been escalated to much higher authority, according to Marais's statement."

"Then I suggest you get onto the bloke and give him what you have had from the guy. Strike while the iron's hot. In fact, If Ted agrees to work with us, we can go to see him and stop at Enzo's place on the way up... what do you think?"

"I think it is a damn good idea! Let's proceed on the basis that Ted will agree. If I know him at all, he'll be with us all the way!"

"I'll get onto Andy now and tell him what's happened. And I'll also tell him that we have to talk to the police in Plaisir about little Vic, or Ted, so it is essential that you come with me, okay? How does that sound?"

"Good. Let me know once it's all agreed. I'll arrange cover here in the department. Let's say we'll need a week?"

"Sounds fine. Leave it to me."

"Hey, Enzo ..."

"What?"

"That bloke they fished out of the lake. He called in here to see you a little while ago."

"When?"

"I dunno. Let me check the book ... here it is, about two weeks ago."

"Why didn't you tell me before?"

"'Cos I forgot. Anyway, Adele dealt with it ..."

"Adele deals with fuck all. Is she in?"

"Yeah. Go and have a look in her office, if you can see her over the pile of fuckin' sandwiches and family-sized cola bottles!" Inspector Enzo Gabin moved to Adele's open door and leaned against the frame.

"Hey, Adele! did some bloke called André, André Marais, come in to see you recently?"

"Might have done ..."

"Hey, don't fuck about, love, did he, or didn't he?"

"Why?"

"Why? Because he was the stiff we pulled out of the fuckin' lake, that's why!"

"Yes, I remember now. Yeah. He wouldn't bloody talk to me, said it was your business. He just sat there for a few minutes trying to chat me up ..."

"Oh, fuck off, Adele, nobody would ever want to chat you up ...!"

"No, really. He wanted me to deal with the business, and I told him I couldn't. It was your case. So he got the hump and left." The woman picked up a Mars bar and ripped off the wrapper.

"Okay, thanks anyway." Enzo turned away to go to his own office. "Thanks." He then took to wondering if any of his contacts would be able to make an exploding Mars bar. But Enzo was far from happy. Then his mobile rang. The detective looked at the screen. It was Marcel.

"Hello mate. How's Italy? Need any police officers down there...?"

"Enzo. Are you alone?"

"Yes, why are you..."

"I've got some serious stuff to tell you. When you can, and you're away from *Madame Boudin* give me a call."

"Yeah? what's it about?"

" André!"

"A...." Enzo looked up at his office door, just catching himself before he blurted out the name. He didn't want Adele or anybody else for that matter, overhearing. "Yeah, yeah!" he said out loud, then cupping the phone with his free hand, very quietly, "Can't talk now ... I'll get back to you when I can." Then the police officer cut the connection. Marcel knew he had got the message across, and that Enzo would be calling him back. Then his 'phone buzzed.

"Marcel? Angie. If you can get a date for the meet with Enzo, we're good to go. I know exactly what we need from Ted, so I'll get onto him now, and I've told the team here that we'll be back within a week. And don't forget, Ted wants you to set up a little training room for him. I'll let you get on with your policeman mate. The sooner we know, the better."

"Got it, Angie. I'm expecting a call from him now."

111

Willis was delighted with the prospect of seeing Angie and Marcel again. He called Connie, asking her to make up two of the spare bedrooms. He also called Rosie and gave her some idea of when the visitors would arrive.

"All the stuff's gone to the lawyers now, so it's just a case of waiting. They've applied for the insurance monies to cover the inheritance tax, so after that you can ... or rather I can ... deal with everything else. Not actually much to deal with. I don't want to send my driving licence or passport back really. Anyway. haven't you got all that stuff somewhere?"

"Doctor Grant had your passport. I'm going to get whatever's left of your property and get it back to you. I'll sign it out for the lawyers, anyway."

When Enzo called, Marcel was sunning himself on the patio outside the exercise room.

"Okay Marcel, talk to me."

"Right. It concerns André. He went to see you some time ago, but he had to see Adele instead ..."

"Yes, I know that. So what?"

"He gave her a statement to pass on to you, 'cos I'd told him that certain issues were going to get messy. He'd been dancing to Pierre Dauphin's tune ... he really had no choice for various reasons ..."

"I know that too."

"I think Adele passed some kind of a confession thing to Pierre ... and Pierre had to get rid of André ..."

"Evidence?"

"I'll email a copy of his statement to you. But not to the office in case it ... er ... gets into the wrong hands ..."

"Right. Send it to my home." Enzo passed on his email address.

"I also have a little tape I'd like you to hear ... but, I'm on my way to England soon, so I want to pop in to see you ... this business runs pretty deep. I'll be bringing one of the doctors from this hospital. She's already been to the SOS place. But I'd like to bet that Adele blew the whistle on André. If she was dumb enough to call the greasy git it'll be on your 'phone system, or else her mobile ..."

"I'll deal with that. I'd like to nail that Pierre bastard ..."

"Wait until I get to see you. But get hold of ... get downloads on Adele's recent texts. You guys have got that technology ..."

"Yes, we have ... but I don't want to alert her ..."

"Don't. Just lift her 'phone, get the stuff downloaded, then just suddenly 'find' her 'phone again. Simple."

"Maybe. Anything else?"

"Yes. I think André sent me a complete download of his PC. I don't wanna see it, but I'll bring it with me. Might be useful."

"Marcel ... thanks. I'll see what I can do. When will you be here?"

"No idea. But I'll give you at least one full day's notice."

"That'd be fine." Enzo was happy. He looked forward to getting rid of *Madame Boudin* and getting the Pierre bastard locked up. In fact, he was rather taken with the idea of keeping them both locked up in the same small cell. After lunch, he looked at the visitors' book again. He noted André's arrival and departure times. He made for his office, and on passing *Boudin's* door, saw her office was empty. And her 'phone was on the desk. He went in and picked it up. He could get everything downloaded in no time.

The 'phone was not returned to Adele, but instead Enzo and two other officers called in to her office.

" Inspector Adele Bonfasse. You are under arrest."

"You're kidding!"

"No, we're not. Stand up and put your hands behind your back."

"Fuck off." Enzo nodded to the two officers.

"Cuff her."

"Piss off, Enzo! We'll have to touch her!"

"Fuckin' do it! Now!" The two grabbed at the woman's arms. She swung her arms wildly around, striking both men.

"Tazer ...!" They tazered her, and she screamed obscenities at them. Quite a crowd of officers had gathered at the door to watch. "Don't just fuckin' stand there, help us get her into the bloody van!"

"Shit, she's bloody heavy!" They managed to drag her into the yard, then unceremoniously loaded into the back of a police van. In the tussle, she had defecated and wet herself.

"Get everything, every bit of paper, everything out of here, into evidence bags. Then take out every stick of furniture then redecorate the place. She won't be coming back!" He turned to another officer. Get to her bloody flat. The same there please. Everything out of it. I want the whole bloody lot in my office by this time tomorrow. This bitch ain't gonna need the place for a good few years!" 'The bitch' could still be heard squealing like a stuck pig.

Later the same day, Enzo gathered a task-force to break into Dauphin's home and business premises. The door-knock was set for four the following morning. There was no resistance. The properties were secured, and search teams virtually ripped the places apart. The result was an impressive haul. Less that forty-eight hours after the raid, dozens of addresses in and around Paris and in other towns in France were raided and seventeen children were freed, and some of the discoveries so angered and upset the police that there were more than a few suspects who fell down the stairs.

Doctor Angelica Scrito and Marcel de Longé were booked to fly Milan to Paris where they had a full day's stopover, then onto London Heathrow. Marcel copied all the stuff André had sent him on the memory stick. The original plus a copy of the taped 'phone conversation and a transcript, all destined for Enzo. Angie had a list of information she needed about Ted Willis, aka Vic, information which would release a huge tranche of money into the hands of those who had some part, large or small, in the whole murky business.

At Paris Orly, Enzo had laid on a police car for his visitors. He met them at the Direction de la Police Judicature on Quai des

114

Orfèvres, virtually on the Seine. The guests were shown into a large office where Enzo sat with two other officers.

"Madame Doctor, Marcel. Nice to see you. May I introduce my colleagues who will be helping me with this case. Let's not waste time. This is a very serious matter. Adele has been arrested and is in custody. A coincidence was it not, that at about the same time as the unfortunate André left my station, Adele sent a text to Dauphin telling him of the statement which André had left with her, and which she denied. In the last few weeks, the woman had sent over forty texts to that Dauphin bastard. And ten my officers broke into his house. Ah! The stuff we found! At first count, he has been involved in the trafficking of many young boys and girls ... "

"Do you know, Enzo, of our interest in this case? Have you any record of a Victor Clément?"

"We have mounds of documents to wade through. It is not, by all accounts, going to be a very pleasant task, I'm afraid. But no madame, no Victor Clément I'm afraid. Not yet, anyway, but we believe Dauphin has been involved with ... in dealing with ... about forty children. We found a lot of money, firearms, forged passports and other documents. We have seized, I believe about twelve mobile 'phones. In all we have seven people in custody, and there have been other arrests and house searches. Adele is going to be charged with many offences of misconduct in public office. It will be nice to rid my station of such an unpleasant smell." Angie spoke up.

"Young Victor was one of his victims. He finished up in China. I can say no more than that at the moment, but this investigation, I have no doubt, will lead there. Or would, but as you know inspector, what goes on in China is not for the general consumption of the rest of the world."

"Well, Enzo, I'm sure you are more than capable of dealing with the French side of things. However, we have the Italy link and the UK connections to deal with."

"Thank you, Marcel. I can see that there is still a lot for you to do, and in due course I shall unearth such connections as there are. Naturally, we cannot keep you informed ... officially, anyway, but maybe the odd 'phone call could be made?"

"Enzo, you're a gentleman. We will similarly ... keep you posted."

"We owe you, madame, and you Marcel, a great deal. The whole business has been most distressing, but I fear there is worse to come."

The meeting broke up; Marcel and Angie were taken to their hotel.

"Well, Marcel, I thought that went very well. Now let's get to the bar for a drink and have an early dinner. Our 'plane leaves for London fairly early tomorrow morning."

"Good morning Sean. I've got the flight times for our visitors. You've got Angie's mobile number, so if you make contact once she and Marcel have landed ... of course, you'll use the Mustang?"

"No problem with that, Vic. And by the way, and further to our various discussions and also with Rosie's agreement, I've been given permission to take this investigation on full time. Been given a kind of indefinite leave!"

"Hey, that's great news! And I suppose here it will focus on our friend Grant? I expect that our two guests will have a load of info to give you."

"No doubt. And the next job will be to see if he's still connected somehow with the business up in Manchester. Anyway, I'd better get my arse down to your place. I'm bringing Rosie with me. She and you can have a bit of time together while I nip down to the airport."

Willis sat in the kitchen looking across the front garden, as Sean and Rosie motored up the drive. He got up and met them at the front porch and pressed the zapper to open the garage doors. Sean pulled the Mustang out onto the drive. Rosie gave him a hug, as he called to Sean.

"You drive carefully, now! don't get pulled up for speeding, will you!" The police officer waved to him.

"No fear of that, Vic!" In a minute or so, he was on his way to Heathrow. Willis took Rosie to the kitchen, where Connie fussed over her as usual. Willis had asked her to book a table for five at the local, expensive restaurant, so Connie could have some free time with her daughters. Then Rosie got serious.

"Vic, I've been doing some research into this business, you know, the China stuff. By all accounts, there's been a load of it going on, and most of it, if not all of it, totally unregulated and no doubt illegal. In fact, I think your case falls into both categories!"

"I think you're right, Rosie. I want you to raise this with Angie while she's here. I have no doubt she's got a lot to tell us. Now, regarding my estate, my lawyers seem to think everything is fairly straightforward. They've applied for the inheritance tax insurance policy to be credited to their client account. There's been no caveats, or anything applied for ..."

"What's that for?"

"Oh, it's in case anybody wants to delay any grant of representation ..." Willis could see Rosie looking at him somewhat quizzically. "Er ... if anybody thinks there are things which have to be addressed before the estate can be wound up ..." Rosie smiled at him.

"You know, Vic, sitting here looking at you, you are just a good-looking eleven-year old, talking like a lawyer again, I think you're going to have a lot of fun especially when you go to school in September. I sincerely hope you don't hold back. And another thing, you'll be worth a few bob, as well. Looking at your probate things, it's going to be tens of millions, and then if you sue the bastards who behaved so atrociously, or if we do on your behalf ..."

"Yes, as my guardians *ad litem* ..."

"There you go again!"

"Yes, as I was saying, as my guardians *ad litem*, which means my representatives in any court proceedings, as in *Cornwall County Council ex parte Cornwall Guardians, 1992 WLR 427...*"

"And again! Vic, promise me ... that you'll deliberately wind up your teachers! And can I please be a fly on the wall? I'm getting so excited at the thought of you sorting out that grammar school, and as for the other kids, God help them if they think they can give you a hard time!"

"That's all very well, Rosie, but what'll really piss me off is having to do what they'll want to do.

"Like what?"

"Watch bloody football, go to their parents' houses for birthday parties, not being able to drive my car, only going on holidays or into restaurants with mummy and daddy! Granted, I'd probably want to have long, engaging conversations with their dads, or screw the mums ..."

"Vic!"

"Well, it's true! but imagine if the kids are all tucking into ice cream, playing on bouncy castles, and there I am with my face into Leo Tolstoy's *'War and Peace'* ... you know, about the French invasion of Russia and the impact of the Napoleonic era on Tsarist society as seen through Russian aristocratic families ..."

"No, Vic, I don't bloody know!" Rosie laughed.

"Or *'And Quiet Flows the Don'* the novel by Mikhail Alexandrovich Sholokhov ..." Rosie laughed again.

"Vic, I reckon you will be classed as unteachable ..."

"Yes, Rosie, that's the problem. They'll regard me as a freak, won't they?"

"That would be the biggest mistake ..."

"But I won't mind that, really. I might even enjoy the somewhat unique challenge. Imagine being interviewed by the careers officer? *'So young man, what do you want to do when you leave school?'* And me saying something like, *'Oh, sir, I won't have time to do a job. I'll be too busy spending all my money'.* I mean, how arrogant! At least, Richard Branson and I do have a lot in in common ..."

"Let me guess. You've both got money?"

"No. We both have a passion for chocolate biscuits! But I would, however, love to go to Uni and study for some interesting but useless degree! "

"But you've already got master's degrees, and now you're well into a doctorate ..."

118

"That's just one of my problems ... imagine me telling anybody that? Or turning up at the graduation ceremony? It's just ridiculous in the extreme! Or me telling anybody that I have a pilot's licence, or a driving licence? Think about it. Me applying for insurance on a car, saying that I have had a full licence since August 1963 ...!"
"Yes, Vic. Although your situation is somewhat unique ..."
"Somewhat! ... That's an understatement!"
"I can appreciate your problem."
"I think ... I think the possibilities for litigation are endless. Anyway, fancy another cup of coffee?"

Sean arrived with Angie and Marcel shortly after Willis and Rosie had polished off their coffees and half a pack of chocolate biscuits. The two guests piled out of the car. Willis and Rosie went to meet them.
"Which of you two were jammed into the back, then?"
"I was!" said Angie, as she gave Willis a hug and a kiss. "But it wasn't too bad."
"Marcel, Angie, can I introduce Rosie? you've spoken on the 'phone."
"We have. Nice to meet you." Connie flashed about looking after everybody as usual, and Willis as ever the good host, took the new arrivals on a tour of the garden. The serious business would not start until tomorrow.

Connie and her daughters had done a wonderful job of preparing the main dining room as a little conference centre, and Connie made it clear to Willis that she would be on call as and when needed by the group and would prepare a snack lunch for whenever the meeting wanted to adjourn.
"You have a lovely house, Ted. What a little jewel so close to London. No wonder you mean to stay here." Marcel, Rosie and Sean all agreed.
"Well, because of the circumstances, I've had to do a bit of work

on inheriting my own property, and of course Rosie and Sean have stepped into the breach ... anyway, who wants to be chairman?"

"You have just been elected."

"Thank you, Sean! Then I declare this meeting open! Firstly, does anyone object to the proceedings being taped? They will be for our use only." The consensus was that it was a good idea. Willis got up and moved to the sideboard and turned the recorder on. He put a couple of microphones onto the table, so everybody's voice would be picked up. "Right, Angie, what exactly do you need from me and why?"

"Right. Here's the deal. And for the purposes of the recording, I'll paint the full picture. You all know what's been going on. It is the general understanding that the Chinese medical team, generously funded by Beijing in what I might delicately call the human tissue experiments, just needs to tie up some loose ends, and have told Andy, aka Professor Vennuchi of the Milan Ospidale San Raffaele, that they need confirmation that the subject is alive and well, and performing totally normally."

"We all see he is. What do they want, to have him back in Milan?"

"No, Rosie. I've already told them that ain't gonna happen. If it did, somehow, I seriously doubt he would ever get back here. At best, they want an idea of the operation of the six brain functions, viz., creative visualisation, memory and learning, executive planning, language and maths, emotional responses and social interaction ..."

"All that and without notes, Angie?"

"Thank you, Ted. There's more. We can deal with the basics, but for some reason these China guys want particular emphasis on the amygdala, the little structure which is alert to basic survival like emotional reactions such as anger and fear ..."

"So you are going to frighten our Vic? make him angry? How are you going to do that?"

"Well, we won't need to do that ... but another reaction they want to test, and they have made the point that provided it seems in order, they will take as read that the others are in order. The reaction we need to test ... is the ... the sex bit. The Chinese go pretty strong on that, so we need to deal with that somehow."

"And just how, Angie, do you intend to do that?"

"Well, Ted ... that's up to you. If you'll just let me work on that one for a while ..."

"I intend that you do, Angie. I'm sure we can arrive at a suitable ... solution."

"You didn't intend any pun there, did you Vic?"

"Sean! ..."

"A little joke, Rosie!"

"Er ... moving on, I will need to take videos of you walking, talking, doing a few sums, running and whatever else is on the list. They must know it is you, so full face identification is essential. If I take more than is necessary, Andy's team can edit. Just so you know, my take will be edited into the whole operation, and I'm told it'll be from when the body of young Vic was first taken to Harbin Medical University. It makes me believe that Xia Renchuan, their lead surgeon, was actually ... actually waiting ... knew that Vic would be arriving. The whole thing is just too awful to contemplate ..."

"Hence the syringe in the boy's room? And where's the body of ... where's my body?"

"Yes, to the syringe, and as far as the body is concerned, I understand it was cremated. In fact, when we asked for a disposal record ... it was one of nineteen cremated that day, all from Harbin ..."

"What a blood disgraceful business! What the hell are they up to?"

"I'll tell you, Marcel. They are going to put the whole thing on show at the next UCSF conference in San Francisco. The subject is *'Pioneering Advances in Transplantation'*.

"When is that?"

"I think, third week in September. This year."

"Do you think I could get a few days off school to attend?"

"Let me just tick the box *'has a sense of humour'*. I think if you do, you would be the guest of honour. You'd go down a bomb!"

"I know who would go! Steve Grant ..."

"That name rings a bell."

"He was looking after Ted in the Royal Berks ..."

"But, Rosie, he's not a transplant surgeon, is he ...?"

"No. He's not!"

"But hang on a minute. The business up in Manchester. That was ... what was it? SOXMIS? That was something to do with organ donation. Remember?"

"So, you reckon he's trading organs?"

"Very possibly, he still is. But I think we really must look more closely at the Manchester deal."

"Okay. Lunch break." Willis stood up and pushed his chair back. Shall we take an hour?"

"Vic."

"Yes, Rosie?"

"Should I talk about the stuff I found on the internet about serious transurgery? and mention what Grant had been doing with our patient?"

"Yes. I think it's all grist to the mill. Do it." The meeting resumed. Angie started the post-lunch discussion.

"Before we move on, I have been asked what's in it for China and Italy, or rather the Italian team. Simple. Money. For its part, Andy and his team will get about two million Euros. China could get billions. It represents the very pinnacle of modern surgery. But it is very much a business for profit."

"Angie, if I can add something. A few years ago, there was a spook news item that some Italians and some Chinese had managed a head transplant, and the reaction from round the world was phenomenal. Then they said that they had also managed to bring the brain-dead back to life using electrically charged metal probes, again wrong. In fact, there had been very many experiments ... a successful one will indeed be a very profitable result, hence Beijing have been financing it for years. And if I may add, there have been cases where a patient has been pronounced brain-dead, but in fact and very probably known to the medical staff, the brain was very much alive. And I think I'm correct in saying that we found some of the drug in Vic's blood, so the doctors had him pronounced brain dead, so making his body available to the trans-team in China ... Angie?"

"Yes, there are about seventeen common-use drugs that can do that. It all adds up to a massive conspiracy..."

"And we believe Grant is in on it?"

"I'll check on his drugs record to see if he had used any of the stuff on Ted. But I don't see how we can rule him out."

"Thanks, Rosie. And I gather that you, Sean have now been given the job of looking into Grant?"

"Yes. And I know where I'm going next. Manchester."

"Right, I think that apart from detail, were about done. Just to make sure we know what we each have to do now. Also make sure we have each other's contact details. Okay?"

"Yes, Ted, I think that's about everything. For the remainder of the day ..."

"*'The Remains of the Day'*. Kazuo Ishiguro. Nobel Prize ... He also wrote the dystopian science fiction novel *'Never Let Me Go'* Published in 2005 ..."

"What?"

"The book. *'The Remains of the Day'* 1989. And the film. 1993. Anthony Hopkins and Emma Thompson. Nominated for eight Academy awards ... It was about ..."

"Ted, Vic, whoever you are, you are utterly intolerable. I wouldn't be surprised if your teachers wanted to give you a bloody good slapping ... you are really going to piss them off, big time!" Everybody, even Willis, laughed.

"I'll really enjoy myself then! And by the way, could we drop the Vic bit and just use Ted? I am easily confused."

"I bet you are! As I was saying, Ted, for the remainder of the day, we can deal with the photos and video stuff. We'll need a copy of today's Le Figaro if you can find one or something equally suitable, and you can read something from it. Right, I think the garden will be a good start. I'll want you to run around and kick a ball about. Let's get out there now while the sun's shining." Angie and Willis exited the patio doors and moved into the large rear garden.

"Angie, just a thought. When I go, or we go, to town for the paper should we also get a porn mag?"

"What!"

"Well, if you want me to ..."

"Stop right there! Neither you nor I are going to buy anything like that!"

"Well how ..."

"I know exactly what you're going to say ... and I do not think you need anything like that. It's my department, so just leave everything to me!"

"That sounds interesting."

"Just behave yourself young man. You're turning into a dirty old man."

"I have been one for ages."

"This conversation ends right now!"

"Yes, miss."

"Okay. let's get this sorted. I need a live recording of you with an erection, and also a sample ..."

"You what?"

"This is strictly business."

"So, what do you want me to do?"

"You know bloody well what."

"You said you would deal with all this ..."

"Okay, I will."

"Rosie, Sean ..." Angie got them both together ..."I'm going to ask Andy if I should pop in and see Doctor Grant at the Reading hospital. I'm sure I can think up some excuse. I'll ask him about his various interests in the business, and I could also ask for his bank details for his payment. I think he'll be very forthcoming, and it might save you, Sean, from having to collect that information yourself. What do you think?"

"Would you want to record the info?"
"If possible, yes. Can you arrange that?"
"No problem."
"Okay, I'll text Andy. If it's yes, I'll let you know."
CHAPTER 12

Angie had a three-day window for her visit to Grant at the Royal Berks hospital. She had sent him a text and they fixed up a meeting at his department. He also agreed to show her round. Willis, Marcel and Rosie had all decided to go and see some London sights. Connie drove Angie to the hospital as she had to some shopping anyway. Grant and the psychiatrist met at reception. Angie had turned on her little recorder, which Sean, having twisted the arm of his boss at the Early Road HQ, had managed to get hold of, together with a small camera.

"Hi, Angie. Steve Grant. Let's go for a chat. What brings you to our little town?"

"I was in the UK to finish an assignment. Had to see one of our patients. Usual thing. You were in on the er ... Willis deal?"

"Yes."

"Ah, good. maybe we could have a chat about that? I am a bit concerned that every year we are cremating or burying tons of possibly good transplant material ..."

"True. That's why I'm always on the look-out ... for whatever I can get."

"So what about Willis?"

"It was an opportunity. I have a little business which is always looking for organs to harvest. Willis just fell into the bracket. Nothing on his driver's licence about organ donation, no known relatives, so I kept him sedated until Andy was ready."

"Was the hospital agreeable?"

"Didn't go there. As far as they were concerned, your team were to try and treat him. Anyway, what I say usually goes. Nobody interferes in my business. It's the old thing, *'trust me, I'm a doctor'*". Grant laughed. Angie was not impressed. The doctor had virtually confessed to murder and seemed so blasé about it.

"Would he have recovered, do you think?"

"Possibly ... he could well have been classed as *'cerebrum mortuus est'* by a doctor in a hurry, then press for disengaging life-support. I chose not to make that decision. I could have. Anyway, what's your role with the team, Angie?"

"I just look after the post-trauma issues. Keeping recipients well-balanced, that sort of thing. And on that, we've had the Harbin Medical guys on to us. They want to tie off the loose ends to get their money. And ours of course, out of Beijing. Then they can prepare all the stuff for the conference ... in the States? It's in September, so they've got to get a move on".

"And my cut as well!"

"Of course. But if you give me your bank details, I'll chase it up for you when I get back the day after tomorrow."

"Great. I'll deal with that. Maybe you want to have a word with my people in Manchester about what else we can do for you?"

"Love to". Angie was thinking fast. "Er ... in fact, better that that. I can always go there with an associate to meet with them? I doubt a short 'phone call would be adequate."

"Great. I'll get my office to fix up a meet."

"Thanks. Will you be there, Doctor Grant?"

"Hell, no! we're so bloody backward in this country, that such things as I would like to get involved in ... are just a big no-no. I have to keep a very low profile in this business. Anyway, I'll get things organised for your chap. What's his name?"

"Don't know who it'll be yet. I'll be the lead name, anyway, so it'll be me plus one. But if I can get a name soon, I'll pass it onto to you, okay?"

"Sure. No problem. Oh, here ... my account details. HSBC. That account is in Milan. Anyway, nice meeting you, Angie. Speak soon."

Angie was impressed by one thing he learned from Grant. His overwhelming arrogance. And he had willingly, though unwittingly, walked into every trap she had set. She called Connie. She was waiting in the hospital car-park. They both drove home.

Angie had a brainwave. She would see if the police would sanction her being an investigator into the illegal harvesting of organs. With the many thousands of refugees turning up on their shores, the opportunities for such exploitation was enormous. If traffickers were totally indifferent to the hundreds of deaths caused by the lack of equipment and serviceable craft with which to engineer successful crossings of the Mediterranean to safety, would they think twice about killing to sell healthy organs? She concluded not. The sheer disdain that doctor had shown of the consequences for the families of what he was doing with their spouses, children and others, shocked her. She did however, feel that she had overlooked, nay, perhaps had not wanted to see, what had been staring her in the face when sat behind her desk at the Ospidale San Raffaele.

Back at Oaklands, Angie took Sean aside.
"Sean, I have the recording. I also have the bank details ...".
"Hey, you've done well! How was he? Co-operative?"
"Very arrogant. However, I took the liberty of inviting my representative, by which I hoped Grant would assume it was from the Milan team, and not just me, to speak to the people in Manchester, where he admits he has a business ... I'm going to run it past Andy first, but if I dress it up as further opportunities for them, I am sure he'll agree."
"So, who is the rep? Do we know him?"
"You. At least, I hope it'll be you. After all, you need to get totally immersed in the whole bloody mess. All I have to do is call Grant and tell him when we can make it, and off we go."
"You said 'we' ... does that mean you as well?"
"Yes, if I can talk Andy round ... shouldn't be a problem. I would think your job will be to look at the criminal aspect, and I can ask all medical questions."
"Angie? You are bloody brilliant!"
"Maybe. Anyway, I'll go and brief the others. How was the

127

London trip?"

"Great. That Vic ... er ... Ted is full of information. He hardly stopped talking all day! After Madame Tussauds, he dragged us round the Planetarium, then around the corner to see Sherlock Holmes' house."

"I thought he would! Let's grab the others and have a chat."

Angie set out what had gone on in the hospital, then the arrangements for the Manchester office visit.

"Our doctor, Grant, that is, struck me as being a bit arrogant. But we have a lot of info from him. And Sean and I will be going up there to have a good look round. And we'll both be wired?"

Within a day after her visit to the hospital, Doctor Angelica Scrito was granted permission to visit Manchester. She had also made up a list of questions she wanted to ask. She planned to be fully prepared. She knew she would not get another chance. While she was away, Marcel and Willis were to visit a gym kit store to purchase all the stuff the trainer wanted to buy to fit out Willis's little training room. That would keep them both busy.

The following day, having confirmed with Grant that the visit was on, Sean and Angie boarded the 09.12 train on platform seven at Reading to arrive 12.41 at Manchester Piccadilly. They took a taxi to the SOXMIS office. It was a first-floor property in an imposing glass-fronted block in Fountain Street comprising a reception area, three separate offices, an admin office and a conference room, a kitchenette, a room marked 'Treatment Rooms' and toilet facilities. Sean estimated the rental would be in the region of £40,000 per annum. Not cheap. The receptionist greeted them, and they introduced themselves.

"We've been expecting you. I'll call Sophie Garner. She's our MD. Please take a seat." Sophie was with them in seconds.

"Welcome. Steve Grant told us to expect you." After the usual small talk about the trip from Reading and the weather, the MD go

128

down to business. "Let me give you a quick tour. The three departments we have here ..." she pushed into the first room ... "... this one is for the AI administration. Everything here is only for that service. We have a very large bank of various men who want to be donors. We categorise by hair colour, job or profession, skin colour, physique ... our clients come here to choose a person and then we arrange the usual. It can either be done in the treatment room, where the fresh samples are ... er ...extracted, and that can either be done by the lady client herself, or by our member of staff or by the man himself. Whether here or at any other mutually-convenient location, the further necessary actions are completed according to our full instructions. Every donor has to go through monthly screen ..." And so it went on. Sean had a question.

"What fee do you charge for the service?"

"About £500 give or take. The donor gets nothing, of course. We assume the processes are sufficient recompense for him. I mean, to put it crudely, if you were keen to engage in similar practices say on the street, you ... the man would of course be expected to pay for it. I think the going rate is about ..."

"Yes, Sophie, I understand. Thank you." Sean noticed another door, slightly ajar. It was marked 'Private'. He looked into the room between the door edge and the frame, to see a slim, dark-haired lady seated at the desk. She looked up at him briefly, then stood up, moving out of his line of sight. Then the door closed. Sophie was still talking. "... and, with our other services, the donors select the status of the recipients. But we'll come onto that in a minute. Let's go and see the treatment room." As the visitors followed Sophie down the corridor, she addressed Angie. "Would you have much call for this in Italy, Angie?"

"Yes. mainly because with so many immigrants there now, recipients have to be sure they're not going to get mixed-race donors."

"Understandable. Steve is very hot on that. We think that's why we're so successful. We give the donors and the recipients a very wide choice. Here. The treatment room."

"What goes on in here, Sophie?"

"Donation collection where we recommend that the donee female extracts the specimen herself. Then we have medical staff on hand to complete the donation. The parties therefore have a chance to talk to each other, but occasionally, very rarely, the donee may not want to proceed with that donor. We have usually matched them fairly but ..."

"At least, they're all better off knowing and having met each other ..."

"Precisely. Let's move on. Next, we have the adoption service. We have a number of couples who sell their babies on. They do it for the money ..."

"A baby factory?"

"Kind of ... Steve set the fee at about £15,000 to adopt. The couple who produce the child and agree to the adoption get about £4,000. The rest goes to us. We did about seventy last year, and this year we've already exceeded that. You can understand that our rules are quite strict. We need baby DNA to ensure parentage ..."

"Who are the clients, generally?"

"Many from overseas. This is the operation Steve gets most involved with. That and the care-home referrals. Some can pay up to fifty grand!"

"And the organ exchange? How does that work?"

"Again, Angie, we're different. The donor before death or his family can stipulate where the organ goes to. For example, some will not want blacks or Asians as donees, Catholics, or Muslims. Only white British ..."

"And how does the hospital take that?"

"Interesting question. You'd be surprised how forceful the donor side can be. Almost violent. However, we ignore it, and take steps to ensure that it doesn't happen. And that the donor family never meet the donee side ..."

"So how do you make money on that, Sophie?"

"They pay us to put them on what we call the Exclusion and Preferences Register. Some stipulate that the donees can only members of their own organisations, like the BNP or the KBW group, or some such, usually very right-wing. The trouble is, they're never gonna win if they took us to court, 'cos we give them no paperwork or anything. They sign the register, here, only. Or it is signed by someone here on their behalf. Then it goes straight into the bin."

"So I take it all this is available to us? In Italy?"

"Of course. We've done a lot of everything there. Organs, sperm collection and storage, care-home referrals. You name it!"

"And I assume Steve keeps a finger on the pulse?"

"Of course. One reason he still works as a surgeon, is so he can access a number of donors. He effectively gets first choice. He's had a few sent to your guys, as you know ..." Sean and Angie had heard enough. They had been in the office for just over three hours.

"Well, sounds pretty good to me. If you can give me your card, we'll get back to Reading. Have to get back to Milan in a day or so. If you can tell Steve thanks."

"Will do. Here, take a few cards. Obviously, we don't advertise our full range of services. But we get many people who wish to avail themselves of our expertise. Have a good trip back. We ordered your taxi. It's just arrived."

In the taxi, Angie just looked at Sean. The policeman put his finger to his lips. Then he spoke. Angie got the message.

"Bloody impressive. I am sure we can do a lot of business with them."

"Very good. I'll get onto my boss and get a few more lines of business set up. Could even open a separate office in Milan. And in Paris?"

"We'll work on it tonight and try and get something going as soon as I get back." The taxi dropped them at the station.

"What do we owe you, driver?"

"Nothing, sir! All taken care of!"

"Thanks." The car drove off.

"What was all that about, Sean?"

"That wasn't a taxi, Angie. It was a plant. I reckon the office just wanted some real feedback on us. I saw the car parked up when we went in. Those guys have to be extra careful!"

"Looks like you saved our skin, Sean, thanks!"

"That's not all. Did you see the girl in that other office? The one we didn't get taken into?"

"No, why?"

"I saw her. She appeared to be Asian. I'd like to bet she was Chinese."

"Wow! That explains a lot!"

The driver returned to the office.

"Sophie! Those two were really sold on the business! In fact, they were talking about opening up offices in Milan and Paris!"

"Good stuff, Eric, thanks. I'll get onto Steve and tell him. By the way, hang on here for a while. The boss wants you to take her to town. I'll tell her you're back." Sophie knocked on the 'Private' door and opened it.

"Miss Ling. Eric's back. He tells me that the visitors from Milan are keen to set up a similar operation in Italy and in France ..."

"They fuck stupid! We already have work there! And I tell you always keep my door shut. That man he see me. Bad. Tell Eric to come take my bags pretty quick!"

"Yes, Miss Ling, of course!"

At seven-thirty or so that evening, Rosie picked up Angie and Sean from Reading station. She was full of questions.

"Well, Rosie, that doctor of yours! He's in it up to his neck. When we get back to Marlow, we'll go through it all, if Sean can work the recordings. I would think the GMC would like to know about this. The net's closing round him!"

"Is what they're doing legal, Sean?"

"No idea. That'll be a matter for the office to decide, or possibly the Crown Prosecution Service! But it doesn't sound to me like a

fully legal, above-board organisation. I'd like to bet there's a fair few pounds in Steve's Milan account, though. And get this, there's a Chinese girl there. I bet she runs the whole bloody show!"
"That sounds interesting! So, where do we go from here? I've just had a thought! If we know where Grant used to work, would it be possible to see if he's done this sort of thing ... I mean nicking organs ... before? I imagine the office keep records somewhere!"
"We'll all hear the recordings, then maybe I should hand them over to the boss and see where we go from there. And Angie, you've got to make a decision. Do you confront Andy at work? Would you ever know what he's been up to with Steve and with poor old André Marais?"
"I don't actually know, frankly. There's a lot to think about. But I'm absolutely sure of one thing ... and that is, that because of the France thing, and now what we know of Steve Grant, sooner or later, the police will be visiting the hospital and going through all the records ... and I want to make sure that I do not get swept up with the bad guys."
"Tell me, is there anybody else you know of who is getting even a little concerned about all this? I mean apart from Marcel, who I think is totally behind you?"
"Yes, Rosie, I think there are two, at least two, who might be. If I can tell them about André Marais, Manchester and Doctor Grant, it might just sway things my way. But of course, I really doubt it will be done before the Chinese release the recordings of it all in September. But at some stage all the shit is gonna hit the fan and that could really mean that the China idea of walking away with all the kudos they hope to get ... will collapse around their ears."
"Be careful, Angie. The Chinese like the Russians, can be pretty nasty ..."
"That's what worries me! I think I'll wait until after September, and just see how the medical fraternity react."
"I think that makes sense". The party got to Marlow and piled out of the car. Sean and Angie spent the next hour briefing the others.
"That Chinese person. It's possible she's the one pulling the strings. Those bloody Chinese steal any damn thing, including

military secrets, like new fighter-jet stuff. I get the feeling that pretty soon the whole thing is gonna unravel!"
Everyone had a last drink, then retired.

In the morning, Angie 'phoned Andy.
"I'm told you were really taken with the Manchester set-up?"
"How did you know that, Andy?"
"Doctor Grant, Steve Grant called me. Wanted to open up in Milan and Paris? Steve thinks it's a good idea!"
"We have to walk before we can run! Anyway, I'll brief you when I get back."
"Yeah, and we need the stuff on the boy. Beijing are getting impatient. They need to get it all edited, organise re-takes if necessary ..."
"It won't be, Andy. I've got miles of footage, don't worry!"
"Okay. See you soon." A thought occurred to Angie. She must copy the footage and keep the copy here, in the UK. She called Marcel.
"Can we copy this stick here, Marcel?"
"Sure, we can. Vic ... Ted ... can do that for you, no problem! I'll ask him." Ted agreed. In a few minutes it was done.
"I've got one for you and I've done another for myself, Okay"
"Perfect, thanks. Now we've got to get back to the hospital. All this has to go the China team. It's gonna be part of a super-slick presentation at the conference. And will no doubt cause a sensation."
"I hope it goes down well. Just one thing, though. We absolutely must get a copy of it. I don't care how, but it is absolutely essential that we do!"
"Ted, I'm sure I can work that! Now I want to give Sean a call. In the car back to the station, he warned me to say nothing in case the driver was a plant. He was, because what we said in the car, some bullshit conversation about opening offices in Milan and Paris, has just been relayed to me via Andy, and he got it from Grant. They must have recorded us!"
"I would expect that from the Chinese!" A full day later, Angie

rang from her flat.

"Ted? Andy's delighted with the footage. The girls loved the bit where ..."

"Don't tell me, Angie, let me guess. Was it the bit where you, you know ..."

"Okay! Stop! That's enough! Anyway, I've suggested that we ... the hospital that is, get copies of the finished article, 'cos I told them we're going to have to run it past our lawyers, you know, the usual nonsense, because we can't really pixilate your face, can we? And it might mean having to get the permission of your guardians or whatever. Make sense?"

"Of course. It's a good ruse to get a copy of the whole business. Guardians? That'll be Rosie and Sean, of course. So you'll have to get some papers sent over to us, okay? I don't think it'll be essential, but I think we ought to do it. It will make a fine addition to the file!"

"I'll get onto it ..."

"And, by the way, what would have happened if the whole thing went tits up?"

"Well, if you snuffed it, or suddenly started acting like an animal, or were sort of eighty-percent paralysed, you would have been finished off and cremated, and nobody would be any the wiser. If you had got as far as the UK, you would have been dropped into the lap of the BIRT ..."

"The what?"

"The Brain Injury Rehabilitation Trust ... as requiring a certain degree of care ..."

"Oh, great! ... anyway, let's get this video thing sorted, shall we?"

CHAPTER 13

Something had been nagging Doctor Steve Grant. It was Willis's estate. He decided to tackle his theatre and ICU nurse, Rosie. He knew she had of late been taking care of his former patient's business. He bumped into her at the nurses' station.

"Rosie. How are things moving on with Willis?"

"In what respect, Steve?"

"His money and stuff, his estate. The house and everything?"

"That's something for Mrs Registrar Blake to deal with, isn't it? Or do you have any special reason for ..." Before Grant could answer, she added, "Anyway, how come you're interested in all that? The bloke's dead. No longer your concern, is it?"

"No, I suppose not. It was just a thought." Grant put it to the back of his mind. Or tried to. But he couldn't. He knew that if there was any family beneficiary, he, she or they would, and quite understandably, want to know about his patient's last few days. Grant felt he could be in their sights. However, he had work to do. He put it on the back-burner. Anyway, he didn't want to give the impression that he had any further interest in his old patient.

Angie had been thinking about her position in Vennuchi's hospital Transteam. She and Marcel had discussed it frequently since their return from the UK.

"I think what we need, Angie, is some idea, some way to get into the records of the whole business, here at San Raffaele. We must know for sure about what's been going on. I can get in touch with Enzo to see what he's been able to unearth, and how if at all, we feature. I do not believe that Andy does not know about it. If anything ..."

"Look, the bloke's picking up a whack of dough from the China connection. Isn't that enough incentive for him to turn a blind eye? Ditto the Dauphin bloke, and the Steve Grant bloke in Reading. But, as you say, until we have proof, and if we go off at half-cock, we're just going to look stupid, aren't we?"

"Yes. Do you have any way ... do you know of anybody we can trust to access those documents? I don't imagine they will be published on line!"

"I could ... I could tell Andy that I have to do, or want to do, a survey or something, a kind of audit if you like, of all the TP patients referred to me over, say the past year? If he suspects nothing, then he's probably going to say, just go-ahead! That should at least get my foot in the door."

"Give it a go. In the meantime, I'll call Enzo to see if Vic comes up on anything." Enzo did have some news.

"Marcel, let me pass you over to my assistant. She's actually looking at all the stuff we picked up from Dauphin. Call her any time you have more info, okay? I'll pass you over now."

"Hi, Vic Clément ..."

"Yes. A request came in to Dauphin for a lad with plenty of hair, well-built and large for his age. Had to be a '*no known family*' candidate. A note on the file said Milan was end destination, via China. A handwritten addition, something about a gymnastics team booked for there anyway. The target could be added as a supernumerary. Fee to AM, which we assume to be André Marais, was 500 Euros."

"Jesus, that's loose change! If you find any more for Italy, or China, please let me know!"

"China, you said? There's a Chinese name, Ling. That's Chinese isn't it? Manchester, apparently. Ring any bells?"

"Fraid not. But we're nowhere near finished ... there might be a chance that she was the woman we saw in the Manchester office. Don't have a name as yet. You've done well."

"You're welcome." Marcel's comment on his notes was '*Bloody hell, kids sold for peanuts*'. He passed the message on to Angie. It really upset her.

"At least, we know some of that should appear somewhere on

the books here. I'm determined to have a damn good look. I'm collecting quite a good dossier on all this! What's this Ling name?"

"Enzo's lot picked it up. They reckon it's Chinese. From Manchester ..."

"Bloody hell, Marcel! That must have been the woman Sean saw when we were visiting SOXMIS! I reckon she's the one who pulls the strings! Wow, I think this could be a breakthrough! I wonder if she attended the same conference that Grant and Andy attended?" It did not take long to establish that she did. Angie called Ted.

"Ted, the Chinese woman we saw in Manchester. We believe her full name is Yu Yan Ling ..."

"Yu Yan? That comes from Yu Xiao Yan Ran, women who have beautiful smiles. I bet she does smile beautifully when she seals another organ deal!"

"Well, another load of really useful information! Is there anything you don't know? Anyway, we seriously believe that she runs the Manchester show ... so she's probably Doctor Grant's boss!"

Angie didn't beat about the bush. In the admin office she went straight in to the head clerk.

"Bella, I'm looking for any information you have on a Ted Willis, from England, and a Victor Clément, France."

"Hi, Angie. I have a notion that we have both ... Yes. Let me look at the index ... as I thought. We do have both. Here." Bella lifted the files from the cabinet and dropped them onto the desk in front of the doctor. Angie looked through the files. Then she had a few questions.

"Odd. The death certificate appears to have been raised two days before Willis went to China. And the Clément lad came here from China. What's that all about?"

"Angie, I have no idea."

"Didn't you ask?"

"If I asked about every odd bloody thing that goes on here, I'd never get any work done. We're supposed to be a cutting-edge transplant unit, and we necessarily become involved in cases where no records, or no accurate records, can be maintained. Those guys move people in and out randomly ... like chess pieces."

"Yeah. Pawns. Is China involved a lot?"

"Yes, it is. I'm not totally happy with it, and I'm not the only one. Whenever anybody complains, they're either moved out or told to shut up, and not interfere with their work."

"Do you know about money due in from China?"

"There's some rumour, yes..."

"I think you and I should have a chat. You know where I live, don't you? ... Good. Then I think you should pop in and see me some time. I don't want to say too much here in case ... well, just in case. But I think we should have a frank exchange of views, okay Bella?"

"Give me your mobile number."

Two days later, Bella pressed the bell to gain access to Angie's flat. Having both sat down with a coffee, and with a pizza in the oven, they two girls talked.

"Angie, there's been a kind of swelling concern about all the stuff going on in the trans-department. The last deal nearly broke through ... er ... we know there's a load of normal ops going on, but Andy feels he could be doing more. He went away on a couple of those conferences and came back with some funny ideas ..."

"Does the name Grant ring any bells?"

"Funny that, yes it does. He was the guy who brought in that old man, Willis, the one we shipped off to China rather suddenly. Apparently, a plane was diverted into Milan to pick him and a couple of Andy's team. But the odd thing was, Andy had already prepared a death cert, and gave it to the Grant bloke, even though the old bugger was still alive!"

"Then what happened?"

"Grant buggers off back to England!"

"So, what do you think's going on, apart from that Willis business?"

"I ... we ... think that the transteam is coming under pressure to work with the Chinese to do ... to do what they did with that lad Vic."

"Which was ...?"

"Well ... you know, don't you! You were asked to look after him."

"I do know. And I can tell you that there was some bloke in France ... well, two blokes in France, one was murdered ..."

"What?"

"Yeah, really, and they were both running a kind of racket dealing with kids ... supplying them for various purposes, and quite a few came here. Or rather, went to China I believe ..."

"Including Vic? Now, that reminds me. Those hair and follicle samples you brought in. The ones from Paris? Where do you reckon they were sourced to?"

"I think I know. Hair etcetera from a Chinaman?"

"Yes."

"And the syringe cover? Also Chinese manufacture? Why are they so important?"

"Because we now believe that our little French boy was deliberately disabled by an injection when he was in China on some sports tour, then shipped over to the Harbin unit ... where his body was stolen!"

"What? You're kidding! Does Andy know?"

"I don't know the answer to that question, Bella. But I'd like to know. Somehow, I don't think Andy would have been told where the poor bugger came from.

"Let's get the pizza." Between mouthfuls of food, the conversation continued.

"So, where do we go from here, Angie?"

"Well, we've already involved the police in the UK and in France. Now I think, we should involve the police here, in Italy. If we don't, and we know what's going on, we could all be considered as conspirators. Has China paid up yet?"

"No. They just want to get some video thing sorted out. I think it's all in hand. Anyway, I know that they won't dare to show it in America without having paid Andy off, because if there's even a whiff of how they managed all this, I mean the truth, there'll be serious consequences for everybody concerned, and the Chinese ... Beijing is in it up to their bloody necks ... they won't be too pleased at losing all the dosh they've invested in the whole business. Frankly, I don't know why we ever got involved with them!"

"Right. And I'm also wondering why we did. Just keep your eyes and ears open. But be careful. Two million Euros is a lot of money! And a quarter of it is going to Grant?"

"Correct."

"And one other thing, does the name SOXMIS mean anything to you?"

"Yes! That's the name of the account we pay Grant's money into, why?"

"There's a business of that name in the UK. They arrange baby adoptions, private sales of semen, care-home referrals and are also in the organ-harvesting caper."

"And Grant's mixed up in all that?"

"Yes, Bella. And it appears that the woman who runs it is Chinese!"

"That explains a lot!"

A letter addressed to Rosie Pollard arrived at Oaklands. Willis opened it knowing it was from his, or rather, Rosie's, lawyers who were handling the estate. Sean, Rosie and Willis decided to just let them finish the job. The letter stated that there had been no difficulties with the payments. The house had been transferred into the names of Rosie and Sean, who were to hold the same as trustees ...'*pending the beneficiary Victor Clément attaining his majority at the age of 18 [eighteen] years, when the property and the remainder of the deceased's estate would vest in him absolutely'. Furthermore, we do not consider it necessary to deplete the estate by seeking potential beneficiaries under the rule in Evans and Westcombe [1999] as, inter alia, we are fully convinced that the signatures on the documents submitted to us are those of Mr Willis [deceased] as we have had dealings with him over a number of years. Furthermore, we have also attended to the winding-up of Mrs Willis's estate, as an essential prerequisite and which we effected prior to the winding-up of Ted Willis's estate'.*

Rosie and Sean were required to sign a copy of the letter and return it to the lawyers at Fountain Court, Reading, together with the details of the Trustee account into which all monies would be transferred in due course. There was the usual nonsense about the lawyers *'offering investment advice'* and every other service under the sun, as it must really hurt them to have to transfer millions of pounds out of their client account and thus beyond their control.

"Well," Willis state aloud, "They would have to try for the extra business, wouldn't they". The lawyers had at least closed all the bank accounts, dealt with Willis's late wife's affairs, in so far as they needed dealing with, so Willis just wanted them to 'butt out'. There had been a minor upset about various withdrawals from the accounts, but it was easily explained away when they were told that the funds were for the benefit of the only beneficiary, point one, and, point two, and as Rosie had told them, nobody else had the *locus standi* to bitch about it. Rosie liked being able to tell the lawyers that. He smiled to himself when he remembered the lawyer's reaction. He called Rosie and briefed her, and she and Sean agreed to set up the account, sign the copy letter, and pass bank details on to the probate lawyers.

Willis poured himself a glass of wine and sat outside in the cool, afternoon air and considered his position. Was he doing anything that was illegal? No. He knew that if he had not done what he had done, the entire estate would be disposed of to the Treasury Solicitor's department in Kemble Street London, just as he had himself done for many of his deceased clients who had, usually, been too mean to leave their estates to some decent charity such as those for the Armed Forces, or animals. What would have happened then? The house would have been sold, and even if he managed to make a successful claim on his own estate, he would never have got it back. Leaving all those years of work he had done in the house and the garden would be lost forever. The moral aspects of it all? Absolutely no question it was the right thing to do and he had every right to do it. He drained his glass. He knew that if he survived long enough, and were he were to institute proceedings against various parties, it would be an interesting case, but a long uphill struggle. He was, however, convinced of one thing. He was most definitely going to give it a go. He stared across his large back garden, beautifully manicured by Alf. This was his heaven. He considered his overall situation. Thanks to the information collected by, principally Angie, he could see a clear pattern emerging. He resolved to set out his findings once all parties were together again.

Doctor Grant couldn't shake of his feeling on unease about Willis. It had been a bit of an unconventional deal, and he had, on reflection acted hastily, but the money was good, and there was a lot of pressure on him due to the proximity of the next conference. He scanned the Willis file for Registrar Blake's 'phone number. He also noticed that the Willis notes were getting a bit of a bashing. He got through to the Registrar's department.

"Doctor Grant here, Royal Berks. Any move on the Willis case?... That's right, the chap who was attacked ... I believe you have spoken to my Rosie ... nurse Pollard? ... Oh, I see. I assume therefore that he left a will and had some beneficiaries? ... Okay, I'll get onto the probate people ... No reason, I just felt I ought to see the matter through ... just something I like to do." Mrs Registrar Blake thought it odd that the doctor seemed so interested. Grant too, had an inkling that his interest was a tad unusual, so he decided to ask Rosie to look into it for him. He didn't want to seem overly interested, as it might raise her suspicions ... again. She had seemed to be too much on the ball, for his liking. He would play it cool.

"I'm not bloody wearing short trousers!"

143

"It's okay, Ted, I don't think you'll have to. But you still need a uniform!"

"The last uniform I wore was that of a Naval Commander..." The assistant in the shop looked up sharply. Willis saw the look. "I was playing in a musical. HMS Pinafore." The assistant nodded knowingly. Then to Rosie.

"Which school is it madam?" She explained. "Size?"

"Don't know. have to have a measure." With a flourish, the assistant produced a tape measure, and did the usual. For Willis's liking, the guy spent too long measuring his inside leg. He moved to a rack of jackets and trousers, produced the uniform of choice, laying it carefully on the counter. He disappeared then came back with three boxed shirts and the school tie.

"Try it on sir?"

"Yes, Ted you will. In there!" Rosie was enjoying Willis's discomfort, so he obliged by sulking. "Or you don't get an ice cream!" Willis would have to have a chat with her. He scooped up the trousers and went into the fitting room. It was a perfect fit. Ditto the jacket when he tried that on.

"Granma ..." If looks could kill, Willis was dead. "Granma, can I wear cuff-links with my shirts?" The salesman whipped open a box.

"Yes, you can, sir, Look." There was a little cut in the sleeve above the cuff buttons."

"Oh, goodee!" Rosie paid for the uniform, thanked the assistant, and went into the high street.

" I'll bloody grandma you, Ted Willis ..."

"Sorry, thought I'd just play up a little. Frankly, I think I'm gonna have a good time at school ...!"

"Don't overdo it, for God's sake! Right, we'll need underwear and shoes and socks."

"I'll try on the shoes, but not the underwear!"

Back at the house, Willis got serious. Sean had been setting up the equipment on the training room, with a copy of Marcel's schedules and diet routines prominently placed on one wall.

"If Sean's finished his little job, can we have a chat? I want to run a few things past you."

"I think he has. I'll fetch him." A few minutes later, all three were sitting round the dining table. Willis had his notes.

"I want to try and get some sense out of all the information you and Angie have dredged up. I think once we can put it into some kind of order, we will know who to approach to start putting pressure on the key players. I've printed off copies of my notes, with, as you can see, little arrows so we have a kind of flow, okay? Right. Firstly, I think that Miss Ling is at the top of the pile in the UK. I think she has been taking orders from China, the place where these ops were all carried out. We know Grant is in it up to his neck, so he's the UK guy. What Ling's got on him is anybody's guess. Then we have that Dauphin bloke in France. He's been contacted by Ling, 'cos that's what Enzo has discovered. Now, the Milan side. Are they just consumers, or are they prime-movers? And I'd like to bet that everybody is motivated by cash. Then we have the China gang. We know their plan is to cash in massively on the ultimate transplant market. China is a country riddled with debt, and in serious need of foreign currency. And finally, but you will appreciate that this is only a short précis of what's in the notes, I think they wanted Europeans because firstly, all or most Chinese look the same, or could very easily be made to do so, and secondly if they are going for a world-wide market, then having European subjects will greatly enhance the value and the reach of the market. Comments?"

"It makes sense to me. Question is, do we move in on Grant like, now? Or do we wait until the conference, and work with the Yanks to raid the Chinese camp and really screw up their ambitious project."

"Makes sense, Sean, but if Ling got wind of anything before the conference, she could get angry ... and maybe deal with Grant? Or Ted here..."

"Yeah, Rosie, it's a thought. But I'm inclined to let the police make that decision. What do you think, Ted?"

"I think you're both right. I'd like to hear Angie's take on it."

"There's something else. Mrs Clarke told me that Grant has been on to her ... about the Willis estate. She wondered why Grant had bothered himself with it. It ain't his bloody business!"

"That sounds a bit suspicious! People are going to ask why he's poking about in Willis affairs. Maybe he thinks things will backfire on him. If I had a choice, I'd act only after the conference. Once half the transurgeons in America had seen the procedure, there's no way anybody can back out!"

"I agree with you, Sean. And if Angie can get us the full record of the operations, together with the recordings we have from Grant and the Manchester crew, I reckon there'll be enough evidence to pass onto the CPS."

"Sounds pretty good to me, Ted. And I reckon it will be a EuroPol job, but there's no way we can rope China in. Or the Chinese individuals responsible, unless they can be arrested when out of China."

"I reckon that's for you and your guys to deal with, Sean. By the way, what does your boss think about all this stuff?"

"He behind me one hundred percent!"

"Good. Tomorrow, I'll get some stuff off to Angie."

It took Angie about a day to respond. Her text suggested that they did nothing until the September conference ...'*and I think the first person to 'hit' will be Doctor Grant because the UK cops are the least corrupt, and because any leaks up or down the line to anybody else involved could mean a wholesale exodus of people, destruction of material and sending money overseas so it becomes irrecoverable'*. Willis thought she had a point, and he told her so. He also told her that he was due to start school soon, but she should copy Sean into to all emails, and speak to Sean as well if anything urgent came up. He forwarded the emails to Rosie. She called.

"Makes sense, Ted. Will you be okay there with Connie and Alf? School's only a walk down the hill. Anything I should do in the meantime?"

"Yes. Secure all my medical records. Get them sent to the lawyers for safe storage. Not to be accessed by anyone except you and Sean. Once it's all blown over, we can have them here. How's our doctor bloke these days?"

"Usual self, but just a bit quieter than normal. Don't think he'll be doing much apart from run-of-the-mill stuff for a good while. He's booked for the conference, anyway. His diary says UCSF San Francisco, is that the one?".

"Yes. Third week in September. This year."

"If there's nothing else, have a good time at school. Take a clean handkerchief ..."

"Don't you start! Or I'll call you grandma again!"

"You dare! Speak to you later, bye."

Early on Tuesday morning, Connie had prepared breakfast; tinned, peeled plum tomatoes on toast. She also made up a packed lunch which Willis stuffed into his backpack, the same one he pinched from the hospital box room, all covered in Italian writing. He also had the usual kit, a sort of everything everybody needs for school in one pack including dividers, different coloured pens and some 2H and 4H pencils. He picked up a set of keys and left the house. Connie gave him a hug and wished him luck.

There was a big sign just inside the main door directing new boys to the assembly hall. Willis reckoned there were about forty newcomers already there. He did his usual trick of picking out the plonkers, the intelligent looking blokes and smart girls, some of whom were quite good-looking, and the other selection was guys who he thought could be trouble. At the far end of the hall was a small table, at which were seated five adults each with a small pile of papers in front of them. They were totally ignoring the newcomers. A small group of older boys were standing in the corridor outside the hall, staring at the new kids, until they were shooed away to their classrooms by a bloke in a black gown. Willis saw it was the headmaster, who then strode up to the tables, turned and faced the group of new boys. Not surprisingly, apart from the murmur of the seated teachers, the kids had not been talking amongst themselves.

"Right!" The headmaster called out, his arms spread wide. "May I welcome you all to my school. I am the headmaster, Dyson is my name. No cracks please about hoovers. Or suckers." There were a few polite titters. "The first lesson you will learn here is respect for your teachers and for each other. Now, when you hear your name called out, please approach the desk and when your form teacher has his or her group, you will follow him or her to your classroom.

After about half the group had joined their teachers, Willis's name was called out.

"Clément! ... Mr Ferris." Willis had already established who Mr Ferris was. He was probably the oldest teacher, and he had a kind of well-worn look about him. Willis rather hoped he'd have Miss Gambold, a little blonde girl. But he walked up to Ferris, eyeballing some of the more attractive of the five girls in the form and extended his hand towards the teacher.

"Clément. Victor Clément. Good morning, sir!" Ferris, although taken aback somewhat, took Willis's hand.

"George Ferris. I'm your form teacher. And I'll be teaching you maths. Then a minute or so later. "Form D. My form follow me please!"

Willis was the second or third pupil into the classroom. He immediately made for the front, left hand chair and desk. He always felt comfortable with his right-hand free and towards the 'enemy'. It was the sort of place he had worked from, the cockpit of an aeroplane. Ferris came in last, having herded his 'flock' from behind. He took up his place at the front of the class on a raised platform. To his left was the classroom door; to his right and behind him was what looked like a stock-room. The front wall of the classroom was one huge white-board. Willis remembered the old blackboards, coloured chalk and the dust that went with it, and board rubbers. Ideal weapons which were from time to time thrown at pupils, sometimes at him. Mr Ferris started on his little

148

welcoming speech, possible for the fortieth time in his career at the school. He then had a couple of the pupils hand out the School Rules. There were to be no mobile phones, no lap-tops, no running in the corridors, no chewing-gum, no sweets, no water bottles. And so on. Looked good to Willis.

"Your formal lessons will start at eleven. Your programme for the week is in the pile of papers you have just received. You will note there will be no PE until next week, to give you all time to see what you will need to bring for those lessons. Nobody will be excused PE unless they have a note from their doctor or parents. The classroom numbers are also indicated. You get there by following the signs. If you see a master approaching you in the corridors, you are to move into the side and stop until the master has passed you. You are not to attempt to engage him or her in conversation. If you see a prefect, you are to execute any lawful instruction he gives you ..." And so it went on. "Any questions? No. Good. Now if you turn to your pile of papers, you will find a questionnaire. Please complete it now and make sure it is placed on my desk as you leave this room for your first lesson. Please start that now." Ferris opened a folder in front of him and started to write in it. Willis got out his questionnaire and his pen. His name and address was easy. When it came to *'Parents / Guardians' Names'* he paused, then wrote *'Sean Johnson & Rosemary Pollard'*. Address was no problem, nor were the 'phone numbers. At date of birth he put 01 December 2006; place of birth: Paris. Then came *'previous educational establishments'*. This would be tough. He wrote *'Primary schools. Felixstowe, Suffolk and Salcombe, Devon. Exams passed: None. Hobbies: Interest in aviation'*. He thought that was enough. To all the other questions he wrote *'You have this information already'* then he folded the A4 sized questionnaire in half and turned in his chair to look around the classroom. Most pupils had finished writing. Then a bell rang, somewhere out in the corridor.

"That's the five-minute bell. When the bell rings again, you go for your first lesson." Willis observed a sudden increase in productivity, the pupils stuffing their bits of paper into satchels. By the time most had finished, Ferris called out "Times up! When the bell goes again, you will leave this room and proceed as per your week's lessons. At the end of each lesson there will be a five-minute bell, then a final bell when you move on to your next lesson. Unless you are having a double period" Ferris looked at his watch. The bell rang. "Off you go!" There was a surge as everybody grabbed their bags, stood up and made for the door. Apart from Ferris, nobody had said a word. Willis was now in the corridor. His destination was room eleven. The first lesson in his new school was English.

CHAPTER 14

Mr Dyer was short and chubby, but amiable enough. He opened his lesson by talking about the value of reading.
"Reading is important. Where would you learn what is going on in the world? Where would you find information on anything? ... anybody got an answer?" There were mumblings about the internet.
"Yes, good. But what are the problems generally about getting all your information from the internet?" The silence was painful. Willis hated embarrassing silences, so he put up his hand. Dyer pointed at him. "Yes."
"There are several. Firstly, there is so much information that some of it is conflicting and very often it is hard to establish the bona fides of those who posted the information. If the author added his name, he can be traced and if he is for example, a well-respected expert in this field or that field, then it is likely that his article can be relied on. However, if you were keeping up with the business of the measles, mumps and rubella or MMR vaccination controversy linking it with autism, and which hit the headlines in about 1998, it is a signal lesson against taking any information at face value. The individual who wrote those articles, Andrew Wakefield, was later discredited after research by the journalist Brian Deer, who found that the author had multiple conflicts of interest and had broken several ethical codes and was eventually struck off the medical register. Does that answer the question, sir?" Dyer was just staring at Willis.
"Er ... yes, I think it ... er ... I think so, yes. A good answer. Thank you. Anybody else got anything else to say on the matter? No? Right homework for this week." Dyer turned to the whiteboard behind him. He scribbled away for about a minute, then turned to face the class. "I want you to pretend that you are the leader of a

political party, and there's an election coming up, so you have to prepare a manifesto which has to convince the general public to vote for you. You have a week. A minimum of five-hundred words. You can produce it on your personal computers. I will mark it for content, spelling and grammar. Copy the homework instructions from the board behind me. Any questions?"

"What's a manifesto, sir?"

"Get a dictionary and find out. Or perhaps you can ask the young gentleman in the front here." Dyer turned to Willis. "Can you tell them?"

"Yes, sir. A manifesto is a public declaration of intent or policy issued by a group of people, in this context it will be by a political party. It is actually an Italian word." Outside in the corridor, the five-minute bell rang.

"Right, class D. Lunchtime. You have a one-hour break then you attend your next lesson. I think I'll be seeing you again tomorrow afternoon. Now put your books away. There was the usual scrabbling about as the pupils shoved their bits and pieces away. Then the second bell rang, and everybody stood up and made for the door. Dyer reached out and grabbed Willis's arm. "What's your name, boy?"

"Clément, sir, Victor Clément."

"Right, thank you."

As was usual on a Friday at the Sir William Statton Grammar school, lessons finished early to allow the heads of department to get together for a run-down on issues various. Mr Headmaster Dyson opened the meeting.

"Okay! How are the new lads doing, any problems? Anything I should know about?"

"Could try Clément."

"What's that?"

"It's a he. One of the new boys."

"What's he done, Richard?" Dyer looked at the notes he had made.

"Well, first of all, he should not be in the D stream. He's too bright. My assessment is that he ought to be at least two streams higher ..."

"Don't question my judgement, Richard. I assessed him as being at that level, and there he'll stay ..." Ferris spoke up.

"I'm with Richard on this, Mike. The lad's just not being pushed enough ...".

"Well push him, George!"

"It's not as simple as that ..."

"Case closed. Shall we move on?"

"No, Mike! At least we can do some checking up on him ..."

"Case closed. Don't bother me with this boy again. Now I have another appointment this evening, so let's move on!" Neither Dyer nor Ferris were going to let it go. After the meeting they decided, Dyson or no Dyson, to check with the schools the boy had mentioned on his information form. They put a note on the school secretary's desk asking her to make the usual enquiries.

Over the weekend, Willis started work on his 'Manifesto for the Common-Sense Party'. And Angie called.

"I've made two copies of the video stuff. There are two versions, a short one they intend to show at the conference, and the full one which runs to just over ninety minutes, and if anybody wants to see it, they can order a copy. The Chinese are asking five hundred Euros for one. Anyway, I've done both for you. I'll get them sent to you by registered post. By the way, Ling is going to the conference, so we'll have her, so she, Grant and Andy will all be there. Anyway, while Andy's away with his lot, that'll be in about a week, Bella and I can have a good rummage around his office to see what we can pick up. By the way, how was school?"

"Tough, really tough."

"How so?"

"I found it hard to keep my mouth shut ..."

"I can tell you now, Ted, it's gonna get tougher!"

"I have a feeling you're right! Some nice girls there. Apart from that, I really ought to hold back on a lot of things. Some of the blokes are so bloody backward, I'm sure they only got in 'cos dad's got some money."

"Well, just leave the girls alone. They're all too young for you for a start, and secondly you'll have enough homework to do without taking any girls to the local coffee bars."

"Yeah, right. Which seems to be a fairly common expression. I'll be saying everything's 'cool' next! Anyway, I'll look at the stuff when I get it. Maybe I should show it at school?"

"That's not a good idea, and you know it. Now get on with your homework!" Angie laughed.

Then Rosie called almost as soon as Angie rang off.

"Sean has taken this business up with the senior bods and they reckon they should put the squeeze on Grant. This Ling girl has obviously got something on the doctor. Anyway, if we pop over and speak about it, he can fill you in on exactly what it's all about, okay"?

"No problem with that. And no cracks about homework, or clean hankies or polishing bloody shoes, alright?"

"Promise!" Willis got back to his PC and the manifesto. He was being constantly distracted by the 'planes from Booker aerodrome flying overhead. He decided to dump the manifesto for a while. he called Rosie again.

"Rosie, can we go to Wycombe Air Park tomorrow? I want to get some flying in. I mean with an instructor, of course!"

"Okay. You book it and let me know what time you want to go. Can Sean come as well?"

"Of course. He might even enjoy it. It he's not working, drag him along. Willis called the airfield. He asked for a four-seater. Preferable a Cessna 172. He called the airfield and booked the trip which he said would be a buzz around the local area, then a trip westward for a bit of straight and level. They would be looking at a midday take off. Sean and Rosie arrived at about ten on the Saturday morning.

"Hi! I'll just back the car out of the garage. if we plan to get to the airfield at say, eleven or so, we can look around the aircraft then go for a pre-flight briefing."

"Okay with that. Are you flying us?"

"I expect so. But I'll have to persuade the instructor that I can fly, first, then we'll see."

"No aerobatics, though!"

"I doubt a Cessna 172 would really be the best ship for that!"

"Well, you might just forget that you not flying a Phantom ..."

"No chance of that!"

The party checked in to the ops desk. There they met their pilot, Bob. He looked more like a vicar than a pilot, a small, bird-like guy, probably Mr Steady Eddy. No problems with that. They were led out to their 'plane a neat little red and white Skyhawk. Everyone strapped in. Each of them had a headset. Willis sat in the front right-hand seat. They called for start-up clearance, then taxied to the runway threshold. The throttle was pushed fully home, and the little Cessna gathered speed over the grass and gently lifted into the air. Bob levelled out at fifteen-hundred feet, set the QNH, and headed west.

"Can I have a go please?"

"Of course! Flown before?"

"Yes. A little."

"Okay. Let me explain the controls ..."

"I think I've got past that stage. I have a few hours on Cessnas. The 172 first flew when, about 1955, probably the most successful 'plane ever made. About 44,000 to date, I think. Cruises at about 125 knots. Stalls at about 50, maybe more with four-up. Ceiling about 14,000. VNE what, 160? 170? Rate of climb can be 700 feet per minute. Wing loading fourteen pounds per square foot ..."

"Hey, you're pretty clued up!"

"Okay, can I fly it please?"

"Yes. Hold the yolk, feet on the rudder and now you have control!"

"I have control. Will you please deal with the radio? I plan to follow the M4 to the Membury mast, then to Swindon then turn north east towards Oxford. We'll remain VFR. Visibility is excellent.

155

Have to watch out for gliders, though. Can you please contact Oxford approach and ask if we can do a touch-and-go? I doubt they will let us if they are busy with the glider tugs flying around. Then we can aim for White Waltham, do a low overshoot then back to base. Did you know that it was at White Waltham that Douglas Bader lost his legs?"

"Hey, you are clued up! And your very smooth on the controls! Ever thought of taking up flying as a hobby?"

"Yes. Like you would never know. I'm probably the youngest person in the whole world to have flown both the McDonnell Douglas Phantom, and the Sea Harrier!" Bob laughed.

"Rosie, Sean? You okay in the back?"

"Yeah, great!" Willis adjusted the throttle settings as the thermals tried to lift the little plane. He just fell back into it naturally. Bob spoke up.

"Oxford is quiet. A roller is okay by them. ETA is what? Any idea?"

"Yeah. We'll be at Swindon in five or so, then ten to Oxford. So be with them in fifteen. Here's the mast. We'll turn round the mast, I'll keep it on your side. Rules of the air! Then keep over the motorway. Watch out for Lyneham traffic or Brize. Anyway, Lyneham's shut, now, isn't it? Shouldn't be too busy at weekends. Bob noted how smoothly the boy controlled the little Cessna. What little turbulence tried to buffet the aeroplane was of no concern to him. He had trimmed the 'plane perfectly, and he hadn't even told the lad where the trim wheels were. He just knew. He had an uncomfortable feeling about the whole performance. At Oxford, Willis followed Bob through on the controls. They did the landing, then Bob applied full power, and took off again.

"Can I do the next one please? But to make you feel more comfortable, you can follow me through on the manoeuvre?"

"Er ...yeah, okay." Willis levelled off, turned onto the cross-wind leg, then downwind onto the base leg. Everything went perfectly. With the wheels kissing the runway, Willis applied full power and pulled away.

"I'll level off at fifteen hundred. Heading for White Waltham ... I'll try 170 degrees. Can you give them a call please? Probably stud seven on the box." Bob was becoming ever-more impressed with the flying skills and confidence of the boy.

"Okay ... Right, cleared to drop in, taxi round and take off again. No problem. You'll see the dual carriageway below us soon, the airfield comes up on ..."

"Should be on the right."

When Willis landed the 'plane at Booker, he taxied it to the parking area outside the flying club offices and shut down. All four on board, climbed into the warm air, and walked over to the office.

"If I may say so, er ... Vic, that was a most impressive performance ... how many hours have you flown, really?"

"About ... three thousand, give or take."

"In what?"

"I've already told you that ..."

"I think I need a drink ...!"

"Maybe. But, when you get some time, look up Willis ... he used to pop in here occasionally and borrow a little Cessna or sometimes a Cherokee ... was last here about nine or ten months ago, I think. Used to fly quite a bit with the CFI Ron Prentice ... the guy who was into music in a big way. He'll remember old Fred Willis!"

"Yes, I'll do that. Anyway, nice to have met you all."

"Well, Ted. I think you impressed that guy ... and we're pretty pleased as well. You did a good job in getting us home. Enjoyed every minute."

"Yeah, so did I. But I expect I'll have to do all my exams and flying training all over again, probably never be able to add all my service flying to my log book. And wait until I'm eighteen to fly solo, do the minimum number of hours to get a licence back. I used to be able to drop in there, do a quick check with the instructors, and hire a bloody 'plane for the weekend! Happy days!"

CHAPTER 15

Sunday turned up, so did a senior police officer, who wanted to discuss a few things with Sean and Willis. He looked like the sort of guy one could trust, but no doubt he'd had to wrestle a few baddies to the ground, and he looked as he would have had no trouble doing it. Willis had just finished a session in his little gym. He had taken off his T shirt and was a bit sweaty.

"Hi, do come in. I'm going to have a shower, be back down shortly. Connie will look after you. Back in a mo!" The DCI turned to Sean.

"How old is he? Eleven? He's got some bloody muscle on him, ain't he?"

"You think that's impressive! You ought to be more impressed with his brain!"

"So I've been told. Anyway ..."

"Can I get you anything? Sean? Rosie ...?" The trio ordered what they wanted. Connie put some milk out for Willis and some chocolate biscuits. He was down in no time.

"So, Rosie, Sean ..." The senior officer stood up and extended his hand.

"Woodward. Mike Woodward. How do you do ...Ted." They shook hands.

"So, where are we with this?" Sean waved his hand towards Woodward who took up the question.

"First of all, the story is just incredible. But we've been approached, and I understand that you, Ted, are more concerned about what's been possibly going on before you were involved, and of course for the poor buggers who might be caught up in the future ... it seems odd that the Chinese are so keen on Europeans ..."

"Not really. It's the European market the Chinese are interested in ... they want foreign currency, and there are plenty of white Caucasians available, and the younger, the more likely they are to be without contacts ... they are easy prey to the likes of Dauphin and his bloody crew! Or maybe they're keen on Brits because they believe we got the Chinese hooked on opium. That is, according to Lin Zexu, who wrote to Queen Victoria in 1839 to complain about it! You ought to read Stephen Platt's book, *'Imperial Twilight'*. Very interesting!"

"Look at that, Mike! He's been to school for a week, and he's a bloody historian!"

"Yeah, well ... I reckon that we are best to let the conference go ahead, then we can drop in and see the French guys, then possibly the Italians. The last thing we want is for something to leak out and then find everybody and everything disappears ... I understand that the girl in Milan, Angie, is keeping an eye on that side of things."

"She and Bella, yes. If fact, they're going to try and download all the stuff of the surgeons' computers while they're away in America. Should be interesting."

"Is that not a bit risky, Rosie?"

"I'm sure they wouldn't do it if it were ... after all, they're both in the thick of it. Bella in the office, and of course Angie as a psychiatrist. Is that right, Ted?"

"As I understand it, yes. How confident are you that Grant will co-operate?"

"Well, we can't be sure, but we can apply an awful lot of pressure on him. We've got his bank details from Milan, there's his taking ... taking people out of the UK, knowing that they were to be used for an unauthorised procedure, we know he's connected to this Ling woman and that he's also on Dauphin's books. Somebody, somewhere is applying a lot of pressure on him ... it'll be interesting to find out who and why."

"I bet it's Ling ..."

"We'll find out soon enough. Anyway, Ted. I have a feeling that when the balloon goes up, or before even, then it would make sense for the bosses of this bloody mess ... might think it prudent to silence you ... you're the only living witness not actually involved in any criminality, and who will be a chief witness ... in fact, just standing in the court and talking is all you need to do. I hope the jury would also see the films ..."

"But we'll never get the Chinese into court ... it'll have to be Ling!"

"Correct. But won't it be another Russian poisoning job? won't it whip up a storm of protest, internationally once the enormity of what they've done comes out ...?"

"As if they'd give a shit! ... but I don't suppose that will be for us to deal with!"

"And what about me? I can't even get on a 'plane alone at this age! Can't have a pint, drive my car, smoke, get married, have sex even!"

"Ted! Behave yourself! That's all bad stuff!" Everybody laughed, except Ted.

"Seriously though, isn't that every lawyer's nightmare? Taking on a case like me? And won't the insurance company want their money back if I am officially declared to be Ted Willis, and aged 73?"

"I bet you'd rather be Ted Willis at eleven!"

"You're not wrong! However, in purely legal affairs that does not diminish the enormity of what has happened to me."

"Well, are we clear on where we're going with this? We do nothing until Grant gets back from America, then we drop in and see him. If he starts to get difficult, then I think we should arrange for you, Ted, to drop in and see him. I think he's the key to a lot of what's been going on. But we need to know exactly what Ling's got on him. Are we all clear on that?" Everybody was.

Early the next week, Willis dropped his English homework onto Richard Dyer's desk. After English there was a double session of PE. Willis had all the kit stuffed into his backpack. The PE teacher, Harper, had the physique of a long-distance runner and he had thick, black hair and glasses. The teacher handed out vests with numbers on, noting each name with each vest. In the gym had rigged up a kind of training circuit.

"Right you lot! Here's the deal. We go outside and run once round the track. That's a quarter of a mile, approximately You should all finish it in about five minutes. Follow me to the track!" Willis thought five minutes was a bit generous, but he decided to just stay back as number three. They all lined up, then Harper blew his whistle, and everybody started running. It was soon apparent that most of the kids were as unfit as hell. But Willis tucked behind the two leaders. At the end of the run, all three were hundreds of yards in front of the others. Some were already walking. Others had stopped and were lying on the grass. The time for the leaders was a respectable three minutes. It took Harper nearly half an hour to round everybody up and get them back to the gym.

"Well guys, that was crap. We do that every lesson. Get fit or don't bother to waste my time, right? Now the rest of the test." There was rope-climbing, high-jumps, standing jumps, weights. Willis decided not to over-exert himself. At the end of the double session, Harper blew his whistle. He had a comprehensive set of notes on every pupil's performance.

"Right. Into the showers!" In the changing room everybody stripped off. The showers were hot, power-showers. Willis noticed Harper standing just outside the showers. He was wearing only shorts and appeared to be watching the boys through the steam, and as each boy left the shower, they had to squeeze past him, so forcing whole body contact, and he stroked their backs as they passed. Willis thought it was totally unnecessary. But he had a plan. He was only one of about three left in the shower, and as he moved towards the exit, he raised both hands to his face as if to wipe away the water, and as Harper moved in on him, and feeling the teacher's body, from chest to thighs, against his, he brought his right elbow down as fast and powerfully as he could into the teacher's solar plexus. Willis knew that the solar plexus controls the stomach, liver, spleen, gallbladder, small intestines and kidneys and that his *yokoempi* strike would have a significant impact on these organs. He was not disappointed. Harper folded up and dropped to his knees, both his arm clutching his stomach. It was his shouting *'Fuck!'* which got the attention of all the boys in the changing room. Willis continued walking as though nothing had happened.

An hour or so later, Harper staggered into the headmaster's office.
"What the hell's the matter with you, Len?"
"Some bloody kid punched me!"
"Oh, really? Who was it?"
"Some little shit called Clément, or something ..."
"Why did he hit you?"
"No idea. Just came up to me and hit me."
"Hard?"
"Yes, bloody hard!"
"Where?"
"In the showers ... in the gym."
"No, Len, where on the body?"
"In the guts."
"Does it hurt?"
"Course it does!"
"A new boy?"
"Yes. He's muscled up like a bloody prize-fighter. I tell you, Mike, the bloke ain't normal"
"I think I know the name. Leave it with me. Now get back to work."

"What the hell's wrong with you, Len?"
"Hi, George. Some fuckin' kid punched me. Some new kid. French name. I'll get the bastard expelled. He can't just do that to people!"
"Seen the doctor?"
"Yes. Got a couple of cracked ribs as well."

"That's a six week heal job, isn't it?"
"Something like that, yes."

"Richard? George here. Have you heard that Clément lad pasted bloody Harper?"
"About time somebody hit him. He's a weird bugger, that Harper ..."
"That may be the case, but I think we ought to look into the kid's background. Has the office come back with anything yet?"
"No. I'll chase them. Leave it with me, okay?"

Willis was not finished with Harper yet. The following day, with about fifteen minutes of lunch hour left, he slipped into the boys' changing rooms. He knew exactly what he was looking for, and he found six of them. He didn't for one moment think he had found them all. But six would do. With the thin screwdriver he had with him, Willis prised the small cameras away from their fittings and put them into his backpack. Then he went to his first lesson of the afternoon. When he got back from school, he asked Connie to take the little cameras to Sean's office. He had spoken to Sean about the incident.
"So I hit the bugger. Expect he's going to go whinging to the headmaster, probably asking to get me expelled, so I want to hold all the cards."
"Sounds like you'll need your own dedicated copper soon, Ted. Yeah, I'll have a look and let you know. The conference starts tomorrow by the way. So be prepared for some shit to hit the fan soon."
"I'm looking forward to it!"

The police officer called Willis on Wednesday evening.
"Interesting shots. You think about everything that can go on in a shower with some bloody paedo, and a couple of kids, and it's on

163

there. The bloke's a dead-man walking!"

"Okay. No need for any detail. So, if I'm called in to see the headmaster, who holds the cards, Sean?"

"You do. A full pack. And there was more than one bloke involved. I think it was the headmaster. If you need us to drop in and have a chat, we'll be there with a couple of marked cars and a van or two. We'll put on a real show for you, Ted!"

"Okay. Can you see the kids who are being abused? And the abusers? I mean, could you get good mug-shots of them? Do you think I could have a few of them?"

"No problems with that. Easy-peasy."

"Thanks, Sean. By the way, do you know where that comes from?"

"What?"

"Easy-peasy. It comes from 1970's TV commercial ..."

"Ted! I don't really want to know. Anyway, good luck with the headmaster. I'm sure you'll floor him. I'll get you some mug-shots."

On Friday morning, there was a note on the headmaster's desk. The secretary had responses from two schools she approached regarding their pupil, Victor Clément. She also spoke to Richard Dyer about the result. Dyer told Ferris. The headmaster picked up the note as he was removing his jacket, then called his secretary. He waved the paper in her face.

"What's this, Elaine?"

"It's what it says." His secretary took no shit from him.

"So, what am I supposed to do with it?"

"Well, at least you could tell Richard and George that they were right. He didn't attend those schools. No record ... ball's in your court, now, Mike."

"What do you think I should do?"

"First of all, you can congratulate Clément for punching Harper, then move him up at least two streams..."

"You're kidding, right?" His secretary moved her face close to his.

"Mike. I am not kidding. I have a feeling about this kid. He's a cracking looking boy, and arseholes like Harper just won't be able to keep their hands off him. Harper has had a lesson. This is gonna get very nasty. Remember just who is paying you to educate their children. Some of those dads are perfectly capable of blowing your fuckin' head off, Mike. It's the ones who bring their kids to school in Rolls Royces, Bentleys ... and new fifty-grand Ford Mustangs."

"What did this lad come in?"

"A fifty-grand, five-litre Mustang. Do you know where he lives? In a four-million-pound property!"

"How do you know all this, Elaine?"

"Because I take the trouble to find out. Now I suggest you call the lad in and have a chat with him, okay!"

"Whatever you say. Send for him please."

"I will. Maybe I should also send for Harper? So we can watch him squirm?"

"Alright. Do that."

Willis was in his maths lesson when he was called out of the classroom by the headmaster's secretary.

"Nothing to worry about, Clément. How are you settling in?"

"Fine thank you. Once I've managed to find my way round, I'll be okay."

"Is the work challenging?"

"No. I seem to be a bit ahead of the others though."

"How about PE?" Willis knew where she was headed.

"The same."

"Is that all you can say about it?"

"You're fishing, aren't you? Well, if you want an honest, no-holds barred appraisal ..."

"Nothing less."

"The PE teacher's a cunt!" Elaine laughed.

"Full marks. However, I think you ought to use ..."

"More delicate language?"

"Precisely." In fact, she was warming to him. He was a big guy, a

165

lovely head of hair and by all accounts very physical. They got to the door of the head's study. Without knocking, the secretary opened the door and ushered Willis in. The boy quickly worked out that the secretary was indisputably the boss of the school.

"Victor Clément, headmaster."

"Come in. Both of you." Harper was in the room, seated. He affected a pained expression. "Now, Clément, I expect you know why you're here?" Without waiting for an answer, he continued. "Mr Harper here, tells me that on the ... on Monday you punched him. Is that true?"

"Not exactly, sir ... " Willis saw Harper look up at him sharply.

"He's lying!" Willis responded before the head had a chance to say anything, or for Harper to continue."

"Mr Harper, I have the floor. So please ... be quiet until I've finished. I did not punch Mr Harper, I jabbed him with my elbow."

"On purpose?"

"Yes sir, on purpose."

"Why did you do that, Clément?"

"Because at the material time, I was being touched by him in what is generally termed, an 'inappropriate manner' and I took ..."

"It wasn't intentional!"

"Mr Harper ... I have told you once before. You will get your chance to speak. I'm sure you are aware of the protocol. When one is being asked to speak, everybody else holds their tongues to await their chance to make their points." Although the head was at that moment looking down at his blotter, Willis saw the trace of a smile on his face. The secretary was looking at him, grinning openly, and with a look that said, '*carry on mate, you're doing a great job'*. Willis continued "... so if it wasn't intentional, how was it that you did exactly the same to all the other boys who left the shower, and how come that you were only wearing a pair of shorts. In my view that was also inappropriate. So as soon as this gentleman touched me, I did what I think all the other boys would have liked to have done, and I defended myself against persistent sexual predator."

"What! How dare you ...!"

166

The History of Victor Clément

"Mr Harper, don't be so tiresome. I have recently passed to the police six spy-cams you or somebody had installed in the showers and in the toilets. I have asked for pictures of all those you have recently assaulted so I can approach them. It's a pity you couldn't have been into girls. They are so much more interesting." Willis thought Harper was choking by the noises he was making.

"Is that it, Clément?"

"Do you need any more?"

"No. Mr Harper, leave us now. We have other issues to discuss and they don't involve you ... you'll get your chance to respond in good time." Harper slunk off.

"Right, Clément. Victor Clément, you mention in your arrival form a number of schools ... they do not seem to have heard of you."

"True. But nevertheless, I did attend them. I do not want to go into any great detail, but I assure you I did. And may I finally suggest ... that you deal with the Harper issue as a priority? Because if I see him touching up any more boys, I will seriously hurt him."

"Thank you, Clément. Elaine, please take the boy back to his classroom."

"Thank you, sir." On the way back to his class, he spoke to the school secretary. "I suppose you can guess who the other bloke was."

"What do you mean?"

"I mean your boss. He was also picked up on the cameras ..."

"I was hoping you wouldn't get to know that."

"Well, you've got a great opportunity to get a new headmaster and a new PE instructor."

"Can we get together and talk about it sometime? And will you also tell me just who the hell you are?" Willis stopped walking and turned to face the secretary. There was nobody else in the corridor. He smiled at her.

"I have no doubt you will learn all about me sooner or later. But just please bear in mind, that until you do, I just want to continue enjoying myself, doing what I'm doing."

"I want to kiss you." Elaine didn't know why she said that to the

167

child, but she felt so close to him, and in some inexplicable way, drawn to him and she also felt that he was wise beyond his years. He was a small man.

"You can't. It might be inappropriate touching. And anyway, I might enjoy it." The woman extended her right arm and put her hand onto Willis's shoulder, and Willis covered it with his right hand, then dropped it down to his side again. Elaine turned and started walking towards the classroom again. Her regard for the pupil was almost overwhelming.

"You, Victor Clément are an enigma ..."

"It's from the Greek, *ainissesthai* ..."

"What is?"

"Enigma. Someone or something that is mysterious or puzzling."

"Can I give you my mobile number? I might need to call you to discuss the national debt, or how to deal with our Donald if he ever plans to visit the UK?"

"Yes, but please do try to deal with less mundane matters initially? I have to decide who will take over as your new boss, and we also need to find a new head of PE."

"Funny that, I was going to raise the issue with you ... once you've decided whether or not to invade North Korea!" The school secretary handed over a slip of paper with her mobile number and email address. The perceptive, intelligent Elaine Coates had a strange premonition ... that her Victor Clément was a man in a child's body.

The headmaster went to find his head of PE.

"Let's go for a stroll, Len. We need to talk."

"What's the point?"

"Don't worry. The kid's bluffing."

"No he isn't, Mike, six of the bloody cameras are missing. And they were last downloaded before the end of the last term, so there's all sorts of shit on them. I had intended to ..." The head interrupted.

"Well, we're fucked then, ain't we?"

"Can't we expel the brat?"

168

The History of Victor Clément

"Don't think so. Anyway, he said he had handed the stuff over to the cops, didn't he?"

"He's bluffing ..."

"Don't keep saying that. All he has to do is show pictures of all the little sods you've been messing with ..."

"Me! what about you?"

"Now thanks to your brilliant idea it's all over the dark web! That little earner is on hold now, probably forever. If the cops come sniffing around, and find it all, we're toast. And I don't want to be left tied up in an outbuilding somewhere with some of their fathers pouring petrol over me."

"What are they gonna do then?"

"How do I know? ... the cops identify them, tell the mums and dads, and I'll tell you, it's more than your fuckin' job you've got to worry about, it's your fuckin' testicles, then probably your head. Literally. You know as well as I do, half the parents who send their kids to this school are gangsters, and the most precious thing they have are their kids!"

"So what are we going to do?"

"First thing, let's wait and see what happens. If things look bad ... I don't know."

"Right. Let's just do that. How long has that kid been here? Two, three weeks?"

"Possibly. At that rate, he'll be bloody prime minister by the time he's fourteen!"

"Fuck that! he's bloody dangerous enough as it is!"

Willis was feeling happier at school now, knowing that he had something to get his teeth into. When he got back home, he found a message on his mobile. *'Conference brilliant by all accounts Andy says plenty of orders for the videos call me when you can xx'*. Willis went to his bedroom to put on his training kit, then lay on his bed and made the call.

"Hi, Angie. Tell me what you've been up to. Spill the beans."

"Right. This thing went down a storm. Everybody saying it's

169

impossible. It's a trick. Anyway, the full-length videos are selling like hot cakes. We've been through Andy's computer, and downloaded tons of stuff. When we've been through it all, we'll lock it away somewhere. Doing a search, the big three come up, Ling, Dauphin and Grant. All I'm concerned about is your position. If we ever have to admit that you are kind of roaming around the UK, like a loose cannon, then as these blokes have got what they want, you could become a ... let's say a target? With you gone, then who's gonna tell them that the deal was done illegitimately? There was an outcry, a few years ago, when the Chinese said they had done something like this. Anyway, now that the conference is over, I expect your guys, like Sean the cop, will move in on Grant."

"That's the plan, yes. Anyway, just keep us informed, okay?"

"Will do."

Doctor Steve Grant felt exhilarated by the obvious success of the conference. The demand for detail was overwhelming. He recalled the words of the Beijing professor who introduced the team and the short video clip.

'The implications behind the process my dedicated team of experts have perfected are without precedent in the history of trans-medicine. We are now looking at the possibility of preserving the most valuable of humankind assets. The pioneering work carried out by the world's most renowned experts in every field of science, technology, mathematics to mention just a few, can be continued by them theoretically for ever. I am talking about ... knowledge ...'

He called Andy, who was somewhere around the conference venue.

"Andy? Steve. Seemed to go down well. But what I really want to know is was the conference aware of what the team in China really want? It's the billions they would collect from the most despotic leaders in the world, who would pay ridiculous sums to extend their cruel regimes ..."

"But Steve ..."

"No, Andy, hear me out! People with physical disabilities could leave their broken bodies behind on the table of an operating theatre to be thrown into the incinerators of hospitals all over the world and walk out of the facility a new person. A man can become a girl or a child. A woman a man. The procedure is so open to corruption that the consequences of having such operations available to the very rich and possibly the most corrupt people in the world doesn't bear thinking about. Demand could be so high that individual persons could be targeted as donor bodies by those who seek to benefit from the procedure ..."

"Steve! Listen to me ...!

"No. You hear me out! Apart from the phenomenally complicated issues of the ethics of the procedures and which now engage my mind and should be engaging the minds of every right-thinking doctors the world over ..."

"I agree with you! We must get together and deal with! But the good news is ... I think there is something fundamentally wrong with the whole damned business! Now, we can address this when we get back home ... I've been working on something back home. I really want to get you involved. But in the meantime, keep it under your hat, okay?"

"I will. See you soon." But there was something else nagging Grant as well. Something he couldn't quite put his finger on. He tried to put it out of his mind, but he couldn't. Anyway, he had to meet with the whole Milan team, and with madam Ling before they all boarded their flight home.

"Well, Steve, what do you think?" Then quietly so as to be barely audible, "Let's pretend we have no issues. You never bloody know who's earwigging!""

"Went down well, Andy. Ling seems ecstatic!"

"She bloody ought to be. All Those guys from Harbin are virtually wetting themselves over it. Did you get to see the full presentation?"

"Not yet ..."

"You ought to. It's a very professional job. Ling tells me they've had over two hundred orders for it. Not bad for a day's work!"

"It's all about the money, really, isn't it?"

"Of course, dear boy! Of course it is! ... Look out, Ling's coming over!" The woman from Manchester homed in on the two doctors. She stopped in front of Grant and poked a finger into his chest.

"You work hard! Nobody wants to be Chinese boy or girl. All be white European. You be busy man!"

"Well, plenty of them knocking about in Spain or France ..."

"You no understand. Your job. France man finished. I think he retired or he dead. Need new man." Grant was getting fed up with her.

"No, Yu. It's not that easy..."

"Course it is ... For you." She again stabbed Grant with her finger. "You very good! You don't give me problems, no?" Then she smiled and scuttled away. Grant wondered just how many people had seen that same smile just before Yu Yan Ling plunged a knife into them. Was he thinking figuratively? Possibly. Possibly not.

"I hate that fuckin' woman, Andy! Why don't you just get rid of her?"

"I'd bloody love to, Steve. Is she chasing you for more models?"

"Yeah ... and I don't think any waif or stray, male or female under about twenty will be safe anywhere in Europe if all this takes off, and my feeling is it bloody will, if my theory is wrong, that is!"

"Now I know just how that bloke who invented gunpowder felt ..."

"Well, I'll tell you now, neither you nor I are going to denude the continent of Europe of unconnected kids just so all those arsehole pariah states can ..."

"You need say no more, Steve ... but I'm afraid I can't just walk away from the woman."

"I might be in the same boat. There's you signing a death certificate for a living body, and me delivering it to you was a bit iffy ..."

"You're nowhere near. By comparison that's picking wild flowers. Anyway, I've got to get to the airport. Keep in touch, old mate, okay?"

"Yeah. Have a good trip."

"I plan to sleep all the way! I hope your trip back goes okay.""

"You're kidding! I'm on the same flight as Ling, I think!"

"Isn't she going back to Manchester?"

"Yes. But she has to pop into her embassy in London first. Probably gonna get a bloody medal!"

"We've gotta put a stop to this, Steve!" Those words rang in Grant's ears all the way to London.

CHAPTER 16

At 35,000 ft or thereabouts, the nagging discomfort Doctor Steve Grant he had felt since he saw the video during the conference, hit him in all its clarity like a hammer-blow to the head. He leaned forward in his seat and held his head in his hands, and through tightly clenched teeth hissed out the words *'Jesus fuckin' Christ'*. He then sat up, his back hard against his seat. He covered his eyes with his fingers and in his mind re-ran the short video clip. There was the lad, prancing about in the garden, with the talk-over reminding the audience that the young lad there, in the sunlight, with a now full head of thick, blonde hair, was without any doubt, living proof of a successful experiment. What had put Grant off making the connection at the time was that inside the house, the boy had held up, and the camera had zoomed in on, a copy of Le Figaro, the French newspaper, clearly showing the date. Grant had himself been in that garden, and in that house, twice. It was Fred Willis's property in Marlow. Rather than coming to Grant as a great relief, he now felt like a hunted animal. He felt physically sick at the thought that there was something afoot, something he ought to have known about, but was not in the loop. He felt hemmed in. Not thirty feet behind him was the tormentor he knew. A few thousand miles ahead of him was, he surmised, another tormentor. One he didn't know. And he was flying towards it at nearly 600 miles per hour. He felt he was moving into a trap. Then he remembered the last words Andy spoke to him at the conference arena. *'We've gotta put a stop to this, Steve!'*. Maybe, if he were to find himself being squeezed, he could save his skin by spilling the beans. But dealing with Ling was not going to be easy.

Richard Dyer, B.Ed., stood in front of Form D. He was holding a bundle of papers in his hand. He watched silently as the pupils sat down at the start of his class.

"Right. I have marked your manifesto homework. Some of it is remarkable only for it's stupidity. This was meant to be a serious look at some of this country's problems. I was not overly impressed by suggestions that sweets should be free, and all schools knocked down. Some were obviously done by parents. Of the twenty-eight submissions, only seven were acceptable. What you must understand is that here you are, on the threshold of the rest of your lives. Whatever you may or may not have done in the past, you, all of you without exception, have the potential to become lawyers, doctors, accountants, airline pilots, concert pianists ... just because you have been dumped in the lowest form in the school does not mean that you will forever be level D. Acting like an idiot, wasting time, concerning yourselves here and at home with anything other than your future, maybe the next sixty years of your lives, will be like dragging an anchor behind you. The sooner you wake up to that fact the better. You do not have to be academically gifted to do well. You need targets and ambition. You have to appreciate that whatever you do with your time, it will pass just the same. You ... most of you I suspect ... have never read a good book. Forget fiction apart from the classics. Dickens, Shakespeare. The war poets. Look at history. Look at the stories coming out of World War one. Autobiographies are full of life. Form your own opinions. Don't tag along with the crowd. We, here, at this school, have made mistakes. We expelled a pupil once. In my view it was a mistake. We failed to recognise that he had unlimited capacity for hard work, so we did not push him. But he went on to become a fighter pilot shortly after he left school, then he became a lawyer and now he has a doctorate. He scored high at every level. What did we do? We should have been proud of him. Instead it became an embarrassment ... for us. And that boy started his schooling here, in this very classroom ... and I can tell you that he didn't put two fingers up at us ... he thanked us. Because being in Form D was for him, a reality check. He was not restrained by these four walls. He was not prepared to just make do. He was not limited by what his mates wanted or what his mates were. He didn't spend his time sitting in front of a television. This boy read books. Hundreds of them. Books take you out into the world. Reading a book takes you across continents and across oceans. It takes you into the air, under the sea. It takes you back hundreds of years, or into space. Knowledge extends your ability to read, to converse, to sensible argument. It does not encourage you to defend the indefensible. With knowledge, you are limited by only the possible. I want you, all of you, to lift yourselves out of the sump to become the A star form at this school. I want you all to become my heroes. We start here. Now. Those who failed this homework will do it again. The seven who passed, I want you to come out to the front, one at a time and read a bit of your manifestos. We'll start with Clément. Up to the front please. Here's your paper. Choose one of your ideas and discuss it please." Willis stood up and made his way to the front, taking the paper from the teacher's hand.

"Thank you." He turned to face the class and opened his homework. "Rather than choose any one of my manifesto points, I'd rather read the introduction first, if I may?" he turned to look at the teacher who waved his hand as if to say, 'Go ahead'. Willis began.

"I have written this manifesto for my Common-Sense Party, sub-titled 'I want my Country back' - not very 'PC' just very 'common sense'

'The whole world laughs at us; they know that we are good people, on the whole, but led by donkeys; we, the indigenous population, the man on the Clapham omnibus know it, but our leaders seem to be oblivious to that fact. They are so concerned with image, being 'PC' and wallowing in their own egos, that they cannot see further than their own noses. Day after day, we are witnessing displays of unalloyed incompetence and ignorance by government Ministers and MPs who are so well insulated from the effects of their idiocy, that they cannot see beyond the edges of the trough and the snouts of those who share their desire to do good for themselves by trampling over the Great British Public. In these austere times, they drain the bank accounts of the populace by ever-higher taxes, to fund ... what? unworthy agendas for some

The History of Victor Clément

personal motive at the expense of more justifiable causes which might benefit the deserving, note, deserving people of this country.

In addition, we are being drawn deeper into the cloying mire of crassness and the deliberate chipping away of our identity by malevolent influences, the fringe minorities into whose pockets we shovel money, and whose raison d'etre is not based on altruism, but unadulterated in-your-face self-promotion, or the promotion of some ideology engineered to bring about the total collapse of our way of life or to succour the growing numbers of 'won't work' individuals kept at ever-rising cost to those who do work. The more we stand by to observe this descent into absurdity, the sooner we will have passed the point of no return. We were a once great nation; our engineers, our civilisation, our politics, our explorers, our army, all serviced our island nation. We have the finest navy, army and air forces in the world, and ...' "

"Thank you, Clément. Good. Can you explain a few things please? What's the Clapham omnibus reference?" He was testing his pupil. Did he really write it?

"Yes, sir. The man on the Clapham omnibus is a hypothetical, ordinary and reasonable person, used by the courts in English law where it is necessary to decide whether a party has acted as a reasonable person would. For example, in a civil action for negligence. It was introduced into English law during the Victorian era ..."

"Thank you. Any questions?"

"Yes sir! What's Clapham?" Clément answered.

"Clapham is a district in London. It was believed that the bus was in fact the route number 88 of a London tram."

"Thank you, Clément. You may return to your seat. Linda! You're next!" The girl delivered her manifesto. While she was talking, the teacher put the next-weeks homework on the board. *'Choose an English classic and copy out a paragraph or two which you find interesting and state why you have chosen it. Minimum 500 words'* The girl finished her bit. Willis thought it was pretty good. So, he thought, was Linda. The five-minute bell rang, and the class started packing away their books. Next lesson was history.

177

Willis moved into the corridor with the crowd from his form. He had noticed over the past week or so the class was breaking up into little cliques now, but as yet nobody had done more than speak a few words to him. He thought it was probably his own fault because he had looked, or perhaps been made to look, a bit 'different'. It was usually the fat boys and fat or ugly girls everybody tended to avoid. And the boys always seemed to steer clear of the really attractive girls, he seemed to remember, because everybody thought that they had dozens of boyfriends. He felt a tug on his arm. He looked round. It was Linda.

"Vic? Can I read your manifesto? I mean, all of it?" Before he could answer, she continued. "Do you like Mr Dyer? I think he's nice and he talks a lot of sense, doesn't he?"

"I'm sure he'll be pleased to hear you say that. And yes, of course you can read my stuff. Do you want me to email it to you?"

"Oh, yes. Let me give you one of my cards ... here." She fished a card out of her pencil case. it bore her email address and mobile number, with *'Linda Bee'* and a small bee sitting in the top right-hand corner. He slipped it into the side pocket of his backpack. "I think my dad would like to see it too. I liked the introduction. It's a pity he stopped you reading more of it."

"What does your dad do?"

"Oh, this and that." Which Willis took to mean 'mind you own business' a preferred answer to the question, no doubt, if dad was either a crook, unemployed or a real high-flyer. He didn't really care because he was rather attracted to the girl who was walking alongside him. Then, surprisingly, she asked. "You don't like old Len Harper, do you?"

"Why do you ask that?"

"You biffed him, didn't you?"

"Might have!"

"I don't like him either. He's odd!"

"What else do you know about him?"

"Nothing, really!" Which Willis again took as a 'mind your own

178

business' answer. They got to the door of the history classroom. Inside, the girl chose to sit beside Willis, just across the aisle between the desks.

Mr Paul Raff knew his Kings and Queens. Willis did not as he had no time for them. He thought Prince Andrew was an arrogant shit, the Duchess of York was a total bloody idiot who needed a good slapping, ditto her daughters. Charles was just round the bend. Harry, William and their wives were okay. He couldn't make out Edward. What he couldn't stomach was how they all dressed up in stupidly OTT uniforms. They just looked like they had pinched something out of Idi Amin's fancy-dress wardrobe. Raff was more interested in the older line. He prattled on about the Alpine Kings of Scotland, all thirty of them from Kenneth 1st 843 to 860, to John Baliol, 1292 to 1296; then the Bruce line and the Stuarts. Willis was more interested in Wellington, Napoleon and the exploits of Nelson. Far better than reading about the murdering royal families down the ages. He decided he could do without knowing any more about the Royals. He would stick to his seafaring heroes and to the bloody, muddy first world war, engendered by the assassination of the heir to the Austrian throne; the act of one man which resulted in the death of millions of men. As Raff droned on, Willis lost interest. He was back with Sean and Rosie ...

"Clément! What did I just say?"

"I'm sorry, sir, I didn't quite get it. Could you repeat for me?" Every eye in the class was on him. Willis thought Raff was determined to make an example of him.

"No. I won't. Does history bore you, Clément? Does it?"

"No sir ... I have a good general knowledge of history ... but I regret I cannot assimilate all of it. My interests lie far from the royal lines ..." Raff had him on the ropes. Or so he thought.

"Okay mister smart guy ..." Willis knew Raff was out to humiliate him. "... you're so clever, you expert historian! Tell me how the year forty-four was significant?"

"I assume, sir you meant to say forty-four and not nineteen forty four?"

"I did indeed, mister smarty-pants, forty-four, four four." Raff was leaning on Willis's desk, his face not six inches away from Willis. he did mean nineteen forty-four, but he didn't want to admit it. Anyway, he thought, four four would be harder, if not impossible, the for boy to answer.

"Caesar was murdered. Do you want to ask me say, two more dates, sir?" If looks could kill, Willis would have dropped dead on the spot. But Raff was incautious.

"Shall we say ... one six five?"

"I can say that between one six four and one six eight the Roman and Chinese empires were ravaged by plague." Raff stood up and walked back to his desk at the front of the class and without turning back shouted to Willis.

"Right! 1808!" Raff carried on walking to the front of the class.

"Napoleon makes ... " Raff whipped round. He was red in the face. He knew he had been made to look foolish. Willis continued, "... Napoleon makes his brother Joseph, king of Spain."

"And? ... Anything else?"

"Yes, sir. Spain and Portugal revolt, and the Peninsular war begins. It was clearly quite a year. Then, in 1809 ..." Raff held up his hands.

"Enough!" The five-minute bell saved him. "Right class. Pack away your things and go for your lunch." Willis resolved to send his manifesto to Linda as soon as he got home.

In the staff-room, Raff grabbed George Ferris's shoulder. Ferris turned.

"Hell, Paul! You don't look at all well!"

"It's that bloody kid of yours, George! What's his case, eh?"

"Explain." Raff explained. Ferris laughed.

"What's so funny?"

"Paul, for God's sake, don't meddle with that guy. He is seriously weird. He's the kid who smacked Len. Now he and the headmaster seem to be on the way out!"

For his lunch-break, Willis found a quiet sunny corner, got out his lunch box and his paper and started to read. After about five minutes, he looked up to see Linda walking towards him. She was eating a sandwich. Willis put the paper away in his bag.

"Hi, Vic, may I join you?"

"Of course. Pull up a chair."

"There aren't any, silly, I'll just sit on the concrete like you. I couldn't help laughing at what you did to Raff. He's a sarcastic sod, always putting us down. I hate him. Was it just a fluke or did you know all that stuff?"

"I just made it up. I don't think he actually know any of those dates anyway."

"You fibber! You were right! I checked on my 'phone!"

"Just an amazing coincidence, I assure you."

"Where do you live?"

"I have a cave in Mesopotamia where I am the keeper of the Sumerian's Cuneiform writing tablets, that is, before they were absorbed into the Babylonian Empire!" Linda laughed. She had a nice laugh and had nice teeth.

"No, seriously, are you local?"

"Yes. I have to be, because I walk to school every day."

"Where?" Willis could not avoid the question.

"Up Spinfield Lane. Where do you live?"

"The Common."

"Wow! In a tent! How cool is that!"

"No, idiot, in a house." Willis knew damn well where Marlow Common was. "What were you reading when I came up? A girlie mag? Is that why you shoved it away so quickly?"

"No. It was a paper." Willis reflected that in his day the question would be more like *'were you reading the Beano or Dandy'*. He marvelled at how things had progressed since those days.

"I don't believe you! Show me!" Willis pulled the paper out of his bag.

"There!" he didn't unfold it. Linda grabbed it and unfolded it.

"It's the Times! My dad reads the Times! have you done the

crossword yet?"

"No, of course not!" She opened the paper.

"Oh yes you have! Nearly, anyway! My dad can't do the crossword ..." The bell rang somewhere in the distance. Willis grabbed the paper and shoved it back into his bag.

"Don't tell anyone, will you. They'll think I'm weird. Even reading the Times can get you strictly isolated, like fat, smelly boys."

"I'll only not tell if you be my boyfriend for a while."

"Okay. Just for today. Come on. we'll be late for class!"

When Willis got home that afternoon, he slipped Linda's card out of his backpack, and emailed his manifesto to 'Linda Bee'.

It dropped into Linda's inbox. The girl opened the attachment and read it. Then she printed it and stapled it together and took it downstairs to her father.

"Dad! here's the thing I told you about. You know, the boy who bashed old Harper! The one who said he lived in a cave in Mesopotamia or somewhere, looking after tablets!"

"Where does he really live, Darling?"

"He said Spinfield Lane, where your friend used to live?"

"Oh, really? Mr Bishop's ears pricked up at that. He had heard that his old friend Ted Willis's property was already reoccupied, but he hadn't had any occasion to call on the new residents. But he was interested.

Grant could hardly say it was a surprise when he found two police officers standing outside his flat. But he tried to pretend for a while that he did not know why they were there. The pretence didn't last for long. Sean Johnson and his deputy, DCI Tug Windlesham, or 'Windy' to his friends, had done their homework. They were not going to be fobbed off.

"Doctor Grant. You are obviously an intelligent man. Just so you know what we're looking at, let me give you a name. Ted Willis." Grant looked at the police officers. Then he turned away.

"I'll put the kettle on. I think you'll be here for a while." When the doctor had moved into the little kitchen in the two-bed flat, Windy gave two thumbs-up to Johnson. And a silent, mouthed 'Yes!' In five minutes or so, all three were sat down. Grant took a sip of his coffee. "Alright, shoot."

Windy started.

"We just want to discuss a few ... issues. We will not at this stage, and probably never will, take notes. It all depends on you. May I call you Steve?"

"Of course."

"Right, Steve. Tell me what you did with Ted Willis. I'm sure you remember him. He was stabbed in the Reading car-park and you kept him in hospital for a few weeks stabilising his condition, then you whipped him over to Milan. Why?"

"Because I wanted to see if he could be more successfully treated by my old friend, Professor Andy Vennuchi of Ospidale San Raffaele, Milan"

"Thank you. Where did you meet the professor?"

"Some conference somewhere, I think."

"Tell me about him. What does he do in Milan?"

"He's a doctor. Look, can I ask you, where is this leading? I had care of my patient, and my opinion was that he should be given the best treatment. He had no relatives to say yea or nay to my plans. So, I made the decision. To move him."

"I am not a doctor, Steve, but when you moved him, was he brain-dead?"

"No. If he had been, there would have been little point in doing anything with him apart from turning off his life-support system."

"So, what was his condition?"

"In simple terms, he had multi-organ failure." Steve knew he had just walked into a trap. He tried to back out of it. "But there was a chance ..." But Windy didn't let him finish.

"So, unless he were to have multi-organ replacement, he was as good as dead? But as your friend Andy is, we believe, a transplant surgeon, he could replace all the failed organs and return your patient to the UK? What was the reason for that Steve? You must be aware that such an idea just doesn't hold water."

"Well, ... er ..." Windy was closing the trap, and Doctor Grant knew it. "Look, you're not medical people, gentlemen, so I really don't think you will understand how these things work, but ..."

"Steve. However, these things work or maybe don't work, and with everything else apart from politics, applying common sense is the key. Would you like to try again?"

"There was hope ..."

"Steve. Do you remember, at or about the time you decided to move Willis, making a 'phone call to your friend Andy?"

"Er ...no, why?"

"No reason. Do you remember chartering a plane call-sign G-ABMM?"

"I chartered a plane, yes."

"When you got to Milan, do you remember a conversation with Professor Vennuchi along the lines of ..." The police officer read from a slip of paper "... er ... *'Looks okay to me Steve. Got his passport there ... I'll get the death certificate signed and you can take it back with you just to close the case. Organ failure and dementia do ... No problem with that Andy if your staff can register the death with the Consul, it'll be a great help. That's no problem.'*

"No. How the hell would I remember things from that far back, for God's sake!"

"Okay, let's break it down, shall we? You delivered Ted Willis to your friend in Milan."

"I've already told you, yes I did!" Windy had been a copper for many years. He now detected in Grant, as he had done in so many other cases, a defence mechanism creeping to the fore. He was backing Grant into a corner, and they both knew it. He carried on.

"You got back to your hospital after your Milan trip and you brought back with you a death certificate signed by your friend. Cause of death given as organ failure and dementia. Who determined the cause of death?"

"Professor Vennuchi."

"How did he do that ... determine the cause of death?"

"Ask him." Again, a defensive response.

184

"To put it simply, Steve, if someone dies in hospital say of natural causes, for example, disease, no autopsy is needed. But if the cause was due to a violent act, such as a stabbing, then an autopsy is required. Of course, you know that already. Ted Willis had been stabbed. In the UK ..."

"Things are different in Italy ..."

"They may be, Steve, but not that different. Shall we just be grown-up about this. You know that when you flew back to the UK with Willis's death certificate in your pocket, that your patient was alive. Am I correct?"

"You'll have to ask the professor ..."

"Okay, Steve. I am on the verge of calling a halt to this ... by which I mean not doing things the easy way, and arresting you ..."

"For what?"

"Let me tell you a story, right? This is just an idea. We have this fictitious young doctor working at some fictitious hospital, and this doctor has lost his way a little bit and comes under the influence of somebody, let's say a bad person, and this person makes certain demands of our doctor. One day, the bad person say, has a need for ... let's not be too specific, but say for human organs. A suitable candidate pitches up at this fictitious hospital shall we say either a short time or perhaps even a long time after this bad person has made a demand for, say, a suitable donor. Our doctor then has to make sure that there is nobody sniffing around our prospective donor, so he ... our doctor goes to his patient's house and makes enquiries about possible relatives. How are we doing so far, Steve?"

"This is all fiction, right?"

"Well, Steve, it may be. It just depends at what stage you get a faint inkling that you may have heard this story before, and perhaps even wake up to the fact that it might even be a true story. Perhaps, Steve, you would like me to just stop wasting your time and cut to the last page of this story? Or perhaps you would like to finish it for me?" The DCI looked at Sean. "Do you think you can give us a few clues, Sean?"

"Yes. Let's say there are out there, quite a few people who know the ending, Steve. I can think of at least ... er..." Sean Johnson started to count on his fingers, as Windy finished his now cold tea. "... maybe ten key players. Or maybe you could add a few hundred more. By which I mean all the clever guys who were at the UCSF conference in San Francisco. I'm going to continue to tell you this story and when you think you can take over the story-line, Steve, then please feel free to continue." DCI Tug 'Windy' Windlesham had done his bit, so he let Sean Johnson continue. They had rehearsed this many times. "Anyway, Steve, this doctor bloke, reckons his patient is a likely candidate, so jumps onto a medivac 'plane and nips over to Milan with his patient, drops him off, then nips back to the UK. Our Willis guy of course, is still alive, and a few days after getting to Milan, he is suddenly picked up again and this time finishes up in China ..."

"Stop!" It was Grant. "You know, don't you? You know every fuckin' thing!" Windy took over.

"Yes, Steve we do. We know, as you so succinctly put it, 'every fuckin' thing'. And I believe, too, that you knew from the word go that the story-line was one you could have explained to us. Now, whatever might have happened, you must, and I underline must, co-operate with us. You are not to make contact with anybody else involved in this, and if they contact you, you are to inform us immediately. We are happy for you to keep working. We will tell nobody about this. If you agree to all this, you will, possibly, come out of it with clean hands. If you try to frustrate our enquiries, or even if we think you try, then you will be arrested. And if you think you are in trouble now, then I promise you, you will be in it as far as we can shove you. In the shit I mean. Do I make myself clear? We want you to be on our side. And, I repeat, just to be clear, we could be looking at the deaths of around twenty to thirty individuals, in the UK, France and Italy. Do you understand what I'm saying?"

"I do. What do you want me to do now?"

"We want you, over the next few days, to write out a statement of just what the hell's been going on between you, Ling, Andy and Xia Renchuan ..." Grant interrupted. He looked straight into Windy's eyes.

"You know everything, don't you? Every fuckin' single thing!" "Pretty much ... What that means, Steve, is that if you try to bullshit us, we'll know. And if you feel uncomfortable now, I assure you, that we can make things a damn site worse for you. Remember what I told you. You could, I repeat, could, come out of it with clean hands. It's up to you now. Well, I think that's all for the moment. We'll give you a week to do your report. Here's my card. All details you need are on there. We'll be on our way now. Thanks for your time, Steve." All three shook hands, then the police officers left Grant alone.

The doctor sat at his desk and stared out of the window. He knew his situation could become pretty bad unless he grasped the nettle and made some decisions. Two things nagged him now. The first was the boy. For some reason he was now, or was until recently, staying or living in Willis's old house. The second was Andy's last words to him. _'We've gotta put a stop to this, Steve!'_. Maybe, just maybe, he and Andy could address the situation together and maybe save their arses. In any event, he would include his feelings on this when he drafted his statement. He also knew that if he were to contact anybody down the line, that he would be failing in his promise to keep stumm about the whole, messy business.

CHAPTER 17

By the time Sean and DCI Tug 'Windy' Windlesham got back to their office, they had agreed a course of action.

"Right, Sean. You ask Rosie to keep an eye on Grant. Talk to the doctor ... Angela? ... brief her. Then the lad. We'll need whatever Angie has dug up from the professor's computer. She can also look out for the lad. As soon as we get Grant's statement, we'll work on our next move!"

"Right. Do you think we ought to put a watch on Ling's mob? I'm bloody sure that if she gets wind of anything, she'll be off like a rat down a drain."

"Good point, Sean. I think the least we should do is put a watch for her at all points of departure. But if she's got a different passport, then that ain't gonna work ..."

"And don't forget, if that woman is on the Beijing payroll, you can bet your bottom dollar that all their telecom and other kit was supplied is courtesy of ZTE ..."

"What the hell is ZTE?"

"It's a communications company owned and run by the Chinese or more likely by their intelligence services. They produce the stuff our cyber-blokes, you know, GCHQ guys, regard as a risk to our national security, so, as I was saying, I doubt any call or email goes into or out of their offices without going to somebody somewhere in China. You must realise, mate, that China is worse than Russia. The boss of Huawei, a bloke called Ren Zhengfei, had contact with China's signals intelligence division when he was an officer in the People's Liberation Army! Anybody who uses Chinese computer kit is asking for trouble. "

"Yeah, so we'd be stuffed. Anyway, I don't think we'll get enough on her for a while yet. So it's gonna be a waiting game, I'm afraid.

What do you think of Grant?"

"I think he'll come up with the goods."

"If he doesn't, Tug, then he's stuffed!"

That evening, Sean briefed Rosie.

"For God's sake don't let Grant know you're watching him ... be discreet. If you have any problems, call me. Tomorrow we can take a run over to Marlow and speak to Ted, and also have a chat with Angie. I'll also help when we get the stuff from their computer.

"I'm just wondering if he'll try to find out who applied for probate on Ted's estate. I mean, does he know the name Clément?"

"Even if he does, I don't think he'll take much notice. He's been warned to back-off from contacting anybody, and if he were to ring the solicitors, they'll tell him nothing. Let's see, shall we? Marlow's on for tomorrow. Ted's agreed that we should speak to Angie."

Rosie and Sean pitched up at Oaklands, and before the hour was out, they had relayed to Willis the outcome of the Grant interview.

"There you have it, Ted. We reckon Grant is running scared. I hope that when he's done his statement, all will become clear."

"Okay. I'll have a chat with Angie." Willis dialled her number, the 'phone on loudspeaker.

"Hi, Ted. How's things?"

"Fine. Just want to update you on the Grant situation ..." He ran through the latest. "How are things your end?"

"Well, our Andy got back from the conference, and by all accounts he is not too happy. He discovered from one of the China team that they had tried this stuff on nearly forty different cases, all Europeans. He thought the bloke was a little pissed and was so full of himself ... Andy knows that there were a few, but it was that woman, Ling he blames. As I told you, they needed to do it that way because they are looking for that market. And I'll tell you something else. Andy reckons that the recent success was just a fluke ... and they couldn't do it again. He's been looking at blood-

189

group and tissue combinations on all the ones he was involved with, and he's asked the Harbin team for more blood and tissue samples, and he plans to run them through the new computer system ..." Willis looked up at Rosie and Sean.

"Hang on a minute, Angie, if Andy's research proves almost conclusively that there is a million-to-one chance or thereabouts that this high-profile case was a fluke, that's going to sink the Chinese ambitions to cash in ..."

"Exactly. And Beijing won't be too happy about it. In fact, they would probably try to wreck Andy's research. And that might mean hitting Andy..."

"So, what do we do about that?"

"I have no idea ... except that we could come clean with him. He hasn't stopped since he got back. He's in that lab all the time. If we had a chat ... certainly tell him to lead the China lot on ..."

"Haven't they got their own laboratories that can do this?"

" Apparently not, nor do they have the technicians ... or the know-how because they were just jumping in with both feet. Little preparation, no serious post-op care, and Andy also feels ... that some partial successes were just incinerated, and they tried again. There's loads of stuff on it. And it's because when they sent stuff to us, they were, or rather the computer guys were, just sending whole files of stuff and not just picking out the information Andy needed. The whole thing is, frankly, just wholesale slaughter!"

"Bloody hell, Angie, maybe we should think about opening up to Andy. But he seems keen to get something off his chest!"

"You work on it at your end. I'll think about where we go from here. Anyway, must dash. Speak soon."

"Well, Ted. Looks like the door is opening. I'll have a chat with my guy, Tug, and see what he thinks about where we go from here. I'll call him now."

"Tug? Sean. We've just had word from Angie ...Yes, that's right, Milan, that the professor there recently learned about all the dodgy goings-on and apart from anything else, wants to bale out of the whole Chinese deal ... he reckons the latest job had a one-in-a-million chance of succeeding, and that from the data he picked up on blood and tissue samples, there's no way it's ever gonna happen again ... the bottom line? That he'll be ready to spill the beans on the whole thing. He's been tricked, he reckons ... alright, when you can. In the meantime, we'll keep the line open to Angie. Cheers." Sean looked up at the others.

"Well ... you heard my side of the conversation, and he seems positive but wants to see what takes place in Milan. I rather hope that the professor takes the initiative ... or Angie will just open up to everyone. Sounds good, either way."

Professor Andy Vennuchi was not happy. He knew Doctor Angelica Scrito had had contact with the boy Victor, but in the urgency to get the video evidence of his condition and faculty control, he had not addressed a major issue, that being where the kid actually was. He buzzed her extension.

"Angelica, can you nip in to see me please? ... Yes, the sooner the better. Thanks." Within a few minutes, the psychiatrist was seated in the professor's office.

"Yes, Andy. You wanted to see me."

"Yes. I'm getting a bit concerned about this whole bloody China deal. As you may know, I've asked for the tissue and blood samples of the work done so far on their latest case. Well, it seems they sent me the whole T&B files going way back, and that they have in furtherance of their experiments, managed to get through loads of indigenous Chinese, plus about forty other people. All European. Ages range from nine to sixty plus. Anyway, I asked them to send the stuff again, in case they gave me the wrong references, but I didn't actually say in my email that I had received anything. Bad drafting on my part, because I only wanted in the first place the ones we were involved with, about four in all. But they came back and said they had sent the files, but in the meantime, I saw just what the buggers had been up to. They also added that they don't have the files any more, and they think that whoever sent them to us must have deleted their records, and they cannot be retrieved, apparently ..."

"So why is that significant?"

"Two reasons. Firstly, I was staggered at how many people they have, in effect, murdered in pursuit of their aims, and by the way, the source, that is, the country of origin, of all the subjects, was on the records. Mainly France and the UK. And according to the info from the files, there were getting on for two hundred Chinese experiments. It looks like they were trying to do head transplants ages ago, but clearly somebody pointed out that there was a fairly limited scope for marketing that process, 'cos it would have to have been male to male, female to female and kid to kid, but imagine the issues if the new addition was an ugly bastard, or totally bald ... you get the point, so as a consequence they changed to what they try to do now. Imagine, Angie, the prospective beneficiary actually choosing who he wanted to be? He only has to kidnap the poor sod ... it doesn't bear thinking about! Secondly, you may already have heard that in analysing the data I reckon that the successful one we all heard about ..."

"Andy, I know what you're going to say, but why couldn't the China guys have done the analysis for themselves?"

"Because they don't have the technology. They've been leaning on us quite heavily recently, which explains our having to keep going over there. They needed our expertise. And now, of course, they don't even have the data!"

"So, to sum it up, Andy, if they ever knew about the fluke factor, it would screw up the whole deal?"

"Technically, yes, it would. But they're very unlikely to disclose that to anybody. If they can suck in billions of dollars, then have a few failures, are they going to tell anybody? We have to assume here, that they will probably never get the right match. Unless we hand our stuff, over by which I mean all their files, and our research. So then all they have to do, is log into the world data bases of DNA and make the choices."

"And if some seventy-year-old Russian oligarch wanted a bit of freshening-up, the Chinese guys access the data base then find a match."

"Yeah. They are hardly going to invite anybody along, are they? More likely kidnap a few and use them."

"And who would stop them?"

"Exactly."

"So what are you going to do?"

"I don't know. It's no good going to the police here, because they won't be in the least bit interested in anything that's not an offence in Italy. If we, as an institution, blow the whistle on them, they're likely to get pretty nasty. But if, say, the lad Vic were to suddenly develop a serious rejection, and it were made public ..."

"Don't tell me that you might find it convenient to kill-off or otherwise incapacitate the boy ..."

"That's one way ... but the other is to just fake it ..."

"But you know as well as I do, they'd want to check the kid themselves ..."

"Yes, if they could find him."

"Then, Andy, we'd have to make bloody sure they don't damn well find him!"

"Angie you're right! But I'll let you deal with that! He's your baby!"

"Then I'll have to warn his guardians. And I also suggest that you talk to Steve Grant. I have no doubt he shares your ideas about this deal. How many times has he come up with patients?"

"Just the once ... as far as I know, anyway."

"So who put pressure on you to find one?"

" Xia Renchuan."

"They wanted to get some deal done for the conference."

"And somebody else came up with the lad? Any ideas?"

"No."

"Ling?"

"Possibly. I expect she has control of all that, and probably put pressure on Grant to come up with Willis."

"So, Ling is the real villain of the piece? Have you met her."

"Yes."

"What do you think of her, then?"

"I think she's a proper bitch. But she's working for, I assume, Beijing. They're pulling the strings, but how they roped Grant in, I've no idea. But I do know that he's met her, so maybe because he was Manchester, like her, she just homed in on him."

"We could ask Steve just what happened ..."

"I think we'd be better off dealing with the tissue and blood match business first. They might just accept it, but somehow, I don't think they will. However, if they proceed with the deal, who the hell will know that they are all going to fail? Nobody. And in the meantime, if, just if, they get a perfect match, then again, it'll be all over the bloody papers, so off we go again!"

"I think you've got it. Anyway, we certainly have work to do." Angie got up and turned to leave. The professor called after her.

"Look after your boy, Angie!"

"I will, believe you me, I bloody well will. Now I suppose I'd better get onto to his guardians and tell them!" Angie did not tell the professor that his researchers had already given her all the information he had imparted to her.

CHAPTER 18

Angie Scrito called Sean and relayed the message to him.

"Okay, I suppose we'd better see what my boss wants to do about that. And of course, Ted. The French cop, Enzo? ... I think we maybe ought to pop over and see them to decide on a plan. I would estimate that most of the poor sods who were used probably came from France, but it's gonna be one hell of a job to find out who they were, isn't it?"

"Possibly, Sean, but I'd like to bet that it's all recorded on Ling's PC. Thing is, if they're using Chinese gear as soon as they get an inkling of what's going on, they'll wipe the bloody files. And if you downloaded them to one of your computers, the spyware would also be sitting in your offices. Unless you used one which was not connected to the internet, or otherwise there could be a built-in wipe mechanism, which is dodgy, because if an authorised person screwed up the passwords it would be damned inconvenient for everybody in the office. Anyway, that's something you're gonna have to work out for yourself."

"Ain't going to be easy. But I see your point about the computers. Tug will know the answer!"

"Possibly. Now, what about the lad? Or Ted I should say."

"Ah! That's another little problem. But I assume he'll be safe until the bad news hits the headlines. Which of course, China doesn't want to happen."

"True, Sean. But I think Andy will be well ahead of them in that he'll know when the dam is about to burst."

"Right. But consider this. If we involved all the police forces, all at once ... that's a hell of a risk because the info will be leaked as soon as we've had our first meeting. I think France should be the first hit."

"But it looks like Manchester is gonna have to be first"

"Okay. I'll raise it all with Tug tomorrow. But I think you should have a word with Ted."

"That's probably the best bet. I expect Manchester's so well organised, and with Ling sitting at the top of the pile in that office. I reckon go for them. Which means Miss Ling!" Sean sat at his desk for a while, staring into space. Then he stood up and went to find his boss.

"Tug. The Willis case. I'm thinking we ought to do a flow-chart job on this one and get organised. By all accounts, the best move would be to take the Manchester office apart. Grab every bloody thing there, and look for the evidence which supports our contention ..."

"Which is?"

"That this Ling woman is sitting on a kind of kidnap business, whereby she's been targeting kids, or young adults, mainly those in care with very few people who give a tinker's cuss about them."

"I doubt there can be that many, Sean, after all, with CCTV, PIN numbers, Facebook and all the other crap people can't just disappear, for fucks sake, especially kids!"

"You're wrong, Tug. In the UK every year, over two hundred people go missing, from OAPs to kids of every age. in America, the annual figure is over two million. Basically, Tug, that Ling woman doesn't have to try too bloody hard, does she? And if she's operating in other European countries, we could be giving her a choice of over a million she could have got hold of!"

"Yeah, but a lot of them are found again ..."

"The number who disappear forever is about ten percent of them. That's a lot of bodies. And another thing, how many stiffs do you think are never identified? In the UK I mean? Go on, have a guess!"

"No idea. Tell me, Sean>"

"Hundreds."

"Wow! So, we go for Ling? I'll arrange a trip up to Manchester and get things organised. We can both go up, okay?"

"No prob. Anytime." Detective Sergeant Tug 'Windy' Windlesham reached for the 'phone.

Commissioner Wallace and two of his DCIs comprised the Manchester team tasked with getting into the SOXMIS premises in the Fountain Street offices. He started the brief.

"Right Al, tell us how we do the job."

"Thank you, sir. We know what we've got to do. So, do we just walk in, arrest Ling and all her staff, then get all their PCs, take them back to HQ and bingo! Would we then have all the info we need to charge them? It ain't gonna happen, Commissioner sir, 'cos by the time the stuff leaves the building, alarms will be going off all over Beijing and suddenly, when you power-up the PCs are all wiped clean!"

"Why? How will they know?"

"They'll know because half the bloody computer kit in the UK and the USA, if not the whole world, has some kind of China stuff in it, and if, for example, the MoD or the US department for defence buy any of the stuff, then you have a team of bloody Chinks looking at it the next day! And that's not all. Do you know how many Chinese and North Koreans are engaged in cyber theft and warfare? Two hundred thousand. And they also do it for a few other government ... all they have to do is pay for it."

"Are you suggesting that we're fucked on that score, Al?"

"Not exactly, Tug. But we have to find a way of getting in and downloading stuff onto a memory device. Takes time, but ..."

"How long?"

"Minutes. But the real problem is breaking the passwords."

"Can you do that?"

"No, but I know a man who can!"

"Who?"

"Can't tell you. But I can talk to him about it, and if he knows it's kosher, he'll do it."

"How?"

"Sir, I am not going to tell you that. What I'd like you to do ... need you to do ... is let me have office locations and layouts, land-line numbers. And your complete assurance that if we need coppers on site to bale us out if there's a hitch, then it's game on."

"Is this a government-run outfit?"

"Of course it is. And when we ..."

"You said 'we' ... does that mean you as well?"

"Yes. But it does not include you except as I just suggested."

"How long with this all take?"

"Days to organise. Once we have all the stuff I've just asked for."

"Sean ... you've got all that stuff you filmed when you and the doctor visited, haven't you?"

"Yes. And it shows Ling's office, and Ling as well."

"Great, we'll need that stuff. The rest is easy." the Commissioner spoke again.

"Right. Currently, the Manchester office don't think they're under threat. As long as we can keep their guard down, it should be fairly easy. What I think we do now, is get the whole team here for a briefing. So anybody who's drafted in to help will know it's a proper, police-organised bust. Let's say we meet here in ... four days ... is that time enough for you, Al?"

"Yessir."

"Okay, gents, that's it for now. See you all here on Thursday."

The meeting broke up. As the group left the Commissioner's office Sean collared Al.

"You one of us, Al?"

"Yeah, used to be. Joined up when I left the Army ... my background was a technician working for the MoD in communications. When retirement loomed, my wife thought I should leave the Army 'cos of all the time I spent away from home. Turned out, the cops wanted me to do all their comms stuff, so in fact I really work for BT. Bet you didn't know that BT employs blokes like me?"

"Nothing surprises me, mate. I bet they employ quite a few other guys whose job is just to fuck-up the ordinary bloke in the street! I suppose the rest of you all work somewhere near Cheltenham?"

"Close." Sean decided that short answer was a brush-off.

"Well, Al, if there's anything you need to know about our Miss

Ling, I can fill you in. Our worst fear is if she gets wind of what's going on, she'll be off in a jiffy!"
"If I have anything to do with it, she won't. The guy I have in mind always does a good job. And if you need to get in touch, here's my card. Don't hesitate to call, okay?"
"Thanks, Al."

Twenty-four hours later, Al Compton had his team together. He briefed them.
"Right this is the deal. Same as we've done dozens of times. The target is a business on Fountain Street, Manchester. The buzz is that there is a people-smuggling business there, run by some Chinese woman. I gather they do all sorts of other border-line stuff which we're not bothered with. You know the MO. We get into the offices. We'll be invited in. Jim, we'll have one of your vans outside, sign-written. The Open Reach job please. Get your head into the bloody box and just piss about for a while. Usual trick. Make sure the van is clearly visible from the offices. The lines go down on the Sunday before the op. Standard crap. So we go in, right? And we need initially to get a keyboard swipe in place."
"What about a back-up eye somewhere in the Ling's office?"
"If you can, yes. But remember, nothing on the PC at all. The closest you must get is the keyboard. Our intention is to break through the passwords. Tec, your job is to be all friendly with the woman as well. And make sure, that when you leave, or before you leave, you tell her to call you, not BT, if they have any more trouble with the 'phones ... which they will of course, or the computers. Do your usual bit about how crap BT is, and that you have your own business. Usual shit. And as usual, we'll man-up your lines."
"This Ling. This Chinese woman. You need me to string her along?"
"How did you guess! That's just what I've been saying. You can tell her how wonderful Beijing is, and how you really want to go home again. You do the homesick routine pretty well. I want her to be taken in,
hook, line and sinker!"

"Got it! Is she pretty?"

"Sorry, mate, a real hard-looking woman, about three times your age!"

"Jim you'll do the usual. We have police back-up arranged in case it all goes tits-up. Any questions?... Yes Jim."

"When?"

"I'll let you know on Thursday. Just getting an up-date then from the Commissioner. Okay? right you can both fuck off now."

On the Thursday morning, Commissioner Wallace was seated at his desk when Al Compton, Tug 'Windy' Windlesham and Sean Johnson filed in. The two DCIs were also there again.

"Morning'. What's the plan then, Al?"

"In brief. The ORCOPs team ..."

"The what?"

"Open Reach Covert Ops team aka the ORCOPs ... will break the lines into the Fountain offices. That'll be on the Sunday. On Monday morning, the ORCOPs will have a van in the street and a small tented shelter round the main exchange terminal. When the office staff call BT about the problem, the calls will be diverted to us. The ORCOPS guys will connect one by one all the other offices except for the SOXMIS lines ..."

"This sounds like a bloody Army exercise, Al ..."

"Well, I suppose it does! Then when we get somebody who comes down and bitches about the SOXMIS kit, and they will, Tec and I ..."

"Who's Tec?"

"He's the whiz kid. He also happens to be from China. He and I will go up to the offices and make a show of looking at all the office lines. While I'm busy doing that we expect that this Ling woman will be chatting up our Tec. Or he will be chatting her up. Tec by the way speaks fluent Chinese. He was born there after all and didn't leave until he was about eighteen."

"Can he be trusted?"

"With my life! He's one of many foreign nationals who ..."

200

"Okay. Al. I'm convinced. What next?"

"He agrees to do Ling's office on his own, and quickly. Then he comes out with all the spiel about how BT are no bloody good, but he has his own business etc. etc., and he'll give her a business card. As usual, all the 'phone-lines shown on his card will be manned. Anyway, when we disconnect the lines again, it's expected that Ling or the other staff will call him."

"So, he fixes the lines. Then what?"

"He picks up his KBS ..."

"A what?"

"A key-board sweep, Commissioner. A small device which records every key pressed over a period of about seven days. It's then easy to pick up any passwords. Because it's also run against a time-base. Like, say at eight in the morning, if anybody types in say DingBat99 then it's probably to open the screen or a file and so on. When we run it through our software, it shows up all the likely passwords, 'cos it picks up lower-case, upper case and number combinations. In other words, ..."

"In other words, exactly what the computer guys expect a password to comprise! Pretty cool!"

"Yes. Now, we won't need to locate the email addresses of the office staff, so ..."

"How the hell would you do that?"

"Screencaster. Takes about four minutes, and I doubt they'll have done a OnDMARC on their PAs ..."

"I didn't get a word of that Al but do please carry on."

"Fine. And also, on first visit, Tec is gonna try and plant an OE somewhere in the place ... OE. ... Stands for Office Eye, a little bug that can cover on a wide-angle scope the PC, you know, a personal computer ..."

"Thanks, Al ... I guessed the PC one!"

"Right. It'll cover the PC screen and the keyboard."

"Where the hell's he gonna plant that little job?"

"Don't ask. The key is, that when Tec gets a call-back from Miss Ling. That's when he and I go in to collect the kit. Or, if no call, we break in. And during the op, we'll need a couple of coppers ...

policemen ... to cover our arses on the first stage in case the office staff get suspicious, or on the second stage, when we collect, especially if we have to go in uninvited. How are we doing so far?"

"Brilliant. I can sleep easy in my bed knowing that bloody BT could be spying on me."

"Thanks for that Commissioner. I think that's about all."

"Hang on, Al. This Tec bloke. I assume he also reads Chinese?"

"Of course."

"Would he be willing to help us with the downloads in case it's all in their language, whatever it is?"

"Of course he will. He's from southern China, so he speaks Cantonese, writes Simplified, I think, as do most other Chinese, so there's more that a fighting chance that he will understand her and ditto. Anyway, we expect most of the stuff to be in English. Except when she sends or receives from China, but even then, it'll probably be in English. After all, and I bet this is something you didn't know, all the Chinese cyber-nerds were all educated at our bloody universities! ..."

"So while the Unis make a killing on the fees paid by these guys, they're all plotting to fuck the UK and probably the USA as well?"

"Probably, but that's not a problem for us to deal with some other time."

"Thanks, Al. Since meeting you, I've been feeling very uncomfortable. Any of you guys got any questions?"

"Do you have a date for this, Commissioner?"

"Al? can we get it started this Sunday?"

"I'd say yes. As far as your support's concerned, police back-up I mean, if you have a couple of cars earmarked for the job on the Monday, were good to go. Our side of it is always ready to go at about two hours notice."

"Sounds good to me. Let's go for it. Thanks guys, back to work!"

"You seem a bit down, Steve. Anything wrong?"

"No, Rosie. I mean yes. Do you remember patient Willis? The guy who ..."

"Of course, I remember him. Why?"

"Well, I think he's gonna come back and bite me in the arse."

"How so?"

"Oh, various things. Did he leave ... any beneficiaries to his estate?"

"Why don't you ask the woman from the registrar's office?"

"Could do, I suppose."

"Anyway, why would that come back and bite you?" Rosie felt a bit uneasy, pretending that she didn't know anything about the Willis business.

"I dunno. Just a feeling." Rosie didn't want to pry further. She would wait until he addressed her on the situation again. If he ever did.

"Want a coffee?"

"Yeah. Have to do a ward-round soon. Get me a couple of chockie biscuits as well, please." Grant had only another day to complete his statement. He decided to finish it that evening then email it to that Windlesham bloke. He was seriously worried about his career.

"Sean? Tug. Just had Grant's statement in. I'll send it over to you. Have a read then we can have a chat about it. I've made a few comments, but I'd like to see yours, so we can get together for a discussion. It'll be with you in the next thirty minutes or so, okay?"

"Yep. I'll get into it today. Thanks." Grant's statement forwarded from Tug, dropped into Sean's in-box. He sent a 'Got it' note then he opened the document, saved it in his task file, and read it. It was about fourteen pages long, double spaced. The grammar was pretty good. It started out with a brief personal history. Then the doctor moved onto the bit that interested him most. Sean read the whole document twice, making notes on his pad as he went through it the second time. Then he called Tug.

"What do you think of it, Tug?"

"He's been very honest. I mean about the two Chinese nurses

and the drugs. but to me it stinks of a set-up!"

"Yeah, and me, but for God's sake, he must have known it was a set-up!"

"Why would he know? You and I as police officers would know, but don't forget any whiff of a scandal, especially with two deaths and the stuff in the back of the car ... what do you reckon it was worth? Fifty big ones? He was obviously pretty scared. Imagine it happening to him ... look at what he says. Firstly, he remembers being at the party, he remembers talking to the nurses, and that's it. Next thing he knows, he's in a bed somewhere. A copper turns up and takes a breath-test, and the nurse takes a blood-sample. Both way OTT, right? ..."

"Yes. Then it starts to get fantastic. Firstly, he has no injuries. Secondly a so-called aunt of the two nurses turns up saying he's killed her two nieces, and she says the Chinese custom is to take an eye for an eye or some other shit, then guess who turns up later and sets up the deal? Bloody Ling! I mean, Tug, what a coincidence? And she is by all accounts, another aunt saying that she wants to forgive him. Then this police officer guy turns up again, what was the name? ... Bakewell ... he turns up and charges Willis with causing death by dangerous driving, driving whilst over the limit, no insurance, possession of a class A drug with intent to supply. Who the fuck was this Bakewell guy? Manchester police force? Have you looked him up?"

"Yes. Couldn't find him. But they had on the force somebody called Boswell, but he had long gone by the time all this happened. But it's an old trick, isn't it? A guy 'phones up asking to speak with Bakewell, the switchboard say 'Don't you mean Boswell' or something like that. Anyway, definitely no Bakewell. Then they tell the guy that he must have been confused over the names."

"Well, surprise, surprise! And what about the two nurses?"

"They were real. Two of them, and they were not sisters! Dead sus! Both really tanked up on alcohol and drugs, the only people in the car, and it crashed and caught fire. Cause of death was smoke inhalation, both trapped in the car. The fire brigade got on scene pretty quickly. Official report, no other person involved."

"So that bit which Grant mentions, is true and he thought the Ling woman arranged that with the police?"

"So then she pressurises Grant into working for her ..."

"Which seemed to be working a treat until SOXMIS thing was featured in a local paper, so Grant had to be seen to break with the outfit."

"But Ling keeps her claws in him, and pulls his strings from Manchester? And who owns the Manchester property?"

"Have a guess!"

"Ling?"

"No, but close. Cash purchase, no mortgage. It's in the name of a company, the directors appear to be resident in the UK. Both Chinese names. The company name is er ... I've got it here somewhere ... Sun Simiao 88 limited or something like that. Paid-up share capital roughly equal to the value of the office block, that's about one and a half million, and the accounts look really healthy, with a turnover in excess of three quarters of a million. New accounts due in about three months time ...."

"What's the Sunsim thing supposed to be, Tug?"

"No idea, but I think the number eight is a lucky number in China!"

"And Grant says that he came under a lot of pressure to find someone. And he found Willis."

"And he seems to be connected with the SOXMIS lot still, but surely he could just pull out? And what about his Milan account? He doesn't mention that does he?"

"So, we ask about the copper's name, and whether Grant might not have got it right, but I'd like to bet it was a put-up job. We'll also have to ask about the account."

"I reckon, Sean. So, this could be a murder case."

"Yeah, but I don't think Grant's a suspect. We can always get it reopened. And I don't suppose for one minute that Grant was ever in the car. But the report might have overlooked something?"

"Possible. Anyway, I'll ask Manchester to look at it again. The car will have been crushed by now, of course, but there's always photographs, probably finger-prints and forensics. But I don't suppose the investigators thought it might have been staged."

"So, what do you reckon, another chat with Grant?"

"Yes, definitely. And shall we let Ted see this?"

"Of course. We'll have to. He's the main man and he's given us a lot of input so far, so he might have some worthwhile comments to make."

"Hi, Ted! Angie! Rosie's been telling me that you have been in a bit of trouble. What went on?"

"Some PE teacher got a bit familiar. So I hit him. So the Head sent a letter to complain about my behaviour."

"What happened?"

"He was groping all the kids as they came out of the shower. He knew he was doing wrong, so I just made the point that he wasn't going to do it to me. You know, Angie, there have been many cases of young boys and girls being abused by all sorts of weirdos, but they didn't know what to do about it, and years afterwards, they were badly damaged, and it made them a but funny as well. Bastards! I also found a load of cameras planted in and around the gym showers and toilets. Sean's got all those. Anyway, it looks like the PEd bloke has now been sacked, or rather resigned, and the headmaster was also involved ..."

"So is there a replacement yet? Because I reckon Marcel would love to work in the UK. And he speaks good French and Italian ... and English of course ..."

"You serious? Really? Hey, that'd be really cool ... Oh shit, Angie, there I go again, beginning to talk like an eleven-year-old! I'll send a text to the school secretary and ask. Now, what's happening with Andy and his crew?"

"I think he's seen the light. He got a load of tissue and blood samples, and according to his lab guys, there's very little chance of any repetition ..."

"So our China friends ain't gonna be too pleased ..."

"That's the point, Ted. For them, it's game-over. And into the bargain, Andy reckons that about forty Europeans and probably several hundred Chinese have been involved in the experiments ... so Beijing are gonna have to write off millions of Euros ..."

"And what about Grant? Did Andy mention him?"

"Yes. He's never been involved before. You were his first."

"And Sean and his mates have already interviewed him. But it's the Ling woman who, I think, is the real driver behind all this. And I have a notion that she'll be the first to feel the full force of the law. Then move on to France, then onto Andy."

"That's about it. Now, see what your school wants to do about a new PE teacher ... and let me know if there's a chance, and I'll go and talk to Marcel. His wife also speaks the same languages, so they could be really useful. I think his parents run a small hotel near Paris, so for the students learning French, it could be a real deal!"

"And of course, he knows a lot about what's been going on with the SOS place, and all those kids!"

"Yeah. Let's hope he's all for it. Speak later."

Sean's email with the Grant statement pinged into Willis's inbox. He acknowledged and asked whether Grant knew that he, Willis, was living in Marlow. He asked Sean to call as soon as he could, but preferably after school hours.

The following day he sent a text to Elaine. *'Please let me know whether you have appointed a new PEd teacher; I have an ideal candidate in mind. VC'* The school secretary replied almost immediately. *'No; talk to me. I'll come and fetch you as soon as you settle into your next lesson'.* The end of break bell rang, and Willis turned off his 'phone and dropped it into the bottom of his bag. He knew he should not have it with him during lessons, but he wasn't too concerned about it. He'd been seated for no more than a few minutes, when the secretary entered the classroom and asked for Clément to follow her to her office. In the corridor she spoke.

"I know damn well that you don't need to listen to a geography lesson. We have far more important stuff to discuss."

"Like religion? Have you heard about my rants at the RI teacher, yet? Wait 'til I get started on the morning assembly!"

"Victor Clément, you are a real trouble-maker! But we need a few people like you around!" The secretary had taken over the headmaster's office.

"Where's he gone to?"

"Sick leave."

"Appropriate. He's sick."

"Firstly, what have you been doing with a Miss Linda Bishop?"

"Bishop? Is that Linda's surname! Nothing. Why?" The name meant something to Willis. Sandy Bishop from the Common had been a frequent visitor to Oaklands. He had to be careful.

"We've had her dad on the 'phone threatening hell and damnation ..." That sounded to him like the Bishop he knew.

"What? That's a bit severe! Preachers motivate their congregations by threatening them with hell. Is her dad a real bishop or vicar or something?"

"An 'or something' is a better description. He wants to know who the kid is who's been making overtures to his darling daughter ... I told him that if either his daughter or anybody else for that matter were guilty of inappropriate behaviour, they would be severely reprimanded ..."

"Except for teachers, that is!"

"Probably. Anyway, this PEd replacement ... tell me about him please." Willis gave her the facts.

"How do you know him?"

"When I was in Milan, he let me use his facilities at the hospital there, and he set up a small gym for me at home."

"Sounds too good to be true. Especially with the languages. If I advertise the post, I'll let you have a copy as soon as it's posted in the TES ..."

"Times Educational Supplement ..."

"You're too smart for your own good, Clément ... and if he's interested, I'll look forward to his application. Give me your email address ...okay, I've already got it. And I still can't work out who you really are. What is it about you?"

"No idea. But I'd like to see George Ferris as your new headmaster."

"So would I. Let's leave it there for now, shall we?"

"Can I go now, please Miss?"

"Yes. Clément. You know, you have a head on you which one could realistically believe is about fifty years old? Your attitude, outlook, presence and general ..."

"Oh, Miss! Never! I would suggest at least seventy!" The school secretary didn't laugh. He just wondered what her favourite television programmes were. The Walking Dead perhaps and those of similar genre.

On Sunday morning, the telephone lines to the Fountain Street glass-fronted office block were disconnected. On his *'work progress'* sheet, Al Compton ticked his box and added the time. 0921 hours.

At eight-fifteen on the Monday morning, the ORCOPs van was parked half-on the pavement and virtually outside the front door of the target block. Some twenty metres away, the engineers, comprising Al, Tec Martin and Jim Swales, had used a small canvas surround to mark out the area around the BT switch boxes. Then all three 'engineers' retired to the van to make tea. And do nothing else. The first reaction was not long in coming. And all three were fully aware of what was going to happen. As the first 'customer' exited the doors from the office, and it was obvious he was making for the BT team, Jim turned his back to the approaching figure.

"Eh up, lads. First customer!"

"Got him, Jim. Looks angry." The man eased up to them.

"Scuse me! Do you guys know that our 'phones are down?" The response.

"Sorry, mate". Jim turned to the others. "Hey, you lot, any of you cut any 'phone lines? This bloke says his 'phone's dead." Al looked at Tec.

"What've you done, Tec?"

"Nothing yet. Not supposed to start yet. Not 'til nine." The visitor looked at his watch.

"Nearly that now."

"Give us a few minutes, and we'll 'ave a look. What's the number?"

The visitor gave them the number. "Company name?" The man gave the name. "Okay. I'll have a butchers." Al sidled off and messed about in the box for a minute then came back. "Try that? Sorry about that. This kit we've got here's been really screwed up. Hopefully we can get it all sorted. If you go back in, you can tell all the others to pop out and we'll try to get them sorted. Might be able to fix their lines. It's only a few we think that's causing the problem. okay?"

"Yeah, thanks guys. Good job!"

"Nice bloke."

"Wait until you get the China woman here! Not so nice!"

One by one, various office workers from each company accommodated in the block, popped out of the building to ask that their lines be connected. The team obliged. Then came the SOXMIS office.

"Sorry, love. No-can-do. It must be in the building somewhere. Could be a couple of days ..." The girl threw her hand into the air.

"Shit! The boss will go fuckin' bonkers."

"Sorry darlin'." was his parting shot to the girl as she retreated into the building. A few minutes later, Miss Ling appeared. Tec moved from the passenger seat into the back of the van, where the woman would not see him. But he heard her.

"Hey, you!" She advanced on the two men, who had managed to put cups of tea in their hands. They, all three of them, knew exactly what they were going to do. It was a well-rehearsed operation. Ling was clearly angry. It was also obvious she had failed her social-skills course.

"Hey you fucks! You fuck-up my phones. You switch them now or I call the police hurry! hurry!" The woman advanced on Jim and tried to slap his tea mug from his hand.

"Oi! What do you think you're doing?" Al chipped in.

"Hey, calm down! If you don't, we'll call the police, and have you arrested for assault! Who the hell do you think you are! go away and leave us in peace or we'll go back to our depot and you get no 'phone for a week!" Jim again, with the code for Tec to appear.

"Clear orf! Hop it!" In a moment, Tec appeared from the back of the van.

"What the bloody hell's going on?" He saw Ling turn and look at him.

"Madame, begging your pardon, what are these men doing to you?" Ling looked at Tec and actually smiled. In Cantonese, she addressed Tec.

"These men bad men. I want my 'phone fixed. They told me to fuck off!"

"Madame, you leave this to me. Tec turned to Al and Jim. How dare you insult a member of the public! This good lady need 'phone. You fix it pronto or I'll have your arses in a sling! get to work!" Tec faced Ling again, and once more in her mother tongue, "These men lazy English pigs. BT is shit. I have this country full of lazy men. Beijing works much better!" Then Al spoke up.

"Tec, the problem must be in their office. All other lines are okay. We have to go inside!"

"Okay. You go inside but you go with me. You keep your mouths shut." Then in Cantonese to Ling. "These men stupid men. I supervise them I fix your 'phone." Then to the two telephone men. "Get your tools lock the van and come with me. But not speak!" He turned to Ling and bowed. "Madame, I supervise. We go now into office and fix 'phones." Ling positively beamed. On the way up to the office, Ling and Tec chatted all the way. it appeared Ling was hooked. Once in the office, Tec took charge.

"You two. Find all the 'phone points and check each one carefully." he turned to Ling. "Madam, I will personally check yours. I assume you boss here, yes?"

"Yes. Come with me please." The woman moved to the door marked Private, unlocked it and beckoned to Tec to follow her. If she was going to hang around him, his job could be difficult. He looked up at the ceiling.

"You have smoke and CO_2 detectors." It was a statement, not a question. But she answered anyway.

"Yes."

"Sometimes these are also connected to emergency services. The good ones are of course. I check them. I expect you have the good ones. But first I do your 'phone sockets." Ling was by now beaming. "I send man to get step ladder from van."

"No, I go and tell man. I need to see what they are doing." In a flash the woman was gone. She was away for longer than it took for Tec to slip open the battery compartment on the Ling keyboard and insert his own batteries. They were good for a week of constant use but could run for a maximum of ten days. Half of his job done already. With his mobile, he photographed the bunch of keys on the desk. There were four keys in all. With a standard AAA battery next to them, the lab guys could work out sizes and make new keys. This was a bonus for him. He dropped down on one knee and started to open a phone socket. Ling returned.
She addressed him.

"Why you work here?"

"You mean in the office? Or in England?"

"In England, of course. It shit place. All men lazy. All get free money. Stupid government."

"My father from Xiamen. When I was eighteen, he meet woman in Hong Kong. Move to England. I very not happy ... I had good business there working on 'phones and computers. I work for Huawei I want to go back. But I have own business now in England. It will be a big business soon working for all clever Chinese people like you."

"Why you work for BT?"

"As soon as I get all latest stuff from them, I leave ..."

"Maybe you work for me?"

"No, no. You must have work done by your man, no? But if you need 'phone work you call me. I fix everything. BT is crap. I move to new house it take BT nine months to put in 'phones."

"You give me your business card, yes?"

"Okay. But don't tell anybody. Big secret, yes?" Just then, Al walked into the office carrying the stepladder. "Al. you done the 'phone sockets?"

"No."

"Well you go and hurry. We must not take all day! Hurry up!" Tec screwed back the face on a socket and placed the ladder under the first ceiling alarm. He climbed up and unclipped the cover, pulled the live wires from the connector block, and eased out the little clear plastic fitting covering the indicator lights and attached a small, wide-angle camera lens. He re-attached a power supply from the body of the alarm box, then snapped the device shut again. It was beautifully positioned to catch the PC screen and keyboard. In the second alarm he repeated the process, but this time fixed a small sound recorder.   Job done. He slid down the ladder, and went to find Al.

"Finished. Nip down and do the job. We can piss off now and test." Al gave the thumbs-up. "I'll go and find Jim." He found Jim drinking a can of Coca-Cola. "I hope you've finished!" Jim turned to face Tec.

"Oh, yes boss! You got the job done?"

"Yes. Al's gone back down to check the masters." Which meant nothing at all but sounded technical enough. "So let's get the hell out of here, okay!" In ten minutes, all three were back in their van.

"Good job, eh?"

"Yeah, but if you'd left me for another ten minutes, Al, I reckon I could've given that girl I was talking to, the blonde, I could've given her a sample!"

"A sample of what, for fuck's sake?"

"Let me explain in great detail, Tec ..."

"No you won't, Sam! Instead get onto the office and see how it's all working. Our job's done now. But for you, Tec, the spooks might want you do talk them through a few things."

"No problem ... But just a point ..."

"Yes, Sam?"

" The blonde I was talking to ... I wasn't just thinking about my dick, Al, because I asked her how she liked working there, and about her boss, you know, the Chinese woman. By all accounts she thinks the woman's a proper bitch. She used words like autocratic, despotic, tyrannical, over-bearing ..."

"Not too fond of her then?"

"You could say that."

"Useful. Could we have her turned to help us? Do you think she'd go for that?"

"I say worth a try. She and hopefully her mates could probably all be useful. I doubt they would knowingly engage in the people-smuggling job."

"Well, we have to get our kit back in about six days or so. We'll pass the INTEL to the pigs and see. Maybe we could use you as bait, Sam, you know, unbutton your shirt, put a huge gold medallion round your neck and let your belly flop over your trouser belt and ..."

"Fuck off!"

"Okay. Let's see if the cops want to give it a try with her. But now we should concentrate on getting the stuff out of there and into the freezer ... and in a few days, we'll see how our Ling woman's getting on."

CHAPTER 19

When Doctor Grant opened his door to the officers again, the two policemen thought he looked weary. The doctor just let his hand slide off the latch, and turn⸍ ᵈ to move into his lounge, and then virtually collapse into his ⁀ᵃⁱᵣ. He said nothing but beckoned the men to take seats. Tug spoke first.

"You don't look too chipper, ⸍ Steve!"

"What do you expect? For the second time in my life, I feel I've really fucked up my career ⸍

"Well, that might not be the case ⸍ Can I ask you a few questions about your statement? Tʰᵉ doctor waved his hand in the air, a very submissive gesture.

"Right. This car accident when the two nurses were killed. Are you sure you got the name of the police officer right? Bakewell was it?"

"Yes. It's because she looked like a tart ..."

"It was a she?'

"Yes."

"How was she like er.. like a tart?"

"Attractive, but too much make-up. Like she was advertising."

"Or maybe a rather thin disguise? We couldn't find anybody on the Manchester force by that name ..."

"So?"

"It might be that she didn't actually exist?"

"Does that make me a liar?"

"No, but it might make you the victim of a scam ..." Grant suddenly came to life.

"So, there was no accident? but I read ..."

"Oh yes, there was an accident. Or at least, it was classed as an accident, we know that. But we don't think you were directly involved."

"But ..."

"Another point." Sean picked it up. "Have you ever been to the Manchester office?"

"Yes, once. Before all this blew up. I'd been to a conference, in Germany, it was, and met Andy ... he's from Italy ... and somebody else from Manchester. The Chinese woman. But they were already talking before I was kind of roped in. We could see by the name tags where they were from. And of course, also on the attendees' list. I was based at the hospital there until the newspapers got hold of my involvement in the SOXMIS thing, so I was advised to move away. Hence ..."

"We know that. Can we show you a short video?"

"Of course." Sean handed over a clip from Angie's and Sean's visit to the office. Grant moved over to his desk and pushed the memory stick into its slot, with his mouse clicked on USB DISK(G) then 'play'.

"That's the office!" 'The clip showed only the office staff.

"Okay, Steve ... if you see the policewoman, shout out." It didn't take him long.

"There!" Grant paused the screen and edged it back a touch. I'm sure that's her! But her hair has changed a lot!"

"Sure?" Look at the whole thing then make sure you can identify her okay?" Grant took the cursor to the start of the shots to play them all over again.

"There ... there again ...and again!"

"Sure?"

"One hundred percent! For God's sake, I spent hours with her!"

"Hours where?"

"It was in a private hospital, somewhere between Uxbridge and High Wycombe, I think. When I was considered fit to travel, I was returned to Manchester. My absence was taken care of by somebody ... at my hospital. I think. Anyway, nobody ever questioned me about any of it."

"Looks to me like we're pulling up a weed with very long roots, Tug. God only knows who's scamming whom. Hospitals, nursing staff, doctors, kiddies' homes ... "

"Looks like it. Anyway, that one's out of the way. Now tell us about the bank account in Milan."

"You know about that? ... I was". Grant paused for quite a long time before he spoke again. He was clearly emotional. "I ... I was planning to save a lot of cash just in case things got too much. I was just going to fuck off and start a new life somewhere else, qualify under another name and start all over again. Probably somewhere on the continent of Africa or possibly in Eastern Europe, then somehow get back to the UK a good few years later."

"That sounds pretty plausible. Thank you for being so honest. Any points you want to make, Sean?"

"Yes, Tug. I think your position is somewhat better than before, but I must emphasise that you are not out of the woods yet. We want Manchester to re-examine the crash. There might be a murder enquiry. But as you know, it is not at all unlikely that something was staged just to reel people in. Like you. What we'd like you to do is get together with your friend in Milan ..." Grant looked up sharply.

"You guys know every bloody thing, don't you?"

"No. But we intend to. And we want your help."

"Count me in. Can I talk to Andy about it?"

"I think that's a good idea. Just keep us in the picture, please."

"Of course. And thank you." Doctor Steve Grant looked a lot happier when the police officers left, than when they arrived.

Len called his team.

"Op China. The pick-up job. It's on for Friday, okay?"

"Times?"

"Plan to go in at about nine in the morning. All know what you've gotta do?"

"Usual shit?"

"Yes. And make sure Tec looks like he's out to impress. This is a once-in-a-lifetime opportunity ..." Tec piped up from the back of the

room where he was wrestling with the coffee machine.

"Stuff that! I'm not out to marry the fuckin' woman!"

"Well just pretend that you are, just play her along. And Jim, you try and tap up that blonde you were talking about, okay? We have plans for her. Right, that's it. Meet up at eight. Friday!"

The three OR men were ready to go by half-eight. They had done their kit check and had run over their plan for the day. They parked up again on the pavement outside the Fountain street offices. Sam nipped out and disconnected the 'phoned for the SOXMIS office. Then they sat and waited. At nine minutes past nine, Jim's blonde left the building and approached the van. Al clocked her.

"This is it, lads. Your move, mate!" Jim wound down his window.

"Mornin' love!"

"Hello again. You guys really want to screw-up my weekend, don't you! Chairman Mao up there will have us flogged unless we get the bloody 'phones sorted! Please do something!" Sam got out of the van and put his hand onto her shoulder.

"Okay, love. We'll get onto it now. Come on, you two! Tec, nip up with this lady and see where the prob is. We'll be up in a moment." Tec followed the girl into the office block. Ling was in reception.

"Hey, you!" She addressed Tec. "My 'phones again!" Tec replied in Mandarin

"I'm sorry, madam. I tell you these guys rubbish. We check all the sockets again. Maybe you have a mouse or something eating the wires. Let me check your room first! I tell other men to come up here to do job properly." Tec noticed the blonde girl looked terrified. Ling then turned to her.

"You go back to work!" Ling took Tec by the arm and pulled him into her office. "You good man. You work for me, yes?"

"Madam, I gave you my card. You must ring me with problems not BT. BT no good. Let me fix your 'phones then I go. Thank you. Please go and see my men behave themselves." There was a knock at the office door. It was Al with the step-ladder. Ling followed Al into the main office. It took a second to change the keyboard battery, so he then attended to the smoke and CO_2 alarms. Job done. He carried the ladder into main reception when Sam called him. He had been fussing about near a wall junction.

"Tec? Found the problem. Somebody wrenched this lead from the wall socket. It was shorting all the other 'phones. I'll go and reset the trigger on the road. Job done." Tec went to find Ling and explained what had happened.

"My people fuck stupid!" Tec decided to call the team out of the office before they witnessed a murder. Jim was beaming from ear to ear. He gave a thumbs-up to Tec. Back in the van, job done, Tec looked at Jim.

"What's all this grinning, Jim?"

"The blonde. Poor girl terrified of that woman. I reckon she's gonna be a lot of use when the cops go in. Must tell them before they strike."

"Great. What's her name?

"Her little desk tag said Sonia Tussel. Big blonde girl."

"Right. I'll pass that on. Now let's get this stuff over to the ORBIT offices and see what we've got for them!"

Nine days after the clear-out, Al called his guys.

"I'm going to find out what our guys have got from the SOXMIS offices. I'll let you know if they've found anything useful." Al rang off. Then he called ORBIT aka 'The Freezer'. Nobody really knew why it was called it 'The Freezer' but it was a name adopted by a senior manager, and as everyone was all for an easy life, they kept the bugger happy by adopting that name. He tried to justify it because as he said, *'the stuff we find sometimes will chill you to the bone'* Al asked to talk to Big Simon, who confirmed that the stuff they found was 'hot shit'.

"Well, can we get it to the Commissioner, Simon? They've gotta arrange a bust if necessary

"No prob. Way ahead of you. It all went off the day before yesterday."

"Bloody brill! Thanks!"

"Okay, Al. 'Ave a good'un!"

"Will do, mate." Next, Al called the Commissioner's office.

"Hi, Al. Can you pop in to see us? Boss wants to see you like now?"

"It's lunch time!"

"We'll buy you lunch!"

"On me way!"

"You've done as damn good job, you lads!" The Commissioner was beaming at the OR man.

"Thank you, sir. Anything you can tell me?"

"Yes. Got all the passwords, audio, loads of screen shots. Now we plan to go in hard with the EuroPol guys and detain every bugger there. It'll be tough. If anybody is away from the office and gets wind of what's going on, they might warn somebody higher up the command chain. There must be no bugger locking themselves in the bog and making 'phone calls. It's got to be slick. Then we'll get the spooky guys into the office to whip out the PCs like quickly, before any wipe-apps kick in if there are any. Can't be doing with having all the stuff wiped. But we expect to disable any funny stuff like that first. Anything you want to say?"

"Yes sir. Do you think it's possible to get someone on the inside to give us the low-down first?"

"Anybody in mind?"

"My mate Sam reckoned so. One girl in particular is really anti. It's always possible she's there under duress, but whatever reason she has, she was dead unimpressed with her boss. The Chinese woman, that is."

"How do we do that?"

"Maybe pick her up after work? If we're going in anyway, I can get my guy to arrange a meeting somewhere? My guy's pretty street-wise and I have every faith in him ..."

"Might it cock-up everything we've done so far?"

"I very much doubt it. This guy is right up there in the common-sense stakes, and if he detects any pull-back by her, he'll recognise it immediately. Her name is Sonia Tussel."

"Give it a go. If it looks like backfiring, we can arrest her immediately and keep hold of her until our bit's over and done with."

"Sir, if you plan to go in in the next few days, do we need to be there?"

"The Commissioner turned to his senior officers. "Well?""

"I doubt it. We can go in on two hours' notice, sir. However, if this inside job looks like a runner, then why don't we pick her up the night before, just in case there's something in there that could hinder our enquires, especially wipe all the hard-drive stuff?" Al spoke up.

"That's a bit unlikely, sir. The danger with all that kit in the wrong hands is, if it's all done accidentally, then resetting their systems would take not hours but days. You would only find that sort of wipe-out stuff in highly-organised criminal gangs, where you have real pros on the job, or in some iffy government departments, so I would say unlikely. Anyway, if you take our guy, he can deal with most of the other low-risk stuff. I think the key is to get in quickly, quietly, and immediately pin-down everybody. You know, on the floor, cable-ties the lot."

"Any comments on that?... No?... Right, you guys ..." the commissioner nodded towards his men, "That's it. Get together with your teams and give me a flow-chart, people, back-up, materials, transport ... the lot. You'll take priority over any other business. I'll give you 24 hours. Build into your plan a questioning of this Tussel girl, at least one day before we go into the offices. Thanks, Al, we'll let you know when we plan to move in. I think on reflection, we ought to have your guys there as well please. Briefing over. Thank you, gentlemen."

Willis opened his copy of Oliver Twist. It was a Bells Continuous Readers edition and had cost the original purchasers, the County Education Committee of the North Riding, ninepence, in old money. It had belonged to Willis's mother, and she acquired it from the County Education Committee of the North Riding, and she had used it when she was at East Rownton Church School 1924, when she was seven years old. Willis had read it many times. But as this edition had been adopted for use in schools, it did not begin with the birth of Oliver, as it was regarded as being too brutal a description for the tender ears and constitutions of first world war era seven-year-olds. Willis returned it to the library and collected another, later edition of Charles Dickens' book. The same volume advertised a Chippendale stained rosewood book case for three shillings and sixpence to hold twenty volumes of Dickens' work.

He opened the book to read the contents, Chapter one. *'Treats of the place where Oliver Twist was born and the circumstances attending his birth'.* Willis started to read. He was once again, captivated by the writing, as much as he was by Shakespeare. He knew that to just pluck out 500 or so words, could not possibly show the full brilliance of the author's descriptive prose. He would pick the opening words of the first few paragraphs. He opened a new word document on his PC and began his draft.

1. Among other public buildings in a certain town, which for many reasons it will be prudent to refrain from mentioning, and to which I will assign no fictitious name, there is one anciently common to most towns, great or small; to wit, a workhouse; and in this workhouse was born, on a day and date which I need not trouble myself to repeat inasmuch as it can be of no possible consequence to the reader ...' and so on.

2. For a long time after it was ushered into this world of sorrow and trouble, by the parish surgeon, it remained a matter of considerable doubt whether the child would survive at all ...' and so on.

3. The fact is, that there was considerable difficulty in inducing Oliver to take upon himself the office of respiration - a troublesome practice, but one which custom has rendered necessary to our easy existence and for some time he lay gasping on a little flock mattress, rather unequally poised between this world and the next ...' .and so on...'

Willis continued with his draft. *'I have chosen Dickens' Oliver Twist, because it is a neat example of that authors' writing. It is also of immense historical value, Dickens being a social critic apart from a writer who created the world's best-known fictional characters. Known for his creative style, flair for language, and impressive insight into human nature, Dickens' novels continue to endure nearly 150 years after his death. it is easy to see why. In the opening chapter of Oliver Twist, it would have been easy for the author to write that 'Oliver's was a difficult birth, and his mother died shortly after the boy was born' But that was not the author's way. the language is quaint and wholesome, it draws the reader in. The fact that it develops into a story is a bonus. Many read Dickens for the power of its expression. Most, if not all writing today, fails to employ such powerful prose, now and sadly a lost art'.*

Another reason for Willis choosing this novel was because he appreciated that he was writing about young Victor Clément, but that was his secret. Willis resolved to ask the English teacher if he could read the whole of chapter one, only in length some four small pages, as he wanted the class to appreciate the power of well-written prose. He finished his draft, read it over a few times, then printed it. He printed four copies, as he doubted whether his friend Linda, or indeed anybody in his class, would have a copy of Dickens' book at home. He carefully stapled the copies and put them into his backpack.

In Manchester, at approximately the same time as Willis shut-down his PC, Sonia Tussel left her office to make the short walk home. Across the road were parked two unmarked police cars. In the front one, sat two uniformed officers, and Sam, from ORBIT. Behind that car, were two plain-clothed officers from the Operation China team.

"That's the girl, chaps! The blonde." One of the officers spoke into the little handset clipped to his left lapel.

"Target in sight ... Blonde girl, fawn coat. Carrying a Tesco bag.

Copy?"

"Got it, sarge. We'll pick-up as soon as she's away from the office windows in case we get eyeballed, roger?"

"Copied. We'll dawdle behind you to keep an eye open for you." The girl crossed the road at a zebra crossing, turned left and continued walking. It was noted in both cars. Then the order to pick-up was given.

Both cars moved, the rear car passing the front vehicle. Two hundred yards ahead, it pulled into the kerb, the two plain-clothes officers got out of the car and stood in front of Sonia Tussel. The woman moved to her right to walk past the officers, but one of them held his left arm out and placed his hand on her right shoulder.

"Miss Tussel? I'm Detective Constable White, and this is my colleague DC Hart. I wonder if we may have a few words with you?"

"What's it all about?"

"Let me reassure you, madam, it is nothing serious. It's just that we need to talk to you about a Miss Ling. And her business? It is just a formality, but we think it would be better if we could talk somewhere quiet where we won't be overheard? And just to put your mind at rest, we are genuine police officers. The vehicle behind us has two uniformed policemen observing us now." Sonia Tussel turned and looked.

"Yes, so I see. You could talk to me at my flat. I'm on my way there now."

"We're happy with that. Can we give you a lift?"

"Very well. I'm only just around the corner." Within a few minutes, the officers and Miss Tussel were seated in her lounge.

"Right, how can I help you?" the officers noted that she was really calm, bearing in mind the circumstances.

"Miss Tussel. You work at the SOXMIS office, with a Miss Ling?"

"I do, yes."

"What goes on there? Apart that is from the services of organ donation, AI and certain adoption processes?"

"That's about all, really. I assume it's all above board?"

"What does Miss Ling do? Is she just the boss?"

"Yes ... but she seems to keep herself away from the staff normally, and as far as I can tell, and if I had to put a name to her role, I would say she is the business development manager."

"Do you like her?"

"No, not really. She can be a bit, shall I say, abrupt? But she pays well."

"What else goes on in the office as far as you know?"

"As far as I know, nothing." DCI White looked as his partner. He shrugged.

"If I told you that we think she is involved in ... in people smuggling, would you be surprised?"

"Not really, but I think it highly unlikely!"

"Well, our evidence suggests that she is ... Or might be. And as a result of our suspicions, we intend to raid the offices tomorrow."

"Bloody hell! Why are you telling me?"

"Because we have reason to believe that you may be able to assist us. We really need to know if there are any areas in the office that may be difficult to access, or any way that staff, particularly Miss Ling, could escape from the building without our knowledge or ..."

"I'm sure there aren't. But you might have trouble getting into the offices because of the security doors. Chairman Mao is a bit tight on security ... she even keeps her door closed all the time ... come to think of it, I suspected she was running a parallel business of some sort. Always talking to Chinese people ... are they the ones you think are involved in the smuggling business?"

"Yes. And the French!"

"That figures. We do or did sometimes get a couple of French guys calling us when Ling was out. So, apart from all that, what else can I do?"

"Just make sure we get into the building would be helpful ..."

"But what about our jobs?"

"It's not what you do that interests us, just the Ling connection ... you others can carry on as normal. But are there any people in the

225

office who work closely with Ling? I mean people whom you think are working hand-in-hand with her?"

"Definitely not. All of us hate the woman. She is so rude and demanding. Trouble is, she runs the place. She's the boss."

"Maybe you ought to set up an alternative management after she's gone."

"Gone ...?"

"Yes. We have enough evidence to charge her with some serious offences ... and to keep her in custody. Is Ling's door normally locked?"

"No. But always closed. Unless someone forgets to shut the door and she's too lazy to get up and close it herself."

"Do you know where she lives?"

"No. But Alf does."

"Who's Alf?"

"He's the driver bloke. He's always having to collect or drop off some of our clients, and she makes him drive her home every day, and pick her up every morning."

"Where can we find him?"

"He hangs around the office when he's not working. Drives a proper taxi, but it's not got a plate. The car belongs to SOXMIS. Now what do you want me to do tomorrow?"

"Go to work as normal. If Ling isn't in by nine-thirty, call me. Here's my number."

"Okay. See you tomorrow." The police officers left Tussel's flat and returned to their car.

"Reckon she's on the level?"

"Yes, I do."

At half past nine the following morning, four uniformed male and one female and two plain-clothes police officers entered the Fountain Street offices. Nobody tried to stop them. No doors were locked. Two uniformed officers went to find Alf, the company driver. The others walked into Ling's office. She was sat at the smaller desk writing in a notebook. She was not on her 'phone, nor was she at her computer. She stood up as they entered her office.

"Who are you? Get out! Who let you in!" Ling was pointing at her office door, as though to show them the way out. "Go or I call the police!"

"Madam, we are police officers ..."

"Show me your cards!" The two officers obliged her. They explained why the police were there. She said nothing except to complain when she was handcuffed. Ten minutes later, the ORBIT team arrived and removed all computer and other communication equipment in Ling's office. Every other item which was not screwed down, all books and note-pads, were collected by SOC officers and taken to police HQ. The remaining staff just stood in a group and said nothing. Sonia Tussel stepped in to take control of the office. Alf, having spoken briefly to the two plain-clothed officers gave them the Chinese lady's home address and a separate team was sent to search the property and help SOCA guys remove all contents they thought would be of use. It was as easy as that. All the PC's were taken to the Freezer.

At the police station., Miss Ling was advised that she could make one 'phone call. She called Tec Martin.

"Mr Martin? I need you. Police have me in cell. I need to talk to you. You come here now!" Tec's initial reaction was 'fuck you' but he thought he could be of more use to Op China by seeing her.

"Okay, I come to see you soon." He then called Al, his boss. "Hi, Al. That Ling woman's been arrested, now she wants to see me in the police station ..."

"Right, if the Commissioner's team OK it, go. Call them direct to save time, and of course they'll have to make sure the cops let you talk to her. The team can arrange that. Let me know what happens." Tec called. The team briefed the Commissioner, who decided that the technician should go and visit the Ling woman.

When he turned up at the police station, he was expected, and led to an interview room, where Ling was already waiting. They conversed in Mandarin.

"What's going on, madam?"

"I've been bad I let the police arrest me. They tell me I have been smuggling people ..."

"Have you?"

"In a way, yes I have. I am told to give them a better life in China. I do it for Beijing. You must not tell Beijing that I'm in trouble!" Tec was always at odds with the way in which the China regime owned its population body and soul. "You are a good man. I have been left here in this horrible city alone. Beijing do not support me. You must take over my work. It is essential business."

"Madam, I cannot do that ... I have no experience in ... in whatever it is you do."

"I think you will." It sounded to Tec like a threat.

"Okay. Who do I call in Beijing?"

"Not Beijing. You have to call Xia ... Professor Xia Renchuan of Harbin Medical University." Ling scribbled a number on Tec's pad. "He's got all the information. He'll get you to work for us. I'm relying on you. I knew from the moment I saw you that you are a good man for business. He explain everything." Tec was embarrassed. He felt that the woman was psychotic and delusional. He decided to agree, rather than face the certain wrath she would doubtless direct at him and no doubt calling him a traitor to the good people of China.

"Okay, madam. I think I can earn good money helping Mr Renchuan. I will go now and call him. I tell you soon. I will tell him that you are very ill. How will he know I'm working for you?"

"He'll know because you call him. I am the only one who has this number. Go now. You have work to do!" Tec knocked on the door of the interview room and was released into the police station corridor.

"Well?"

"The woman's a nutter. Wants me to run her business. Pass this number on to the Commissioner's team. They might be able to tap into it. Then let me know what the hell you want me to do!"

The following morning, Tec got a call from the police station.

"Hi, Tec. That woman you saw yesterday, Yu Yan Ling. She's topped herself. She'd taken off her tights whilst she was in her bunk in the police cell, and wrapped them securely round her neck, then pulled her sheets over her head, and died by choking."

"Crikey, that's a bit of a bloody nuisance! nothing we can do about that. I assume you passed the number I gave you yesterday to the Commissioner's office? ... Good. I'll check in with them as I think we ought to try and tap it."

The guys at Operation China were not pleased.

"That's a fuckin' pain. I'm positive we could've wrung some info out of her."

"Possibly. But we might have another one. Got a call from the Reading office. By all accounts, one of the girls there was part of the plan to put pressure on their doctor, the Grant case, remember? It concerned the two little Chinese girls, who were killed in that car-crash a few years ago. So, they want us to pick her up. We've had an email in telling us all about the job. They want to come up and question the woman. I imagine it'll be a fact-find job first, then possibly a charge, or maybe and if she spills the beans, then a let-off. Can we do it?"

"Yes. Get on with it. Call for the Reading team to come and see us. And try and get some info from the Freezer, so we have something to throw at her. There must be tons of stuff on those computer things. Had a girl call from SOXMIS to see what's going to happen now that Ling's been arrested. I told her the woman was dead we and need any information they had on her. Also told her that she can carry on with what she was doing. Didn't seem too concerned."

"Okay with that. But let's see what the Reading blokes dig up! I'll call the computer blokes to see what if anything they've found."

They had found a lot. "Okay. Please send us a summary, not too long, and if possible, within the next two days? ...Thanks."

Willis did not get called into morning assembly. Instead he was taken by Elaine Frost to reception. She handed him two letters.

"Open them, Vic." Willis opened the first one and he read it.

"You're taking me up to form B?"

"Yes, not least because you are embarrassing some of the teachers, when you clearly know more about their subjects than they do. Especially Paul Raff! He was so embarrassed that he was thinking of punching you!"

"It was his own bloody fault! Anyway, I don't think punching me would be a very good career move for him! So I'll have to work harder in this new form?"

"I doubt it. But give it a go. Your new form takes you in as from Monday."

"Thanks. I won't let you down. I promise. I'll take it as a challenge."

"I'm sure of that. But I doubt it will challenge you in any way. Now you'd better get to your lesson. Mr Dyer. He's your greatest fan, along with George. Now open the other letter."

"Wow! it's the job advert! For the post of a P. Ed teacher! I'll get that sent to Marcel later today! Thanks!"

Mr Dyer was not happy. Form D filed into his room for another English lesson. All the pupils sat and waited for their teacher to do something. He did something eventually. He spoke.

"Quiet! ... I really fail to understand what it is about the word 'classic' that most of you appear to not understand. Classic literature means authors like Dickens, Shakespeare, Conan Doyle, R. M. Ballantyne. It means poetry such as that produced in World War one. Although a classic work to one person may not be a classic to another, there is an easily accessible definition of 'classic literature'. I doubt that many, or any of you have looked it up. The internet makes it easy. Easier, perhaps, is just to ask dad. I doubt even then you will get a proper answer. If you are going to go through life without taking any trouble to take it upon yourselves to do some research, then the information you will have in your heads fails you on several counts. Firstly, you will never rise above from those whom you seek the information. Secondly, your information will be, or will become, stale, and finally, if you can find nobody to ask, you're finished. Classics does not mean copying from Spider-Man comics. Nor is it, as one of you believes, a paragraph from Fifty Shades of Grey, that 2011 so-called erotic romance novel. You are at school to study, and to learn, not to amuse yourselves and your friends by engaging in idiotic, pathetic attempt at being funny. As I told you a few weeks ago, you don't get a second chance at school. Is there anybody here, in this room, who can give me an example of a classic novel? Before any of you answer, and I am not in the habit of picking on people, there is probably only one person who can. I am going to ask him. And the reason is, that this is his last day in this form. I for one will sincerely regret his leaving, but I know that he knows things, because he reads books. Lots of them. I want you to follow his example. I told you all, I want you to be the best form in the school. I do not want a bunch of idle slobs. Clément, please come up here and tell us what classic literature is?" Willis stood up and walked to the front of the class. He was nearly as tall as Dyer.

"Thank you, sir. A classic is an outstanding example of a style. Something of lasting worth or with a timeless quality, of the first or highest quality, class, or rank. Something that exemplifies its class. The word can be an adjective, like a classic car, or a noun, such as a classic of English literature. Let me give you some examples of what is regarded as classic literature. J D Salinger's The Catcher in the Rye; Dickens' Great Expectations; Mary Shelley's Frankenstein; Dumas' The Count of Monte Cristo; Fyodor Dostoyevsky ... Crime and Punishment. There are very many more."

"Thank you. And congratulations on your promotion!"

"Thank you, sir."

"Class, this young man has been elevated to form B. He has been here only because of an administrative screw-up, now rectified."

Linda Bishop was not happy. At lunchtime, she found Willis in his usual place, reading his usual paper. She was crying.

"Vic, you can't leave us ... leave me!"

"Linda! come here and sit down! I am not leaving you. I didn't ask to leave the form, but I have no choice ..." The girl gripped his hand.

"I want ...my dad wants me to be as clever as you are ... he says you can teach me a lot ... if you go then I will have to stay with the idiots, as Mr Dyer calls them ..."

"No you won't. Those idiots are rungs on a ladder. Use them to elevate yourself. In the next form exams, you must come top. We'll do it together!" For a moment, Willis thought she was going to kiss him. Her eyes were wet and sparkled as she looked up at him and a smile spread over her face. She really was a stunning-looking girl.

"I'll tell my dad then. He'd like that!" Willis was a bit alarmed at the idea. He knew the bloke, and there was a serious possibility that he, Willis, might somehow and unwittingly give too much away. If he was right. Bish, as everyone called him, was a large-scale importer of goods from virtually every country in the world, goods which he sold on directly from the docks into the trade at a handsome profit. But the general impression was that he was an OK guy. The bell rang again, summoning Willis and the girl to their afternoon lessons. As he and Linda walked to their next lesson, the girl addressed him again.

"Why don't you come over to my place sometime this weekend? My dad would love to meet you. But for God's sake don't do his crossword! Please say you will!" Willis was not too enamoured of the idea, but then he didn't want to upset either Linda or her dad.

"Okay. Just let me know when. Send me a text ..."

"But what if you're busy, like waiting for a call from Donald, or Vladimir?"

"Don't be ridiculous! My social and business secretaries take all the unimportant calls!" Linda had a beautiful smile and a wonderful

232

laugh.

That evening. Willis emailed the job advert to Angie, then he called her.

"If you can help Marcel complete it, I expect you can be one referee, and there's bound to be somebody else who would give him a reference."

"I'm sure there is. Anyway, how are you getting on at school?"

"Fine. They've just sent me up two streams, to the B stream, so I must be making an impression on somebody!"

"That has to be an understatement! I reckon you're blowing them away! Let me deal with Marcel. he told me he really would like a job in the UK and this suits him down to the ground. Now, any movement on the Grant and Ling case?"

"Seems that. as Ling has gone, there's nobody here they can chase, so I think they want to hand it all over to the French guy, Enzo, in Paris. I also think that Grant and Andy should get together and open up to their own guys or go and see Enzo. I expect they could help clear up quite a few matters between them."

"Sounds good to me. I think I'll just go and see Andy and be totally straight with him and get him to contact Grant."

"Okay. But remember, Marcel first ... then Andy and Grant!"

"Of course, love ... I'll keep you in the picture. Bye." Angie sent the job application to Marcel. She warned him to be 'circumspect' regarding his dealings with Vic Clément.

CHAPTER 20

Officers Sean Johnson and Tug 'Windy' Windlesham were shown into the Op China briefing room.

"I assume this is about those Chinese girls again, Tug?"

"Yes. We want to establish the relationship if any, between that Ling woman, and the girl. She was by all accounts the woman who was partially responsible for setting up the Reading doc, Grant ... it'll be interesting what she has to say about it! And of course, she might know more about what the Ling woman was up to!"

"Keep your fingers crossed on that one ... we need all we can get, now that Chairwoman Mao's dead!"

"Yeah, and who let the woman keep her tights on?"

"A sensitive point ... don't ask!"

"Anyway, what did you get from the computer kit?"

"A lot. A hell of a lot. It appears that about thirty individuals were picked up and sent to China eventually. In the UK alone, we have to look at about eleven who were taken over to France, then disappeared. All details are there. Everything's well documented. Even have copies of passports. From France, some guy Dauphin took over. I'll get full info later."

"That guy is already in police custody. The bloke handling it over there is Enzo Gabin. He's a good guy, based in Paris. Give him a call."

"Will do. Now your mystery girl."

"Yes. We don't have her real name as far as I know, but I think we could use your friend Sonia Tussel to try and get a tag on her. Could we drop in on her this evening?"

"Don't see why not!"

Sonia Tussel had just put her key into the front door of her flat, when she turned to see a familiar figure climbing the stairs to the first floor. DCI White and officers Johnson and Windlesham had been sitting in their unmarked police car across the road from the block and had seen the SOXMIS girl arrive then enter the building. White reached the landing then called out.

"Sonia. Sorry to trouble you once more, but we would like a few minutes of your time again ..."

"Oh, hello again! I have no problems with that. I suppose it's about Ling?"

"Yes and no..." White introduced Sean and Tug. "These two are from Reading. We're looking at a few issues surrounding Doctor Grant He used to be based here, in Manchester, but now working in Reading."

"Oh, right. Come on in ..." The woman walked into the flat and held the door open for the three men to follow her. "I'll just put the kettle on ... " She called from the kitchen "Anybody else for tea?" She returned to the lounge with a tray bearing four cups of tea a milk jug and a sugar bowl. "Right, fire away!" Sean produced a picture of their target, as the other two policemen stirred their tea.

"Sonia, do you recognise this person?" Sonia took the pictures.

"Yes, I do. I work with her. Nice girl."

"What's her name?"

"That's Val. Valerie Bakewell ... she is into amdram. Always wanted ..."

"Sorry, amdram?"

"Amateur dramatics. Always wanted to be an actor. But a bit naive."

"Er ... right." Sean turned and looked at the other two men. They were both grinning. "Now, do you know Doctor Grant?"

"Yes, of course. He's involved in the business, here in Manchester."

"In what capacity?"

"He's a doctor, and he refers clients to us. Or we ask him for advice. Usual stuff."

"Does ... did ... Ling have any influence over him?"

"Ling had influence over everybody ..." Sean turned to Tug, who leaned forward in his chair and looked at Sonia.

"Sonia, do you think Ling could have something on Grant such that she could force him to ... er ... break the law? Or do something which he maybe didn't or would not normally do?"

"To be blunt, almost any bloke can be forced into doing things he would not normally do. You'd be surprised how much influence a nice pair of tits or nice legs can have on a bloke, but clearly Ling has neither of those, but Val does. So ... and it was you who paired them up, I mean Valerie and Grant ... so maybe ..."

"Ah! I see where you're going on that!"

"Val might be a nice, obliging girl, but I doubt very much that she would actually ... er..."

"Well, I think that about explains things. Do you think she ... Val would be happy to clear things up?"

"What exactly do you mean ... things? Maybe I am missing something here?" Sean spoke up.

"Tug, maybe you ought to explain."

"Alright. Do you remember a few years ago a couple of young Chinese nurses were killed in a car crash ...?" The girl nodded. "Well, we think that somehow, your Ling roped Grant in on that, and made Grant think he was responsible, because he wanted to pull away from the SOXMIS operation ..."

"So, you think that Val was used somehow? I remember she said she had done a small part for a film or something ... some years ago now, but according to her, it didn't come to anything, but she was paid a few thou for doing it. Do you think that could have been it?"

"Possibly. But we'd like to talk to her, just the same."

"Okay ... I'm sure I can arrange that for you. Tomorrow be alright? We've set Ling's office up as a quiet room, so you can do it in there. How does that sound?"

"Great. Well, Sonia, you've been a great help. We'll pop in tomorrow. Thanks."

Back in the car, Sean voiced his feelings.

"Well, I don't know about you two, but I think we're gonna get nowhere on this. It's a great big flop ... so far. Anyway, it'd be nice to go and see her just the same. What do you two reckon, eh?" White looked at Tug.

"I reckon you're right. But as we're here, might as well do it. Ten tomorrow do?"

"Yeah. Then we'll get our arses back to Reading."

At five minutes past ten the following morning, officers White, Johnson and Windlesham arrived at the SOXMIS offices. Sonia met them.

"Can I help you gentlemen?" She had the wit to realise that it would not have done any good it had she appeared that the men were known to her.

"Yes, good morning. If possible, we would like to have a word with your Valerie Bakewell. We are from the Manchester and Reading police."

"Please take a seat." Sonia pointed to the chairs in the reception area. "I will call her for you." The girl moved into the main office area, and soon returned with the girl the officers were keen to talk to. The immediate impression she gave was one of being attractive, rather young-looking, but concerned about meeting the police. "Val Bakewell, gentlemen." Sonia put her hand on Val's shoulder. "Would you like me to stay with you, love? Or are you ..."

"Oh, please stay, Sonia. I have no idea what this is all about ..." Sonia looked at the officers. They seemed to indicate that the two girls could say together. White opened the questioning.

"Val ... may I call you Val? ... Do you remember an incident a few years ago when you played the part of a police officer investigating ... looking into a young man's involvement in the death of a couple of women in a car crash?"

"Oh, yes. I do! I didn't get the part, but I still got paid for it. Do you want me to tell you all about it?"

"Please do!" The feeling that DCI White had that this was not going to get them anywhere, was shared by the other two policemen.

"Well, there was this chap who had been dragged from the wreckage of a car ..."

"Were you involved in that bit?"

"No. The first time I saw him was when he was in hospital. It wasn't anywhere near here, but near London somewhere ..."

"Was Miss Ling involved?"

"She was in and out. She didn't speak to me much. But it was all very well organised. There was a Chinese doctor looking after the victim. As I understood it, there were gangsters involved, and murder and drugs I think as well ... it was great fun. I think I was on location for about four days ... the patient was sedated and had some bandages ... and was supposed to wear very dark glasses but sometimes he managed to shake them off ... so we had to replace them occasionally ... and I had to wear loads of make-up."

"Were you there when he was eventually allowed out of the hospital?"

"No."

"Did you know the name of the doctor in the hospital?"

"No. I don't think he was a real doctor. There were cameras all over the place ... and I think the production hired the room from the hospital, or something ..."

"Thank you, Val." DCI white turned to Sean and Tug. "Well, any questions you want to ask?" Sean stuck his finger into the air. "Yes, Sean?

"Two questions, Val. Firstly had you seen this patient before the filming, or subsequently?"

"No."

"Secondly, did the patient seem very ... er ...groggy? Like heavily sedated or something?"

"Oh, yes! He played his part very well!"

"Thanks. I have no more questions."

"Thanks, Val. Thank you Sonia. I think that's all"

"Can I go now?"

"Yes, Val. You have been very helpful. I think you did a grand job. Sorry you didn't get the part!" The girl stood up and left the reception area.

"What do you think, guys?" DCI White answered her.

"I think she was one hundred percent above board. Miss Ling

chose her well! I don't think she had any idea of just what the hell was going on. At least, we can cross her off the list! So what does she do here, Sonia?"

"She's part of the AI team. She occasionally has to extract ..."

"Well, I reckon she'll be good at that!" Sean interrupted her. Well, are we finished here?"

"Yes. But one more question. How are you and the other girls getting on now Ling's ... er ... moved up in the world?"

"Actually, rather well. We have an extra room, we don't have to pay her wages, and the girls are a lot happier. Well, if that's all..."

"Yes. And very many thanks, Sonia, you've been most helpful."

All three men got back into their car.

"Well, that was a bloody waste of time. But unless we did come, we would forever been asking exactly what happened to Grant. It seems Ling was an expert manipulator. However, I'd like to take that Val girl to a party ..."

"Tug! You're a married man. But I see what you mean!"

"Stop it you two! Just let's get back to the fuckin' station and get you two back onto the bloody train, and out of our hair! And if it's any consolation to you, the boss has decided that he needs to hand the whole business over to the Paris cops, so they at the very least can work out exactly what happened to the poor bastards who doubtless finished up on some operating table somewhere in China!"

"I agree. There is nobody here in the UK we can pursue. As far as we're concerned, and until something else crops up here, or from anything they find out from that French guy, we have no case against anybody. I also reckon Grant's off the hook as long as he can explain to the medical ethics board, or whatever it's called, he's innocent."

"I second that, Tug. Now let's leave Manchester to the Manchester cops, and let's get back to civilisation!"

"Hey, watch it you two ... Right, here's the station. Take care guys, and thanks for all you've done for us."

"Thanks mate, have a quiet weekend!" Officers Johnson and Windlesham made it to the platform, and hardly spoke another word until they got back to the Reading police station.

"Can you come over this Saturday, Vic? You'll be in your new class next week, and I might not see you for a while."

"Let me see. I'll have to try and get out of my invitation to Buck house, and then ..."

"Buck house?... what's that?"

"Buckingham Palace. My great-aunt Liz wanted me to pop in for a chat ..."

"The Queen? Oh, just cancel it ... If you don't, I'll have a word with Theresa for you ... I'm sure she would sort it out!"

"You, Miss Bishop, have DoG disease, aka delusions of grandeur!"

"So, you'll come?"

"Yes. I'll get Sean to drop me off."

"Oh, thanks! My dad will be pleased." Willis wasn't so sure about that. Linda was getting very tactile. She would loop her arm around his when they walked anywhere together, and always looked out for him during breaks and lunch-hours. He knew he could handle it, but he was concerned for her. A brother and sister relationship he could manage, but it just could not get any closer than that.

"Ted?" It was Sean and Rosie. "Got time for an update?" Willis had been back from school for a few hours, and Connie had just started to clear away the dinner table. He ate with Connie and her two daughters, as it was a more sociable arrangement, and it was also good for the children.

"Hi, Sean. Yes, of course. How's Rosie?"

"She's fine. Can we pop over later this evening? Quite a bit to tell you."

"That's okay be me, why don't you stay the night, both of you. Anyway, I've been invited to Linda's place on Saturday, so could you drop me off? It's only at the Common. I can walk back, of course."

240

"Okay. And it'll give the Mustang a run. Hasn't been out for a while. See you shortly.

Within the hour, Sean, Rosie and Willis were seated in the little meeting room, and Connie fussed over them as usual. Sean set out the latest position, then he summed up.

"So, until and if we get anything from France, there is nothing we can do here. All the documents and records from Ling's office seem to indicate that although she was in it up to her neck, there was nobody else involved in the UK apart from Grant, and he was more-or-less being forced into it, but even so, there is still a cause of action against him. If, that is, we choose to take it up ..."

"Then would it not be a good idea if Doctor Grant was encouraged to speak to Andy, the Milan bloke, to try and tidy up that end? From what Angie tells me, he's virtually on the point of doing that anyway, and they could both get onto the Paris cop, Enzo, and work something out."

"Sounds good to me, Ted. But I have no doubt that somewhere along the line, somebody here in the UK will have to answer for what happened to you ..."

"I imagine a civil action against the NHS would succeed, but who has the right to do that? I have an idea, but if the courts don't accept that I'm Ted Willis ... and treat me accordingly, then I'm stuffed ..."

"That looks like being the mother of all civil claims, frankly, but as you've said before, the first step is to be recognised as Ted, and if you're not ..."

"Then I'm certainly not Vic Clément! I think it'll be the most unusual case ever to hit the English legal system, and I have no doubt that there will be expensive lawyers on either side just in it for the money ... so what's changed, eh?"

"Don't worry, Ted. I don't think you should beat yourself up over it. But as you say, it's going to generate media interest all over the world. And what a story it will be!"

"No, what you mean is, there will be thousands of people who'll make a lot of money over it. Unless the hearings are held in camera. And the plaintiff can remain anonymous. But some shitbag will leak the name somewhere along the line. Well, I'm all for hitting the sack."

"Okay. What time do you want to go to this girl's house, Ted?"

"Ten, say? It's Bish's daughter. I knew the guy. He'd been here more than a few times. Nice wife. I also have a feeling that I saw the girl when she was new-born. She's certainly grown up now! And that's another thing, if I really fancied her and ever got the opportunity ..."

"Don't go there, Ted! I know where're you're going on that one! It's one hell of a can of worms!"

"I agree, Rosie. Best left alone. Anyway, as I said, I'm off to bed."

Sean pulled the Mustang into the sweeping drive at Linda's house. It was very much as Willis remembered it. He climbed out of the car, just as Linda appeared at the front door, and ran over to him giving him a big hug. He turned to Sean, who was grinning, and gave Willis the thumbs up.

"See you later. If you need a lift back, just call, okay?"

"Will do, Sean!" The yellow sports car disappeared down the drive.

"Come on, Vic! Meet my mum. Dad's busy right now, but we'll see him later. And you are going to help me do something ..."

"What exactly?"

"Not telling. Just you wait and see!" Inside the house, Linda's mother appeared and strode up to Willis. She was a very attractive, elegant lady, not looking a day older than he remembered her. She extended her hand to him.

"Vic. Welcome to Linda's home. I'm Nancy, Linda's mother." She was taller than Willis, so he couldn't kiss her, but instead, and after taking her hand, he hugged her.

"Nice to meet you, Mrs Bishop. You have a lovely house, and a lovely daughter ..." He turned to the girl who was blushing deeply.

"Vic Clément, you are a creep!"

"No, he's not, darling, he's a lovely boy too! Now you both go to the summerhouse and I'll bring some cold drinks and biscuits. The paper's in there already."

"Thanks mum. Come on, Vic ..." She took his hand again and led him out of the house across a beautiful lawn into the huge, glass summerhouse. The Rottweiler sitting in the corner in the pool of sunshine, lifted her head as they entered, and briefly wagged her tail. "That's my best friend, Jade. She's okay, but she tends to chew the post!" Willis walked over to the dog and stroked her. "Now you must show me how to do crosswords. You sit next to me and explain how it all works, okay? Then I can help daddy with his puzzles when he has time to do them."

"Linda, of course I will be happy to help you ... but it takes years to learn ..."

"Well then, you'll have to marry me, won't you?"

"What, this morning?"

"No, silly. After lunch. I'll tell mum to organise it!"

"But only if we complete the crossword first!" Willis was actually beginning to involve himself in childish banter, it was so innocent, meaningless and stupid but it was a relief from the sometimes ersatz seriousness which enveloped many adults which they used as a cloak to conceal the fact that they were themselves mostly engaged in inconsequential affairs, and sought to impress not only others, but also themselves, by this veneer of importance where their lives were in fact otherwise, and overwhelmingly, pointless.

"Do tell me that your dad doesn't have a beard or a moustache?"

"No, he doesn't. Why?"

"'Cos facial hair and tattoos and lots of jewellery on a bloke is a signal. It says 'I'm a plonker, but I try and hide the fact by having a beard or ..."

"My dad says that as well ..."

"What's that darling?" Nancy had come into the summer house with a tray of drink and biscuits.

"Vic was saying how men with beards and tattoos and jewellery were weirdos!"

"Quite right too, darling. Now I must go and deal with your dad and his guest. I'll let you finish your crossword."

"Thanks mum. After lunch Vic and I are going to get married."

"Of course, dear!" Nancy smiled and left to go back to the house.

"We have to finish the crossword first, Linda."

"Then we'd better get started!" She opened the paper to find the crossword. "Right. Where do we start?"

"One across is a good place ... let's see...!"

"Shall I read the clue?"

"No, Linda. We have to look at the words to work out an answer. Come and sit next to me. ...right, some you can look at and almost immediately work them out ... here's one. *'One dealing with gender-fluid performer'*. Ten letters. I think that is an LGBT thing ..."

"What?"

"Lesbian, gay bi-sexual and transgender stuff ..."

"Oh! I see ... sort of!"

"Right, so we can assume that gender-fluid is transgender. Now another word for performer?"

"What, like in films and stuff?"

"Right. Thespian? doesn't fit. What else?"

"Like Tom Cruise? actor?"

"Yes! so add actor to trans ..."

"Actor ... trans ... No! transactor!"

"Yes! See, it's easy! Now do one more ... before the drinks get cold ..."

"They're cold already, silly!"

"So they are! And we have loads of time, don't we! Right, the next one. *'Does one hold up one who is late'* four and six. Here I assume late means dead. Like the late Mrs Smith, or Mrs Smith, now dead."

"Who's going to hold up dead people? When is a dead person ever held up by anybody? Maybe when they are carried?"

"Like into the church for a funeral?"

"Yes! So what are they called?"

"Funeral directors ... pall bearers!"

"Yes! Brilliant! you can now have a drink and a biscuit." Willis and the girl took long pulls on their glasses of sugar-free coke and munched some biscuits. Right, one more, okay?"

244

"Yes!" Just then, they heard the summer-house door open. Willis turned to see Bish and, he assumed, his guest entering the house. Willis stood up and approached Bish. He extended his hand to the man, who took it.

"Nice to meet you, sir!"

"And you, Vic ... how did you know I was Linda's father? It could have been my friend here." Bish turned towards his guest and nodded to him. He knew immediately he was under examination.

"Quite simple, sir, by the way you opened the door and ushered your guest in first. Only the owner, or host would do that ..." Bish turned to his guest again.

"Told you, David. Sharp cookie this lad." The guest stepped forwards and offered his hand to Willis, who shook it.

"Hey, you've got quite a grip there, young man!" Bish then looked down at the table and saw the open newspaper. "Hey, you two, not doing my crossword, are you?"

"Yes, we are daddy! You always need help with it, and Vic is helping me, so I will be able to help you with yours!"

"Oh, I see! Right go ahead! Let's see you do the next clue!"

"Okay. We were just looking at twenty-three down. I'll read it. Four letters. *'Place to eat in Times Square'.* Any ideas, daddy?"

"Er ... can I see the clue please?" He bent down to look at the crossword. "Er ... no idea at all ... not really ... Vic?"

"Four letters was it? Mess? It seems to fit in with twenty-six across, *'disproportion'"*

"But we haven't done that other one, yet Vic, have we? twenty-six across?"

"No, Linda, but I did it when you weren't looking. Anyway, that's enough of school today!" Willis was quite annoyed, as he felt he had been set-up, kind of made to perform for Linda's dad. He decided to just cool things. But there was no escape. Then the guest spoke up.

"Vic, as I said you have quite a grip ... you obviously keep fit, don't you?" Before Willis could answer, Bish spoke up again.

"He does, Dave. This was the lad who punched that paedophile teacher ..." Willis knew immediately that Bish had had contact with

the school secretary, Elaine Coates.

"I didn't punch him, sir, I elbowed him. He was being ... too familiar. I used a yokoempi, a very basic elbow strike. There are ten empis in all, mae empi, age empi, yoko empi, tate empi, otoshi empi ..."

"Whatever you did, it was a damn good job ..., eh, Dave?"

"You can look after yourself then, Vic?" Willis decided it was time to finish the conversation.

"Sir, I have been looking after myself, in every respect, ever since I was born. Nobody ever did anything for me. Ever. I had to learn everything I know, both academically and physically. I never knew when to stop. It is a matter which causes me the greatest concern and upset, and ..." Willis doubted it was very wise to continue, but he intended to anyway "... and had it not been for ... Mrs Willis's interest in my case, I would not be able to now have the advantages that arise as a result of a good education ..." There was silence. Then Bish spoke up.

"I'm sorry, Vic. It really is none of my business. Shall we do one more clue, then we'll leave you alone. He picked up the paper. "Here we are ... er ...eighteen across. '*Substitute monarch posed with Zulu'*. Seven letters." Willis counted on his fingers.

"I make it six letters ... ersatz." He saw the guest's jaw drop and he turned to Bish.

"This is Quora site stuff. Quotidian ..." Willis butted in.

"You are a psychiatrist, sir? Quotidian. Middle English from *old French. From Latin quotidianus, or* cotidianus, comes from *cotidie* meaning daily." Willis thought Dave was going to pass out. He and Bish both were taken aback. The message Willis was politely trying to convey, was *'fuck off and leave us alone'*.

"Yes ... er! Yes ... Vic. You are indeed very perceptive ... now, how do you work out the crossword answer, Vic? I mean what are the thought processes, there must be a logical sequence."

"Just the same way Linda and I worked out the other ones. Look at the clues and take them apart, apply a little thinking and ... hey presto!" It seemed Dave wasn't happy with that answer.

"No, I mean ... "

"Okay. Monarch ... can probably be interpreted as ER. Posed with, say 'sat with', Zulu. Zulu is 'Z' in the phonetic alphabet. So, we have ER, then SAT then a Z. Ersatz. Or substitute. The first word in the clue. You threw me at first with the seven letters, so it was a long shot, then I realised it could be nothing else."

"Well done!"

"Thank you, Mr Bishop." Without another word, the two men left the summer house. As Willis watched them walk across the lawn to the main house, he could see they were engaged in animated conversation. He turned to Linda. She flew at him and hugged him tightly.

"Oh, Vic! I'm so sorry! I didn't want dad to come in here with that man! I wanted you to just be here with me, so we could spend some time alone. Can I kiss you?"

"Yes, Linda. But only once!" She kissed him. It was a long kiss. Then Willis pulled away. He felt things could get seriously out of hand.

"Let's do one more question, that I think you've had enough for today, okay!"

"Yes. Then we'll have some lunch, I think."

"Could I just have a pint of Guinness, do you think?"

"If that is beer, then no. However, I think dad has some stuff he gives me. looks like beer, tastes like beer, so it's okay."

"Right. Six down," Linda read, "*'Lost vegetarian goats sure to stray'*. Nine letters."

"Let's take it to bits. We need a vegetarian species. Lost probably implies that it is an extinct kind. That leaves us with what, *'goats and'*? You said nine letters, didn't you?"

"Yes. So, we can assume that the word we need is actually in those as yet unused words. As it's extinct, the words *'saur'* are in the word. So where would the remaining letters be with *'saur'*?"

"Before *'saur'*? Like dinosaur?"

"Yes! Brilliant! So, the remaining letters are g, e, t, s, and o. So if you make up a few words using those letters, then go to the dictionary and look at the words you made up, you'll find the whole word!"

"You know it, don't you!"

"Yes, I do. But I am not going to tell you."

"I don't want you to! I'll find it myself!"

"Good. That was the best answer."

"Yes, I remember what you told me the other day ..." There was a long silence, while the girl worked the pages of the dictionary. Then "Got it! Now you tell me your answer!"

"No. You write yours down first! .... Right, have you got Stegosaurus?" She had. "It's from Greek *'stegos'* which means roof and *'sauros'* which means lizard. A genus of herbivorous, thyreophoran dinosaur. Lived about a hundred and fifty million years ago, late Jurassic-Albion. Ate moss."

"Vic Clément, sometimes you could seriously piss me off! Do you know every bloody thing? Let me write it in then let's go back to the house. And what's Kate Moss to do with it?"

"Not Kate Moss ...ate moss! Like, for food."

As Bish and Dave entered the house after leaving Willis and Linda, Dave grabbed his host's arm.

"Shit, I'd love to psychoanalyse that boy!"

"No, Dave. I have a better idea. We don't know where he bloody well came from. According to Elaine, he was born in Paris. He's looked after by guardians, and he lives in Ted Willis's old house, you know, up Spinfield Lane way. I've been there dozens of times. I plan to find out exactly where the kid comes from. I don't give a fuck how long it takes, or how much it costs!"

"You'll have to import more sex-toys and wine then, Bish! Do you have a picture of him? It might help. And a date of birth."

"I can get all that from Elaine. And they're not sex toys, Dave, they are marital aids!"

"That's what I said. Sex-toys! Anyway, who's this Elaine you keep mentioning?"

"The school secretary. We get on pretty well. She looks after my Linda, and I look after her!" Bish paused for a moment, standing stock still. Then he slowly turned to his guest. "You know, Dave, there is something really funny ... really fuckin' odd going on. Old Ted. He was into that karate stuff, he got a black belt when he was in his late sixties, and he was also ... he had a really sharp brain. He never stopped reading stuff, I mean the most way-out literature, always factual, never any fiction. He was eventually banned from all those pub quizzes, 'cos his team were always winning. It's almost as though ... no, forget it."

"What? Forget what, Bish?"

"Oh, nothing. Just a stupid idea." But Bish was not utterly convinced that it was a dumb idea. But it nagged him all the same. To avoid being badgered about the 'dumb idea', Bish raised a point. "Do you think the lad found the crossword answers before he came here? I mean, he wasn't here until just after ten, so he could have, couldn't he?"

"He could, but it's very unlikely. He was able to explain his answers ..."

"Right. But if I could find a copy of the Times, say one about three or four weeks old, then gave it to him and Linda, what do you reckon the chances are of his completing it?"

"Quite high ... but you could give it a go. Why don't you find one you started but didn't finish? Ask him to complete it."

"That's a good idea. I'm sure Nancy has some stacked up somewhere. We'll spring a little trap on him next time he comes here!"

It was late afternoon when Willis left Linda's house to walk home. He'd had a longish chat with Bish and Linda's mum, and had toured the house and gardens. He had no doubt that Bish was a straight guy, but he felt, too, that the bloke was not entirely happy about him. He resolved to keep away from the Bishop residence for a while. And to watch what he said to Elaine Coates.

249

When Willis had gone, Mr Bishop ambled over to the summer house. He picked up his Times, and as he turned away to return to the main house, he saw a small pad on which his daughter and Willis had sketched out ideas for the crossword. He noted that for an eleven-year old, the lad's writing was extraordinarily mature. He slowly straightened up and gazed through the summer house windows focussing on nothing in particular. Then he raised both hands to his head.

"Fuckin' hell!" He almost ran back to the house. "Nancy! Nancy have you got any of those old invitations to Ted Willis's old place? Have you?"

"Of course, darling. In the albums. Why? What's up?"

"Er ..." He did not want to share his idea with her in case it alarmed her or Linda. "Nothing, dear. Just wanted to ... just wanted his postcode, that's all!" Bishop dodged into the office where all the albums were stacked on the shelves, shut the door behind him, and lifted down an album. His third selection contained all the various invitations he and his wife had ever had, including those from the Willis's, at Oaklands. He compared the handwriting. There was no mistake. It was identical to the scribbles on the pad he had found in the summer house. He started to shake. It was almost violent. He moved over to the drinks cabinet, poured himself a stiff whiskey, and sat in his armchair. He sat for a while with all kinds of utterly unreasonable, impossible thoughts racing through his head. Why do I need to get involved? If I am right ... I just can't be right. His last thought clinched the deal. With his daughter's help, he could make a tidy sum out of all this. Then he spoke aloud.

"Right, Vic, or is it Ted, where the fuck do we go from here?"

"In the new class on Monday? I'm sure you'll find it more to your intellectual ability, Ted, but somehow I doubt you would be at all put out even if you were at university!"

"Rosie, your faith in me is not misplaced, I hope. What I am more concerned about is, first of all, will Marcel get the job at the school, and secondly, what the hell is happening about those two teachers and their dirty going-on, any idea Sean?"

"Yes. We passed it onto our sex-crimes people, and I gather they have been busy on it. The hardest thing is to get all the poor kids identified, then get onto the parents, take statements, all the usual crap. It takes time, and in the meantime the blokes are out on bail. No doubt it'll crop up soon. Anyway, more to the point, how was the visit to Linda's place?"

"It was okay. However, I think I over-cooked it a bit. She got me to help her with the Times crossword, then dad popped in with some guest bloke, turned out to be a psychiatrist or something. Anyway, I think they're both a bit sus about me. Maybe I ought to give it a break, like not go there for a while, then maybe they'll have forgotten about all the crossword nonsense. What do you think? ... Anybody?"

"I think you ought to be natural. Do what you want. To be frank, Ted, you ain't going to hide it forever, so just enjoy it."

"You could be right. I am what I am, and even if the whole thing blows up what the hell difference will it make? The big issue is ... getting the courts to accept me as Ted Willis and allow me to do all the things I could do before the, you know, before the incident."

"What you have to bear in mind, Ted, is that you are currently below the age of criminal responsibility, so you can get away with all sorts of things. At the moment. But if they, by which I mean the courts, return you to the status quo, that'll go out of the window!"

"So, if Linda and I wanted to have sex ..."

"Do it now!"

"Sean!"

"Well, Rosie, it's true!"

"Maybe ... but you don't have to put it in such crude terms, do you!"

"How would you put it, Rosie?"

"I probably wouldn't put it at all. Ted. You just have to work things out for yourself!"

"Okay, then, what if I wanted to have sex with Linda's mum? Would she be prosecuted if I did?"

"Look you two, there are far more important issues to be settled before anything like that arose. So concentrate on them."

"I think you're right. In fact, I think everybody's right. We just concentrate on different issues, that's all."

"Well said. Now I think Connie and the girls are ready for some food."

CHAPTER 21

"Victor Clément!" Willis knew it was the school secretary, who, it appeared to him, was now the boss at Statton Grammar, at least until a new headmaster was appointed. The school secretary walked up to him and placed a hand on his shoulder. "Morning. Two things. Here's your programme for form B. Your form teacher is Mr Westbrook. He's a science teacher. And your friend Marcel de Longé has sent his application for P. Ed vacancy. Looks ideal candidate, but we'll have to see who else applies. How was your visit to Mr Bishop's house?" The woman immediately knew she should not have asked that, as it meant to all but the dullest, which Victor most certainly was not, that she and Bishop had a kind of 'special relationship'. Vic knew that anyway, so he was not surprised by the question. He turned it to his advantage, however.

"Ah! Yes. It was okay. Mr Bishop seems keen for Linda to move up a form or two as well. We spent a lot of time looking at crosswords. And I think Mr Bishop regards me as being a little ... a little odd? I can't understand it!"

"Nonsense! I'm sure he likes you. You'd better go now, you're in room seventeen." Elaine Coates knew damn well Bishop thought the pupil was odd. But Bishop had not confided in anybody just how odd he thought the boy really was.

Willis knew that he was going to have a hard time in his new class, initially, anyway. As always, when a new boy arrives at school and after all the classes had settled in with each of their classmates, the new arrival could generate curiosity, resentment or

even, if he shows any nervousness or other weakness, become a target of the class bullies. Willis had no concerns about anything which came his way. When Peter Westbrook introduced him to the class, he saw almost immediately who he had to watch. They were the ones who were leaning back in their chairs, one arm dangling down on one side, the other hand on the desk, playing with a pencil or pen, and with a kind of smirk on their faces. He picked out three, all sitting close together. Also, it didn't help that some of the girls were elbowing each other, which to him meant *'Hey girls - I fancy a bit of that!'* which doubtless engendered in some of the other boys another reason to 'get at' the new boy. In fact, Willis was looking forward to *'being got at'*. His desk was at the front, which suited him. The register was called, then the bell rang indicating
that the form had to move to their first lesson of the day.

At lunchtime, after a series of lessons which Willis found were of an academic standard seemingly no more challenging that in his earlier form, he took up his usual place outside, eating his sandwiches and reading the paper. He was hoping that Linda would turn up, but instead he noticed out of the corner of his eye, three of his new classmates approaching. He ignored their advance, apart from making the usual observations as to who the ring-leader was, their sizes, and of his own readiness to respond to any attack. He concluded that he was ready and waited until they or one of them made a move. The biggest and the ugliest was the one who made the first move. As far as they were concerned, the new boy had not observed their approach. Willis's legs were stretched out on a small area of concrete, his back to the wall. He appeared to the boys that he was still reading, and oblivious to their presence. Then he heard one of them call out.

"Go get 'im, Nick!" Nick approached Willis, then stopped in front of him. His feet were about two feet apart, with one leg to the left of, and his other leg to the right of Willis's own right leg. He said nothing, but then 'Nick' started to throw peanuts, one at a time, at

Willis's paper. Behind him, his mates sniggered. Nick spoke.

"Wanna peanut, mate? They're good for you!" Willis looked up at the thug.

"I'm sorry, Nick, they're not gonna be good for you if you continue to throw them at me!"

"What are you gonna do about it then? You're the clever fucker ain't ya? Go on, cunt, fuckin' stop me!" His mates sniggered again.

"Look, please don't be so tiresome." As Willis spoke, he gently moved his left foot to make contact with Nick's right shoe and planted his heel firmly on the ground. Nick turned to his mates.

"Hey, guys, I'm being fuckin' tiresome!" Willis suddenly lifted his right leg and dug his heel sharply into the liver key point nine, the pressure point located half way between the knee and the crutch. The intention was to create intense pain. Nick's reaction did not disappoint. With Willis's left leg anchoring Nick's right foot, the young thug squealed in pain, and he fell sideways onto his right shoulder, his head also striking the ground. His shoulder was dislocated. And it really hurt him. The lad lay still, but his mouth was busy.

"What the fuck 'ave you done! I'm hurt! Help me!" Willis stood up and called to the other two.

"Hey! Come and help your mate! I think he's hurt!" As Willis approached them, they ran away across the playground. Willis picked up his bits and pieces, then bent down to speak into Nick's ear.

"I told you, Nick. Peanuts can be bad for you." Then he walked away.

The bully was not at any more lessons that day. Or for a while afterwards. Then Willis was called to reception for the inevitable interview. It was Linda again.

"What the hell have you been up to, Vic?"

"Nothing, why?"

"You apparently injured our school bully. Well done. The whole episode was observed. We think your response was wholly

justified. Provocation. Hopefully you won't ever have to do that again."

"I hope so too." When Willis had gone, Elaine Coates called Bishop.

"Hi, Elaine, what's up?"

"Victor. He's just beaten up that Nick Bourne kid, the bully who was trying to mess with your Linda ..."

"What did Vic do to the little shit?"

"Gave him a really bad cut on the head and seriously dislocated his shoulder."

"Make him head prefect! Sounds like a grand job to me. How's Vic?"

"Totally unmarked."

"What was the Bourne bloke doing to the lad?"

"He and two of his mates were chucking peanuts at him, by all accounts. Somehow, the kid suddenly fell over, and landed on his head and right shoulder. The whole thing was witnessed by a member of staff. When Vic stood up, the other two ran off."

"Sound even better."

"Yes, but what about Bourne's dad? He's a thug of the first order. He'll be round here soon demanding to see Vic ..."

"I can take care of him. That is, if Vic doesn't! By the way, that bloke from Italy. The one you might employ to replace Harper? What's his connection with the boy?"

"Marcel? If I remember correctly, he let Vic use his gymnasium at the hospital in Milan, where he works now. Vic was there for quite a while, actually." Bishop immediately saw an opportunity to gain further information about Vic's past.

"How does his CV look?"

"Actually, very good. He's also quite a hunk. He and his wife own a guest house near Paris, and he speaks good English, French and Italian, and he is a qualified ski instructor, so possibly we can get the ski holidays sorted out again. So he'll be a damn good all-rounder."

"So why did they stop in the first place?"

"Because that wimp we sacked for his unhealthy interest in

children, didn't know how to ski, and he didn't want to look silly, so he cancelled them!"

"Then employ this guy, Marcel ..."

"I can't just ..."

"Of course you can. When he comes for interview let me know. As a school governor, I ought to have a say, especially in view of the mess made by Harper and Dyson!"

"Very well. I'll let you know when he comes over."

"Right. Something else. And this is strictly between you and me. There's something very disturbing about that boy. I knew old Fred Willis, whose house the boy now occupies, and the boy seems to have all his traits, mannerisms, high level of intelligence ... did you know, he was banned from all the pub quizzes round here? He knew all the bloody answers, and on Saturday, he was showing Linda how to do the crossword ..."

"So? What's odd about that?"

"It was the bloody Times crossword, Elaine, the bloody Times crossword ... I can't do it! The brat's eleven bloody years old for God's sake!"

"Well I can tell you, he's seriously disturbed a number of teachers here ... some are threatening to refuse to teach him!"

"That's stupid! But I intend to find out everything I can about him. I don't care how long it takes, either. Do you have a copy of his passport?"

"I do, but ..."

"Just send me a copy ... I've got to start somewhere. I think the Marcel guy will be helpful..."

"But don't link me in with that ... I wouldn't be at all surprised if quite a few other people have an interest in him as well, and I cannot afford to tangle with them!"

"Ted!" It was Rosie. "Angie called when you were at school. Marcel has been invited to attend an interview. He's coming over here with his wife and with Angie. I've taken the liberty of assuming that you would accommodate them here? At Oaklands?"

"Hey, yeah! No problems with that! Any dates yet?"

"Yes. They arrive in four days' time and will be here for two days. What I think we could do is get Sean and me over there as well, to just have an update on things at this end. I've asked Angie to fill me in on what Grant is doing with Andy, and also she has some info on various loose ends, okay?"

"Of course, so I'd better get Connie and Alf to work on the meals and drinks plan. She loves all these meetings, and I think your idea is brilliant. And one more thing. That Bishop bloke. I think he smells a rat. I over-did it a bit when I was at his house with Linda, and he seems well-in with Elaine, the school secretary, so I must be careful about what he gets out of me. Anyway, I'll keep you informed of issues if he gets a bit too close."

"Makes sense. In the meantime, I'll get on to Connie if you can agree everything, 'cos we don't want her to have to race around at the last minute!"

Sean had the floor. Present were Rosie and Angie, with Marcel and his wife, and Willis.

"Right. Miss Ling. We understand that if the activities she was up to were sponsored by the Chinese government, which is highly likely, then we may have an entitlement to seize their asset in Manchester, being the office block, and also possibly the flat Ling lived in depending on whether she or the Chinese government owned it, or whether it was just rented. By all accounts, it is quite a palatial place! There are no other avenues to pursue in the UK as far as we know. The French police are chasing up the information we passed to them. Your Enzo, Marcel, seems a good guy. We know Grant and Andy are talking to each other. It's just possible that Grant must take the rap for what he did, but with the extenuating circumstances, and the fact that Ted would probably not have survived the punishment he took at the hands of those thugs in Reading, and by the way one of them is still at large, he might be lucky. But it's touch and go. I have no idea what the situation is with Andy, but that's not our business. Any news on that, Angie?"

"No. But I do know that he is worried. He acted in good faith, but his real crime if you like, was signing Ted's death certificate, and knowing that the guy was still alive ..."

"Again, that's not our business. But it might be of some value to the French cops if Andy were to send them the files he got from the Harbin place, as it might let them to work out exactly what happened to the poor kids and others who went to the operating theatre ... what took place one can hardly imagine. Could you suggest that, Angie?"

"Yes, I certainly will. Have you got anything to add, Ted?"

"Nothing, really. But if you get this job, Marcel, it won't be too long before the staff at the school will tie you in with me. What you tell them is up to you. However, I understand from our Bish ... by the way old Bishop and I knew each other long ago, and his daughter has taken rather a shine to me, could be taking a keen interest in me ... a pretty close interest too! He's no dummy, and with his money he could dig quite deeply into my past. I don't think anything we say will stop him, except that the more we try to put him off, the more determined he will be ... "

"So, how do we play it, Ted?"

"I suggest we just go along with him. Don't forget he will be looking at Vic, not at me ... yes, Marcel?"

"What if he asks me, Ted?"

"Answer his questions honestly, but do not volunteer information apart from what the asks. As a cop, Sean, does that make sense to you?"

"Yes, it does. But if he finds out the whole story ...?"

"If I know Bish, he'll want to earn money from it. However, his daughter Linda is the biggest thing in his and Nancy's life, so Linda will try and put the brakes on that if it means she will lose me. And besides, I've undertaken to get her into the same stream as me ... and that means me and her spending a lot of time together in the next six or so months ..."

"And what if he manages to find out exactly who Vic is and

where he comes from? It could be opening a can of worms ..."

"It might, Angie, but on the other hand, I expect that at least one of his parents was pretty upset when the baby was dumped. And I for one would like to know the circumstances of how that came about! As I understand it, the name on my label or whatever it was tied to me, was Victor Clément ... now as those are two Christian names in France, maybe it was a clue as to who the father was? Does that make sense, Marcel?"

"It does indeed!"

"And as you guys have my DNA stuff, maybe that'll be somewhere to start?"

"So, Ted, if this Bish bloke should go that far, should I just refer him to you, Angie? Bearing in mind what Ted has just said?"

"If Ted is agreeable, then yes."

"I am. I would really like to know ..."

Marcel may or may not have been the best candidate of all the applicants, even though there were only a few, but with all the school secretary's votes, and all of Bishop's, he was the clear leader. He was appointed. His estimated start date was eight weeks after interview to allow for all the usual checks to be made. Accommodation was provided. Marcel was delighted.

"Linda?"

"Yes dad?"

"That manifesto, the one done by young Victor ... do you think it should be put onto Facebook and all that other social media stuff?"

"Why?"

"Because for an eleven-year old, it shows a remarkable degree of understanding of not only UK but also international affairs ..."

"Won't you have to ask Vic about that?"

"We won't use his name. We'll just ask for comments. I expect that some will be stupid, but others might be more positive."

"I still think we should ask him, though."

"Alright, ask. Let me know what he says." Bishop had every intention of putting it out on the media sites, whether the boy agreed or not. He knew that sooner or later, somebody would find out the name of the author, and that was when he could start to work on the lad's background. He would still be happy with the opening paragraph of the manifesto, which started with the thought-provoking assertion that *'The only law we need in this country is ... the law of common sense...'.* It had been buzzing round Bish's head ever since he read it, and the more he thought about it, the more he realised how profound it was, and try as he might, he could find no situation where an application of common-sense would not solve a problem or prevent one arising. He doubted he would include the whole manifesto, as it ran to three thousand words, over six pages. He would be selective.

"Sir, I am not trying to be awkward, I promise you. I do not believe in your god. It's simple." Willis had chosen his day of protest and had been sitting at his usual place in the playground reading his homework answers for the first lesson of the day. And he had chosen that day because he knew the first lesson was RE.

"I'm sorry, but you will attend morning assembly and prayer."

"No sir. I will be happy to attend assembly, but I will not join in prayers or hymn singing."

"Yes you will, boy."

"No, sir, I will not."

"What's your name, boy?"

"My name is Clément, sir. And with respect, addressing me as 'boy' is redolent of Dickens' time when boys were beaten for minor misdemeanour's, or indeed, no misdemeanours at all, as you are no doubt aware if you have ever read the author."

"Clément? ... Clément ... I should have known. Of course I have read Dickens. Follow me to assembly."

"I will, sir, but I will not remain for prayers ..."

"You will because I shall prevent you from leaving the hall."

"If you are suggesting that you will physically restrain me from leaving, then frankly sir, that is ill-advised." William Pitts, the Religious Education teacher glared at Willis.

"Very well er ... Clément, I will pursue this later!"

"Of course, sir. Thank you." Willis sat down again and continued reading his homework. When the morning assembly finished, Willis walked to his first lesson.

"Right, everybody, settle down! Quiet!" When the room was silent, Pitts spoke.

"How many of you here do not believe in God?" No hands were raised. "Clément? I thought you were a non-believer?"

"Well firstly, sir, your question was somewhat difficult to interpret. I believe that you should have specified which god you meant. For example, the Hindu religion probably has millions of gods and goddesses, approximately three hundred million, by some accounts, plus the pantheons of famous mythologies which number about one hundred and forty, and the God of Abrahamic religions. So, if you had meant the god the Christians believe in, there is only one and you should have asked that specific question. According to some estimates, there are roughly 4,200 religions in the world and the word 'religion' is sometimes used interchangeably with 'faith' or 'belief system', but religion differs from private belief in that it has a public aspect ... so if I were to ..."

"That's enough!"

"But sir, I have not finished yet ..."

"I will hear no more! many men have died for their belief in God, Clément ..."

"I believe so, sir, but a thing is not necessarily true because a man dies for it ..."

"Is that one of your little sayings, boy?"

"No sir. It comes from Oscar Wilde. And Albert Einstein said *'Learn from yesterday, live for today, hope for tomorrow. The important thing is not to stop questioning'*. Einstein, sir, a German theoretical physicist. Born 1879. Died in 1955. I am merely questioning, sir." Pitts was clearly very angry. There was no sound in the class.

"If you do not want to listen to my lesson, then you had better leave the classroom!"

"Not at all, sir. I am perfectly prepared to hear your arguments in favour of your god. I am not a bigot." Pitts ignored Willis's last comment. In fact, the teacher ignored Willis for the whole lesson. But the boy listened intently to what Pitts was saying.

The end-of-class bell rang. The pupils stood up and left the classroom to go to the next lesson.

"Hey, Vic! Well fuckin' done mate! That Pitts is an arsehole. A real sarcastic bastard. You put him in his place! Fuckin' brill!"

"Glad you approve guys! But I expect he'll go bitching to the school head. If they had one! Anyway, let's leave it there, shall we? Thanks for your support."

Willis was right. Pitts burst into the school secretary's office.

"Bloody hell, Elaine! You know some kid called Clément?"

"Yes. What's he done now?"

"What's he done now? Just humiliated me in front of the class! Spouting all that anti-Christian stuff! I'm sure he makes it up ... If I didn't ..."

"William! Calm down! For one thing, he does not just make it all up. He is absolutely genuine. Do not ever argue with him. He'll rip you to shreds..."

"But he also refused point-blank to go into assembly, said he would get up and leave when the prayers and hymns started. When I told him ..."

"William! You will not win. Leave him alone. Discuss things with him by all means, but do not try to be smart with him. For a guy who can quote acres of Shakespeare, who does the Times crossword, you ain't got a cat in hells chance of ..."

"He does what? You're bloody joking!"

"No, I'm bloody not. Please, do not try it on with Victor Clément!"

"What's with the kid?"

"Good question. He's not a kid ... anything but. But that's another story. You've made your point, there's no more to say! And take a lesson from this. Be a little more laid-back. Relax. Don't take everything so seriously, okay?" Pitts turned on his heel and walked out. The secretary made a mental note to ask the boy what he'd been up to.

"Mr Bishop?"

"Yes, speaking."

"Bob Nathan here, Weatherly and Tuck. You spoke with my secretary recently regarding the late Frederick Marshal Willis?"

"That's correct. Did you find the information I wanted?"

"Yes, we have all the information you requested. We'll write to you, of course, but we have established that he left his entire estate to a Victor Clément. Estate value was around ten million give or take ..."

"Was that a young lad? Any idea of age?"

"No. But of course, if the beneficiary were a minor, then the estate would be held in trust ..."

"Was there an address for him?"

"No address given for the beneficiary ... but the deceased lived at some place in Marlow ..."

"Is it possible to obtain a copy of the will?"

"Of course. We could obtain a copy now probate, or rather letters of administration, has been granted. I'll get onto it immediately. And I'll put all this in writing shortly with our fee note."

"Thanks, that information is really useful. You've been very helpful, thanks."

"Not at all, Mr Bishop. I am glad that we have been of assistance."

A letter containing a copy of the will arrived a few days later. Bishop took it to his office where he had a file marked 'VC' and which contained a copy of the boy's passport. The will gave him no more information that what the solicitor had already told him. He decided the next step was to find out who applied for the passport and their relationship to the boy. He picked up the 'phone and dialled a Paris number.

"Roland? Bish here ..."

"Hi. The wine has already been dispatched ..."

"I'm not interested in the fuckin' wine. I need a favour. I have a copy of a French passport here. I need to know who applied for it ... it was for a child. Is that possible?"

"Anything's possible. Which office dealt with the application? It'll be bottom right, on one of the pages, I think ..." Bish looked at the document.

"Paris, I think ..."

"Email a copy to me. When do you need the information, Bish?"

"Yesterday."

"As usual. I can do last Wednesday, but yesterday might be tough!"

"Just get on to it, okay? The sooner the better."

"You'll pay?"

"Of course. Just don't top it up with your extortionate fees, right?"

"Okay. send the info to me and I'll get onto it as soon as it arrives." Roland put the telephone down and reached across his desk for his 'phone book. The merchant was nothing if not organised and knew every dodge bloke in town. He did not list names in his book, but professions. He flicked through to *'Passeport'*. Nothing. He went to *'Escroc'* and picked out a few names. Then to *'Faveur'*. One of the two names came up again. He picked up the 'phone once more.

"Marianne! Roland here! How are you my lovely! I need a job ... no, darling, that's just your filthy mind ... but we'll do that some other time ... I need someone in the passport office ... of course I'll pay. It's for my UK dealer. So it's urgent ...I don't care how you do it, just get onto the guy who brings in all your girls ... he's bound to know someone there who deals in all your bent documents ... I'll email a copy of the passport to you. Need to know who applied on behalf of the holder ..."

"Why didn't he apply?"

"He was a kid, apparently, so he couldn't, could he! Still is. I'll give you three days. Just do it ... same to you, love ..." He knew she would do the job. Bringing in to France the number of girls she did, all with bent passports, she must have someone who worked in the passport office. It was his best bet. And Bish was the last person he wanted to upset.

Marianne got back to Roland within hours.

"Hi, love. The passport was obtained by some guy called André Marais. Gave an address as SOS Children's Village at Plaisir."

"That was quick. You can forget half of the money you owe me for the booze bill. And by the way, when is the next party?"

"No good you knowing that, mate ... you ain't invited to the next one. You got too familiar with the girls. And, by the way, that André Marais bloke ..."

"Yes, what about him?"

"Somebody whacked him. drowned him in the *Etang de Saint-Quentin.* Rumour has it that it was some fuckin' crook by the name of Dauphin, now in jail facing charges of people trafficking ..."

"Not Pierre Dauphin?"

"That's what I heard ..."

"Did he work for you?"

"No. And mainly because he was getting them out of the country, and usually it was youngsters. He had that bloody woman cop, Bonfasse, Adele Bonfasse, in his pocket, and she's also in the can. I'd just hate to think of her getting her fat fingers into the pants of the kids! Poor bastards!"

"She's a big girl! So, any more about what this bloke was up to?"

"Look mate, I've got you the info you wanted, right? Any more you pay me up front ... I can come over tonight. The information I have is more or less as a direct result of my supplying your expensive hooch to half the cops in Paris ... tongues wag when they've been close to a wine glass!"

"You're a hard one, Marianne! Get your arse over here tonight!"

"Do you want me to bring one of my girls over?"

"No, you'll do!"

"Have both of us ... you're paying!"

Roland called the Plaisir children's home. He pretended to be a police officer needing information to cross-check with a person who claimed to be his mother. The information was freely given.

Roland had a headache in the morning. He found the two women still in his bed when he woke up. He prodded them into wakefulness.

"Right, you two! Fuck off! This ain't a bloody bed and breakfast joint!" He pulled his dressing gown over his naked body and went downstairs to his office, leaving the women to shower and dress. The night had been fruitful. Bish would be pleased with all the info he had elicited from Marianne before she collapsed into his bed. She and the young Polish girl she had brought with her had been equally entertaining. The night had cost him a lot of good wine, and a thousand Euros. He sat in front of his computer and started work on an email. It began *'Bish; re our last conversation ...'* With a few breaks for coffee, and after about an hour's work on the email, Roland was satisfied. He clicked *'send'.* The email dropped into Bishop's in box. It was opened at lunchtime the same day.

Bishop read the email three times. It seemed too detailed to have been made up, and in any event, he knew that Roland would have obtained the information from sources he knew and trusted. The next step was to engage a DNA detective. But he needed a DNA sample. He would need saliva or blood samples, he had no idea which, so he decided to engage the specialist tracing agents, then follow their advice. He called his Paris warehouse manager. In view of the fullness of the information Roland had passed to him, he thought that his wine wholesaler's contacts were probably not the ones he really wanted to deal with. The man was shit-hot on wine ... but the company he kept was probably best avoided.

"Jacques! Hi, Bish. I need a favour. Can you let me have the names of a couple of DNA detectives in Paris? You know, the guys who can work out where a person came from, genetically speaking?"

"Why, Bish, have you forgotten who you are?"

"No, cheeky! It's just that Nancy wants to start getting into the family history in a big way, and she apparently has connections in

Paris somewhere ..." Bishop didn't want to have to explain anything which would seem a bit unusual, and anyway, what he did with the DNA people was nobody's business but his own "... so I'm just trying to help her."

"Okay, I'll get someone onto it today. When will you be over here again? Don't forget we've got all the new stuff in now, so ..."

"Yeah, send the dates ... I'll bring the family over, okay?"

"Of course. The new wine release should be a good show. I'll get back to you shortly. Chow!" The parties rang off. Bishop made a note on his VC file. He was starting to make progress. He was just leaving his office when a thought struck him. He searched for a web page on *'Ancestry & DNA Detectives'* and left the one he liked best, open on the screen. He knew Linda sometimes used his PC to do her homework, and if she saw the site she might ask if she or the family could do an ancestry search. He would then suggest that she and her new boyfriend both do one. He thought the boy could hardly refuse. He set up the PC then left for his trip to Willesden to seal a big order for marital aids. If he knew his clients, he would be back long after his daughter arrived home from school.

Bishop's plan worked. He got back late, but his daughter was in her pyjamas cradling a cup of Ovaltine.

"Daddy! Are you going to find out if we are related to somebody famous? Like Nelson or Hitler?" Then Nancy butted in.

"Heavens, darling, she hasn't stopped going on about this since she got home from school! Put her out of her misery, please!"

"Well, I was thinking about it, because a friend of mine did it recently and he had relations all over the world. So, if everyone is agreeable, I can of course ..."

"Oh, yes! I might have brothers and sisters in nice places like the Caribbean, or even Russia!"

"Well, I damn well hope not! But maybe distant cousins or something" added Nancy.

"Okay, okay! I'll deal with the application tomorrow if I get time. Who knows, you might even be related to your young man, Victor."

"Hey, that'd be nice! Shall ..."

"No, love, I don't think it would be all that nice, but if you want me to do his ancestry stuff, you'll have to ask him yourself."

"I will! I will tomorrow!"

"And if he agrees, we'll need a sample from him."

"A sample of what!"

"Saliva, Nancy, just saliva. What had you in mind, blood?"

"No, not exactly! ... Right, now get off to bed or you won't have a tomorrow!" When Linda had gone to bed, Nancy tackled her husband. "You're a crafty bugger! It's really that boy you want to look at, isn't it! Ever since he came here, you've been walking around like a dog who's lost his bone."

"You ain't wrong, love. There's something about him and old Ted Willis, you remember him of course. The boy is either a son or a very close relation ... the two are practically identical in everything except looks ..."

"I know what you mean. And he's a smashing looking kid. If I were Linda's age, I'd ..."

"I know. You'd do just what Linda's doing, wouldn't you!"

"Yes, I bloody well would!"

As soon as Linda broached the subject, Willis knew exactly what Bish was up to.

"Just think, Vic, we could be related! We could be brother and sister ..."

"Definitely not ..."

"Or maybe related to a famous person like Tom Cruise, or Theresa May ..."

"I think Tom Cruise is a jerk! And I don't want to be associated with the prime minister, either!"

"Who would you like to be related to then?"

"I'd just be happy to ... to find my mum and my dad."

"You mean you don't know who your mum and dad are?"

"Right. But it's a long story. Well, I do, and I don't. But it's a bit complicated really ..."

"Oh, you poor thing ..."

"Yes, that's right. I'll have to ask Sean and Rosie ..."

"Are they your parents?"

"Well, again, Linda, yes and no. As I said, it's a little bit complicated. Can I tell you tomorrow? About whether I can do this thing with you? As I'm a minor, I have to get permission to do these things, okay?"

"A minor?"

"Yes. That means I am under eighteen."

Pitts was not going to let his humiliation go without getting back at Victor Clément. He had a plan. As form B filed into the class for the next RE lesson, he was ready. When he saw Clément take his seat, he actually felt nervous.

"Morning. Today I am going to talk about our beliefs, and God's messages to mankind. We know He created heaven and earth. We know He performed miracles and that he is a jealous god. His words, *'Thou shalt worship no other god but me ...'* " He expanded on the subject, rambling on for virtually the whole lesson. Willis felt a bit sorry for the guy and was a little alarmed when he insisted that *'the only book we need for life, is the bible'*. Then he set homework. "I want you ... all of you ... to go away after this lesson and next week, we will each stand up and tell the class why we believe, or maybe in some cases, why we do not believe. Not just in God, but the particular form of your beliefs. Some of you may be Muslims, or Jews, or Christians. You should talk without notes. Each of you will talk for no more than five minutes. You can of course ask your parents for help. Have you all understood that? Good. And after each one of you has spoken, any member of the class can ask you questions. Is everything clear? Good" The second bell rang. Form B filed quietly out of the classroom.

"What a cunt! Why the hell should we waste time on that?"

"I think you should. It'll give you the chance to tell him that you think religion is all bollocks. It takes guts to do that, but I wonder how many of the class will? And for the blokes who say they believe it all, how many are actually telling the truth?"

"Yeah, that's a point. I'm gonna spread the word. Everybody has got to be honest."

"It's good training for life. If you're honest, you can't go wrong. If you tell lies, you'll never remember what lies you've told, so it gets easy to trip you up, okay?"

"Yeah, makes a lot of sense to me, Vic! I'm going to ask the class who actually believes, and those who don't, then I'm going to put my findings into my talk somehow. That'll catch them out!"

"It will. But don't name names. Don't need to. They'll know themselves who they are, and they'll learn something!"

"Bloody hell, Vic! You're a fuckin' wizard!"

"Very possibly, Mike, maybe I am!"

"Rosie, remember me telling you about Bish? I was right. His daughter, or more likely he, has suddenly become interested in family history, and Linda asked me if I wanted to have her dad look at my side, by which I think he really wants to look into my DNA to find a match ..."

"Why not let him? Sooner or later you are no doubt going to do the same, surely?"

"You're right, and I'm not too bothered but all I am worried about is if he finds something, will he involve me and, more to the point, bloody well broadcast it all over the place? He can make money out of anything!"

"The decision is yours, of course."

"I'd like to bet that it was the mother who dumped me. And that I was illegitimate, and that the father was either a penniless moron or had some interest in keeping his son away from his house ... or his friends and employer. And that the mother was very probably married to somebody else or was an employee of the father. Why else would she dump me? I'd really like to know. So, all in all, I'm happy for him to go for it."

"That's settled then. By the way, Grant and Andy have passed to the Paris police all the stuff they got from China. Angie reckons that with that info and the stuff found in the Ling raid, the whole picture will come out. Some of the people they dealt with were apparently useless for their purposes, so they disappeared. Others ... finished up probably exactly where you did. But they didn't get home. Ever!"

"Much as I suspected. Now what happens?"

"They've got loads of people in custody, another lot on bail and it's going to take the judges ages to decide if there are any cases to answer ... and of course there are."

"So where does Grant stand?"

"No idea. It'll be the subject of an investigation and as soon as Sean's boss gets the word, he'll move in on him. It'll be months, probably, before anything happens on that front, anyway. And a message from Sean. The thug who attacked you has been given fifteen years. Manslaughter."

"You are kidding me! He'll be out in a couple of years! What I ought to do is get Sean's guys to do an artist's impression of the other little shit who attacked me. Couldn't do it at the time, could I?"

"Good idea! I'll mention it to him ..."

"Another thought, Rosie. Do you think I should meet with your Steve Grant?"

"Well, I don't really know. I suppose that if you pursue your court action, a meeting is inevitable."

"Is that a yes or a no?"

"it's a definite maybe ..."

"Does he know your involvement with me?"

"No, I don't think he does ... but he will learn about it sooner or later, that's for sure."

"Why don't we arrange a visit? Or even better, why not get him over here? I don't think you need worry about your position at the hospital. However, there is one drawback and that is, if he is going to be the subject of any proceedings by either the police or the NHS, then maybe we should not meet?"

"Yes, Ted, I think that is the best option. However, I only think it reasonable that we have aired the issue."

"That's it then ... if he finds out of your involvement by other means then at least we would not have been in any way responsible for that. I think we should leave it. He will of course be referred to in my claim for recognition."

"That's inevitable."

CHAPTER 22

"You have to give me a sample. Next time you come and see me my mum can do it. My dad's away for a while, gone to Japan for a week or so. So why don't you come down on Friday after school? And I know it's boring, but mum wants you to finish some of dad's old crosswords."

"I don't see why not. Doing crosswords isn't boring, Linda, it serves a number of purposes. They exercise the brain, they show you just what little you know, and it improves your vocabulary, your mood, reduce stress, improves verbal skills, and it's nice to do them with someone else. Like pretty girls."

"Oh, yes, which pretty girls have you in mind, Victor Clément?"

"Far too many to name ..."

"You are asking for a slap ..."

"But I have one particular one in mind ... now you're blushing!"

"No, I'm not. Mum'll pick you up with me after school, okay?"

"Okay. No problem. I'll ask Rosie first. If I'm not allowed, then I'll tell you immediately."

Mum's car was a Range Rover Vogue.

"Nice car, Mrs Bishop!"

"Yes, love. Good for shopping and school runs, I suppose. Right you two, as soon as we get home, I want a sample from you, Vic. I suppose Linda's told you?"

272

"Yes, she has." Rather mischievously, Willis added, "I'm glad she explained it. I was worried about what kind if sample you wanted ..." He was sure Nancy blushed, but given his apparent age, Nancy doubted whether the lad was thinking along the same lines as she had been earlier. "You know, blood and stuff?" Nancy laughed, more with relief.

"Oh, nothing like that!" Willis would not have objected to whatever Nancy wanted. He rather fancied her. "What do you want for tea, you two?"

"Pizza! Or steak and kidney pie and beans!"

"That's you sorted, Linda! Vic?"

"I'll go for same as Linda, please. And a Guinness ... or two!"

"Well, that's a definite no! To the beers, I mean." The car pulled into the drive. "Right, you two go and dig your dad out of a hole and finish his crossword please! Then we'll do the sample thing, okay?" This time, the two of them sat at the dining table, at the far end of the large lounge. The Rottweiler, Jade immediately ambled over and lay across Willis's feet. Nancy appeared with the old crossword. Linda snatched it up.

"Hey, mum! This one's about a month old! And dad's only done two clues! Right, Vic, let's finish it!"

"No prob. We'll need the notebook and a pen each. Let's have a look." Nancy was in the kitchen, and she opened the little serving hatch doors, so she could hear what the two were talking about. Her husband had briefed his wife to listen and report back to him, and he was clearly hoping he would catch out the lad who was so, or seemingly so, annoyingly smart.

"Right, Linda. Look for the obvious ones first. Here's one. *'Disallows screwdriver, say, used by supporter in pub.'* Three and five. Take it to bits. Think out of the box. Disallows. Forbids. Denys. Prohibits. Bars. Make a note of them. Then *'screwdriver, say.'* That in crossword-speak means something like a screwdriver. A screwdriver is what your dad keeps ... where?"

"In his tool box?"

"So, it's a tool?"

"Yes, silly!"

"So, put tool with one of the words you've written down, to make up something that supports something in a pub?"

"I think its *'bars'* and 'tool.' That makes up bar stool?"

"Right!" Nancy listening to Vic, was reminded of her university lecturer. She knew, as did her husband, that there was something special, something rather disturbing about this boy. She immediately understood her husband's deep interest in him. He was abnormal. She listened with renewed interest in what was going on. She would let him complete one more clue, then she would serve the food.

"Here's another easy one. *'One would be respectful to this national anthem - or mean.'* Five and three."

"Let me do it! Be respectful ... when the anthem plays, people stand up? and if *'or mean'* it is possibly *'to mean'* like mean something. Another clue, then it's ... 'stands for' or 'stand for! Two clues in one!"

"Right! Well done!"

"Come and get your food! But do the saliva samples first please, Vic! Linda, you do yours later!" Vic gave the sample in the small plastic envelope provided with the kit.

After eating, Linda and Willis cracked on with the crossword. They had done more than half of it, and time was running on. Nancy called a halt. She was utterly convinced that the boy was genuine. There was no doubting it. Their little plan had worked. She bundled them both into her car and drove to Oaklands, to drop Willis at home.

"Wow, Vic! What a lovely house! It was all lit up, with the drive illuminated round the edges, and bright security lights illuminating the large front lawn and flower beds."

"Thank you, Linda ... it took ..." he nearly said *'took me years of hard work'* but stopped himself just in time ..."somebody a lot of work." He said his farewells and watched the Range Rover drive out of the gates.

"Mum, do you think Vic is weird? And very rich?"

"Yes, to both, love. And you must look after him."

"Of course, I will mummy. I think I love him, actually!" Nancy just smiled. She wished she were eleven again.

Ten days before Marcel took up his new post at Sir William Statton Grammar school, all his furniture was stacked in the garage at Oaklands. A week before start date, Marcel and his wife Jeanne moved into the Marlow house until they could take up residence in the accommodation provided by the school. Willis, Sean, Rosie Connie and her daughters and Alf were delighted. As everyone said, it was great to have the place full of people and come alive again. Marcel was overjoyed.

"Ted, you have a nice place. I'm so glad to be able to work at the school. I've asked if I can spend a couple of days at the place just to look at the lesson plans so, by the time I start I can present a new programme. I think I can improve it ... I want to start a new thing ... but translated from French it looks like a silly PTWAP, or physical training with a purpose ... what can we call it here, Ted? we have to have a better name for it!"

"I don't know, but maybe we can have a competition ... the winner gets a prize!"

"Great idea ...!"

"And we'll work on a programme to include something like JAM EVERY DAY ... 'jog a mile every day! Get everyone running a mile a day. Also, do some basic self-defence and choose a new sport ..."

"Hey, Ted! you are stealing my ideas!"

"I know, Marcel! I remember you told me about that sort of stuff back in Italy!"

"Vic! ... Your Marcel is just brilliant! He's going to work on a ski holiday, a week in a resort in Austria ..."

"St Anton...?"

"That would be nice, but not cheap! However, I expect some parents would be happy with it. Maybe just after the new year, so the children can spend the Xmas at home with their families."

"Sounds good to me!"

"Right we'll go for it. Now, the real reason why I want to talk to you. The head and his P. Ed. master look like pleading guilty to a number of sex offences. Some of the kids have been interviewed, and all have said more or less the same story. But one of the abused lads was Bourne ... his dad is livid, and that explains a lot about his lad's behaviour ..."

"Yes, I managed to see the boys on the films ..."

"Well, the old man is grateful for what you did ... and wants you and the lad to make up. He admits what the boy did was wrong ..."

"Let's get him out to Austria, then?"

"Can't. He can't even afford to pay the terms fees, 'cos his dad's lost his job ... he wanted to invest in his son's future "

"What did he do for a living?"

"He worked for a scaffolding and roofing business, but had an accident, but he got compensation but ..."

"I er ... I know you shouldn't be talking to me about this, and I also know that ... hang on a minute, would he qualify for a bursary or something?"

"He could if he improves, he isn't stupid, but he won't if he has to leave through non-payment of fees ..."

"I'll pay them. Send the bill to my guardians. But you must not let ..."

"What? How the hell ..."

"You shouldn't ask. But nor must you tell Nick Bourne or his dad, alright? I'm sure you and Mr Bishop know too much about me to have to ask that question. Just make sure that the boy's attitude improves, and that he does well in class. I'm not going to pay for him to piss around and upset the other pupils. And into the bargain, he'll have to sort out those two plonkers he hangs around with, okay ...?" Without waiting for a reply, Willis left the office.

"I believe in God because He created heaven and earth. It says so in the bible and it must have been made by somebody. And

276

when Jesus was killed, he rose again from the dead and pushed the big boulder away from the cave where he had been put when he died. And I say my prayers every day before I go to bed."

"Thank you, Oliver. Robert?"

"Me and my mum and dad are Christians. So we look after people and love our neighbours and all of God's creatures. We go to church every Sunday because we have to pray to God and thank Him for His love and we want to go to heaven when we die so we will be together again as a family. Thank you." Mr Pitts was beaming.

"George ... your turn." The boy stood up.

"I believe in God. There is only one God and he created the universe and He control it. God is spiritual not physical. Jews believe that God in none. A unity. One whole complete being."

"Thank you. I think you mean 'God is one', not 'none' ..." George looked down at his notes.

"It says 'none' here, sir."

"Very well. Stephen."

"I am not sure about God. A lot of really bad things happen in the world. I think that if everybody in the world just got on with their own business and left everybody else alone and didn't force people to believe in any god, then everybody would be happy. I don't think anybody created the world. I think this because he lived only just over two thousand years ago, yet we can find things that are millions of years old ... I think that a lot more research has to be done on him before I believe ..."

"Michael."

"I agree with Stephen."

"Is that it?"

"Yes, Mr Pitts sir."

Very well. Adrian?"

"In assembly, we learn about the miracles God performed. Loaves and fishes, bringing people back to life, making sick people stand up and carry their beds, the parting of the river Nile, Jesus rising up to heaven in a chariot of fire, it is all too hard to believe. And I know of many famous and clever people who do not believe in God. They have probably looked at it and decided it is all rubbish ..."

"Victor…" Pitts was anticipating a victory.

"Sir, when I see an aeroplane fly, I look at the theory of how that works, and I see logic. It is science. I see roses grow, and I see eggs hatch to produce young. I see storms sweep away houses and sink ships, I see skyscrapers being built, and in every case, there is an explanation. I have, as yet, seen no science to support a god.

Those who have invested most in the belief in God seem to be the ones who are keen to perpetuate the idea. They ingratiate themselves into people's lives, and in many cases frighten them into believing in, or at least professing a belief in Him. In church they will tell their congregation ..."

"Thank you, Victor ..."

"Sir, you said we have five minutes to talk. I have been talking for probably less than two minutes ..."

"You've said more than anybody else already."

"May I ask the class with a show of hands if I should be allowed to continue?" Without waiting for a reply from Pitts, Victor turned around to face the class. "Who would like me to continue? Please raise your hands." A few hands shot up. Then more, slowly at first, then virtually all the class raised their hands. There were a few shouts of "Let him finish!" Willis faced the front of the class and carried on talking. Pitts looked as if he were about to explode. "... in church they will tell the congregation that the souls of sinners, after physical death, or those ultimately destined for heaven must first 'undergo purification' so as to achieve the holiness necessary to enter the joy of heaven'. It frightens some people, which is the intention of many religions. Is there a choice? Muslim parents want their children to be Muslims, ditto Catholics and Jews. What I have said is a very short resume of my thesis. Finally, I do not believe that anybody with a logical mine can conjure with the mysteries of religious faith. Thank you."

"Thank you all. Just for the record, schools are obliged to teach religious studies and to provide a daily act of Christian worship, so

278

whether you like it or not, all of you will have to have lessons in RE."

Willis put his hand up. "Yes, Victor?"

"With respect, sir, a school is obliged to provide a daily act of worship, but parents have the freedom to remove their children from RE classes. It is the National Association of Teachers of Religious Education, otherwise known as N A T R E and who clearly have a vested interest, who seem very keen to ..."

"Thank you!"

"Elaine ... that bloody Victor Clément kid ... so help me, I'll kill him!"

"What's he done now, Bill?" The RE teacher explained what had taken place in the class.

"I told you, didn't I? Do not meddle with him. There are many reasons why you shouldn't, and until you ... and I and the rest of the school find out why not, he is best left alone. I really cannot put bit more succinctly than that!"

"Okay. But I still think he's bloody weird!"

"That's pretty clear to me and the rest of the staff. But please do not antagonise him, or try to get one over on him, because if you do try it ... you will fail. And if you want it from higher authority, speak to George ... George Ferris. He's going to be appointed as the new head!" As Pitts turned to go away, there was a knock at the door. "Thanks, William. Come in!" It was Marcel. Pitts walked past him without any acknowledgement.

"Thank you, Mrs Coates. I just wanted to know how the new programme looked to you. And maybe it's time I got a parents' letter together regarding the proposed skiing trip?"

"Oh, Marcel ... our arts department can do that, no problem. I would like to go myself, and I think one of our governors would also like to go with his wife. They have a child here, Linda. A pleasant girl, very friendly with your young Vic ..."

"Well, that's nice! Should I go and see the arts teachers with place and dates? if I can get a certain minimum number, I can arrange some good discounts at the resort, on hotel, lift-passes

279

and instruction!"

"Sounds good! I'll alert the department to expect you. Grand job!" Marcel determined to speak with Ted about the proposed trip and poster.

"Thank you. By the way, who was that who just left the office? I don't think I have met him yet."

"That's William Pitts. Teaches religious education. I think he was having a small personal crisis. Nothing uncommon in that, so don't take him too seriously!"

"Thank you. I have to run. I have a class in five minutes." Marcel made it to the playground, and jogged round to the gym. The changing room was busy as he walked through into his office to collect his new programme for P. Ed.

Marcel looked like the kind of guy you would expect to find in the French Foreign Legion, tanned and big. The kind who would take no shit from anybody but was in fact a kind and gentle man. So when he called his first class into the gym for a briefing, everybody did as they were told. Immediately.

"Right boys. We have a new system now. We will run a mile every PT lesson. We will also introduce a basic self-defence programme, and train for any sport you individually want to take up or are already doing. So, next lesson, I want you all to give me a note of what sport you have chosen. I don't want any comedians wanting to do knitting. Right, outside to the running track. I will lead the first run. Four laps. No chatting. Follow me."

Elaine Coates appeared at the door to Marcel's little office in the gym. As she entered, the P. Ed. teacher stood up.

"Elaine ..."

"Marcel! You've been here for just over a month, and it looks like your new regime is paying off! Parents are reporting that their children slept better, had good appetites and generally appeared to be fitter and teachers have noted that the pupils are more focussed and attentive. And the list of those who want to go skiing is filling up! Some parents are booking independently, and some wanting to extend their stay to two weeks. You are doing a grand job."

"Thank you. You have good facilities here, and it's a pity they hadn't been used to the full. I'm sure the ski trip will be one of many. And all the different sports the boys and girls want to do are all being accommodated, and as for the self-defence, I've been talking to a local karate instructor and he's agreed to run low-level self-defence classes, on the basis that he will pick up some new members for his own club, so that's looking good. He can do his first lesson today, if you can agree it"

"Thank you, Marcel. Go ahead on that one. This should have happened years ago."

Willis was looking forward to the self-defence lesson. He was not going to hold back and pretend he knew nothing about karate or self-defence. The instructor's name was Dave. He was wearing a pair of black jeans, and a white gi top. He had a belt round his waist, which showed him to be a second-degree black belt. He gave a quick talk about being able to look after oneself. Then he got down to the practise.

"Right, anybody done any of this stuff before?" One lad put his hand up. "What have you done?"

"A little Tai-quon-do. I'm an orange belt."

"Well done. Anybody else?" Willis stuck his hand in the air. "Yes?
and you've done ..."

"Some Wado Ryu ..."

"Oh, that's good! Same as I do. What katas have you done?"

"Er ... my next one is Rohai ..."

"Really? so you've done everything from Pinan Nidan through to Bassai?"

"Correct, yes."

"So, you are ... a black belt?" There were a few 'Wows' from the class. Willis felt that the sensei didn't believe him.

"Okay, show me the Naihanshi kata. Class! watch this! This is an advanced kata such as a person might do for maybe his purple belt!" Willis stepped forward, turned to face the class and the instructor and bowed, then took up the Naihanshi stance, and commenced the moves, looking slowly to his left, then his right, before stepping left foot over right ... The whole kata took no more than about half a minute. Willis finished, went to the yoi position, then bowed again.

The instructor clapped, then the whole class joined in the applause.

"Very good. But you look a bit young to have done all of that!"

"But I am big for my age ..."

"You are. Now, if I can use you please to demonstrate some wrist locks ..."

During lunch break, Linda grabbed Willis's arm.

"Hi, Vic! My mum and dad are taking me on this ski trip. They love skiing, and I really want to learn! Have you been skiing before?"

"Yes. And I'm sure you'll enjoy it! How's your dad getting on with the family research thing, Linda?"

"Oh, he's sent it all off. Takes a bit of time but it'll all happen sooner or later. And guess what! I came very nearly top of the class in the term exams!"

"So, will you move up a class?"

"Probably, yes. Dad and mum are very pleased. And they're going to get me some really cool ski gear!"

At Oaklands, Willis tried to get Sean and Rosie to join the group, but work prevented them from travelling. Willis would be going with Marcel and Angie would be attending from Milan with a doctor she was dating. it was going to be some week.

"Rosie, now that things have settled down, I think I ought to see if I can get the courts to recognise me as Ted Willis ... and Vic."

"I think that's a damn good idea. There are many things you are, things you have done, which as Victor Clément, you cannot be. It would be grossly unfair if all your achievements were binned because of actions beyond your control. How do you start?"

"Engage solicitors. Probably personal injury and medical claims specialists ... and we'll have to show them the short video the Chinese guys were handing out in America ... but I cannot do it, you and Sean will have to be my guardians ad litem, so the lawyers can ask the court to appoint you both as necessary. Then it's full speed ahead!"

"Let's go for it then, okay?"

"And by the way, how is it that I've got a bill for the Bourne boy's school fees?"

"I told the school secretary that I would pay them, that's way. His dad had a bit of bad luck, and I don't want the boy to lose the benefit of a good education."

"Sounds a good enough reason. However, imagine if a Court of Protection appointed deputy was running your trust ..."

"Yeah, I know! What a bunch of arseholes they are!"

CHAPTER 23

Willis had a favourable impression of the solicitor allocated to the case, and as Sean and Rosie between them outlined the issues, Willis could see that the lawyer believed little of what he was hearing. He wondered, then, if the guy would just tell his clients outright that he thought the story was utter nonsense, or make noises of approval, and take a sizeable sum of money on account. However, the lawyer did not disappoint. When Sean and Rosie had finished putting their case, the solicitor sat for a while, picked up his spectacles, and swung them gently in his right hand and looked from one client to the other for what was no more than a minute, but felt to everyone in the room like an hour. During that period, however long, nothing was said by anybody. He finally put his glasses back onto the desk, leaned back in his chair, and, looking down at his hands, carefully, one at a time, steepled his fingers, joined the tips of each finger one at a time and then the thumbs. Then he looked up again, firstly at Willis, then to Sean then to Rosie. He looked back at his fingers, then he spoke.

"The story is incredible. You have told it with a degree of sincerity which inclines me towards belief. I will now make some assumptions. Firstly, that you have evidence to confirm the story, and secondly, that no court will even consider listing the case unless the evidence you produce is overwhelming, irrefutable, utterly convincing and backed up by all the various professionals who were, according to your story, involved at some stage in this saga to a greater or lesser degree." The lawyer looked up again, to each of his clients in turn. Then back to his fingers. If everything can be proved, and if counsel with the necessary expertise can be found, then the case will very probably be one of the most extraordinary in living memory. The consequences for those who ... shall we say ... facilitated this ... this extraordinary business, and those not beyond the reach of the law, will pay dearly. I can fully understand your desire to keep your names out of the media, and it follows, to hear the case in camera, and I'm positive that any judge would grant that wish. Subject to the above, I'm going to recommend that my firm takes on this case." Willis reached forwards and placed a CD case on the lawyer's desk.

"I think you should look at this. It is not for the faint-hearted. In addition, we will send you a list of the prime-movers in this case. Or at least, those we can identify. There can be nobody in this world who will endeavour to deny the truth of this ... business."

"Thank you. What does this CD show?" Sean answered.

"Look at the title on the CD. If you have no more points, I think we should leave you to look at this ..." Sean pointed to the CD ... "And I warn you, it is not pleasant viewing. We have a longer, nearly two-hour version if you really want to see it. As regards fees, might I suggest that the persons we are pointing the finger at should be ordered to cough-up. But I'm sure, as the business progresses, you will come to a similar conclusion." The lawyer leaned forwards, and picked up the CD, and stood up.

"Thank you. I think that is as far as we can take it now. Once we have received further evidence of this ... frankly incredible ... story, we will move it all up a notch." Sean, Rosie and Willis stood up. The consultation was over.

It was ten days before the lawyers wrote to Rosie. She slit open the envelope, scanned the contents of the letter then put it aside for her and Willis to go through together. Her first impression was that it was positive, but there was work to do. As Willis walked up the drive, Rosie fetched the letter and put it on the kitchen table, then poured a chocolate milk for him.

"Ted, a letter from the lawyers. Shall we go through it? Sit down. Here's your drink. Willis sat down and opened the letter. He read it through once, then asked for a notepad.

"Right ... they've checked out all the doctors and other professionals we mentioned, Steve Grant appears to be a fully-paid-up member of the MDU, so that's fine. Regarding other stuff. Point one. They want to see the full two-hour tape. We'll get onto Angie for that one. Two. Has Sean seen any connection between Ling and Grant? Let Sean answer that one. Three. Did Ted Willis ... me in other words, show up in any documents from Ling's office. Again, Sean will have to check. Four. They want all the medical information that Andy got from China. That's a job for Angie again, I think. Now he mentions my estate. Wants to know how I was the sole beneficiary. Take a rain-check on that one. I can deal with it if he pushes, but I don't think it's very relevant. Next point. How was it that I was sent to Milan from China? Angie, again, to ask Andy if he knows. I have ideas, but just ideas aren't going to be enough. Now, here's a funny one. I quote 'How does Vic feel about the whole business, and what physical damage, pain, expense, pecuniary losses, stress, inconvenience, discomfort, disruption to his former life ... Rosie, this is bollocks! It's so bloody obvious!"

"Ted, he won't understand, will he? He wants a few clues from you as I see it. Doubtless, he'll expand on it all." Willis took a long pull on his drink.

"Yeah, I suppose so. A few clues? I could write a fifty-thousand-word thesis on that! I'll answer it to say ... whatever, but it'll be a long answer. Next. Why does the client want recognition as both Vic and as Willis? Because I am both of them ..."

"You are. I suggest that tomorrow I'll get onto Sean and Angie about these points. Maybe we could get the guy to contact Enzo, the Paris cop? I expect he'll have something to say, won't he?"

"Yes. But I expect Sean and the Manchester guys will drag him in anyway. I'll read the letter again tomorrow, and no doubt think up more stuff he'll find useful."

"Well, he seems to have decided that there is a case!"

"Either that or he'll ask for a huge deposit against fees, run it for about a year then drop it as a hopeless case."

"Would he?"

"My dear Rosie, it is the recognised *modus operandi* of all law firms. They'll take on hopeless cases ... as long as the client has the dosh to pay them!"

"Do you know what a cynic is, Ted? ... I'll see Sean shortly, and I can ring Angie for you."

"Ted?" It was Angie. "I've sent a load of stuff to Rosie and Sean, all the stuff you needed for your lawyers. Andy has agreed to make a statement, obviously mentioning you but nobody else. I don't know whether Steve Grant would be willing to make a statement, but I know Andy asked him to. And of course, the long CD video thing is already available. Glad we got a copy. I also think that it might be useful if we sent all the data from China, I mean from the hospital there."

"Thanks. I'm sure more information is better than too little, and I don't think much will happen until the new year, but these things do take time. And I'm really looking forward to the ski trip! Marcel is doing a great job, and St Anton is my favourite resort ... you been there before?"

"Yes. Loads of times!"

"So, with your pretty fluent German, you'll be a hit!"

"Maybe. But I'll have to forget the beer and the schnapps!"

"I dunno! If you sneak into my room maybe I'll have a bottle for you. But just one, mind!"

As November approached, Marcel and Willis worked on the itinerary for the ski trip.

"Marcel, I have a plan. I want to offer one free place to be won by Nick Bourne. He's the kid whose shoulder I dislocated ..."

"Okay, Ted, I can arrange that. In all, then we have fourteen persons, include Mr and Mrs Bishop, me and Elaine. Angie and her doctor friend Roman will meet us out there. Then we have eight pupils including you. A couple of parents are travelling out independently and will be staying for two weeks. They've made their own arrangements but will ski with us for the first week. You can ski pretty well, so you keep telling me, but even so, for the first few days I think it would be sensible if you to stick with our instructor. I know the guy very well, and he'll only be teaching our class. Maybe after that, you can ski with Angie and me and probably the Bishops as well, if you like. He seems like a nice guy, does Sandy Bishop. He's quite keen finding out about you ..."

"I know. He's pushing ahead with this DNA detectives thing. I doubt he'll find much, but as he's paying, I don't really care!"

"Right. back to business. We take the school minibus to Gatwick. The Bishop group are meeting up with us at Gatwick. All flights booked, me being the lead name. When I get the last passport details, I'll put names onto the seats. Roman and Angie will act as out medical team. I understand that they've already spoken to the local hospital. Insurances ... all sorted. All of us have EHIC cover, anyway. Anything else?"

"Yes, a couple of things. I had better get some jeans, socks and gloves as well as a decent ski-jacket. I can probably use my old gloves, I'll just have to try them on. And what have you arranged snow-wise?"

"Not telling you. I want it to be a surprise!"

The party landed at Munich airport bang on time and the transfer buses were parked up with the drivers ready to drive the group to St Anton. They arrived to see the old church lit-up as usual. The snow had been falling all day, which was a blessing as it deterred the German skiers from driving down overnight to clog up the slopes at the weekend. The show was thick and fresh, and the cannons had been firing all day to bring down the snowdrifts. Most of the school party retired early. In the morning, the sky was cloudless, and the sun shone brightly. The group knew the programme. Meet at the Vallugabahn no later than nine on the

Saturday morning to be fitted up with boots and skis. Then meet with the instructor. Willis was first in the queue for boot and ski fitting.

"I'll have one-seventies, please."

"Okay. You skied before?"

"Yes. A few times."

"Okay. Choose some skis, and we'll fit them to your boots." Marcel was well known at the resort and was really helpful with getting all seven of the other pupils fitted up. In no time they were back at the cable-car ready for a morning on the lower slopes. The whole party gathered, the adults having one day of instruction, with the pupils being instructed for the whole week. Willis quickly found his feet. Angie sidled up to him and put her arm round his shoulders.

"Like old times, Ted?

"Yes! I'm lovin' it!" The girl beckoned to her doctor friend to join them.

"Meet Roman." Willis removed his glove and shook the doctor's hand.

"Nice to meet you. I can tell you, Roman, I'm as jealous as hell!"

"Don't worry, Ted. I'll get bored with her soon, then you can have her back!" For that remark, Angie shoved her doctor friend over into the snow and from his recumbent position he called out to Angie and Willis.

"Am looking forward to getting away tomorrow and exploring the deep snow. Maybe I'll manage to bury Angie!"

"No chance! Anyway, the instructor's calling us over now, so no messing about!"

"God morning, English friends! My name is Hans. How many of you have skied before?... seven. Right, you seven stay with me. The others over to my assistant, the beautiful Ingeborg. The rest of you follow me to the cable car station! When you get there, take your skis off and get into the car. make sure ... " And so the briefing went on. All successfully made it to the top of the ride, from where the peaks of Jahnturm, Riffler and the Fernwallgruppe were visible. Outside the station, the perfectly-groomed pistes stretched away down the mountain-side.

"Right, ladies and gentlemen, Line up here please, one line. I'm going to ski down about two hundred metres, and I want you to then come down to me one at a time. Wait for my signal before each of you comes, okay? And if anybody knocks me over, they pay for all the lunches. And one other point. For lunches you must not have more than one beer or one schnapps, alles verstanden, ja?" Willis, without thinking responded.

"Ja, dankeschön, Hans, alles klaar! So jetzt los gehen, nicht war?"

"Ah! Ihr name bitte?"

"Vic."

"Ach so, Vic, du hast gut Deutsch, ja?"

"Leider nur ein bißchen, aber gar nicht perfekt!"

"Gut! I go now! Watch for my signal!" Hans shot off down the piste, legs together, carving perfect curves in the loose snow. He stopped in a cloud of powder snow, then raised his ski-stick. Roman took off. Again, good controlled skiing. Willis was three from the end. Once all but he and Angie and Marcel, had gone, it was Willis's turn. He pushed off, remembering to keep one knee tucked behind the other, the weight on the lower ski, upper ski tip just ahead of the lower ski-tip, and the knees bent, pushing his shins against the ski boots. He thought he did a good job, swinging across the piste, from side to side. His skis were clamped together. He grinned as he came to a perfectly controlled halt with the others. It seemed that Hans was going to converse in German with Vic.

"Bravo, Vic! Das war wunderschön! Du has sehr viel schilaufen gemacht, nicht war?" Vic answered in English.

"Yeah, quite a bit! Mostly here in St Anton."

After a good morning's skiing, the party stopped for an early lunch. Gulashsuppe, a beer and some Apfelstrüdel and cream. Bish and Nancy sat at a table with most of the other parents. Willis, Angie, Roman, Marcel and Elaine were sat at another table. Hans was inside the cafe getting his free mean as usual. With the eating done, Bish spoke up.

"What's with that kid, Vic? He talks like a fuckin' lawyer, he does the Times bloody crossword, he speaks fluent German and skis like a bloody Olympic champion? And by all accounts, he's also a karate black belt?"

"Darling, why don't you ask him?" Another member of their party spoke up.

"He's so self-assured. He acts as though he's about what, thirty or forty years old? I expect he's probably rich as well, and that would really piss me off!" Everybody laughed. Except Bish.

"He fuckin' is ..."

"Darling, watch your language!"

"Sorry, Nan ... he is rich. To the tune of about ten million quid!" As he said it, the man at the end of the table who was taking a long drink of his beer, spat it out in a stream, fortunately into the snow, and not across the table.

"What!" he shouted, then in quieter tones, "Ten bloody mill! You're kidding!"

"No, seriously." Nobody said a word, but just sat looking at each other, then over to Willis at the other table.

"That really pisses me off!"

"And into the bargain, he's a bloody good-looking kid!"

"Yes, Nancy, so you keep saying!" Everyone laughed. Then Hans called out.

"Okay, English! Skis on!"

As per briefing, the whole party met at the bottom of the Vallugabahn at between three thirty and four in the afternoon. Everyone had a good days skiing. All were looking forward to tomorrow. The beginners would have Hans, and Ingeborg would play leader to the senior class. Hans approached Willis.

"Vic, can you spend tomorrow with the beginners' class? With me please? You can be a deputy instructor with me. I think the kids like to see the skiing done by one of their own, you know, I think!"

"Of course, Hans. Kein problem! Und veilleicht übermorgan lauf ich mit der andere Gruppa?"

"Natürlich, Vic!" Willis knew that tomorrow he would be skiing with Linda and with Nick. He was looking forward to it.

After a day on the slopes, and in the sunshine, once the skiers had gone back to their rooms and showered most of them lay on their beds and fell asleep. The plan was to meet and eat, at least on this first day, in the hotel dining room, and thereafter as the week progressed, and if they wanted to, they could eat in the town provided one adult accompanied each group. After their meals, most went to buy postcards and stamps to send home to parents and siblings. Willis bought cards for Connie and Alf and one each for Connie's little girls, plus one for Sean and Rosie. He got to bed at nine-thirty and slept like a log. He woke to another clear, blue sky, the sun illuminating the peaks before it rose further into the sky and filled the valley with sunshine. he was looking forward to the day with the junior class on the lower slopes. The skiing conditions were perfect. He was joined on the walk to the Vallugabahn by Angie, Marcel and Roman.

"Ted, that bloke Bish seems to be taking a great deal of interest in you! How do you want us to play it? Ignore him?"

"No. I think answer the questions ... but little detail. You might suggest I had surgery, even in China, but leave out detail. He's actually been doing this DNA detective stuff on me and his family, mainly I believe because Linda was keen on it and I was just an afterthought. I don't believe that ... because I've known Bish for years, and he sees in me what he saw in the old Ted ... and he ain't gonna let it go, either. Could be a good thing. Could be a bad thing, but he has contacts all over the world, so he's a good guy to do it!"

"Okay with that. He also asked why we called you Ted! Maybe that didn't help too much!"

"Yeah. He's no idiot, our Bish!" Willis stepped into his skis and skated over to where Hans was talking to his pupils. "I'll tell you something, guys! That Ted skis like a bloody pro!"

"He does that, Marcel, he sure bloody does!"

"Yeah! I hate the guy!"

"I think we all do, really, Roman!" Everybody laughed as they entered the chair-lift station.

As Willis approached Hans's class, the instructor turned to watch him, as a couple of the class called out to Willis as he approached.

"Ah! Morgan Vic. Wie geht's?

"Danke. Ausgeschlafen! Dir?"

"Auch gut!" Hans turned to his class, now in one long line. Right today we turn, ja? Vic will watch you all try it, and maybe he can help me a little with you lot. You did good yesterday. Today we make better, ja?" Willis joined the line. He was standing next to Nick.

"How are you getting on, Nick? Okay?"

"Oh, yeah! Brilliant snow. I've skied a little before. But you're a bloody ace, mate! You must have been wearing skis when you were born, eh?"

"I don't know, Nick. I never knew my mum, I'm afraid."

"Oh, shit! Sorry, Vic, I didn't know. Anyway, you're fuckin' good skier. Can you look after me today?"

"Of course, Nick. I'll look after everybody." Willis was impressed at the change in the former bully. He was going to work out okay.

At lunchtime on the upper slopes. Bish made it his business to make sure he and Nancy got a seat outside in the sun at the same table as Marcel, the doctor and Angie. Nancy had gone into the restaurant to order the lunch and beers. He reserved a place for her at the table.

"Hey, Marcel, that Vic sure can ski! Did you see him the way he skated over to the other group? Like a pro!"

"Yeah, he's a good all-rounder."

"You looked after him for a while, didn't you? In Italy?" Marcel together with Angie, knew that such information must have come from Elaine, as she had asked Marcel directly some time after he had been engaged by the school, and he knew too that having discussed it with Vic and his friends, they felt it was time to drip-feed information which, they knew, would come out into the open sooner or later. It had been rehearsed in the privacy of their rooms at the hotel, engendered by the level of interest Bish had generated in the whole seniors' group.

"Yes. That's right. He was recuperating after a little operation. Poor lad. I think it was something to do with the brain, wasn't it Angie?"

"I believe so, yes ..." It was all Bishop wanted to hear. But he resisted the temptation to obviously rejoice that his suspicions were, or apparently were, well founded. He tried to make light of it, and to allude to what was perhaps, so patently motivating the lad's interest in everything and his knowledge of all.

"Oh, yeah, what happened? Some geezer managed to get the complete set of Encyclopaedia Britannica into a syringe, and inject it into his head? The lad's a bloody Einstein! Give me the surgeon's address. I might get the same treatment!" There was a fairly unimpressive attempt at laughter from the others. Then Roman chipped in.

"Yeah, something like that! But you'll have to go to China, 'cos we don't do that sort of thing in Italy." Then everyone became intensely concentrated in finishing their lunches. it was something of a relief when Ingeborg gathered them together for the final few hours skiing that day.

"Okay. Now we play 'follow the leader' I will lead. You must all keep behind me, in my tracks. Marcel, you take the walkie-talkie bring up the rear and buzz me when anybody falls. Then I stop, all right?"

Later, during the evening meal, the senior team agreed it was the best day's skiing any of them had had in years. Immediately after the meal, Bish disappeared. He went to his room to put in a call to his Beijing contact.

"Pau? Bish. Tell me, and this is a serious question, if you wanted brain surgery in China, where would you go?"

"Fuck, Bish! Don't come anywhere near China! Try ..."

"No, Pau, I mean if you had to have any brain surgery in China, with no other options, where would you go to?"

"That's easy. I'd go to Harbin. It's a widely known secret that hundreds of patients go there, a few voluntarily, but fewer come out. They've been doing all sorts of shit there like trying to transplant heads ... it's a real death sentence, going there ..."

"Where's Harbin?

"It's Harbin Medical University. Run by some arsehole called Renchuan, Xia Renchuan."

"Where's that exactly, Pau?"

"Taiping. Not far from Taaikpaania International Airport ..."

"Could you get there?"

"If you wanted me to, yes. What's the deal?"

"Got a piece of paper handy?... Right. I need to know if they had a patient called Clément. Victor Clément. We ... that is my company, is interested in availing itself of their medical services. Use the real name, as they are bound to check it out. Say we are moving into medical procedures and equipment. Import. So it's Check Mate Global, okay?"

"Yeah. This guy, Victor, do you know any more about him?"

"About eleven or twelve years of age. Blonde kid. Good looking. After the operation whatever that was, he was taken to Milan, okay?"

"Is that it?"

"Yes but keep me updated daily. But don't call me until Friday of next week. Currently out of the country. And of course, I'll foot the bill."

Bishop heard nothing from Pau until he returned home. There was an email asking Bish to call him. The note added that he had been at the University for two days, and things looked positive. Bish retired to his office and left his wife to unpack and get the washing machine going.

"Hi, Pau. What's the gen?"

"Pretty good. Met up with the office guys. They remember the lad alright. Turned up with another European fellow. Apparently, everything was dealt with by the boss, Xia, as I suggested it might. Tried to get into the right department but was intercepted by a couple of his thugs. Told them I was really interested and all that. Anyway, offered to meet them for a drink, usual shit. According to these blokes, and by the way one of them is blind in one eye, said the kid did it to him. They told me their job is to make sure that the guys who get wheeled into Xia department don't cause any trouble. Then they deal with the bodies afterwards. He said it was a load of prisoners, mostly dissidents, plus more recently a number of Europeans, most from France and the UK. The lad Victor was shipped out to Milan about a week after the op. Shortly after that, a high-level delegation from Beijing came to the unit. Loads of partying and stuff, so they must have made a big hit. Anyway, I convinced them that my boss was really interested in working with them, just as you said. They're trying to fix me up with an appointment. I might have to give them your 'phone number ..."

"Yeah, do it. Keep at it. Very helpful so far." Pau was no fool. He knew as did Bish, that all calls were probably intercepted. Hence, nothing was said that would in any way alert the listeners that things were not quite 'right', nor were addresses or other 'trace' information ever disclosed. After trading with Russia for years, Bish and Pau knew their stuff.

Pau got a call sometime later that day from the University medical department.

"Please attend and we can discuss your requirements, okay?"

"What time do you want to see me."

"About two in the afternoon. We will go to see the medical facilities." From the moment he arrived at the university, Pau knew that his hosts were interested more in Victor Clément than he was, and knew instinctively that once they had that information, his little journey round the hospital would be over. Xia was fishing.

"I have to immerse myself in the medical ethics of other civilises, western countries if I am to export my expertise as I believe my world-exclusive procedures have raised certain ... issues but currently I am not winning the struggle against the rest of the world. We have no problem with North Korea or some African countries ...so far only the regimes which had similar disregard for the niceties of medical procedures had shown real interest in the Taiping unit. But of course, we have our standards, not quite as precisely defined as some Europeans, the big money. And we want Victor back, so we can log his progress, firstly, and secondly, update our DNA and tissue records which I badly need. So, your boss knows our Victor?"

"Yes. He's spent some time looking into the boy's history and background, and he appreciates the value of becoming involved in your business. He wants to set up a hospital concerned with the ... er ... medical procedures and equipment."

"Good. Your company?"

"Check Mate Global."

"Thank you." Pau knew he had now run out of information for Xia, so he made the man an offer.

"When I get back to the hotel, I'll call my boss and ask him to send some stuff to you. We need to get moving on this. He has a very substantial amount of money to invest." When Pau left the facility, he walked to a nearby taxi-rank and asked to be dropped off a good way from the hotel, then pretended to do some shopping. He knew it was likely that he was being tailed. Eventually reaching the hotel, he left enough cash with the front desk to pay his bill, explaining that he would be making one more trip to the university, early, then going direct to the airport to fly home. Later that day, he left the hotel again, carrying only his essentials ... money and ID documents. He took a number of taxis on a somewhat circuitous route to the station and boarded a train.

It took him two days to arrive home, confident that he was not being followed. Twenty-four hours after Pau boarded his first train, Xia called in his two thugs.

"Find out where this company is based. Check Mate Global. Go and find that boy, Victor, and get him back here. Once you have him, let me know and we'll get a 'plane to fly him here. Do not fail."

One shared characteristic of Xia's Chinese thugs was lack of intelligence. They failed to appreciate that they could not just behave as though they were in China, bullying, throwing their weight around, with no fear of the consequences. They found the address for Check Mate. It had a registered office in the Cayman Islands. Historically a tax-exempt destination, the government has always relied on indirect taxes and has never levied income tax, capital gains tax, or any wealth tax. Bish knew that and found it convenient for his businesses.

Xia's two men flew Air China to Owen Roberts International airport. The flight time was fifteen hours and when the two men arrived, they were tired. As they waited to go through customs clearance, one of the men called their China contact in George Town.

"Chi? ... we've landed. Make an appointment today for us to call on this company. We need to locate this boy ... no, you do not need to know ... see you shortly." Chui made the appointment. The staff at the Check Mate offices called Bish to confirm it was okay. When the arrival's baggage was searched, the firearms and 'kidnap kit' the customs found, landed them both in the back of a police van. Chi, who did not know the two men he was to take to the offices of Check Mate Global, had to cancel the meeting, explaining that the visitors had been caught with firearms in their luggage. The office put a call through to Bish.

"Hi, Bish ... forget this meeting. The Chinese guys who were supposed to attend have both been arrested for importing firearms or something ... yes, they'll go to court and I suppose I could take a snap of them ... it'll be in the papers, anyway. I expect the hearing will be in a week or so, but we'll keep an eye on the court lists, okay?"

A week later, Bish got the pictures of the two men. The Cayman office also called.

"These guys claimed they were supposed to arrest a fugitive from justice, and that they were authorised by the Beijing government. One of the blokes only had one eye, and a huge chunk of his hair missing above his blind eye. The men each got a ten-year stretch, because I don't think the Cayman government is all that enamoured of the Beijing crowd at the moment. Also, the jails in the Cayman Islands are, inconveniently for the prisoners, not the most comfortable of prisons in the world, by a long way."

"Well done. I have a good idea of what they were up to, but I don't think you'll be bothered by them again." Bishop was collecting a substantial portfolio on his daughter's friend. He called Nancy into his office.

"I'm working overtime on this Victor lad. I'm still missing one vital piece of information. Details of the operation. I have an idea, but it's too damned outrageous to contemplate, frankly, utterly implausible. But I'm not going to rule it out..."

"Why don't you approach Sean and Rosie. See if they will provide any further information, but first I would wait until we get some response from the DNA detectives. Then you could use that as an excuse to drop in on them, you know, a reason to ask all the questions. As you are doing it with Victor's knowledge and blessing, you should get some answers."

"Yeah, I suppose that makes sense."

The day after the news from Cayman, Bishop received notification from the DNA detectives. They could find no match. But Bishop was not down and out. He called his Paris agent again.

"Jacques! Bish. remember our last conversation? I need another favour. I'm gonna send you a little bit of copy ... You know, an article for a newspaper ... and a photo of the boy Vic ... and I want you to translate it into good French and get it into a newspaper ... Le Figaro? Yes, that'll do I suppose. But you can only hint that the boy lives in Paris, but and for obvious reasons, you cannot say exactly where ... and when's that wine thing laid on for? ... That's in three days' time! Okay, I want you to take any 'phone calls ... no Jacques! They'll all have to come via the paper, not direct to your office, because apart from the security issue, the paper might want to run a follow-up article, okay? What I'll do is arrange to be out there to meet anybody who takes the bait, so I can sus them out. That's right. You've got it! I'll send a draft to you sometime today, with the passport photo." Bishop hung up. Then he opened a new page on his PC and started a draft. An hour later, he had it. The title was *'A 2007 Paris Foundling - a 2018 genius'*. The text commenced *' A little blonde boy, abandoned in the Paris suburbs by his mother, with just a note of his date of birth and his name, Victor, and wearing a tiny baby-suit, and believed to be dumb, has been found to be a brilliant and intelligent young man. Now aged twelve years, he is an articulate, blonde child whose literacy and numeracy skills far exceed those of other children of his age. Initially looked after in a home, he is now with a family who allow the lad full reign to engage in the advanced academic stream at his school, where he continues to amaze his peers and his teachers. He has also a memory which can absorb, and recount, long tracts of Shakespeare plays and the English author, Dickens ...'* Bishop's copy concluded *'Victor is understandably anxious to make contact with his parents or either one of them and if anybody knows of who they might be, please contact the news editor of this paper.'* Bishop read and re-read the draft. Then he sent it to Jacques.

Helen Vascal's eyes scanned over the small *'Foundling'* article on page two of the day's edition of Le Figaro, before she turned the page, scanned the page three articles then dropped the paper onto the floor, stood up, and left her quarters on the upper floor of the château to carry on with her duties. Her daughter had gone shopping as usual and would not be back until about lunchtime. With her employer confined to bed, looking after the big house was a considerably easier task for her and her daughter to manage. It was as she was loading the dish-washer that she let out a yelp and raced up the stairs to scrabble through the paper. She found the article again and read it at least three times. It finally sunk in.

"Oh My God! Oh My God!" She fumbled for her mobile 'phone and called her daughter. "Sarah! For God's sake answer! Please! Please ...!" The girl's 'phone warbled.

"Hold on, Peter ... it's my mum. Sit here while I talk to her. Probably forgotten something. She and the chauffeur sat on a bench in the main street and Sarah answered the call.

"Yes mum?"

"Oh Sarah! For God's sake ..." Helen struggled to get the words out. "Sarah, stop whatever you're doing. Go ... Oh My God! Go and get a paper ...!"

"Mum! Will you calm down! What's happened?" Her mother took a deep breath to try and control herself enough to get out the message.

"Sarah, my darling, darling, Sarah, go and buy a copy of Le Figaro. Page two. I think it is about him!"

"Mum, who is 'him'?"

"Your son, Victor! Your son!"

"Mum! Are you feeling okay? Are you alright?"

"Sarah ... just go and buy the paper!"

"Okay, okay! I will ... what did you say? My son?"

"Yes! Yes! Get the paper!" Sarah stood up.

"Peter, wait here and look after the shopping. I'll be back in a minute. I think my mum's gone mad." She wondered what her mother was up to. Sarah remembered her son. She had dumped him all those years ago, and although she never forgot him, she never expected to see him again either. It must be a mistake. At the news vendor's booth, she fumbled for her Euros, bought the paper and walked back to the bench. Was it page two? She opened the paper and read the caption above the picture of a stern-looking kid with a shock of blonde hair. *'A 2007 Paris Foundling - a 2018 genius'.* She had no need to read further. She knew it was her son. She let out a scream. Peter jumped.

"Peter! Get me home now!"

"We haven't finished the shopping."

"Fuck the shopping!"

"The boss will go mad ...!"

"Fuck him too! Let's get back to the car, now!"

Back at the château, Sarah ran into the palatial hallway.

"Mum! ... Mum!" her mother practically ran down the stairs. Both were crying as they embraced. "Let's call the paper now, mum! Now, please!"

"Bish? Jacques. The paper has had about twenty hits. I bet they're all bloody scammers!"

"No worries, mate. Invite them all to the wine tasting stuff. Bet fewer than half of them turn up."

"Okay. You paying?"

"Of course. Now, I've got things to do!" He left the agent to deal with the paper. No doubt they would insist on being present at the party, so they can out the scammers, and do a big article on the reunion.

"Helen! We're off to Paris for a couple of days. Leaving the day after tomorrow."

"Of course, darling. Shall we bother to tell Linda? What's the deal?" Bishop told her.

"Oh, darling! Really, Vic's parents?"

"Or parent. It could be a load of chancers, smelling money or else it's going to be the story of the century. Linda will be really pleased. Can she come?"

"No. Nor can Vic ... I'd hate it to be a false alarm."

"Perhaps we could tell them anyway?"

"No ... only if we're happy that we've found mum, or the father ... or both."

CHAPTER 24

"How many turned up, Jacques?"

"Of the twenty-one who made contact, seven. They're over there getting pissed. On your tab." Bish and Nancy looked over at the table.

"I can tell you, darling. None of them qualify."

"You're right, nan. They all look definitely wrong! Jacques, but let's go and talk to them. You never know."

"Just a minute!" Nancy pulled on her husband's sleeve. "Who's that, over there. Just come in the door." Bish followed his wife's gaze.

"Fuck me, Nan! That has to be her!" Peter the driver, Helen and Sarah entered the room.

"God, darling, she's beautiful! She looks too young, though!"

"Follow me, Nan. It has to be!" Bish pushed through the crowded marquee. He approached the group. "Excuse me ... are you with Victor's party?" Peter replied.

"Sorry, no English!"

"Nan ... go and get Jacques. Hurry up! I'm almost wetting myself!" Nan hurried off and was back with the agent in no time.

"Jacques ... what do you think?"

"A definite maybe, here!" Then in French. "Come over to my table please. He escorted he group to the large table at the far end of the tent. It was laid with a floral-patterned cloth, cut-flowers and as yet unopened bottles of wine. And the chairs were padded. The Figaro guys were still busy interviewing the seven guests at the other Victor table. Bish opened a bottle of wine.

"Right, Jacques. We need to know the following. Their names first. Then Victor's date of birth, where he was abandoned, the colour of the little kiddie's suit and his full name. Got it?"

"Yes." He asked. Then he relayed the answers. The girl is Sarah. Mum is Helen Vascal. Peter is their driver here to make sure it's all on the level. Born. December one. Abandoned in Paris, in a Zone Urbaines Sensibles. Suit was blue. Full name is Victor Clément. It should have been Victor Clément Lechairre ... I know that name he could be the guy who made his money in insurance ... bloody loaded!"

"Why no Lechairre?"

"I'll ask." He asked. "It's quite a story. Mum wants to tell you but not in front of Peter. I'll ask Peter to take Sarah over to get some soft drinks and nibbles. I'll call my secretary to look after them ..." When they had gone, Helen opened up.

"I work for the Lechairre family. Have done now for nearly thirty years. I used to work for the old guy, Victor, and he was a real gentleman and when he died, his own son took over the house. He's not a very nice bloke. My daughter, Sarah was born when I was there. My husband, Clément, also worked there for many years and we lived in the big house, the Lechairre family château. When my new boss's son got married the ceremony was in the château, and my daughter was a bridesmaid. We were always a little concerned by the interest my boss took in my daughter, and there were occasions when it got a little out of hand. At the wedding, Sarah was wearing a sweet little dress. She was fourteen then, always a very pretty girl. When the bride and groom had left for their honeymoon, I noticed she ... my daughter ... was missing so I went to find her. I found her in her bedroom crying her eyes out and my boss naked from the waist down. He had raped her in her own bedroom. I screamed at him and attacked him. Then he threatened to sack me and my husband, who was ill even then, if I ever told anybody about it, and he promised to pay twenty thousand Euros into an account for Sarah ... and then Sarah told me that since the boss's his wife died a few years earlier, he had been touching her and taking pictures of her ... so I and my husband went to our boss's bedroom and found all the pictures ... and destroyed them. Then we found out that my daughter was pregnant. He later told Sarah to get rid of the child, but it was too late to abort ... and under threat of losing our jobs, and facing trumped-up charges of theft, Sarah, in a foolish moment, dumped her son. She did it for ... for me and my husband. The baby had never cried. One day, she took it out to a suburb of Paris and left the child in a small cafe where she knew, nurses from the nearby hospital always went for lunch. She heard no more, and ever since assumed, the boy had been taken into care for adoption. She regretted it ever since. Then my boss's son and daughter-in-law went to America, and both died of an opiates overdose. The son had never worked and was deeply into drugs and prostitutes ... that boy had never done a day's work in his life. Now, nearly eighty years old, my boss is bed-ridden and needs full-time care. And when he dies, we have no idea what will happen to all of us, his staff. And we didn't want to take the money he offered. That would have my daughter a whore!" Helen broke down in tears. "I'm sorry. I should be happy that our Victor has been found. But what will become of us?" Bish looked from Jacques to Helen. Then he noticed the Figaro guys had noted every word.

"Jacques. Tell these press guys I want to talk to them, please. In private. The agent did. Bishop took them outside the tent.

"Look, gentlemen, you've heard this story. I would like to see any copy you do for the paper. I want to fuck this Lechairre bloke as much as you do, but I also want to protect young Victor. If I'm right, under French law, the boy is the sole beneficiary of the bastard's estate ... if we can get him hoisted for rape, or statutory rape, that is sex with under-age girls, or whatever in France, then I'll be all the happier. So, if you can hold the story until I give the say-so, I'll guarantee you a bigger exclusive, okay?"

"Yeah. That's alright with me. But can we run the stories those jerks in the tent gave us? Those ones pretending to be the mother? And can we see them being chucked out?"

"Probably. I'll have to see what Jacques says first!" The agent was happy. The press got some good pictures. Bish found his wife.

"Come on Nan, let's find our girl. We need to know if she wants to meet Victor."

"Well, darling, what do you think?"

"It's a no-brainer. But we'll ask. We'll go over to their VIP table."

"What's the score, Jacques? Are they any happier?"

"Yes, now they know it's not a scam. Come and talk to them."

"I need you to ask them three things. One. Do they want to meet Vic and two, are they going to tell their boss about the boy? The third is can I take photographs of Vic's mother and grandmother." The answers were yes to a meeting. And yes, they were going to tell the boss and yes to the photographs. It was all Bishop wanted to know. He took their address, then decided he shouldn't prolong the meeting any longer. He looked again at the girl. She was slim, good legs and hair just the fair side of golden, and thick. She looked younger than her twenty-six years. Vic would be very proud.

"Sarah. Can you please send me a photograph of Victor's dad?" He got another yes. After lots of hugging and promises to meet soon and swapping of 'phone numbers, the party broke up. And Nancy cried. And call us if anything happens, okay?"

"Darling, you've done well. I hope Victor meets his mum soon."

"I'm sure he will. When we get back home, I'll contact his guardians first. I think the school secretary has their number."

Twenty-four hours later, Bishop was back home. He called Elaine at the school.

"Hi, Bish. What can I do for you?"

"First, what a great holiday. We all enjoyed it. Now, sensitive subject. I would like to speak to Vic's guardians ... just between you and me, I have located his mum and dad. I was doing this DNA detective thing, which the lad was happy about, 'cos we asked him, but that came to nothing, so I went to Paris on business and found the family. Please keep this confidential! I don't think it is the kind of information the boy wants to hear first in the bloody playground ..."

"Why don't you just drop in to see them? They ain't far from you, are they?"

"No. That's a good idea. I take it Vic is at school now?"

"Yes, of course. Probably teaching his teachers a thing or two!" Bish called his wife.

"Nan! how about coming with me?"

"Right, let's go."

Nan drove up to the house. The Mustang was parked in the drive. Nan and Bish parked their car and rang the front door bell, but it was opened as soon as they pressed the bell. Connie stood there.

"Mr Bishop! Hello. Rosie and Sean are in. Please come this way!" Connie showed them into the dining room which had for some time now been the kind of operations centre for the Willis and Clément affairs. As they moved into the room, both Rosie and Sean appeared from the kitchen.

"I'll arrange something to drink. Coffee? Tea? Anything?" It was coffee all round. Connie closed the door behind her. Inside, it was introductions all round. Eventually, after some small-talk, and after Connie had delivered four coffees, milk-jug and sugar-bowl, Bishop got down to business.

"Firstly, may I apologise for coming up like this without any warning, but I thought it better I spoke to you both first about your young Vic." Bishop opened a bulky folder he had with him. "Right, let me explain. As you know your Vic and my ... our Linda have been on pretty good terms ..." Bishop set out the various meetings they had had, and Bishops being captivated by the boy's various talents. "Anyway, my daughter was interested in doing one of those DNA detective things, as my wife was keen to do some family history. So Linda asked Vic if they could also do one for him. Nothing came of it, so when I was in Paris recently, I had my Paris wine agent put a small article in Le Figaro ... " Sean interrupted.

"How did you word the article ...? You must have known more about Vic to choose Paris? Why not Rome, or Zurich?"

"Vic's passport ... was issued in Paris. The application was done by a ..." Bish referred to his papers "A Mr André Marais, and the address was a kind of children's home. And as I understand it, poor Andre came to a rather sticky end ... at the hands of apparently, a bloke called ... Dauphin?"

"What do you do for a living ..."

"Just call me Bish ..."

"Okay. What do you for a living, Bish?"

"I'm a bulk importer. I have agents all over the world, and they tip me off from time to time on stuff I can buy cheaply and in bulk ... "

"Agents in Paris?"

"Yes."

"And in China?"

"Yes. All over. Anyway, we got about twenty hits from the article, and we checked out everyone. And before I continue, I want to assure you that I do not propose sharing this information with anybody else. If you choose to tell Vic, then that will be your decision. Well, we found these two ladies and heard their story. The young girl is Victor's mother, the older one his grandmother." Bish slid the photographs across the table.

"My God! She is beautiful! Look Sean!"

"Wow! She is too!" Then Rosie started to cry. And that got Nancy going as well.

"Oh, Sean! Vic will be so pleased. Let's have some more coffee."

Rosie dabbed her eyes, loaded the tray and took it to Connie, ordering more drinks. After everyone was resettled, Bish continued.

"Here's a picture of the father." He slid it across the table.

"He's a bit old!"

"Yes. Let me explain..." Bish went through the story of the rape and the mother's reaction. "Now, and this is what I think may happen. He ... the father, could be charged with numerous offences relating to Vic's mother. Also, and this is the good news, the old man is the son of a bloke who made a fortune in insurance. It gets better. He has no living son or other relative we know of, and this is subject to checking, which under French law makes Vic ... subject to DNA evidence ... the sole heir ..." There was a long silence. "Even if he had made a will, under French law, the children cannot be disinherited. As far as I know. Must check it out. What I think we should do, is let me take charge of all the DNA evidence and stuff, and check the French succession rules before you even mention this to Vic. We do not want to find that our Sarah is not the mother, or the old man the father. How does that sound?"

"It'll be hard to not tell him. But, as you say, we really ought to wait until all the checks are done. Maybe we could get Enzo onto it, Rosie? You know, the Paris cop?"

"That's a brilliant idea, love ... we know a copper out there. He dealt with the two guys you mentioned. He can give us some advice on all that. If you list the questions, we'll ask and relay the answers to you, okay?"

"Fine. By the way, one more thing. Do you recognise these two men?" Bish slid a copy of the press cutting which his registered office had sent him from the Cayman Islands. "They are the guys who said they dealt with our Vic when he went to China for the gymnastics stuff." Rosie picked up the picture.

"Sean! Look at that man's head! He looks like someone ripped his hair out. Remember the DNA stuff Marcel and Angie got from the trainer at the home? The hair found in Vic's hand when they went to his room?"

"Yes! What a mean-looking bastard! Serves him right! How did you get this, Bish?"

"I believe they were sent to the Cayman Islands because they knew it was my company dealing with Vic, and they wanted him back for various reasons, or so I believe. Anyway, they screwed up big-time and are now serving ten years for importation of firearms and other stuff."

"Good outcome then!"

"Right. You can keep this folder. I have a copy in my office. I'll

309

update my file whenever I receive new information."

When Bish and Nancy had gone. Sean put a call into Enzo, in Paris.

"Enzo? Sean. Regarding the Dauphin case ... I have some more information for you. It concerns the boy, Victor Clément ..." Sean related everything that he had learned from Bish. The police officer was really interested.

"Okay, Sean. If the case is reported, I shall try and muscle in on it. Of course, old man Lechairre is well known here. But that won't get him off the hook. And as you suggest, the son cannot be disinherited. Anyway, I'll keep my eyes peeled and let you know of any developments." Next, Sean called Angie. She was delighted and promised to tell everyone who had an interest in the case, so Sean emailed the pictures. Almost by return, Angie sent a text response.

"Vic's mum is really pretty! It's no wonder Vic is so good looking, and the hair is to die for! I want to be there when all this information gets to him. Maybe we should arrange a party and spring it on him, getting mum and grandma there. I can tell you, I will be crying my eyes out!"

"What a great idea ... Bish has promised not to do any more on the case unless he gets our permission first, so we could organise that. But of course, as Rosie has reminded me, we have the court case to get through, but I think that will take second place to the reunion!"

"Great. Keep me in the picture, please Sean!"

Back at Château Lechairre, Helen, Sarah and Peter had been busy. Helen went up to her boss's suite of rooms and confronted him.

"Monsieur, we have found your illegitimate child! The one born when you raped my daughter. We have no choice now we have the evidence, but to report you to the police on charges of rape!" The old man lay for a while, not even looking at his faithful housekeeper. Then he spoke very quietly.

"I am too old and sick for all this business. Leave me alone. Do whatever you want. It won't bother me. And I can sack you, all of you. Now go away! leave me alone!"

"I'll go now. But I'll be back soon with the police. You have to pay for your filthy crimes!" Monsieur Lechairre raised a thin arm, then let it flop back onto the bed. "Wait ... Helen. I understand exactly what you are saying to me. I know I have been a bully, but I am now beyond that. I have been bad to all of you ... I have inflicted pain on you all. I knew too, and ill as I am, that your salaries are made by the trust my own father had set up to ensure your continued remuneration, and I had no control over that. Nor could I have sacked you unless you were convicted of any crime against me or the estate. I am now against the wall. There, I have told you. I have done wrong. My father, rightly, never trusted me with his business or his money. My own son and his goings-on proved that my father was right." Helen could see the old man was struggling to talk, but he had carried on despite the pain of speaking and the mental anguish he was suffering in setting out the painful facts he had kept to himself all those years. He coughed into his handkerchief. "Anyway, it will all come right in the end. Now go!" Helen hesitated, still staring at the weak, pitiful figure lying in bed. She felt no sympathy for him. His eyes briefly met hers as he lifted his head slightly. Then he raised his voice. "Go! I told you to go! Get out!" Helen turned and left the bedroom, closing the door behind her.

Once his housekeeper was gone, he rose unsteadily from his bed and went over to his drinks cabinet. He selected the last two bottles of his finest brandy, Grande Champagne Cognac Delamain. Landed 1974, bottled in 1995 by Justerini and Brooks of St James's London. He slowly and carefully carried them, one at a time, out onto his large, private patio, setting them down on the low table next to his lounger. He returned to his room to fetch a corkscrew, the tooth-mug from his bathroom, then a small box from his bedside table. He set these, too, next to his lounger. He returned to his bedroom once more, to shrug into his thick,

311

towelling dressing-gown and to set his CD player to play Tchaikovsky's first piano concerto on 'constant replay' and lit his last fifty-dollar Louixs cigar. Now struggling for breath, he made it to his lounger and opened the first bottle of brandy. On his father's death, the old man had only a life-interest in his father's estate with generous allowances during his lifetime. He knew his dad regarded him as a wastrel, not to be trusted with money. On his death, he knew too that the entire estate would pass to the nearest living relative or relatives. His father was hoping to be a grandfather, and he would have been had he survived. Then his own son, another ne'er-do-well had died, along with his wife. It now struck him, as he downed his second glass of cognac, that if indeed the bastard child of that lovely girl Sarah, whom he had abused, then raped all those years ago, had been found, then on his twenty-fifth birthday, the entire Lechairre estate would pass to him absolutely, held in trust for him until that age, with the same generous provisions which applied to him while he was living. It would be his own son, Victor.

To him, that fact became a great comfort to him, one thing fewer to worry him. As the piano concerto played in the background, tears rolled down the sick, old man's cheeks. He reached out to the note pad on the little table and scribbled a short message. By the time he had drunk half a bottle of cognac, he was beginning to feel the effects of the alcohol catch up with him. He opened the little box and emptied its contents into his hand. He looked at the various medicines he had collected over the years he had been virtually bed-ridden. It comprised quantities of codeine, morphine, zopiclone, venlafaxine and mirtazapine. Other stuff there was unknown to him. It had probably been prescribed years ago for his wife, but he didn't really care what it was. Half of it he reckoned would do the trick. He stuffed his mouth with a handful of it, chewed and swallowed it, then tipped the remainder into his mouth. He chewed and swallowed again. Then and now somewhat less steady than before, refilled his mug with brandy, and gulped it down in one go. He knew he had done what he wanted to do. He knew he was old and practically helpless, and that his life would not get better. He lay back in the lounger, the music still playing.

He managed one more glass of brandy. He was feeling light-headed, almost euphoric and within no more than forty minutes, he was unconscious. Hours later, as the weak evening sun kissed his face for the last time, he died.

[handwritten: 1 And I saw his pic ! (Eyol)]

Helen found him the next morning and she knew even before she made it to him on the patio, and with the music still filling the bedroom, that he was dead. She then saw the little note, held down with an empty brandy bottle. The note said '*Helen, Sarah, je t'en prie, pardonne-moi.*' Helen replaced the note and the bottle on the table and returned to the bedroom, closing the sliding patio doors, turned off the CD player, then went down to see Peter and Sarah to tell them what she had found. Peter called the police. Then Helen called the Lechairre family solicitors.

CHAPTER 25

"Ted? The lawyers want another meeting. That's all their letter said. If I can fix one up, I'm sure you can get a day off school, so I'll just go ahead and do it. Sean will have to be there as well, of course, but that's no problem."

"Okay, Rosie ... just arrange it please. Thanks."

On the second day of the new month of March, at two in the afternoon, Willis, Sean and Rosie were shown into the conference room in the solicitor's office. Their lawyer was there with another person. As the clients entered the room, the solicitor stood up, as did the stranger.

"Ah! Good afternoon, may I introduce Mordecai Levant? He is the barrister we have instructed in this case..." The elderly barrister shook hands in turn with Rosie and Sean, bowing slightly as he did so, then he did the same with Willis. He said nothing. When all five persons were seated, the solicitor opened the proceedings.

"Thank you for all the information you've sent. It is most interesting, and very full, very comprehensive. Mordecai here has spent many hours going through it with me, and whereas we will have certain ... ah ... difficulties with the fact that this is a case with

313

no precedent, an entirely new, ground-breaking exercise. However, what we have decided to do is look at it from the angle that we should go for a declaration by the court ... a declaration along the lines of what you are asking. However, and whether before or after we are heard, there is going to be a large number of issues to settle. And I ... we ... that is Mordecai and I ... have no doubt that we will be ordered by the court to consider extensively every aspect of this application ... yes, Mordecai?"

"Sorry to butt in, Robert ... if I might just explain the situation. There is no doubt whatsoever that certain criminal offences have been committed by others and we appear to have a very substantial body of evidence to support this contention, and no court, once aware of this, is going to ignore that fact. They will order that all necessary action be taken to investigate the actions of the wrongdoers, and where appropriate instruct the CPS to charge those concerned. Whether or not the court will delay making any declaration until those persons have been brought to justice, is another matter. My own view is that they will very possibly make an order along the lines we seek, and then deal with the ... er ... other issues. Robert?"

"Yes. Frankly, we don't yet know which court will hear the application ..." Willis spoke up.

"Chancery division, possibly?"

"That seems most likely. Anyway, we propose that Mordecai drafts the application for the Chancery court to see where it gets to. The trouble might be, that the case is so unique they will themselves have to apply to the Lord Chancellor for permission to hear it ... then of course, there is the problem of publicity ..."

"That might not be an issue. As a minor there is no right for the media to have full information, but just in case we have to deal with the more aggressive elements of the press and other media outlets, it might be an idea for there to be an application that any publicity carries with it the threat of contempt of court proceeding"

"Good point, Victor. And very substantial fines to boot!"

314

Bish could hear his 'phone ringing somewhere in his office. By the time he picked it up, it had stopped. It showed a missed call from Helen. He immediately called Jacques.

"Hi, mate! Had a missed call from Helen. Can you call her please and see what she wants? Probably not urgent. Thanks."

About fifteen minutes later, the Paris agent called Bish.

"The Lechairre bloke has topped himself. Helen found him this morning. His lawyers will be having a meeting with Helen and Sarah tomorrow. By all accounts, the randy bastard told the lawyers ages ago about Vic ... as soon as she hears anything, I told her to call me so I can relay everything to you, okay?"

"Thanks. Speak soon, I hope." Bish called Rosie and told her to wait until he had more info. Now things were beginning to hot-up. Bish made a note in his file.

Two days after speaking to his Paris agent, Bish received a letter from a firm of Paris lawyers. It was written in English. It read ... *'Dear Sir, we act in various matters for the Lechairre estate inter alia and have been informed by one Madame Helen Vascal that you have custody of, or are otherwise in touch with, one Victor Clément. If you are his legal Guardian and can confirm this with the usual Court documents could you please contact us as a matter of urgency. If you are not the legal Guardian, we would be obliged if you could pass this letter to her / him / them or otherwise furnish us with her / his / their contact details if you are aware of who they might be. We thank you in anticipation of your co-operation in this matter.'* Bish immediately called Rosie's mobile. She took the call at the hospital.

"I'm at work, Bish, but I would be obliged if you could scan it and send me a copy. I'll deal with it as soon as I can. The email address is royalberksnhs.gov. Thanks." Bish scanned and saved the document and composed a short email marked FAO Rosie Pollard. Then he pressed 'send'.

The inbox pinged in the Royal Berks admin office. The clerk

opened the attachment, read it, then printed it off then left it on the counter-top having called Rosie to collect it.

"Is that for Rosie? I can take it up to her ..." It was Doctor Steve Grant.

"Oh, thanks, Steve." The clerk folded the A4 sheet and handed it to the doctor. On his way up the stairs, Grant read the letter. He read it twice. Then again. He stood stock-still on the landing.

"What the fuck ... I don't believe it ...!" But he knew the game was up. It had been Rosie all the time who had been harbouring the boy, and, by implication, he was in Reading or somewhere near.

He found his A&E nurse at the nurses' station. There were other nurses and doctors at the station as well, but Grant threw caution to the wind. He thrust the letter towards her.

"Rosie! What the fuck is this!" Everybody present turned to look at Grant. Rosie took the letter.

"Thank you, Steve ... I have been expecting this."

"I don't give a fuck what you've been expecting, Rosie, I want to know what ..."

"Steve!" It was the senior staff surgeon. "Do not talk to anybody like that. If you have an issue to air, then go to a private room. Rosie, do you want me present for this matter?" Rosie, still looking at Grant, spoke to him.

"Well, Steve? Do you want anybody present?"

"No."

"I think that was a good choice. But if you raise your voice to me again, I will want somebody present. Quite a few people, I expect!" Grant seemed to cool down. He knew his balls were in a vice.

"Right. Let's discuss it quietly, in private!" The doctor and the nurse left the station to go to a private consulting room. Rosie took charge.

"As you know, Steve, there has been quite a bit of to-ing and fro-ing between you and Professor Vennuchi ... on the issues of young Vic and ... Ted Willis. Some time ago, the boy called on me, here, in this hospital. He knew what had been going on. From the moment you carted him off to Milan and returned with a death certificate ... right up to today. Implausible as it may sound, he could recall every word that passed between you and me, the flight to Milan and the brief conversation you had with Andy before you left to return here, and, Steve, I mean every word! Yes, Sean and I have been legally appointed as his guardians. I was the only person, apart from you, he knew. You know he was taken back to Milan ... he escaped and came here ..." Rosie told Grant the whole story. "Now we have found his mother, and his father. This is what this letter is all about. As far as you are concerned, and I know you have been approached by Vic's lawyers on this, what you do now is entirely up to how the court views the evidence that has been submitted in pursuit of an application Vic is making to the courts. What that application is, is something that needn't bother you at the moment. The general consensus is that the files will be sent to the CPS ... and whether or not they bring any prosecution is up to them. And I would tell you that you are by no means the only person who may be in their cross-hairs. I can give you no advice on the matter. What you do is up to you. That's all I can say at the moment."

"But, Rosie, how ..." The nurse held up her hands.

"I'm sorry, Steve ... I cannot answer any questions. Nothing I say will affect the outcome of the case or the court's decision on what they do with the parties involved. It's up to you now." Rosie picked up the letter and left the room. Grant sat for a while looking at the floor. Then he went home. Rosie went to the nurses' station and asked for the rest of the day off. She went to Marlow, and sent a text to Marcel, asking him to meet her after work. Then she sat down and drafted a letter to the Paris solicitors. Marcel would translate it into French when he came to the house after school. The letter was emailed to Paris that evening at about nine pm UK time.

Three days later, the email was answered by letter addressed to

Messrs Sean Johnson and Ms Rosie Pollard. The most interesting paragraph read *'Subject to satisfactory evidence of identity, we are able to confirm that your Victor Clément [Lechairre / Pascal] is the sole beneficiary of the Lechairre estates. As yet, we have not determined the extent of the Deceased's holdings, but his father established a trust before his death, and on the above beneficiary attaining the age of 25 [twenty five] years his interest will become absolute, but pending the interest vesting absolutely, the trust provisions as to advancement etc. are wholly generous ... DNA evidence is now the only issue to be determined and should this be forthcoming, we will immediately commence acquainting you with details of the estate.*

Rosie called Bish outlining the content of the letter. She added. "Maybe now is the time to organise the party. Would you be happy to make all the necessary arrangements, Bish? We are going to be busy dealing with the Milan people, getting the DNA sent to the Paris lawyers ..."

"I've no problem with that. Just let me know who to invite. I expect it'll be over a few days, so maybe I can book a set of rooms, maybe at the Holiday Inn at the High Wycombe and Marlow junction on the M40? maybe we should hold the party there, and get a marquee on the Oaklands garden as well?"

"Sounds like you've got the job, Bish!" Next, Rosie called Angie to deal with the DNA issue. Angie got onto it immediately.

"Bish? Sean. The Paris lawyers have accepted the DNA evidence. I think we can organise the party. I suggest we get the rooms at the hotels booked for say, three days. Arrival day one, party and meetings day two, and slowdown on day three before everybody departs. How does that sound?"

"Good. Give me some dates. If we say in three weeks' time, I can make contact with everybody to see how the date fits. I can get Jacques to deal with Helen, Sarah and Peter, and he can come as well. He speaks perfect English. I'll do a list and send it over, okay?"

318

The guests gathered at their allocated hotels on the Friday before Saturday's reunion party. It was an appropriate name. Earlier that day, Willis was informed that he was required to meet some special guests. In the meantime, Helen, Sarah and Peter were to join up with Marcel in a small room at the hotel. They knew it was to meet Vic. Willis would turn up with Rosie and Sean. It was to be a private affair. Sean parked the Mustang in the hotel car park, and as the three passengers climbed out, they were being observed by the three French guests. As they watched the three passengers head for the main hotel entrance, Marcel put his arm round Helen's and Sarah's shoulders.

"Look. There he is, Sarah ... your son!"

"I knew that as soon as I saw him!" The girl was shaking, and she could not control the flow of tears. "I want to hold him ... again!"

"He'll be here in a few minutes, Sarah." Helen moved over to her daughter. Helen too, was shaking.

"Very soon, darling, very soon ..." The door to the small meeting room opened, and Rosie stepped inside. She was holding Willi's hand. She stopped, then put her arm over the boy's shoulder.

"Ted ... I want you to meet your mother, Sarah." Willis looked at Rosie.

"What?" But before he could say anything else, Sarah ran up to the boy and hugged him. Her tears were flowing freely now. Rosie and Helen also welled up. Marcel and Sean tried to not cry, but they both succumbed a little.

"Oh, my darling, my darling Vic!" There was no need to interpret that. "Vic!" She said no more, utterly unable to talk. Helen also closed in on her grandchild, too emotional for words. Neither Sarah nor Helen would let Vic go. They both clung to him. Eventually, they all sat down, Sarah holding his hand on one side, Helen on the other. Both gazed at him.

"Vic, you are ... beautiful!"

"As soon as I saw you, I had a feeling that somebody would tell

319

me that you were my mother. There could have been no other reason for the secrecy." Sean and Rosie took orders for drinks, then once delivered, retired to the bar with Peter to leave Marcel, Sarah, Helen and Willis alone. They had a lot to talk about.

It was nearly midnight when Willis managed to drag himself away from his mother and grandmother. As Sean drove home, Willis managed to speak after a seriously emotional meeting.

"I think my mother is beautiful. I suppose you both know about the circumstances of ... of my birth?"

"We do, Ted. We had to be absolutely sure about her before we had you meet her. We did a lot of checking and were certainly not going to tell you about it then to have it all snatched away. I hope you do not hold that against us!"

"Of course, I don't. Apparently, my father died recently? I saw his picture. Apart from that, I know nothing of my mother's or my grandmother's circumstances."

"Well, we can probably fill you in on all that. I think we have about everything, don't we Rosie?"

"I think so, Sean."

"One other thing. The photo-fit thing we did. Look at this. We've managed to identify the other guy who attacked you. He is a Polish bloke, with form for fraud, violence and robbery. It's just a pity that we couldn't have had the photo-fit any earlier. I expect the bugger's cleared off back to Poland. Or else, he'll think by now that he's got away scot-free! He'll be on a murder rap, I expect, if we can get hold of him!" Willis looked at the picture.

"Hey, this is pretty damn good! He's a short-arsed, pot-bellied little shit. I expect the security cams picked that up. He was wearing a hoodie, but not when he attacked me, so he probably pulled it up before he left the locus-in-quo! Hence, your guys not being able to see his face."

"Anyway, Ted, he's a marked man now."

Bish was not one for doing anything by half-measures. A dinner was arranged for all guests at seven-thirty for an eight PM start.

Willis was seated next to his grandmother, with Peter on his other side, opposite Marcel and his mother Sarah so they could chat with the P. Ed teacher translating. All were within hearing distance of Angie and Roman, her boyfriend. Sean, Rosie, Bish, Nancy and Linda, Connie and her two girls and Alfie were also present. It went on for two hours, then Connie, Alfie and the two girls retired early to Marlow. After the meal, in the private room at the hotel where everybody had the chance to relax and talk amongst themselves, Sean sidled up to Willis.

"We, how do you feel now, Ted?"

"Complete. Very happy to know that I've made Sarah and Helen also happy people again. They have quite a story to tell. And I'm sure I haven't heard all of it, either!"

"I can tell you that you haven't. You know that old man Lechairre lost his only son who died without issue. And his own father wasn't prepared to let him have free-reign with the family assets, either. So, as it appears that you are the only living heir ..."

"Where are you going with this, Sean ... as if I didn't already know?"

"Well, in a nutshell, it appears that you are in line to take the whole shebang."

"What's that going to amount to, Sean, any idea?"

"Sit down and I'll tell you."

"That bad?"

"There's château near Paris, which sits in about twelve acres of garden. A number of London properties, commercial and residential, there's an income from various insurance franchises ..."

"Do Sarah and Helen feature at all?"

"Not as far as I can see ..."

"Well they damn well ought to! I think once we know for certain, I feel duty-bound to improve their lives more than a bit. Maybe we should get together sometime next week for a discussion. The last fuckin' thing I need is more bloody money!"

"Ted ... people your age shouldn't swear!"

"I know, Sean. Sometimes I forget that I'm only twelve. I'm going to find Linda!"

He found the girl talking to Marcel and Rosie. As Willis approached, she looked up and rushed over to him.

"Vic! I didn't know anything about all this! You are a man of mystery! And I think my mum is in love with you!"

"Well, that's two people then, Linda ..."

"What, me as well?"

"No. I love me, and your mum loves me ... that's two!"

"You are ... a cheeky little boy, Vic! And don't let me find you kissing my mum!"

"You watch too much porn, Linda, I would never do that. Or anything else, unfortunately!"

"I'll slap you if I ever found you ..."

"You wouldn't ... let's go and get some more alcohol-free beers, okay?"

CHAPTER 26

Just one week after the party, it was agreed that there would be a meeting in Paris of all interested parties, and others, who were now closely involved with the Victor Clément case. Sean and Rosie went through the list.

"Right. It'll be me and Rosie, Bish and Nancy, probably Ted ..."

"Hey! what's this 'probably' bit?"

"Okay, you as well then ... and Bish has arranged for Jacques to attend as well. He is by all accounts a pretty sharp businessman ... so nobody is going to get one over on us, as we don't speak the lingo. We'll have to meet with the trustees, which means the lawyers, and I think we have all agreed that Helen, your mum, Ted, and Peter. He's there really to look after the two women. happy with that, Ted?"

"Yes. It's going to be quite a meeting! I gather we're all going to be accommodated at the château?"

"Right. It is by all accounts a pretty impressive property ... you are one lucky guy, Ted!"

The whole party flew out of Heathrow. The lawyers had

arranged for cars to collect them from the airport and drive them to the château. It was not a long drive, south-west to the area no more than four miles from the centre of the city.

"Wow, look at that!" This is impressive!" That was an understatement. "This looks a lot like the Château de Champs-sur-Marne! An eighteenth entry structure probably once restructured by Destailleur. And the gardens ... probably initially about a hundred acres, and looking at the style, I imagine initially by Duchêne! What a place! I can say, my grandfather certainly had good taste!"

"Hey, Fred!" Rosie and Sean were laughing ..."Is there nothing in this world that you don't know about?"

Helen Sarah and Peter had made a wonderful job of preparing the bedrooms, many of which had not been used for probably years. They had brought in outside caterers, and it was good to see the girls relaxing, but at the same time, ensuring that everything was tip-top. And they were all relaxed, a situation normally alien to them. Willis was determined to make sure it stayed that way. He also wanted to learn French.

"Well, that'll take you about a week I expect, Ted." quipped Sean.

"Maybe. Or a fortnight at most!"

"Thank you both, Sean and Rosie ... but it'll have to wait. There are more important things to consider. We have to meet the lawyers tomorrow. may I suggest a meeting of us all tonight? I need to know a few things, and I want to pitch a few ideas ..."

The meeting went on for many hours. There were facts and figures. Options. Ideas. But after all the discussions, there was a draft consensus. Everybody knew the main criteria was to make the château a permanent home for the mother, grandmother and Peter, who had stuck to the two women through thick and thin. And neither he nor the two women had anywhere else to go, and no other life. There futures were to be secured. And they were all invited to the meeting, and all three had input. Jacques translated. It was great to see them being looked after by the caterers. They were relaxed and happy. The draft agreement also made them happy, only more so.

"So, Ted we have as follows." Jacques read it out, before he translated it into French.

"That the château be altered as sympathetically as possible to accommodate disadvantaged children from Europe for holiday, learning and sporting pursuits. To be managed by Helen, Sarah and Peter to engage staff as required. Costs to be met from the deceased's estate, and all income of the London properties until sold, and net proceeds also to be applied for that purpose. Trustees to be Helen, Sarah and Peter with the current lawyer trustees to act in an advisory capacity. The upper accommodation to be reserved for the staff and occasional visitors, with one suite to be reserved for Willis aka Victor Clément and his guests. There are various other clauses such as some profit to go to children and animal charities and those which support, engage and assist with the project. And finally, the above provisions to be subject to bi-annual review and so on. Are we all agreed on this as a draft?"

There was a consensus to agree. The meeting finished. Helen, Sarah and Peter were ecstatic. Willis wanted to make a point.

As far as I'm concerned, all the Lechairre estate and income goes into the project. I have enough back in the UK. What happens after my death? A property trust be set up in perpetuity for the purposes as set out earlier. Now, as a young man, I need to get some sleep."

The next day, the proposals were placed before the lawyer trustees. They agreed to deal with administration in the coming months, and to engage architects to obtain the necessary planning permission. For everybody else, it was party time.

The Paris visit was a success. On return to Oakwoods, there was a letter from the application solicitors confirming that the hearing was to be at the Royal Courts of Justice in The Strand. The parties had six weeks' notice and Willis had time to sketch out his own contribution to the proceedings. Willis knew the Royal Courts well. He told Sean about his earlier visits.

"When I was at court there, usually with a barrister, or when he

The History of Victor Clément

was paying the stamp duty and getting the conveyance documents impressed with the stamp-duty, I use to use a motorcycle to travel. A big Kawasaki 650, all done up to look like a police bike! I used to chat with the Australians who would park their old VW campers round Australia house, trying to flog them before they returned to Oz ... or sometimes so they could get a bit of cash to buy one that worked, having done some bodged repairs on their old ones. In those days, I could park virtually opposite the embassy, just a short distance from the courts! Good days!"

On the appointed day, Willis met with his team just before ten. They had booked rooms at a convenient Holiday Inn, and as the hearing was listed for five days, it was the only sensible arrangement. On the lawyers' benches there was a pile of legal bundles. clearly marked each with little numbered yellow and red tags. One bundle was marked VC. There were others for Ling, Doctor Grant, Professor Vannuchi, Sean and Rosie, Enzo Paris Police, Doctor Angelica Scrito and one marked 'China'. Three judges were sitting. The senior of them, sitting between the other two, opened with the usual. warning about leaking of the proceedings to the press and warned of the dire consequences which would befall anybody who transgressed. Then he looked up at the barrister.

"Yes, Mr Levant." The barrister stood up and in his strongly accented tones, opened the proceedings. The content of the opening speech was such that nobody was inclined to nod-off. Willis hoped he would more than earn his estimated brief fee of twenty thousand pounds. He was not to be disappointed.

For five days on and off, the barrister spoke. There were other speakers called to clarify certain points, but in each case, Mordecai was always on his feet. There was constant reference to statutes, reference books and certain precedents for small issues. Then there were hours out of court, as the judges had to look at the two Chinese videos. After the main representations had been heard, Willis was invited to speak. Willis got to his feet.

"May it please Your Honour, I'm greatly obliged." Willis looked round at the various lawyers and clerks in the court-room, at each one individually. Then back to the Chancery judge and the other two judges, one on each side of His Honour the Lord Justice Rinck, QC. Willis had made many speeches in his time as a lawyer, but this, he knew, was going to be the one which would have the greatest outcome, one way or another, on his own life, his own circumstances. He spoke without notes. "Your Honour, what we are dealing with here is not some dystopian drama, no Dickensian fiction. We are dealing with ... the ultimate identity crisis. I am not Ted Willis. I am not the young Victor. Here, we, I speak for Victor and for Ted ... we who address you now, jointly, are dealing with a society, a regime which seems to be utterly unconcerned with ethics. China. China does not engage with moral philosophy at any level, and whose actions, which have been so eloquently set out have been facilitated by some persons and bodies who in the main work in the medical profession, should have known better. But this is not what I wish to address now. I am concerned for Ted Willis ... and the young Victor Clément. What you have heard over the past five days has to be without precedent in any court in England and Wales. Indeed, I can confidently say, any court anywhere in the world. You have seen evidence which at times was distressing not only for you but also for ... for us and for our lawyers. But there can be no doubt in your mind, or in the minds of right-thinking people wherever they may be and whoever they are, that when you look at the body you see standing before you now, it is precisely what my learned friends have described to you and in every detail. There is, in my submission, every reason to look upon him as one might look upon a piece of realty, or any other kind of property, owned jointly, with the distinction in this case that there is no possibility of severing that joint ownership, to use a convenient description, as we are inseparable. Without one, the other ceases to ... exist. Each of us, Ted and Vic, is the trustee of the other and of ourselves. This is nothing which either of us sought to bring about. It was rather a case of our being manipulated by the persons from whom you have heard, or from those whose statements you have read in their absence, and what they have done was in many respects unethical in the extreme and undoubtedly in many cases, illegal, illegal that is, as would be judged by any reasonable person. We need not ask why it was done. In the light of evidence to the contrary, it was done for motives of ... greed. This is a situation far removed from the circumstances set out in Charles Dickens' Oliver Twist, where circumstances beyond that boy's control left him alone in the world. With every individual involved in this circumstance, hard cash was paid, or was anticipated by the perpetrators. And for that they will be judged in due course. I do not wish to dwell on or rehearse matters which have already been well aired in this court. I stand here to put the case for the application, for the declaration, and on which you have to decide, and which will be made ... or not made. Notwithstanding that your Honours cannot make any declaration which shall bind any other countries apart from England and Wales, but which may, very possibly, and bearing in mind the high regard which most other countries in the world have for justice and equity as handed down by the English courts, be recognised by foreign regimes, it is understandable that we ... hope that such order as we seek will be the result of your deliberations."

Willis stopped talking and took a sip of water from his glass. He did not rush to continue, aware as he was of the value of silence in such circumstances as those in which he now found himself. "Vic and I ... or Ted and I, are joint property. Each one of us is obliged to do the best for the other and it follows in this particular situation, what is good for one is good for the other. If I may, I would like to ask a few questions, which will, I hope, help to clarify some points with respect to mental capacity and physical being, the two principle issues in this case. The law, and with the greatest of respect to your Honours, I seek here not to teach you anything about the law, but I think I may be able to clarify a number of issues to bring into focus the points you will have to address. Let's look at ... Mabel. A fictitious being invented for my purposes. She is a woman of twenty-five years. She has the body of a young,

327

attractive girl. Her body is adult. She can go out to clubs and pubs. She can have boyfriends. She can quite legitimately engage in sexual activity if she and her partners so desire. On the face of it, all quite legitimate. Unless, that is, she has the mental age of a seven-year old. In such a case, therefore, it is her mental capacity which makes the rules as far as society is concerned and governs her relationship with other people. We know that. Let us now consider a reversal of this poor girls' situation. A young, attractive girl of twenty-five years, a very bright girl who has done well at school, possibly, and subject as I shall set out later, in gainful employment. But by some genetic quirk she actually has the body of a minor, say ten or twelve years of age. Does the law say that she cannot have sex? No, of course it does not. Taking this example to some less palatable level, she might become a target of paedophiles. But all this illustrates, is that it is capacity which is the factor. And, yes, in this country, until a girl is eighteen years old, or in other aspects, sixteen years of age, she is deemed to not have capacity ... now, here's the crunch. I want you to consider ... the situation where we have a twelve-your old girl with the brain of a twenty-five-year-old. Has she capacity? Yes, of course she does. May I give you a slightly less entertaining example. We all know about the M'Naghten Rule. We know too that here was a case of a person who was severely mentally disabled, yet he was an able-bodied man, Daniel. I trust you will forgive me if I presume that you are ahead of me with this example. I am suggesting that in every case, it is capacity which governs, not age, sex or physical disability. May I give you one more example. But before I do, I shall remind you that the words you hear from the mouth of this twelve-year old boy ... child perhaps, the words you hear are generated by the thought processes of an elderly man. It is this brain which now governs everything that the boy does, all he knows. The final example now if I may. As you will have heard, I, Ted, have had the great fortune to have done many things, and perhaps have achieved much which only few of my age have been able to attain. This includes very interesting, exciting and, in some cases dangerous experiences in flying ... fighter jets. When my 'planes ...

any 'plane ... is shut-down, put to bed, it is still a 'plane, be it a Royal Air Force Voyager transport 'plane, or a Royal Navy Phantom or a Sea Harrier. A very experienced pilot, pre-World War one aviator, was constantly pointing out that the brain of the aeroplane ... was the pilot. But the airframe, the engines, the controls and instruments do not die when the 'brain' is in the bar having a drink or having lunch. It might be with this analogy that I am stretching the point maybe a little. I understand that, and I would remind myself that in all my dealings hitherto and in whatever of the myriad capacities I have at various stages taken on, I have always shied away from using analogies."

Willis paused again to take another sip of water. Another magic pause. Nobody looked away from him. Nobody was writing or looking at a lap-top. Indeed, nobody moved. Willis was on the home-straight, and to him it looked good. "Thanks to the involvement of Mr Bishop, seated in this court today ..." Willis turned to acknowledge Bish's presence ... "... in my ... our ... affairs and who took it upon himself to discover the roots of the young Vic, we know he did not have a good start in life. He was, we have learned, dumped by his mother ... under severe pressure from his father, and for reasons motivated purely by the father's selfishness and thereby he ruined ... or very nearly so ... the lives of Vic and of his dear mother, also of whom we have learned so much. You can imagine the consequences if we had not the current arrangement, but the undoubtedly awful, other possible combination which might have been the outcome of the iniquitous dealings of the Chinese Communist Party, tolerating no opposition and often dealing brutally with dissent. Several hundred unfortunate individuals, many from Europe thanks to Ling and Dauphin whose activities have been set out in this forum. We know why they did it. Money. The China economy is heading towards disaster. Read Dinny McMahon's book *'China's Great Wall of Debt'*. What else, your Honour, can we expect from a regime which ... produces twenty cadavers and more than two hundred human organs on display at the National Exhibition Centre in Birmingham, and where there are no documents of any kind to show that the bodies and organs were donated with permission of the deceased themselves or their personnel representatives, viz, legally, and where there are serious concerns that the bodies were from a laboratory in the Dalian complex, which included those of political prisoners detained close to that facility and that organs were from members of the oppressed Falun Gong movement. We know how young Vic tried to fight off the men who entered his room, when the boy was there, in China, and again thanks to Mr Bishop's enquiries, the assailants were traced to the same unit where the Professor Xia ran his murderous series of experiments, financed by Beijing. How the lad fought. He blinded one of them in an eye and pulled out great chunks of his hair. We know that those two are now, due to their own stupidity and arrogance, serving a ten-year jail sentence in the Cayman Islands. The lad, in China to attend a gymnastics tournament, but who was brutally deceived by those he came to trust over the nearly eleven years he was in their care, supposedly to look after him. What greater breach of trust was that! And what a risk those Chinese medics took. The result could have been paralysis in the hands and lower limbs and loss of control over urination and defecation, to put it simply, another failure. In which case, two cadavers would have been wheeled out of the operating theatre to the incinerator, because the incapacitated patient would have been put to death, to join the several hundred others, European and Chinese, who had gone before in Beijing's pursuit of the undoubtedly lucrative market for their grisly surgery..."

Willis paused again to let his words sink in, to let his condemnation of the Chinese facility strike home. "I want justice for Vic and for his mother. I wanted to have invested in me, the blessing of this court to proceed in the English courts against the substantial assets the boy's father has amassed here, in London. However, and again thanks to Mr Bishop, and by a quirk of fate, this has now been accomplished. I want to put right the wrongs perpetrated against his mother. I also want the right as Ted

Marshall Willis to retain all he has achieved and where possible, obtain adequate recompense for what has happened to my ... his ... life, where, we have heard, he had more than fair chance of recovery in the Reading hospital but was instead shipped overseas to be disposed of by Xia and his teams. He, Ted, wants his estate, His university degrees, to continue with his doctoral studies, to have a full driving licence, his pilot's licence, his right to have sexual relations with any willing, of age, partners. To be able to live as he did before he was attacked all that time ago in the car park in Reading. Finally, I appreciate that there are certain things I shall probably never recover, and for obvious reasons, but it is up to this court to use their discretion in such matters. May I thank you for your time, and for all those who have turned up here every day to assist me in this application. Thank you." The judge looked up after scribbling a note.

"Thank you, that was a most comprehensive speech. If there are no questions, you may stand down." There were no questions, just ... silence. Willis bowed slightly towards the judges' bench, then left the witness box to take his place next to his lawyers, his barrister Mordecai and his solicitor. Both reached out to touch his arm as he took his place. He noticed some of the women were wiping their eyes. Good. He must have got his message home. The judge looked up again, scanning the court and looking at each person present. "As we have heard during this sometimes-disturbing case, it is undoubtedly a fact that criminal prosecutions will arise in some cases. That is up to the Crown Prosecution Service, but I shall be forwarding my files to them in due course. However, the outcome of this application will not be dependent on the outcome of any criminal hearings. I believe, and subject to my learned friends' submissions ..." The judge indicated to his left and right ... "I believe that we have heard sufficient to determine this application. "Now I need hardly remind you of the circumstances of this hearing. There will be no release of what has taken place here over the last five days, and no names of either the applicant or any witnesses who have appeared, or of any the written evidence.

Failure to comply with this instruction will mean the most severe of penalties will apply." The judge then looked first left then to the right to his panel members. Each in turn nodded their agreement. They had nothing to add, nothing to ask. "One final remark if I may. I wish to congratulate Mr Willis and or Victor Clément on the standard of his delivery and the content of his contribution to this hearing. I have not forgotten that he was once a lawyer himself, but notwithstanding that fact, his performance was remarkable just the same." He looked directly at Willis. "Well done young ... er, well done, sir. I expect to make a decision by one week from now. All parties will be notified of the time and date of my ... our decision. This court will now adjourn." The court clerk then spoke, as the judges rose from their chairs.

"The court will now stand!". Everybody stood, and the judges left the court via the private entrance behind their bench.

"I'm bloody glad that's over!" was Mordecai's remark, one with which everybody agreed.

The judge's decision was to be announced one week later as His Honour Judge Rinck QC had stated. It was short, and to a degree disappointing. Willis did not attend the court. When he got it, he read the Order out loud.

'It is Ordered as follows; That the Applicants Edward Marshall Willis and Victor Clément be invested with all rights to which Edward Marshall Willis is rightly entitled to exercise subject to his obtaining the confirmation from the relevant authorities of fitness to exercise the same. Viz.; the DVLA and the Ministry of Aviation; further he shall be permitted to engage in such pastimes and enjoyments or such of them as in law demands a minimum age to so exercise and that he shall be and is entitled to benefit from his Estate as was his to deal with absolutely at the time of his death all subject to his attaining the age of 18 [eighteen] years at which stage in law that he is legally able to take an absolute interest under a will. Compulsory education; the applicant shall decide for himself if he wishes to attend school, and I shall make a separate

Order accordingly. Further this court hereby invests in the Applicant the right to pursue the estates of such of those individuals who shall on their conviction in a court of law or on being sanctioned by their respective governing bodies such sums as the court shall authorise in respect of any loss of amenity, enjoyment, profit, rights under law as set out supra.'

"So, what does that mean in simple terms, Fred?"

"What this means is, in a nutshell, that nobody will see a twelve-year-old drive to school in his yellow Mustang. I cannot fly solo for years. I could, however, be the only school boy in history to hold two master's degrees and has been accepted to study for a doctorate. So, basically, I cannot do anything which I am prohibited from doing due to being a minor, until I attain the age of 16 or 18 years. But I can sue those who were responsible for putting me in that position, for loss of enjoyment I would otherwise have had. I suppose it's a result. But at least, I am not under the age of criminal responsibility.

"So you couldn't I suppose, kill somebody?"

"That's a point, Sean. But I can't fuck Linda's mum!"

"Ted!"

"Sorry Rosie ... that was uncalled for. Sorry."

"Okay, love. I understand. But you could fu ... you could have sexual relations with Linda."

"Rosie!"

"Well! You two started it. It's all you think about, isn't it?"

"No. Not all the time, but ..."

"That's enough. Subject closed!"

"Yes, dear."

"Need your help, Ted."

"Okay, Sean, what is it?"

"Rosie's birthday soon, and she rather likes the colour of your fences, so if I can, when she's away at work this weekend, I wanted to paint our fences the same colour."

"Right. Have you bought the paint yet?"

"No, why?"

"Don't buy the fence paint, because it's too runny and doesn't cover too well, so you might need two or possibly three coats. Use masonry paint."

"Did I hear you right?"

"Yes. Masonry paint is much thicker, doesn't run and only needs one coat, honestly."

"Well, as you've done it before, I'll buy masonry paint. We'll nip into Reading, buy the right colour, and get to work. I have to pop into town first to go to the bank, so we can have a coffee and a slice of chocolate fudge, then we'll go to the DIY store."

"Right. See you tomorrow."

"Park under the hotel. I can't bear parking in the multi-story job across the road, Sean!"

"Okay. Then we'll stop in the Butts centre for coffee. When we get to the cafe, you find a table and I'll buy the coffees. Flat white do for you?"

"Yep." Sean disappeared into the coffee shop, and Willis found a vacant table. He sat down and fiddled briefly with a newspaper someone had left behind. He didn't find it interesting, so he just gazed around, and his attention was caught by a man seated only a few yards away from him. The back of his head looked familiar. As though the man was aware of being studied, he briefly turned and looked straight at Willis. It was his other attacker, and he seemed ready to leave the table and, probably, disappear from Willis's sight. Willis was not about to let that happen. He stood up and moved over to the same table, sat down He addressed his attacker.

"Hi, mate. Stabbed anybody else recently?" The bloke looked a bit taken-aback.

"Fuck off, you little shit!"

"You're Polish, aren't you? Is this your picture?" Willis took out a copy of the photo-fit picture and held it, so the man could see. Remember a yellow Ford Mustang ... the one you and your mate were so interested in? I saw you stab that old man. You know he's dead now, don't you?"

"I 'ave no idea what the fuck you're talking about. Now piss of before I fuckin' hit you."

"Or stab me? You carrying a knife now? Stuffed down your right sock is it?" The man stood up abruptly, so did Willis, and as he did so, he saw Sean emerge from the shop, and carrying a tray. He was searching for Willis and would certainly see him within seconds. The Pole extended his right hand and grabbed Willis by his shirt collar. Willis swung his whole body sharply to the left, and at the same time, brought his right hand down hard onto the inside of his attacker's elbow, the force of the blow making the man lean forwards, leaving Willis free to bring his right hand sharply back up to the attacker's neck, effecting a perfect shuto punch to the man's carotid artery. The man staggered forwards and down, his head almost hitting the table. Then Willis saw Sean appear on the other side of the Pole. He slipped the tray onto the table with his left hand, put his right arm onto the Pole's left shoulder.

"I'm a police officer. What's going on here?" As Sean said that, Willis saw the Pole reach down to his right foot, fumbling for the knife Willis believed was tucked into his sock his knife. In a moment, the knife was firmly in the attackers' right hand, and the whole of Sean's body was exposed to an attack. Willis swung his right arm in an arc to impact the Pole's Adam's apple. The man seemed to freeze, as Willis then drew his arm backwards to grip the attacker's chin, and at the same time put his left hand on the side of his head and jerked the neck sharply to the attacker's right. There was not much of a crack when the neck broke, but the Pole fell onto the table, sending it flying, then slid to the floor, with the nine-inch blade slipping from his hand and dropping onto the ground. Sean kicked the knife away and leaned over the recumbent figure. A man stepped forwards.

"I've called the police. I saw everything."

"Thank you, sir. I'm a police officer and I'd be obliged if you could give me your name and address." In what seemed like no time, there were policemen and medics everywhere. They were certain that the guy was dead. Broken neck.

335

"Thanks, Ted. Saved my bloody life. I owe you one." The cafe did a roaring trade that day, mainly from police and ambulance men, and Sean and Willis were given free coffee and chocolate fudge cake to replace the stuff the Pole ruined. Sean and a few witnesses explained what had happened. Then both he and Willis were released "Right, let's go and buy our paint, Ted! And try to go for the rest of the day without killing anyone, please!"

The Reading Chronicle was full of the story. It referred to an unnamed police officer and a teenage boy *'engaged in a frightening attack by an enraged knife-wielding thug who had convictions for murder and was wanted at the time for a knife attack on an old age pensioner, who has since died of his wounds. The attacker was restrained but died at the scene. The police praised the bravery of the off-duty police officer, Sean John, and a young lad who cannot be named for legal reasons, but who was instrumental in saving the officer's life ...'* etc.

"You seen this, Ted? Wasn't you there, was it?"

"Good lord no, Sean! I was nowhere near the place! I wouldn't get involved in fights ... how's the fence by the way?"

"Rosie really likes it. Glad we got the masonry paint. As you said, works out better than the other stuff."

"Sean, I've been thinking. Why don't you move ..."

"Move? Move where?"

"Look, you and Rosie will be my guardians for at least another what, six years? I want to keep Oaklands as my main residence, and I thought you might want to ..."

"No, Ted. If I am getting the message, we still want our independence, and I don't think ..."

"Hear me out, Sean. You could have your own house, of course, but closer to Marlow. Yes, Waverley road is near the park, but I'm sure ..."

"Let me discuss with Rosie. We don't want to be tied to anything that isn't going to tick all the boxes, and she might want to stay ... I'll do within reason, whatever she wants."

"That's fair. But remember. Without you I would really be in the shit ... you've both spent a great deal of time with me, and I think I

336

owe you."

"Bollocks! Anyway; let me talk to Rosie about it."

"There are all sorts of things I have to consider now. With the France side of things ... it will require careful planning, and I need to have ... if you like, a family. No man is an island, Sean ..."

"No man is an island ... where did that come from, Ted?"

"You want the whole lot? *'No man is an island, entire of itself; every man is a piece of the continent, a part of the main. If a clod be washed away by the sea, Europe is the less, as well as if a promontory were, as well as if a manor of thy friend's or of thine own were; any man's death diminishes me, because I am involved in mankind, and therefore never send to know for whom the bell tolls; it tolls for thee.'* It comes from John Donne's *'Devotions'*. About mid-seventeenth century ..."

"I thought you would know ... do you think you could be the exception ...?"

"No, seriously, I have mum and grandma. I know who my father was, and that's it really."

"Ted, you're going to need help with your French project. Rosie and I will always be here to help you with that, at least for as long as you want us. We're your family already."

Bishop did not think it would be appropriate for him to fully apprise Elaine or the headmaster, George Ferris, about what had taken place over the weeks when Willis had been off school. He explained to Nancy.

"We've been so deeply involved in his affairs, I don't think it fair or right to just tell everybody. And I most certainly don't want Linda to know ..."

"That seems fair enough, love, we'll just have to be very careful. But what about her friendship with Victor? What do we do ..."

"I know where you're going on this, but remember, they are ... Linda's very young, and I think Vic is aware of his situation overall, and don't think he would take advantage ... he would probably be more like a brother, or an uncle, I suppose. So, I don't propose to do any more apart from let matters drift ... and he's very good with her, especially for school work ..."

"Okay. we'll do nothing?"

"I think that's the best bet, yeah."

"Also, he's going to be pretty well off, and it follows that if people knew that, they would really cosy-up to him, so if they know Linda's there, they might back off."

"Good point. Now, how about a coffee?"

"Yes please. I think we should have a meeting with Vic and Rosie and Sean to just reassure them that we are on their side. Linda could take some convincing about all this stuff about Vic, but it certainly is not something we should burden her with just yet."

"Dad! Have you seen the paper? Was that the Sean who looks after Vic? It is isn't it! And I bet that the boy was Victor as well!"

"Let me see that, love ... no, I don't think it was that Sean. Anyway, Victor wouldn't get involved in fights, would he?"

"I bet it was! He's a hero, dad! Do you think anybody else knows?"

"I doubt it. And if it was Victor, I don't suppose he'd tell anybody, so just in case, Linda, keep it to yourself. It might embarrass the lad!"

"But dad, didn't he bash the paedos at our school? You know, Harper the PE teacher and the headmaster, old Dyson? Do you think he is really an alien? Or superman?"

"Of course not, love, he's just a clever boy. Everybody who reads a lot is clever because they don't have horizons ..."

"By the way, darling, what happened to those two?"

"I don't know, Nan. I seem to remember they got jail. Something like ten or fifteen years? Anyway, it's not important really is it? I'll ask Sean, he's bound to know!"

"Well, I think Vic is a real hero. I am going to write his life story. He can help me."

"Okay, Linda. I'm sure he'll help you with that. But in the meantime, you have to get good marks in your next end of term exams if you want to get into his form."

CHAPTER 27

"Right, Sean. Damn good show with that Polish chappie, Pulsak! Nasty piece of work ..."

"Oh, that was nothing really, Tug! Just a minor inconvenience!"

"Minor inconvenience or not, it's just as well we got him off the streets when we did, because he had a veritable arsenal of weapons in his house. Serial criminal, he was! The bastard lived in Zin Zan street, just around the corner from the car park where Willis was attacked. Now, we have closure on this bloody Ling business. Apart from the politics of it all, which we don't get involved with, we've had a result on the doctor bloke, Grant. He's been removed from the medical register for two years. The board were given all the info re the two Chinese nurses ... so all in all, I thought that was fair. No criminal prosecution."

"Yeah, seems good to me. Not a bad bloke really. How about the French lot?"

"A really big deal. Loads of shit uncovered there. But as far as the Manchester property is concerned, the word is that it will be seized under the PoC Act to recompense the UK victims. Again, not our business. What are you and Rosie doing with Vic now, any thoughts on that?"

"Actually, yes. Rosie's been telling me that she's finding her workload at the Royal Berks getting her down, so once Vic's château project gets off the ground, it'd be nice for her to move to France and work there ..."

"Sounds good! What about you, Sean?"

"Yeah, I'd go too of course."

"You're one lucky sod, mate!"

"Vic! I want to write your autobiography ..."

"If you wrote it, it'd be a biography. If I wrote it would be an autobiography."

"Okay. I want to write your biography." Linda opened a new exercise book, flattened the pages by running her hand up and down the spine, and in her right hand held a black biro. "Right, now tell me your life story!"

"How long have you got?"

"All day. Go on, start!"

"Right. You have a choice of starters. First one. I'll tell you at normal talking speed, then later I'll slow it down for you to write it down."

"Alright, begin." Willis looked at her pretty face. She had lovely eyes, a very pale blue. Her hair was thick, and dark, naturally curly. She had a slim, athlete's body, lovely legs, and beneath her T shirt he could see the outline of her breasts just large enough to be obvious, and doubtless of interest to all the boys at school. He knew she would grow up to be a very beautiful girl. But he knew with more than a pang of regret that it would not be fair on her to have a deeper relationship with her than he currently enjoyed. Once she went to university, there would be boys falling over her, when she would forget him, and move on with her life. He knew though, that he would be watching out for her and God help anybody who tries to take advantage of her teenage innocence.

"You have a choice of beginnings. Here's the first one. *'The young girl left her parent's Paris château, and in the baby pouch*

340

slept a baby boy, wearing a tiny, blue babygrow, pinned to which was a note giving the baby's name and date of birth. When the young girl returned home just over one hour later, she no longer had her son with her.'

"Oh, that's sad! Now the other beginning."

"Okay. Here's the other option. *'Hardly a year had passed since Adolf Hitler committed suicide in his bunker in Berlin, when Vicki, a young nurse working in a military hospital in Ismailia, Egypt, gave birth to her second child. She and her husband decided to call him Ted.'*

"You're mad. Hitler died years ago! I don't like either of those beginnings." The girl shut her exercise book and placed the biro on the desk. "I'll tell you what, let's take Jade for a walk down to the river, and if you have any money, you can buy me an ice cream. And if you do, I will let you kiss me." Willis smiled. He was enjoying being twelve again. He found the simplicity of youth, unburdened with woes and the essential worries of life, and being immersed totally in a mightily appealing adolescent simplicity.

"I'd like that."

"Do you like me?"

"Yes, I do. But not if you smear make-up all over your face and start having boob-jobs, and lip-fillers and all that ..."

"I'd never do that! My mum never wears make-up or does that. Do you like my mum?"

"Yes. A lot."

"Then I'll tell her that. I think she likes you too."

"Maybe it might not be a good idea to tell her, Linda."

"Why not?"

"Well er ... let's just say it wouldn't. Shall we get down to the river for those ice creams?"

The End.

Printed in Poland
by Amazon Fulfillment
Poland Sp. z o.o., Wrocław